"5 stars! *The Volatile Amazon* brilliantly and surprisingly ties old story lines in to Sarita and Ian's story. Not only giving us a good dose of the characters we've come to love but astonishing us by pulling in the ghosts from the past."
—*Tome Tender*

"5 stars! I just need to say, AMAZING!! I was hooked from the beginning and managed to devour this book in one sitting."
—*Musing and Ramblings*

"Ms. James really packed a punch with this book and took a woman who was looked at as the weakest and made her the strongest of the bunch—such a great dichotomy."
—*Tracy's Place*

"Sandy James has written a wonderful conclusion to her Alliance of the Amazons series—a series with strong female leads who are empowered by the men and women in their lives. I am looking forward to what (I hope) is a spin-off series focusing on the Sons of Gaia."
—*The Reading Cafe*

THE VOLATILE
AMAZON

SANDY
JAMES

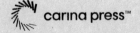

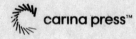

ISBN-13: 978-1-335-01683-6

The Volatile Amazon

Recycling programs
for this product may
not exist in your area.

www.CarinaPress.com

Printed in U.S.A.

Nan Reinhardt—this one's for you.
Thank you for being a great critique partner
and a wonderful friend.

Acknowledgments

A HUGE thanks to my editor, Mallory Braus.
You've been a dream to work with on this series,
and I can't thank you enough
for all you've done for me and my Amazons.

As always, I need to thank my critique partners—
Leanna Kay, Cheryl Brooks and Nan Reinhardt.
I don't know what I'd do without you ladies!

I have to give my appreciation to my husband, Jeff,
for tolerating hour after hour of me ignoring him
to write. Love you, sweetheart!

Special thanks to Deepika Garg for her insight
into Indian culture! Love you!

To the members of Indiana RWA—thanks for
your continued support and encouragement.

THE VOLATILE AMAZON

ONE

THIS PLACE WASN'T HEAVEN, and it wasn't hell.

In the beginning, he'd been grateful and more than a little relieved. He hadn't lived the most noble of lives and had committed more sins than he cared to acknowledge. He'd died with a mortal sin staining his soul—the sin of wishing a man dead—but no fire licked at his skin. No brimstone sliced into the tender soles of his feet. Demons weren't prodding him with sticks and pikes.

Of course, there were no angels singing eternal hymns of praise, either. There were no harps being plucked with a soothing melody. His weight wasn't borne by a fluffy cloud. Yet he had been thankful to be in this place.

But only in the beginning.

Time stood still here. There was food, but only salted pork and rough potatoes. They didn't taste bad, they simply didn't taste at all. There was drink, but only warm water. There was rest, but only on the hard ground.

He didn't have to labor.

That, in the beginning, had seemed a blessing, especially after the earthly struggle to keep his clan fed. Yet the boredom stretched from day to day to day. While there was no labor, there, too, was no amusement. He passed time aimlessly walking in a dusty field with no heather or clover to brighten the path.

He wasn't alone. There were others in the field, in this place with no time. They neither spoke to him, nor he to them. He had no will to give voice to his mind. His thoughts remained his own, but they gave him no solace. Memories were torments, reminding him of his life—one lost in an act of betrayal and ending in agonizing pain.

Marking time was done in movements across the barren field. Left to right. Right to left. Too many times to count, yet he couldn't stop to do anything except eat, drink or sleep. Even if he found the will to stop walking, it wasn't long before he started again. He had no drive of his own.

Maybe this *was* hell after all.

"I can take you from here," a woman's melodious voice called from a great distance. "I can free you. You are what I seek—someone who was also betrayed, who thirsts for revenge. Let me help you."

Now, I'm in hell.

Now, he'd have to endure the torture of promises that could never be fulfilled. Now, he would hear a beautiful, lying voice telling him this torture might one day end.

"Pledge yourself to me," she said. "I can give you the vengeance you seek."

He kept walking, staring at his bare feet as they plodded on the dirt and wishing the taunting voice would return from whence it came.

"Serve me," she purred, "and I will bring you back to the world to complete your goal. I know what lies in your heart. The man who destroyed you will die at your hand, just as the women who destroyed my plans will die. Be my weapon! Be my right hand!"

His steps slowed as a spark flared in his heart, reminding him of the hatred and the wish for another's demise that had followed him in death.

"Promise yourself to me, and I will make you whole again. I will give you all your heart desires."

He stopped walking and clenched his fists at his side.

"Worship me," she sang, "and I will give you what you never found in life. You will have your revenge. I swear it."

With a shuddering sigh, he turned away from the voice and shook his head.

A bolt of lightning sliced the air a stone's throw from him, striking another walker. The man screamed as his body was engulfed in flames before disappearing in a cloud of black smoke.

"I can do all I say—and more. Come to me."

Hatred burned inside him, consuming what remained of his soul. His revenge might finally be within his grasp, yet he hesitated.

"Promise yourself to me!" Her voice was thunder, making the earth tremble beneath his feet.

An agonized cry spilled from his lips as he fell to his knees and placed his fist over his heart.

If he did this, he was forever damned.

Yet he had no will to stop himself.

He bowed his head then spoke for the first time since he'd been sent to this place. "I am yours."

With her laughter floating around him like a whirlwind, he watched limbo fade to what it had truly been.

Nothing.

In the bayous of Louisiana...

THE GODDESS GANGA frowned at the oracle. While Freya praised her prophecies and insisted there was need of her, Ganga had little inclination to listen to the ranting of a crazy old woman who called the swamp home. "Are you sure?"

"I am quite sure." The oracle ran her wrinkled hand over the small, oddly-shaped crystal, the prophetic stone that hummed loud and long.

The woman's cabin was dank, dark and covered with moss that seemed to drip from every surface. Decorated with the bones and skins of swamp animals, the walls had gaps between the boards that probably accounted for the chilliness pervading the air.

Although Ganga normally loved water and the creatures that called it home, swamps were an exception—probably because they were favored by people who seemed to do more evil in the world than good.

The light inside the crystal pulsated, changing from the blue of the ocean to the black of the night sky before it shifted to white and fell silent.

"The sign is often difficult to read," the old woman insisted. "But in this case, the message is clear. You must send the Water Amazon. You *must*. It is the only way to save them all, the only way to heal the hurt that fuels this threat."

Ganga frowned and smoothed her hands over her ruby-red silk sari. Her role in this prophecy was clear. So what made her hesitate?

Why did a nagging guilt fill her at the thought of sending her Amazon after an insignificant demon?

Because the Fates held more in store for Sarita

Neeraj than a mere fight with a lowly demon. What she ultimately faced could easily be the end of her— of *all* the Amazons.

Of the world.

Ganga hated death. She'd granted the power of healing to her sacred Ganges River to halt the loss of so many people. She'd endowed her Water Amazon with the ability to heal her injured sisters. Now, that Amazon faced a future shrouded in loss of life. Including, perhaps, her own.

Sarita's death would cut like a knife. There would be another to step forward, another Amazon to replace one who fell. Ganga sighed, realizing it wasn't that simple this time. She'd developed too strong an attachment to Sarita Neeraj.

She'd seen the other patron goddesses make the same mistake, yet she'd thought herself immune. Perhaps it was Sarita's hidden strength or her boundless love for her sisters—although other Water Amazons had displayed the same honorable traits.

No, Ganga was drawn to Sarita's heart—one that was pure in every way.

The Amazons had been created by four strong goddesses who wanted to help humans despite the insistence of the other Ancients that none should interfere with what the Fates had in store for humankind. Amazons were like shooting stars. Few mourned their loss. Not the four goddesses. Ancients didn't grieve over something as mundane as human death. No, only the sister Amazons and the Sentinels who trained the Amazons felt the loss when the warriors perished.

In her pact with the other goddesses, Ganga became the patron goddess of the Water Amazon, just as Rhiannon championed Earth, Freya empowered Fire and Ix Chel supported Air. As if thinking about the other three deities was enough to bring them to her side, they emerged from the ethereal mists surrounding the old woman's Bayou cabin.

Rhiannon led them with her typical arrogance. Dressed in a sky blue velvet dress, she smoothed her long, blond hair over her shoulder. "Have you heard the old woman's words?"

"I have."

"Heard but not heeded," Freya said, crossing her arms over her breasts. Her typical smile had disappeared, and her blue eyes narrowed. "I told you, Rhiannon. She feels too much for her tiny Amazon."

"Tiny, yes, but Amazon nonetheless," Ganga replied. "I tire of you constantly preaching that my Amazon is the weakest of the four."

Ix Chel scoffed, such an ugly sound in contrast to the goddess's exotic good looks. Long, straight black hair. High cheekbones. Skin the color of caramel. She'd long been Ganga's ally as they faced Rhiannon and Freya in disagreements. "Ah, but she is, is she not? Timid creature. I see little promise in her."

"An Amazon's traits reflect those of her goddess," Freya commented.

The implication hung in the air, making Ganga fight the urge to slap both of her compatriots. Not that one Ancient could hurt another without ramifications to the grand scheme of the fickle Fates. Ix Chel had never before spoken to her in such a condescending tone. While she ached to ask what had soured their alliance, she didn't wish to let Rhiannon and Freya know how close they'd become since this generation of Amazons had been called. "You are too harsh to Sarita."

"Am I?" Ix Chel arched a dark eyebrow. "Does she have the powers of my Air? Can she leap to great heights like Gina? Can she command the clouds in the sky to make lightning to smite her enemies?"

"No, but—"

"Has she been the savior of the world like my Fire Amazon, like my daughter, Megan?" Freya asked, smirking.

As though Freya would *ever* admit that her daughter was less than perfect. Megan should have been a demigod, but Freya had channeled her power into becoming the Fire Amazon because of some old prophecy by this very same oracle. Even then, Megan had her mother's temper, often losing control and blasting fire from her palms when someone angered her. Freya would never admit that, either.

"No, but—"

Rhiannon straightened her spine to draw to her full impressive height. "Water is much weaker than my Earth, much less talented than my Rebecca."

"My Sarita has powers, too," Ganga insisted.

Rhiannon gave a rueful laugh. "She can *swim*."

"She can heal *your* Amazons," Ganga said, her anger rising steadily. "You should remember that."

"Aye," Rhiannon replied. "She is of use after a fight. But *during*…?"

Freya shook her head. "Turning water to ice is of no use in a battle. And your Sarita cannot seem to harness her fear of revenants. How can she help her sisters if she quakes with fear when those mindless minions

of evil attack? How can an Amazon be afraid of creatures already dead?"

"She is not afraid. She is—cautious." Ganga sighed.
All they said rang true. So why had she not pushed
Sarita the way she had her other Water Amazons over
the centuries?

Because she'd developed an attachment—a deeply
personal attachment—for the woman. Sarita's heart
was so pure, so loving. She gave of herself freely and
without reservations to personal cost. Although badly
injured, Sarita had been the one to step forward to save
Gina's life when Helen had tried to kill her.

Why couldn't they see what Ganga did?

The old woman slapped her hand on the velvet-
covered table, causing the snake on its surface to
slither onto her lap. Silence would've reigned had not
the sounds of the swamp swirled around them. The
songs of frogs and crickets punctuated by the cries of
birds. Her eyes fixed on Ganga, sending a shiver up
the goddess's spine.

The oracle picked up her crystal and held it on her
palm. Then she shoved that hand in the air and frowned
at the goddesses. "You are all wrong."

Rhiannon bristled, swishing her velvet skirt in an
angry motion. "I am never wrong."

The woman shook her head until her gray hair began
to pull free of the red and gold scarf binding it. "And
yet, you *are* wrong this time."

"How dare you speak to me with such insolence?"
The Lady of the Lake narrowed her eyes. "I should
strike you down."

"*I* dare," the old woman replied, picking the snake
off her lap and setting it on the wood floor. "I am an

oracle to all Ancients. None may harm me. Only time may claim my body, and it has had no inclination to do so yet."

Rhiannon did nothing to the old woman despite her impudence.

"She speaks the truth," Freya said. "Perhaps we should listen to what she is prophesying. If my daughter is involved—"

"I tire of your constant reminders that Fire is your daughter," Rhiannon snapped. "She is no better than any other Amazon."

"My point exactly," Ganga said. "My Water might not be as strong as all the other Amazons, but—"

The oracle laughed, long and loud. "You, too, are wrong. The Water Amazon is the *strongest* of the four—stronger than any Amazon who came before."

"The woman is too tiny, too timid to be a great warrior," Ix Chel retorted.

"Great warriors are not found only on the battlefield." The oracle swept her hands in invitation to the goddesses.

They reluctantly stood before her.

The oracle's eyes glazed, turning dark and iridescent as black pearls as she held the crystal high. "See the color of the crystal?"

"The blue of my Water," Ganga said. "The blue of my Ganges."

The oracle gave her a curt nod. "Now watch what it predicts for the future of humankind."

The light inside the crystal began to glow and throb until it became a bright white light before it suddenly ended as if someone had snuffed the flame of a candle. Smoke rose in wisps from the crystal as it darkened to black. With a loud pop, the gem exploded. Bits of it rained down at the goddesses' feet like confetti.

"Nay," Rhiannon whispered. "Nay, they cannot *all* die. 'Tis not possible. Our Amazons will stop this."

"No. *They* will not." The old woman leveled a hard stare at Ganga. "*She* will. Only she may find a way."

Rhiannon dismissed the notion with a typical wave of her hand. "Water has not the power. My Earth, my Rebecca, shall save the humans. I shall send my Rebecca."

"Nay, let my Fire take this important task," Freya insisted. "Let my Megan save humankind yet again."

Ix Chel shook her head. "Gina is the right Amazon for this threat. My Air is strong. She shall be the savior."

Ganga closed her eyes and drowned out the continued boasts and brags of the other patron goddesses. When the crystal representing humanity had exploded, she'd understood what the oracle meant. She opened her eyes, glanced up and met the old woman's dark eyes.

"Now you see," the woman said. "Now you know."

Ganga nodded. The time to protect Sarita had ended. There was no way for the tiny woman with the pure heart to avoid her destiny.

Water would face this threat.

Alone.

There would be no help from her goddess. No help from her sisters. No help from the two honorable men who trained the Amazons.

Sarita's trial by fire had arrived.

TWO

As WARM LIPS touched her breast, Sarita arched into the caress. Strong hands stroked her arms, brushing down shivering skin until fingers entwined with hers and lifted her arms above her head.

"So beautiful," the deep voice whispered against her skin.

The heat was almost unbearable as the man drew her nipple into his mouth. One of his hands pinned her wrists to the cool sheets. The other tickled down to settle on her other breast. She couldn't hold back the moans that spilled from her lips, wanting more of his touch, wanting more *than* his touch.

The hand moved lower until it caressed her hip then trailed across her leg to stroke up the inside of her thigh. How was she able to stay on the bed when those fingers reached the part of her that ached and burned for that touch?

"Easy, loving," he murmured.

The timbre of his seductive voice rushed through her in a wave of heat. She strained to see his face. Eyes like emeralds. Red hair that almost brushed his shoulders. Although *red* wasn't quite the right word. Not brassy or bold, but more like a pleasant mixture of red and a rich brown.

"Only your love can save me," he whispered.

She couldn't find the words to reply to his enigmatic

statement as tension knotted her body. A light sheen of perspiration coated her skin, causing more shivers to race over her. A long finger penetrated her, forcing her hips to meet the thrust. The tension spread and muscles tightened until she thought she'd go mad. About to find the release she craved, she arched her back and cried out... Only to suddenly awaken.

Her heart pounded, whooshing loudly in her ears. Sarita was no longer in the dream—the same dream that had haunted her for a long, torturous week. A groan escaped as she rolled over and buried her face in the pillow, feeling the hollow ache of unfulfilled desire.

Why? Why did that man come to her every night, torturing her and teasing her until she wanted to scream in frustration?

Were the dreams simply her loneliness and her long-term celibacy? She was, after all, a healthy woman who'd never taken a lover. Perhaps the heated dreams were nothing more than curiosity.

Maybe she just needed to take advantage of the gifts the goddesses gave to the Amazons—the protection from catching diseases or that they couldn't get pregnant if the man was meant to be nothing more than a partner for a romantic tryst. Maybe she should go out, have a few drinks, a few laughs and finally get laid.

Her Indian culture—one of respect and honor—had been deeply ingrained by her "aunt" Kamala—a high priestess to her goddess Ganga. More so by her nanny, Lalita—another Indian who followed the old ways and customs. Sarita couldn't brush all that off and have a fling. Her whole life had been steeped in tradition, and a week's worth of haunting dreams weren't enough for her to throw away all that made her who she was.

When she took a lover—*if* she took a lover—the man would be her soul mate. Her husband. If not in truth, then the husband of her heart.

Where could she find this Prince Charming? Amazons seldom had the chance to meet new people, let alone spend enough time to get to know someone.

The erotic dream lingered like a haze in the air. The temptation had been there all week—the lure to surrender to the dream and never wake up. To forget her duties and her destiny and be a woman.

A light exploded in the room, and Ganga appeared. All thoughts of sleep vanished.

Sarita rubbed her hands over her face to shake the last of the fog from her eyes. "I'm so glad to see you, Ganga."

"As I am you."

Ganga's dark eyes seemed sad, something Sarita had never seen before. Goddesses tended to hide emotions, often to the point they appeared to have no feelings at all.

A cold lot, Artair MacKay always called them. The man was a Sentinel, so he would know. The fact he'd spent four hundred years in their service gave him far more knowledge of the Ancients—the gods and goddesses of every culture who shared the powers of this world—than any other person.

Before Sarita's overwhelming curiosity forced her to ask why Water's patron goddess sought her out, Ganga spoke. "I have a mission for you. The demon Marbas is loose and we wish him brought to heel." She smoothed her hand over the iridescent skirt of her purple sari as Sarita pushed aside the covers and got to her feet.

"Isn't he a lion? That would be Earth's domain. Rebecca always captures the animal demons." The hair on the back of her neck bristled. Ganga had never come to her like this, nor had she ever sent her on a demon hunt with no backup. What made Marbas so special?

"I wish *you* to go, Sarita. Marbas breathes fire. What better warrior to send than one who can quench that flame? There are children missing, and the voices of their parents cry out for justice."

"I could take Gina and—"

"The aid of your sister will not be necessary," Ganga snapped—another thing highly unusual for her.

"Yes, but… Helen is getting more and more powerful. I thought we'd agreed no one goes on a mission alone."

Helen. The newest of the Ancients.

A former Earth Amazon, she'd murdered her own Amazon sister—the last generation's Fire Amazon, Sparks—as a sacrifice to ascend to being a goddess. Once given a taste of power, Helen had become a megalomaniac who wanted absolute control of the human world. Which made her the main target of the Amazons.

The cult Helen established just over a year ago— The Children of the Earth—had grown by leaps and bounds. She'd burst on the scene with the power of a hurricane, and her image and voice were everywhere. Billboards. Television. Radio. She'd developed a new tactic—hiding in plain sight. Temples were built in her honor all over the world as the Children recruited more and more members. Some of those members even served in Congress, helping push through bills that shielded the cult and their money from local laws. At least Helen was easy to track now, whereas in the past she'd tended to pop up at the most inopportune moments.

With each new follower, Helen's power grew, their worship feeding her like gasoline thrown on a fire. The last time the Amazons had checked, the COE flock had spread to twenty-two countries and had close to half a million people believing Helen held the answers on how to save the world from being destroyed by pollution, famine and war. She preached an appealing gospel much like cult leaders who'd come before her—peace, hope and charity.

If only her followers knew her as well as Sarita did.

So far, she hadn't come after the Amazons. But she would. None of them doubted that. It was merely a matter of time. Her hatred of them—because they'd defeated her three times in her attempts to gain power—ran hot and deep.

She would come after them.

Soon.

Ganga ignored Sarita's comment as though unconcerned about Helen's potential threat. "I shall send you to Scotland to face him." The goddess nodded at the sapphire-encrusted sword standing next to the oak bureau.

"Scotland?" Sarita asked as she walked over and picked up her weapon.

"Yes, my child. Marbas awaits. Be well." The goddess snapped her fingers before Sarita could ask why in the hell Marbas could be found in Scotland.

Her goddess had given her this mission. Sarita would give Ganga no less than her best.

As she dressed, she called to her closest sister, Gina,

telepathically, letting her know she had a job and that all would be well.

"You don't want me to go, too, Sarita?"

"No. Ganga said I should go alone."

Gina sent waves of confidence Sarita's way, and she added a wish that they see each other soon.

MARBAS CAUSED MORE trouble than she'd expected.

Normally, an Amazon would go in, get the job done by either killing the creature or using magicks to incapacitate him and get right back out. Since Ganga hadn't stated a preference, Sarita would go for the capture. No matter that she'd been an Amazon for a few years, the kill bothered her.

Still, this demon was a major pain in the ass.

Sarita ducked behind a boulder as Marbas belched another stream of fire at her. She imagined herself some warrior of old battling a dragon with nothing but a sword—although in this case the enemy was really a fire-breathing lion with a taste for children. She'd make sure his child-munching days were over.

A shame Helen wasn't so easily subdued…

Once she found out which damned idiot had set Marbas loose, she'd give him a piece of her mind before she beat him senseless. The thought that the demon had something to do with Helen was quickly dismissed. She was busy running her cult. She wouldn't stoop to something as petty as setting a demon loose to eat kids. This was just a routine demon hunt. Nothing more, nothing less.

When the stream of fire petered out, Sarita charged from behind the rock, sword ready.

Marbas inhaled sharply, obviously preparing to roast her.

She never gave him the chance thanks to a small puddle at the demon's feet. As his mouth opened, a flick of her wrist expanded the water and sent it flying down his throat, drowning the flames. She ran her sword through his chest as he choked.

Not that a stab wound could kill him—not a demon of Marbas's level. He wasn't immortal, but he could only be destroyed by magicks wielded by an Ancient. She could only subdue him until some spell could be spun around him. As his body dropped to the dirt, she sheathed her bloody sword and jerked the lasso from her belt. She had the demon hogtied before he could rally.

Marbas growled at her.

She snorted a laugh, a habit she couldn't seem to break despite her sisters' teasing. "You lose. It's demon jail for you."

The dumbass might have gone undetected for quite a while, and he might have been true to his evil nature and gone for victims.

Although *her* nature was usually more reserved, Sarita found herself wanting to crow like a rooster over her success. This one felt damned good. She would please Ganga. She'd also please her sisters.

Perhaps she might stop feeling like the weakest of the four. Capturing Marbas with her Water powers took some of the sting away.

Her sisters didn't look down on her. They'd never once told her she had the wimpiest powers. That was Sarita's own baggage. While they'd grown in their powers, she'd been standing still, waiting for an evolution that might not happen. It just got old to feel like the others protected her and pushed her to the back of every fight because her powers weren't as strong as theirs.

Her sisters had the really cool powers.

What could Sarita do? She could swim forever without taking a breath. She could freeze liquid with the touch of her finger. And as she did with Marbas, she could send water flying from one place to the next.

Whoopee shit.

How many demons needed a good drowning?

At least her powers had come in handy once. The last time they'd faced Helen, she'd tried to kill Gina and her husband, Zach. Sarita had been the one to end the crisis. Diverting water from a fountain, she'd encased Helen in a solid block of ice until they could all escape. Not a capture, but *her* powers had saved the day.

Sarita jumped over Marbas, grabbed his head from behind and wound the slack of the rope around his jaws to keep them shut. She could have been a cowboy who'd just won the calf-roping competition.

What she needed was a cocky reply—like *Buffy the Vampire Slayer.*

Instead, Sarita sighed and pulled her cell phone out of her pocket. Being closest to Gina, Sarita could communicate some things simply by thought. But for Rebecca and Megan, she had to use her phone.

Punching the speed dial, she waited for Rebecca to answer. Since the Earth Amazon acted as Guardian to the other three, Sarita, Gina and Megan had to report back to her after any mission.

"Sarita! That was quick. Things went well?"

"All done. Marbas is tied up and ready for transport. Tell the warden he's all hers."

"Sure thing. I'll call for Kampe to come and get him," Rebecca's voice buzzed in Sarita's ear. "She can take him back to demon jail at Tartarus. I feel weird that I didn't take care of him. He's a lion not a walrus."

"My goddess asked. I came."

"Are you coming back to Avalon?"

"Not right away." She needed some time alone. She rushed to add, "I've never been to Scotland before. I'm going to stay and explore for a bit."

"It's beautiful there," Rebecca said. "Artair took me last summer to see the Highlands."

Yeah, thanks for the reminder of how happy you are, Rebecca. A vacation with a loving husband. Something else you've done that I haven't and never will.

As if she would admit to the Guardian that jealousy ate her alive, that she resented the other Amazons so much it twisted her stomach into knots.

Sarita would never hurt her sisters like that, although shielding her thoughts from Gina was sometimes next to impossible.

"How long are you gonna stay?" The Guardian's voice held a note of hesitation that said she felt some of Sarita's restlessness.

Sarita swallowed her feelings to keep them from Rebecca, a skill she'd rapidly perfected. "Do you need me back soon?"

What a lame question. Earth, Fire and Air rarely needed Water's help. From Sarita's perspective, they spent too much of their time in battles checking to see if she was safe.

I'm an Amazon, too, damn it!

She might be ridiculously short, and she might not have all of their powers, but she could use a sword. And her martial arts skills grew every day, thanks to Zach spending so much time instructing her in tae kwon do. The man had five black belts, after all.

"No, we're good," Rebecca replied. "You have a good time. Just call when you're ready to come back to Avalon. I'll get Rhiannon—"

"I have a goddess, too. She'll send me back when I'm ready."

There was a long silence. "Are you sure?"

"Look, I know she's not around as much as your goddess, but—"

"Not as much?" Rebecca's incredulous tone struck a nerve. "Sarita, she's *never* around."

Even though the other goddesses liked to meddle in their Amazons' lives, that didn't mean Ganga was neglectful because she gave Sarita space. Rebecca didn't understand the relationship she had with her goddess because Rhiannon and Freya constantly stuck their noses in everyone's business. Even Ix Chel was known to interfere more often than necessary.

Ganga gave the Amazons space to do their jobs without interference, and Sarita had grown damn sick and tired of explaining that. "I need to go."

"Stay safe."

Sarita ended the call without a characteristic farewell, which Rebecca would be sure to notice. She didn't normally lose her temper. Maybe the extended summer drought drained her Water powers.

Something had been prodding at her, poking at her normal, easy contentment. She loved being an Amazon. She loved being a part of fighting for the greater good. But lately Sarita had been out of sorts. Discontented. Restless.

Sitting down on a large boulder, she stared down at Marbas. "Time for me to have a real vacation." She sniffed the air. "Ah, the heather smells heavenly."

The lion snorted some black smoke out his nostrils.

"Yeah, whatever. You're too pissed to see the beauty around you. Fine. I need to get you to—"

The world went black.

THREE

SHE WAS MUCH smaller than Ian expected. Short. *Very* short. Standing next to him, she wouldn't even come up to his armpit. Weighed next to nothing. Just a little bit of a thing.

Her skin was the most beautiful shade of brown, her hair the color of a raven's feathers. He wondered if her eyes were as dark and exotic as the rest of her.

He kicked the sword she'd dropped aside and stepped over Marbas. While he could probably have untied the angry demon, Ian left well enough alone. Marbas had served his purpose. The other Amazons could decide his fate.

Ian's job was to collect his precious bundle, guard it with his life and hope she didn't awaken to try to kill him before he got her secured at *dorcha àite*.

It shouldn't have turned out this way, having to use a woman as live bait. He'd have to push aside the guilt that nibbled at his soul. Once justice had been served, he could leave this world behind. The fact that he would find himself bound for the fiery pits of hell didn't sway his commitment, nor did it honestly frighten him. That had been his fate all along. If justice was served in the end, he'd welcome the fire and brimstone.

He preferred hell to being sent back to limbo.

Once he reached the clearing, he leaned against the same boulder his captive had used as he prepared to call to his mistress. She'd be delighted things had gone so smoothly. Not that he honestly gave a damn whether she was pleased or not.

He meant to hold her to her promise. By capturing the Amazon, he'd fulfilled his part of the bargain. When he delivered this tiny woman, his mistress would give him what he desired.

Justice.

Or revenge?

He'd lost track.

After propping his captive up against his shoulder so he could see her face, Ian smoothed her black hair away from her cheek. Her skin was satin beneath his fingertips. He couldn't resist the urge to rub the pad of his thumb over her full lower lip, wondering how much she'd hate him when she awoke. A pawn in a dangerous game, she was a means to an ends. Nothing more.

So why did his quest suddenly seem like a betrayal of the very feminine figure he cradled?

Allowing himself to go soft now wasn't an option. He stopped wishing things could have been different. He'd wasted that kind of fruitless hope long ago... Back when he'd been laird and tried to hold his clan together after the English gutted their village. Back when he'd been nothing but a man faced with the impossible— to keep the men, women and children of his clan from starving and from dying.

He'd succeeded at neither.

Thanks to one man, Ian's clan had suffered as no one should suffer.

And in the end, the very people he'd tried to save had attacked him.

Threats of hell's fire didn't frighten a man who'd been tied to a stake as he burned to death.

Ian would have his justice. He would kill the man who had destroyed his clan and turned them against their laird. That man had been gifted with immortality. Ian would find a way to end that. Maybe then he could release the hatred he'd held for so long. His soul might be in hell, but at least he'd be free of the rage that drowned him.

His burden groaned and stirred in his arms. The hard tap on the head had done the trick to render her unconscious, but he needed to get her back to the castle before she regained the strength to fight him. He didn't want to hurt her again.

"M'lady!" Ian called as he stood and held the Amazon close. "I have her!"

Light engulfed him as his mistress transported them to the dark fortress Ian called home.

SARITA OPENED HER eyes to mere slits, fearing any light would increase the pounding in her skull.

"Here, lass," a deep voice with a thick Scottish brogue said. A cool cloth slapped over her eyes. "'Twill help with the pain."

She breathed a sigh, grateful to know she was back in Avalon.

Why was Artair caring for her instead of Beagan and Dolan? The changelings had the healing touch and had always nursed her through any injury.

"Thanks," she said. "What hit me? Did Marbas get loose?"

"Nay. He was still tied as I carried ye away."

That made no sense. "You were there? Geesh. Don't you trust me to do my job?"

"Hard to deal with a demon when you're out cold."

His unusual tone, one of amusement at her predicament, sent a shiver of concern racing over her skin. "Something hit me."

"Not *something*, loving. *Someone*."

That teasing voice didn't belong to her Sentinel.

Snatching away the wet cloth, she came face to face with someone she'd never expected to meet. "Oh, my God. It can't be…"

Quirking his eyebrow, her dream lover stared at her as though she were the oddest creature he'd ever seen. She knew that look well, having seen it before. Many, many times on many, many faces.

Back in her childhood when at age five she'd surfed like a pro, as if born in the water.

Back when she'd worked at Sea World, as though an Indian woman shouldn't want to wear a wetsuit and train seals.

Back in Avalon when she'd managed to bring Artair down for the first time in hand-to-hand combat like a woman her size should never be able to fell a man of his size.

Her dream lover had that same expression now. And goddess, if he wasn't more disgustingly handsome in the flesh.

Red hair, something that often looked goofy on a man, had a different effect on *this* man. The candlelight sent shimmers over the thick, shoulder-length mane. He wore a white shirt and plaid the way Artair always did, albeit this kilt was solid black not tartan. Nor did the cloth reach over his shoulder to rest against his heart.

Candlelight?

Dragging her thoughts away from the man who'd haunted her sleep, she took in her environment. The room was foreboding, the dark stone walls giving the place the ambiance of a prison. Or a tomb.

There only five pieces of furniture in the enormous room, including the bed she rested on. Two chairs sat in front of a large hearth, a wooden bureau rested in the corner and a table stood next to the bed.

A bedroom.

The man took the cloth from her grasp, his fingers brushing her hand. His sharp intake of breath echoed hers. A suspended second passed before he dipped the cloth in a bowl of water, wrung it out and handed it back to her.

"How's yer head feeling?" he asked.

"Like someone hit me with a club." She pressed the wet cloth to her forehead.

"Nay. Not a club. The hilt of my sword."

It took a moment for the blunt words to register. Her dream man had hit her? Why would he have a sword? No one other than Amazons or Sentinels carried one as a weapon in this century.

After his confession, she should have been afraid. She wasn't, but she didn't have time to ponder the oddness of that.

Sarita couldn't help but ask, "Why would you hit me?"

"Seemed easier than trying to hold onto you while I explained that I had to kidnap you."

"Kidnap?" His bluntness was as harsh as a slap.

"Aye. You're now my prisoner."

The hell I am!

She sprang out of bed fast enough it would probably have impressed Gina—a jump worthy of Air. She launched the cloth at him as she moved, the slapping sound it made as it hit his face giving her a small thrill of victory.

Her eyes combed the dismal room, searching for anything she could use as a weapon.

Where's my sword? Where's his?

They stared at each other from the opposite sides of the bed. His stubbornness seemed every bit as strong as hers.

"Seems we have ourselves a stalemate, lass. You've got nowhere to go. Accept this and 'twill go easier on you. I mean you no harm." His gaze gave the room a deliberate appraisal. "Maybe 'tis not grand as what you're used to, but 'twill be comfortable. You'll have food. A bed. Shelter." His grin made her temper rise. "And the pleasure of my company."

"Until when? Until you decide to murder me?" Her raised voice echoed through the cavernous room.

His mouth dropped to a harsh frown. "I would never murder a helpless lass. Especially such a wee one."

The man had a talent for pushing her buttons. It took all of Sarita's self-control not to let her pride grip the reins and declare she was an Amazon and not a helpless *wee lass*. He might already know, but she couldn't be sure. Then again, why else had she been targeted for kidnapping, especially while on the hunt for a demon?

Her curiosity slipped out again. "Why me?"

"A means to an end."

"Who are you working for?"

"'Tis not for you to know."

She mentally ran down the list of usual suspects and kept coming back to the same name.

Helen.

But this was far different than any of her other attempts. She'd never lowered herself to use humans for anything other than minions and cannon fodder. Her allies so far had been Ancients.

Sarita went for broke. "Helen arranged this, didn't she?"

"Pardon?" His confused expression was far too genuine.

"Quit playing dumb. Helen's behind this."

"Nay, lass. Yer spittin' in the wind."

Between the man's strong brogue and his drought of words, she wanted to scream her frustration. Instead, she seized the only advantage she had. Surprise. She might be *wee*, but she was damned fast. Although she probably wouldn't make it out of the room and had no true plans beyond a simple escape attempt, she had to try.

She darted to the door, grabbing the handle. His responding steps smacked against the stone floor.

Sarita jerked the heavy door open before his arm snaked around her waist, hauling her back against his hard, warm body. Her fingers gripped the doorknob like a falling person clung to a ledge. His hands slid to her hips as he pulled her lower body off the floor. Her backside rubbed immodestly against his groin. If she let go of the knob, she'd fall and smash her face.

Yep, I'm good and stuck.

"Next move is yours, lass." The laughter in his voice was a blow to her ego. This guy didn't even know her, and he didn't respect her abilities, either.

She'd have to show him otherwise.

Sarita let go, bending forward until her hands pressed to the cold floor. His grip tightened on her hips. Knowing he'd underestimated the strength of her small body, she wrapped her feet around his knees. Then she pushed off the floor, tightened her abdominals then reared to bash the back of her head against his face.

A loud crack sounded when her skull connected with his nose, and yet, he didn't drop her. He uttered a Gaelic curse, the same one she'd heard slip from Artair the last time she'd accidentally caught him between the legs when they'd sparred. She really couldn't savor the small victory because she'd managed to hit him with the already sore part of her head. The world rotated and swam in her eyes, enough she feared she might be ill. She unlocked her feet from behind his knees.

The man released her.

She took a few stumbling steps and realized she'd go down hard. Before she hit the floor, she found herself scooped up into his arms and placed back against the cool sheets.

He retrieved the cloth, refreshed it and pressed it to her face. "Ye are resourceful. I'll give you that. But 'tis no use, loving. You're my guest for now."

Until I can find a way to get out of this hellhole.

"There's no way out," he said.

"You're telepathic."

He snorted a laugh the same way she always did. Despite her anger, she found it an endearing quality, and it dawned on her she felt no fear of this man. Perhaps because he'd been intimate with her for a week in dreams, showering her with passion that made her body respond simply remembering it.

"I'm not," he said.

"Not what?" Heavens, but the memories of his touch turned her brain to oatmeal. "Oh, not telepathic. My name's—"

"Rebecca. I already know yer name. I'm merely trying to think as you would were I in your place."

Her head spun ever more. *Sweet goddess.* This man had no idea he'd taken the wrong Amazon. For now she'd let him assume she was Rebecca. Maybe then she'd learn his game.

"So you know me. Yet you don't reciprocate."

He quirked a red eyebrow.

"Tell me your name!" she demanded.

"Ian. Call me Ian."

The dizziness subsided, and she focused on his face. A small trickle of blood came from one nostril. She sat, took the towel from his hand and stretched up to wipe the stain away.

He didn't flinch, standing there as she finally rose on her knees and crawled closer to be able to reach him.

My, but he's tall. Taller than Artair.

With gentle strokes she cleaned away the blood. "I didn't mean to break your nose."

"Aye, you did."

"Are you always so blunt?"

His smile hit her like a red hot branding iron, her body sizzling and burning with need despite all her efforts to tamp down the arousing memories. "'Tis my way. I'm a man of few words." He lightly touched her hand, pressing the cloth against his nose. "'Tis not broken. Merely sore."

She almost recoiled when his other hand rose to touch the right side of her face. His fingers rose to trace

the dark scar—a "gift" from the goddess Sekhmet—
that ran from her eyebrow to arch around her cheek and
end at the small cleft in her chin. Then he touched her
mangled right earlobe. The one Sekhmet had jerked a
hoop earring from, ripping it right through the skin.

It took every ounce of her strength not to turn away.
If her disfigured face disgusted him that was his problem, not hers.

His eyes met hers again, but he said nothing.

"I'll escape," she promised.

"You'll *try*. But now, you'll rest. I'll come for you
when supper is served." He nodded toward the bureau.
"There are gowns should you wish to dress more in
harmony with our present location."

Sarita waited until he was gone before relaxing her
guard. Her head pounded, and while she wanted nothing more than to sleep, she concentrated on reaching
out to Gina.

"Sis? Are you there?"

Her mind stayed silent—an eerie stillness that
marked the first time the women hadn't been linked
since Johann and Gina had waltzed right into Sea
World, where Sarita worked, and announced both of
the women were some kind of superheroes.

Sarita had been working with her favorite pet—a
harbor seal named Toby—when they'd found her. After
babbling some ridiculous story about Sarita's new destiny, they'd inform her it was time to go. She'd lost
her temper and sent Toby chasing after Johann. Not
that the seal could hurt him. Watching the big animal
hound Johann all the way to the spectators' bleachers
had made both women laugh aloud.

Then Gina proved everything they'd said was true by jumping an entire story in the air.

Sarita had *felt* her joy. Since that day, Sarita had a bond with Gina that transcended friendship.

"Gina, I need you. I'm in trouble."

Despite call after call to her sister, none were returned.

She'd have to find a way out on her own.

IAN QUIETLY SHUT the door when what he wanted was slam it so he could hear her startle at the noise. At least a startle would show she felt *something*.

His heart pounded a rough cadence, and although he'd barely touched her, he could smell her jasmine scent.

The dreams wouldn't be silenced. For a week, a woman had come to him, shrouded in the darkness of the night. He hadn't known her name then, thinking she was some spirit spreading erotic fantasies through his hours of sleep, perhaps a torment ordered by his mistress. That would be her type of mischief. In those dreams, Rebecca had made him burn in a way he'd never felt before. Not even in the days before his murder—the days when he'd been a mortal. The days before revenge consumed his heart.

Each time, she'd touched him, kissed him, she'd led him to the brink of ecstasy, only to leave him unfulfilled by disappearing in the fog of his dream. He had to be the most frustrated man in Scotland. Knowing she was real and that she was within his grasp made it almost impossible not to take her and satisfy the promises she'd made those nights of sweet torture.

No! No tender feelings for his prisoner despite the

emotions that had gripped him when he'd first realized his prey was his dream lover. He had a job to do, and this woman, no matter how badly he wanted her, had a job to do, as well. She simply didn't know it yet.

Revenge and passion mixed about as well as fire and water.

When he reached the kitchen, he stopped. The staff wasn't there.

Ian snuffed the panic gathering in his chest. The ghosts hadn't left him. He knew better.

When he'd returned to *dorcha àite*, he'd been thrilled to find the two of them haunting the keep. They'd told him they'd been waiting for him to return, somehow knowing his story wasn't yet over.

They wouldn't have left him now...

His ghosts were the only two members of his clan who'd stood by his side as the rest roasted him like a fattened hog. His last clear memories before limbo were of seeing the nooses slipped around his loyal servants' necks. He'd mourned their deaths while he'd lost his own battle to survive.

"Show yerselves," he demanded, needing their reassuring presence.

Old Ewan appeared first, nothing but wisps of white smoke until he solidified into a more human form. His appearance hadn't changed from the day he died. His gray hair looked wind-ruffled and his green eyes shone with wisdom. "Laird?"

"Where's Sile?"

"Here, Laird." She popped up at Ewan's side, dressed in the clan's tartan.

Ian frowned. "Ye know I don't wish to see that

plaid again. You'll not wear it around our guest. Understood?"

She bowed her gray head as her plaid shifted to a black wool gown. "Yes, m'laird."

"Dinner shall be in the great hall."

"As ye wish," Old Ewan replied with a bow. Formality had been such a part of the man, it didn't come as a surprise that he continued the respectful habits as a ghost.

"And stay in your own skins. I don't want to frighten her."

Both Old Ewan and Sile nodded.

"Are we allowed to speak to the lass?" Sile asked.

"Aye, but only pleasantries. Tell her nothing of our mistress or of what is to come."

"May we speak of the clan or of *dorcha àite?*" Sile's smile seemed so damned hopeful. The woman had been the memory of the people, keeping all the births and deaths in her typically meticulous fashion. Her question spoke of loneliness.

Did ghosts get lonely?

Such a simple question, but no easy answer. How much did he want his captive to know? "You may speak of the clan but do not use our name. You may tell of history, but you're not to discuss me. Not my name. Not my life. Nor my family's history."

Sile's smile fell to a frown.

"Understood?"

"Aye." But her frown remained.

"Two hours," Ian ordered.

Then he strode out of the kitchens, seeking a swim in the cold pond to quench his lust and wondering how often he'd have to repeat that ritual in the days to come.

FOUR

A SOFT KNOCK made Sarita jump down from the dressing-table chair. She'd been searching the walls for trap doors—the type of bolt-holes all old castles were supposed to have. "Ian?"

"Nay, ma'am. 'Tis Sile. Yer maid. May I come in?"

She brushed her dirty hands against her thighs, trying to hide her latest escape attempt. "Suit yourself."

A maid? An ally perhaps? At least she wasn't alone in this dismal place with only Ian as company. Being alone too long with that man probably wasn't a good thing. He had a way of affecting her she couldn't fight.

That, or she might be tempted to beat him senseless to get away from her prison.

The heavy door opened, and an older woman took hesitant steps into the bedroom. She gave Sarita a visual sweep from head to toe. "The laird will be displeased. You have not dressed for your meal."

"Laird?"

"The English word is *lord*. Lord Ian. Your host."

She glanced down at her pink—and now dirty—yoga pants and gray t-shirt. "I have no intention of pleasing *Laird* Ian. In fact, I plan to make his life as miserable as possible until he turns me loose. You do realize he kidnapped me, right?"

"Och, aye. 'Twas necessary, ye ken."

Although used to Artair's brogue, Sarita had to

think hard to understand Sile's words. "No, I don't *ken*. Why was taking me against my will *necessary*?"

"You'll have to be asking the laird, m'lady." Sile walked to the bureau and opened the door wide. Her fingers tripped over the row of old-fashioned gowns. "Are ye sure ye donnae wish to dress nicer? We donnae have other clothes for ye. Only gowns and plaids."

"What I *want* is to get out of here." Not that Sarita thought there was a chance in a million Sile would do something to anger her laird, but she had to try. "If you help me escape, I'll see you're well rewarded."

Sile shut the bureau and clucked her tongue. "Nay, lassie. Ye'll not be playing that game with me. I'm loyal to the laird, as is my Ewan. Ye're to be our guest. Best resign yourself to that fact. 'Twill make yer stay here easier. Now, if ye donnae wish to change yer clothes, please follow me to the dining hall."

About to refuse the summons to dinner, Sarita winced when her stomach growled loud enough to make Sile throw her a knowing smile. "Fine. I'll eat a little something."

"Follow me, m'lady."

Sarita tried to take in everything she could about her surroundings, unsure of when she'd escape again to seek possible ways out of this ancient mausoleum.

At least the long corridors were beautifully decorated as opposed to her austere bedroom. Several ornate yet old tapestries hung from the stone walls. There were a few places where paintings had once hung, judging from the faint shadows left behind. Heaven knew why they'd been taken down.

Unfortunately, there was nothing to help her know more about her prison.

"What happened to the missing pictures?" she asked Sile.

The servant didn't stop her pace. "The laird ordered many of the clan's portraits taken down."

"Why?"

"Ye'll have to ask the laird."

"What clan is this?"

Sile shook her head and kept walking until she led the way out of the corridor into a new room.

Sarita's first glimpse of the dining hall took her breath away. Enormous and cavernous, with vaulted ceilings much like an old cathedral, the room was dominated by a large wooden table that could seat more than twenty people. The chair at the head of the table had a place setting, as did the chair to its right. Three silver candelabras with white candles graced the table, but only the one closest to the captain's chair was lit. A small fireplace held a banked fire that provided light and plenty of warmth.

Had this been any other circumstance, the setting would be romantic.

Ian stood close to the fireplace, speaking softly to an old man. Sile moved across the room, listened to whatever Ian was saying, and then she and the old man left the dining room.

Ian glanced up as Sarita strolled to the table, a fierce frown fixed on his handsome face, probably at her choice of clothing.

Sarita smirked, savoring the few tiny victories she could earn over her captor.

Without a word, he went to the table and pulled out a chair.

She eyed him warily but settled in the chair, telling herself she was merely there to satisfy her hunger. Not to spend time with him.

Her best plan was to maintain her distance and keep a sharp eye open for a way out of this mess.

After he'd left her earlier, she'd paced every inch of the bedroom that served as her cell. The heavy door wouldn't budge—not that she'd expected to have free run of wherever she was imprisoned. The view from the window told her no one could escape that way. Three stories up at least, and far too small for even Sarita to fit through.

The heather spread across the field like a blanket declared she was still in Scotland. That and Ian's hypnotic brogue. Guessing her prison might be some old castle, she'd searched for a way to disprove that notion. A light switch. An electrical socket. Anything that spoke of this being anything but a centuries old stronghold.

All she'd found—or all she *hadn't* found—only solidified her theory.

She'd run her fingers over the hearth, looking for latches to secret entrances. *Bolt-holes*, Artair had always called them when he and Rebecca had shared their pictures of the places they'd seen on their Scottish vacation. Every castle was supposed to have a way for the occupants to sneak out if an attack against their fortress became successful.

Sarita hadn't found one, but she had plenty of places to search when Ian placed her back in the room for the night.

She *would* find a way to get home.

Then she'd find out who was behind this—whether Ancient, demig or demon. Artair and Johann would know where to search for clues, but she was going to steer them directly at Helen first.

None of the psychic calls to her sisters, even those to her closest sister, Gina, were answered. She was in this alone.

Although she wasn't sure how Ian managed it, some kind of enchantment had been spun around the place to keep her from getting a message to anyone. That meant he was already connected to her world, the world of gods, goddesses and magicks.

The time had come to stop trying to reach out for assistance and help herself.

She launched her attack with one pointed question. "How long before Helen comes her to see whether you captured me?"

"Helen? Who is Helen?"

"Oh, please. Don't play dumb. Helen—the one who put you up to kidnapping."

"I know no Helen."

Although she still wasn't convinced, she tried another tack. "If Helen isn't behind this, which Ancient set you up here?"

He took the chair at the head of the table to her left. "Nay, lass."

"No? No, it wasn't an Ancient who had you drag me to this Godforsaken rock or no, you won't answer my question?"

The stubborn shake of his head almost made her growl in frustration. Picking up her water glass, she took a sip, biding her time and sizing up her foe.

The old man walked back into the room, carrying

two plates of food. He set one in front of Ian and the other in front of her.

One look told her she'd be hungry a while longer. "I can't eat this."

Ian glanced at her food then at her. "Why not? 'Tis a beautiful piece of lamb."

"I'm a vegetarian."

"A what?"

"A vegetarian. I don't eat meat."

"No wonder you're such a wee lass." He pointed at her plate with his fork. "You'll eat the meat."

Who the hell did he think he was? "I won't."

Ian's face flushed red. "You'll not argue with me. You'll eat the lamb."

Sarita reached for a piece of bread from the platter Sile set on the table. "This smells wonderful. Is it homemade?"

Sile knitted her brow. "I'm not understanding the question. What is *homemade*?"

Such an odd question. "You know, from scratch—put all the ingredients together and stuff instead of from a box of mix."

Sile shrugged. "I kneaded it meself, if that's what ye're asking." With another shrug, she followed the old man out of the room.

"You'll eat more than bread, lass." Ian grabbed a couple of pieces of bread for himself.

"You might be my kidnapper, but you're not my boss. I *don't* eat meat."

His narrowed eyes and low snarl were surely meant to frighten her, but they didn't.

They ate in silence as Sarita sized up the man. Trying to read him was akin to throwing herself against one of the stone walls surrounding her.

The potatoes and carrots were tasty, as was the bread. She pushed the lamb chop to the side of her plate and wished there were some greens somewhere on the table. The thought of asking him to accommodate her with a salad or some zucchini crossed her mind and quickly fled. Requesting something from Ian seemed too much like begging, and she would do nothing to give him the upper hand. If all she had to eat were potatoes, carrots and bread, she'd get by.

Not that she planned on staying long anyway.

The old man came back to clear away the dishes. As he exchanged pleasantries with Ian, Sarita surreptitiously stuck her index finger in her glass of water. She almost blurted out a curse when she couldn't freeze it. Damn it if she couldn't even lower the temperature enough to cool it down.

The man glanced back at her as she dried her finger on her linen napkin, frowning as though he knew what she'd been trying to do. He couldn't, of course, because that wasn't one of Rebecca's powers.

Did he know Rebecca was the Earth Amazon?

He knew. She was sure of it.

She broke the silence, figuring she needed to find out more about her captor and his servants. "What's your name?" she asked the old man.

"They call me Old Ewan, ma'am." His voice was soft, almost as ghostly as his appearance.

"Old Ewan? Why not just Ewan?"

Ian chuckled. "With six Ewans in the clan, we had to find a way to keep all from coming when one was called."

"Are you Sile's husband?"

"Aye. I have that honor."

Ewan nodded to Ian and carried the remnants of the meal away.

Pushing his chair away from the table, Ian stood. "Would you like to stretch your legs? Perhaps a turn around the courtyard?"

Anything was better than being put back into her mausoleum of a bedroom. "You mean you're not confining me to my room?"

"Nay. I only ordered that earlier to see you got some rest since you'd been hurt. You are free to come and go as you please. At least within the castle walls." He offered his elbow.

She pushed away from the table and pointedly left her chair by sliding out on the side away from Ian. Not exactly sure which way eventually led outside, she decided to head toward the large room right off the dining hall. She didn't have to look over her shoulder to know Ian followed.

Guarding her reaction to the room, she wouldn't give Ian the satisfaction of knowing how impressive she found it to be. This castle was nothing short of enchanting, making her feel as though she'd found herself in a different time.

People actually lived in places like these?

More flames greeted her, this time a roaring fire in a massive stone hearth. Several chairs formed a half moon around the fireplace, and she was sorely tempted to curl up in one and relax, hardly remembering a place where she felt so much at home.

Not that she'd moved around as a child. Her "aunt" had spent most of her time in London, leaving Sarita behind in Los Angeles with a nanny. At least Lalita had loved the ocean as much as her charge, and they often spent hours enjoying the fresh air and the spray of the waves. The house they'd moved into on the Malibu shore finally gave Sarita a place where she could commune with the water, but they'd only lived there a few months before she'd left for college to study marine life.

Once she got the job at Sea World, she'd never gone home again. Lalita had left—moving back to India—and with her went the only thing tying Sarita's heart to her aunt's house.

Instead of parking herself in front of the fire, Sarita headed toward the double doors that she hoped led outside.

Her shadow of a host followed, chuckling when she had trouble opening the heavy doors. With a mere flick of his wrist, he pushed one open and gave her a condescending bow. "You'd be strong enough to open my door if ye ate meat."

She ignored the barb and stepped out into the chilly night air.

The wall caught her attention. Tall and imposing, it would take some effort to scale. Her eyes found stairs to reach it, which didn't surprise her because the thing had a catwalk—a way for guards to have been able to keep an eye on possible attackers in days gone by.

She shifted her gaze so Ian wouldn't know she searched for possible escape routes. Although he had to already know she was sizing the place up, she wouldn't be too obvious. Pacing away from the main building, she indulged her curiosity and climbed to see what was on the other side of that wall.

The stone steps were slick and mossy, but she nimbly made her way to the walkway. How embarrassing that she had to stand on tiptoe to peer over the side.

A hand grasped the back of her T-shirt and pulled her back when she strained to see if there was a dirty moat surrounding this side of place. Ian's frown could have melted the polar ice cap.

"What?" Sarita asked.

"'Tis no use." He leaned over the wall, stretched his muscular arm out and smiled. Blue sparks surrounded his fingertips, but he didn't wince. "Try all you like, lass. But you can't breach the barrier. This place is surrounded with an enchantment, so 'twill be no use to try your powers."

"Powers?" she asked, feigning innocence by batting her eyelashes.

His chuckle told her the ruse wouldn't work. "Ye might as well accept your fate. Perhaps my home doesn't have the luxuries you're accustomed to, but you'll be kept comfortable until you can be of use."

Sarita crossed her arms under her breasts and glared. "What do you want from me?"

He looked out over the wall.

She thought about following his gaze, but she couldn't seem to take her eyes off him. The moon waxed close to full, casting quite a bit of light. His features appeared softer, perhaps from the moonlight or perhaps because he liked what he saw as he stared at the property surrounding his castle.

"As I said, you're a means to an ends."

"And what ends are you seeking?"

"Revenge."

The man certainly didn't mince words. "How could

I possibly help you with revenge? I've never wronged you."

"But someone you love has."

Sarita almost posed a question about who in her life could possibly have pissed off some stranger from Scotland then thought of Artair.

Yet he'd been a part of the Amazons, serving as their Sentinel, for hundreds of years. He had no connections with the modern world. Anyone Artair might have wronged would be nothing but bones in a grave long since forgotten.

Had one of her sisters crossed paths with Ian? The Amazons always debriefed each other after every mission. None had mentioned a foray into Scotland or a tangle with a handsome hunk of Scotsman before.

"No questions?" Ian asked.

She shrugged. "You'll tell me when you're ready."

"You're so sure of that?"

"I can tell you're lonely. Otherwise you wouldn't have called me down for supper." She kept her voice soft and coaxing. "How are Sile and Ewan related to you? Aunt and uncle perhaps?"

He shook his head.

"Friends?"

"Members of my clan."

Since he was letting down his guard, Sarita pushed a little harder. "Which clan is that?" She swept her arm out to the courtyard. "Where are the rest of the clan members?"

"Long gone." His voice had grown harsh. "Dead. Every last one of them. Rotting in their graves."

Nothing he said made any sense. "You talk in riddles, Ian. You're young. How could people you were laird to be gone that long?"

"'Tis nae your concern."

"Goddess, you frustrate me."

"Angry that you can't call forth your vines, tie me up and make your escape?"

"Vines?" she asked, trying to keep innocent curiosity in her tone.

"Give it up, lass."

"Give up what?"

He narrowed his eyes, set his hands against his hips and frowned. "You're Rebecca MacKay. You're Earth. You came for Marbas because *I* turned him loose. Animal demons are yer domain."

"Why in the hell would you free a baby-munching demon on purpose?"

"To lure you out so I could capture you. You're here so that I can bring that bastard you claim as husband to justice. Artair MacKay must die."

FIVE

IAN WANTED TO give Rebecca a good, sound shake. How dare she stand there looking all sweet and innocence when she married the man who'd destroyed everything he'd believed in? "Have you nothing to say?"

Her shrug pushed his control to the snapping point.

Rebecca had pledged herself for all eternity to the man Ian wanted dead with every fiber of his being. Artair had the right to kiss those full lips, to touch that tempting body.

Had she borne him children?

Had she nurtured his seed in her womb and given him a child to carry on the MacKay line?

Had she gifted Artair with the one thing Ian always wanted but was denied—a family?

A raging jealousy weighed as heavily on Ian as his need for justice. He should be disgusted with himself for wanting her, for desiring a woman who'd spread her thighs for Artair MacKay. She was damaged goods, spoiled by the touch of a man who wasn't worthy to lick a true Highlander's boots.

Yet Ian wanted her anyway. If his fantasies had their way, he would toss her on the closest bed and make passionate love to her throughout the night until the sun rose again. Her taste had been branded on his lips. Her shape would be familiar to his hands. He could almost feel her tight heat surrounding him.

"Well?" he shouted, trying to scatter his lecherous thoughts by focusing on Artair's sins.

She cast a cool eye his way. "Well *what*?"

"You won't defend him?"

"How can I defend Artair when I have no idea what you're talking about?"

Gripping her shoulders, he pulled her closer, lowering his head until he stared directly into her dark eyes. "He had me murdered."

She'd tilted her head back to return the stare, her gaze every bit as unwavering.

No woman had ever possessed the courage to stand up to him the way she did. Being laird made women fear him. Not this woman. She matched his intimidation tactics and reflected them right back at him. And damn if that didn't make him want her more.

"Funny, but you appear alive to me," she drawled.

"Magicks. I was resurrected by magicks." Dark magicks brought him back to the Highlands, and this time the Seior—the forbidden magicks—was practiced by the goddess who'd pulled him from the barren land he'd called home for far too long.

"Seior."

For a quick moment, he feared she'd read his mind. He knew little of the Amazons' abilities, only that they were endowed with powers of earth, fire, air and water and had some special skills revolving around those endowments. His mistress told him she had once been an Earth before she became a goddess, but she hadn't told him whether Amazons were able to know another's thoughts. "How do you know about that?"

"Let's just say I've given it *a lot* of study. Figured

the more I knew about the scary side of magicks, the better off I'd be. So where did you come back from?"

"What?"

Rebecca's mouth fixed in a frown. "You say you were resurrected. From *where*? Heaven or hell?"

The question caught him so off guard, he blurted out an honest answer. "I'm nae sure. Limbo perhaps? 'twas nothingness. Just…nothingness. I despised it."

"Who brought you back?"

He shook his head. "'Tis not for you to know yet, lass. I'll not be telling you my story merely to satisfy your curiosity. You're to be held here to draw Artair out so that I may have justice."

"Sounds more like revenge." Her arms rose between his and pushed out, breaking his grasp.

"Call it what you will. The man might as well have murdered me by driving his own dirk into my heart. 'twould have been a kindness compared to how I died."

Pain flickered across her face, but at what? At hearing the callousness of her husband? Or at sympathy for Ian's suffering?

"How did you die?" Her voice was a raspy whisper.

Although he vowed to never speak of that horrible day again, something about her made him open up the old wound. "My clan became convinced I was a witch. Do ye know what they did to witches in the Highlands in my era?"

"If you knew Artair, you would've lived around, what—the eighteenth century?"

Ian's voice rose with his anger. "So you have no doubt I am alive even though I also lived so long ago?"

"Who do you think you're talking to?"

"Think then, lass. What punishment was given to one who practiced witchcraft?"

Understanding dawned on her, making her eyes fly wide. "No." Her breath quickened. "No, they wouldn't have… They didn't—"

"Aye, they *did*." He pointed to the vast grassy courtyard. "Bound to a stake, I burned to death down there as my clan cheered. The same people who I worked hard to keep fed with a roof above their ungrateful heads. May they all rot in hell. And know this, Rebecca MacKay—I plan to send your husband to join them. Soon."

"Artair would never have done something like that! He's not that kind of man."

"The hell he isn't!" It took everything Ian had not to grab her again and shake some sense into her. His frustration overwhelmed him, and he wasn't sure he'd walk away from this confrontation without inflicting some of his anger at Artair on the man's wife. "Because of him, my clan suffered. Then I suffered. I mean to pay him back for each ounce of pain."

He had to get away. His rage and the passion he felt for her were drowning him. Stepping around her slim form, he hurried to the stairs.

SARITA COULD SENSE the tumbling emotions in Ian and was pleased she'd drawn more information from him. Unfortunately, those strong emotions were making him careless.

She called out a warning, but it was too late.

Ian's foot slipped out from under him the moment it came in contact with the moss-covered steps. His butt hit first before the back of his head bounced against a stair with a resounding thud. He lay as still as death.

Turning away, she only took a few steps before she ran into a wall of compassion. Torn between leaving him there to try finding a way to escape and seeing if he was badly injured, she clenched and unclenched her fists. Then with a frustrated growl, she hurried to his side, crouching next to him.

"Are you okay?"

No response.

Sarita ran her fingers through his reddish-brown hair, searching for any injuries. What would happen to her if he died? Would she rot forever in this magically protected castle? She knew nothing about Sile or Ewan except that their loyalty was to Ian. Would they help her if he were gone?

"Ian, wake up." Panic rose in her voice. *"Please."*

She started breathing again when he groaned.

As he tried to push himself up on his elbows, she put a hand against his chest, as though someone as small as she could hope to hold down a man as large as Ian. "Let me make sure you don't have any injuries."

"The only injury I have is to my pride." He smoothed his rumpled plaid back in place, covering his well-muscled thighs. "And perhaps my arse." He brushed her hand away and sat up. A smile crossed his lips and soon lit his whole face. "I havenae fallen on those stairs since I was a boy of five. Artair would always—"

The change in him happened so fast, it left her breathless. His grin had been so inviting she'd almost leaned in to kiss him. That was what had drawn her to him each night—his warmth and the way he enjoyed all of her touches, each tender kiss. His irresistible smile.

She'd seen that warmth a moment ago, but a ferocious frown swept over him when he'd said Artair's name.

Dreams were nothing but fantasy. In reality, this man would use her to hurt Artair. *That*, she wouldn't allow. This man wanted the Sentinel—the Earth Amazon's husband—dead. Her loyalty remained with Artair and her sisters. If she couldn't divert Ian from his path of revenge, it would eventually destroy him.

Oh, who in the hell was she kidding? Somehow this frustrating Scot had already wiggled his way into her mind. Every night he'd spent with her, every time he'd reached for her, he'd claimed more of her. And if that wasn't stupid...

"Can you get up?" Sarita offered him her hand.

"I'm nae crippled." He ignored her gesture and got to his feet. Then he brushed the dirt and bits of moss off his backside before heading down the rest of the steps.

She followed. "Watch your step. Don't want to fall again."

Feet on solid ground, he whirled to face her, catching her when she stood on the last step. Although she was still shorter, it was easier to look into his eyes. At least she didn't have to tilt her head all the way back to glare.

"You've a sharp tongue."

"A sharp tongue? Why? All I did was tell you to watch your step."

"Don't pretend that innocence with me. I *know* what you meant. That husky voice of yours—"

"Husky? You think my voice is husky?" Yes, it was a bit on the deep side, but it wasn't masculine.

She thought of her sisters' voices. Rebecca always sounded like Mary Poppins because of her motherly tone. Megan and Gina didn't come across different than any other women. They had feminine lilts, but nothing that forced men to comment.

Seemed like every time Sarita opened her mouth to speak to a man, he felt compelled to make mention the huskiness or roughness of her voice.

"I don't sound like a man." She tried to step around him.

Ian blocked her and set his hand on her shoulder. "'Twas not an insult."

"Husky." She huffed an angry breath. "Sounds like an insult to me."

His hand rose so he could run his fingers over her braid. "'Tis a voice meant for seduction, lass."

"Excuse me?"

"I love to hear you speak. Your voice is as warm as a good swallow of *uisge beathea*."

She'd heard Artair call whiskey *uisge beathea* more times than she could remember. "So now my voice isn't just *husky*, it sounds like *liquor*?"

Tugging her braid, he pulled her closer. She allowed it until his lips came close enough that his breath brushed her face. "Aye. It sends heat through me."

Ian's mouth captured hers.

Sarita wanted to resist, but then his familiar taste and scent flooded her senses. She was powerless to keep from threading her arms around his neck and kissing him back. Goddess help her, she heightened the exchange. Her tongue tickled against his lips.

He smiled against her lips and opened up to her. Her tongue invaded to stroke across his, and he growled, his chest rumbling with the sound that sent heat swirling between her thighs.

Memories of her dreams interfered, making her feel as if she'd always been this man's lover, as if they were meant to see this kiss through to the promise it made to her body.

IAN PUSHED HER back against the cold stone wall. He buried his face against her soft neck. He hated himself for wanting her so much, but he was losing the fight to keep his distance. The memories of those incredibly erotic dreams made it impossible for him to put her out of his mind.

"Artair..." she whispered.

That name hit him like a bucket of ice water.

He stepped back, furious with himself. At least she gasped for breath with the same intensity, saving his pride.

"So you were thinking of your husband, aye?" He lashed out, his own emotions so tied in knots he wasn't sure he'd ever work them loose. Jealousy. Anger. Longing.

That thought made his scowl deeper. No matter how much he wanted to make love to her, he wasn't about to do so while she fantasized about another man. Especially that bastard Artair MacKay.

"Why did you kiss me?" she demanded. "You can't just kiss me whenever the mood strikes!" Her eyes had narrowed and she'd clenched her hands into fists at her sides.

"You kissed me back."

She sputtered in protest.

"I promise you this, Rebecca."

"What?"

"When I take you—when it's *my* body joined with yours—you won't be thinking of any man but me."

On that, Ian stalked away before he lost the last piece of his discipline.

SITTING IN FRONT of the fireplace, Ian sulked.

Things were already more complicated than he'd anticipated. He hadn't expected to feel anything for his captive Earth. She was supposed to lure out Artair for him and the Amazons for his mistress. Yet Rebecca haunted his every thought and guided his every action.

Waging a battle between going to his own bedchamber or seeking her out and finishing what they'd started in the courtyard, he startled at a bang on his front door.

Only one person would come to the castle, and he wasn't much in the mood to see her. Unfortunately, turning her away wasn't an option—not if he wanted to fulfill his quest. "You best let her in, Ewan."

"She wasnae invited. I say let her rot on the doorstep."

Whoever was at the door pounded again. Harder.

"Ewan…please."

"As ye say, Laird."

Old Ewan moved at a snail's pace, his ghostly form floating above the floor. He muttered about rude guests loud enough for anyone to hear, which came as no surprise. The man was as loyal as a summer day was long, but when he had an opinion, everyone was made to know it.

The pounding continued until Old Ewan finally opened the huge oak door.

Helen swept inside, the hem of her pink medieval

gown caked with mud. As she strode over to Ian, she left a trail on the clean stone floor.

Sile would have a fit. She kept the castle as clean as any ancient building could be, and when she saw the mess, she'd probably go full banshee on the goddess. He smiled at the notion. Ghosts weren't bound by the spell Helen had cast on the castle. Sile would scare the piss out of Helen if she reverted to her banshee form—not that Sile could do any real harm. Her wails, however, could be ear piercing.

Ian couldn't let Helen's abuse go without inflicting a barb. "Ye brought most of the Highlands in the door with you, m'lady."

Taking her cloak off with the flourish of a troubadour, she flung it at Old Ewan.

The old man let it fall to the floor and floated away.

She scowled after him. "Why would I care?"

"My servants will be angry and—"

"As if I care what servants think. Yours, in particular, are far too rude for my taste."

Says one who expects others to serve her. From what she'd shared with him, Helen had no shortage of followers. Her "children," as she called them, numbered in legions, and each believed she was their savior— the one who would keep the Earth from destroying itself. Her charisma, no doubt, easily won people over.

Since Ian had been restricted to the castle, he knew only what she told him of her plots and plans. Not that he cared for the future of the world, although her ambitions rivaled that of Alexander the Great. Helen wouldn't rest until every human worshipped her. Those who resisted would meet with swift deaths.

Once he found his justice and faced his brother,

Ian wouldn't be long for this world, either. There was nothing to hold him here. He would die. Again. By his brother's hand or his own. Or Helen's.

"They should be punished," Helen insisted.

"Nay. They are loyal and good servants. Besides, how does one punish the dead?"

Even as laird, Ian had always worked alongside his clan members as they labored. He'd planted fields, delivered lambs and starved with his people. Only one who'd never known labor dismissed the efforts of others, even if they were ghosts who marched to a different drummer.

"Your gown's ruined," he said. "A pity you can't pop in instead of the making the hike across the moors."

Helen looked down at her dirty hem. "A small price to pay to be sure this castle's secure and our prisoner can't escape."

"Why do you wear gowns? I thought you were living in the modern—"

"That's not your concern," she snapped.

"Mere curiosity."

"Don't question me, Ian. *Ever.* I'm fighting for my birthright—for the worship and reverence this world *owes* me. I'm an Ancient, and I should be treated as such. My own kind has ignored me for far too long. I intend to remedy that. One day soon, the world will be mine." Her eyes narrowed as she put her hand against her bosom. "Mine!"

Nerves already stretched close to breaking, he didn't want to spend more time with her than he had to, especially if she was going off on one of her rants. Yes, she was helping him reach his goal, but he didn't like her. Not one bit. Nor did he trust her. "What do you want, Helen?"

Her blue eyes narrowed. "Dare you take that tone with me?"

He wanted to tell her he dared all when in *dorcha àite*. Were he inclined, he could live out whatever mortal life he had left within the walls of his home, and she couldn't harm him with magicks. Unless, of course, she chose to break the spell.

But that would allow the Amazons to sense their sister. She'd lose her bait.

Whenever she was in his castle, Helen was trapped by her own hand.

Still, he needed her. If he wanted justice, this neo-Ancient represented his best chance. So he'd pretend fealty when his real loyalty lay only with the burning desire of revenge.

He bowed at the waist. "I'm sorry, m'lady. To what do I owe this pleasure?"

"Has Rebecca settled into her new home?"

"Aye. She's nae happy, but she knows there's no way out."

"Good, good. Where is she?"

"Abed. She fled my company."

"That won't do. I have plans for the two of you."

"Plans?"

"Yes, Ian. Plans. Patience will be rewarded."

Since she was in the mood to play her petty games, he quit the topic. For now. "Are the Amazons searching for her?"

She smoothed her hands down the front of her velvet dress. "Of course. They're bound to be in a near panic, and far too busy to be concerned with my children." Her eyes roamed the great hall. "Have you seen any attempt by them to pierce the protection spell on the castle?"

"Nay. Not a single spark."

"Good, good," she said again. "Such a tricky spell. I'm not as strong in Aramaic as I am in Latin. A shame the spell can only be given in that cumbersome language."

"An effective enchantment, nonetheless," he said, hoping to stroke her ego so she'd say what she had to and then leave. "Rebecca will be my captive as long as she remains within these walls."

"Keep a close watch over her." The sly smile spreading across her beautiful face raised his hackles. "Even in the darkness, as you dream. Tell me, Ian—have you had her yet?"

"I knew it!" His hands became fists. He'd had more than his fill of her mischief, and now that his suspicions had been confirmed, he unleashed his anger on Helen. "You sent her to me in the night!"

"Of course I did."

"Why? Why would you torment me when I serve you?"

Strolling to the hearth, Helen sprawled over one of the wooden chairs as though she intended to stay for a good long while. "I decided it would suit my purposes."

Ian marched over to set his hands against his hips and glare down at her. "Torturing me suits your purposes?"

"I didn't intend to torture you. I simply hoped to inspire some...*closeness* between you and your captive. I want to deal Artair MacKay one final insult before I end his life."

"You mean before *I* end his life."

"Of course," she replied, although her tone was far from apologetic. "I want you to cuckold him. By sending her to you in dreams, I sought to tempt you into wanting the woman." She stopped, crinkling her brow. "Do you want her?"

"She's beautiful. Any man would want her."

"Not you, Ian. You're a man of—" she shuddered "—*conscience*. I needed you to desire her to the point of casting aside your restraint and taking her. So tell me…was I successful?"

"I haven't bedded the lass."

"But you desire her, don't you?"

He saw no reason to lie, though appalled with himself for wanting his enemy's wife. The passion he felt for Rebecca couldn't be pushed aside. "Aye. I desire her." More than he would let Helen—or Rebecca—know.

Helen popped to her feet. "Then do me this service. Take her. Have your way with her. Should you wish to truly hurt Artair MacKay, there's one more thing you can do."

"And what is that?"

"You can steal away her love. That blow would hurt him more than a dirk through the heart."

SIX

SARITA WAS RESTLESS. Pacing the length of her room and back yet again, she could have snatched at her hair like some crazy person.

The lack of water didn't help. The "toilet" was called a garderobe. Disgusting but serviceable.

Water missed water. No bathroom. No bathtub. No shower.

Sure, Sile brought her fresh water in a ceramic pitcher every evening so she could wash up. But what Sarita wanted—what she *needed*—was to soak in a tub full of rejuvenating water until refreshed and able to face Ian and the possibility of escape with some renewed strength.

The three days she'd spent in his company were heaven. He was witty and charming when he wanted to be, although his moods shifted quickly whenever reminded of the past. Most of the time, he was solicitous and treated Sarita less like a captive and more like an honored guest. Not that she felt she could open up to him about her identity. Not yet. Nor had she found the nerve to ask if he'd dreamed about her the way she'd dreamed about him.

He stole kisses often, leaving her increasingly frustrated and vulnerable. How much longer could she hold out against his attempts at seduction? Even when she reminded him she was a "married woman," he reminded her she enjoyed his attention as much as he enjoyed hers.

Did he truly desire her or did he only want to use her as a tool for his revenge?

Goddess help her, she didn't know.

Yet every cell in her body cried out to give in, to let this man make love to her. She ached, knotted up in sexual need—more than she could have imagined.

Unfortunately, while her stay in the castle might be heaven, it was also hell. She would have to leave. Soon.

This wasn't a vacation in the Scottish Highlands. Sarita was a prisoner, and her sisters and the Sentinels had to be searching for her. Who knew what had happened in their world while she was gone? Helen might use this weakness to make her move—whatever move she'd been building up to with her expanding cult. Perhaps in her absence, her sisters had figured out Helen's plan of attack.

Whoever had trapped her here wanted the Amazons compromised. Even if she was the weakest of the four, they were formidable when together. She needed to find a way back to her sisters.

She used much of her far too plentiful free time to seek out ways to break through the magicks holding her inside the walls of her prison. Spell after spell had no effect—even the black magicks she probably shouldn't have tried. But she was desperate. Although she'd yet to find a bolt-hole, she wouldn't give up.

Once the escape route presented itself, she'd take it.

"M'lady?"

From where she sat on the window's ledge, Sarita glanced back at Sile. "I told you, you should call me Rebecca."

"Nay, I cannae." Sile moved to the wardrobe and opened it. "Have ye chosen your gown for the day?"

Sarita shook her head, sick and tired of wearing the only clothing available to her—gowns. Not just gowns, but the same kinds of gowns the goddesses Rhiannon and Freya preferred.

Helen wore them in her appearances for the Children of the Earth as a way to show her followers she was "special." To Sarita, it spoke of her desire to be equal to Rhiannon—her former patroness. According to Rebecca, the jealousy had been there from the beginning. Helen continued to let that jealousy fester. One day the Amazons might be able to exploit that weakness.

To Sarita, the gowns were cumbersome and pretentious, and she longed to wear a pair of good, holey jeans and a ratty sweatshirt. At least the cotton nightgowns Sile had for her were comfortable.

Today, her yoga pants and shirt were clean. "I'll just wear my own things, thank you, Sile."

Sile clucked her tongue, something she seemed to do often. The woman acted like a grandmother rather than a servant. "The laird willnae like that."

The woman made no secret of the fact she'd been matchmaking from the moment Sarita arrived. Sile nagged at her to look her best whenever the couple would be together. She fluffed Sarita's hair and pinched her cheeks to add "a wee bit of color."

Sarita had discovered that Sile was far too free with her tongue. If asked the proper questions, the servant would open up and provide details that Sarita tucked away in hopes of using them later. So far Sarita had learned that Ian had been a good laird, that *dorcha*

àite had been built by his great-grandfather and that
Ian had never married. None of that could help her, but
perhaps Sile would let something valuable slip soon.

"The *laird* will get over it," Sarita replied. "So.
Sile…how is it that you are here?"

"I'm not understanding the question, lassie."

"Ian said he lived a long, long time ago and that you
were one of his clan. How are you still alive?"

Sile shook her head.

"Tell me about your clan. What name did they use?"

A smile lit her face and she opened her mouth only
to quickly shut it again.

"What's wrong?" Sarita asked.

"I cannae speak of the clan."

But she wanted to. That much was plain. "Were you
and Ewan resurrected? Like Ian?" It was a rare happening, and Sarita had her own idea on how the servants came to be here. She needed some confirmation,
though. "Ian came back because he was murdered.
Were you murdered, too?"

Sile's body shimmered, slowly becoming transpar-
ent as her legs became wisps of smoke.

So she was a ghost.

"We were hanged for fighting to save our laird's
life," Sile said, her voice choked with emotion. "'Tis
why we've stayed here. We waited for the laird to return to seek his justice."

"Justice? Against whom? The people who killed him
are all long gone."

Sile clenched her hands into fists and tipped her
head back as she floated higher and higher. Right as
she reached the ceiling, Sarita worried she'd leave.

Sile might be a ghost, but at least she was someone to talk to.

"Wait. Sile, please. I'm sorry. I shouldn't have said that."

The ghost drifted back down. "I cannae speak of the past. It pains me so."

"I know. I'm sorry."

Sile's form solidified. "Thank ye, lassie."

Sarita changed the topic. "I'm *so* bored. What is there to do in this castle?"

Damn if Sile didn't pull out a gown of ice blue out of the wardrobe and drape it over the bed. "Bored are ye? Mayhaps I can help. Can ye read?"

That got Sarita's attention. "Yes. Oh, yes. I love to read."

"Have ye not found the library as you search the castle for a bolt-hole?" Her green eyes lit with a smile.

"Who said I was looking for… What did you call it? A bolt-hole?" She kept her tone inquisitive and as innocent as possible.

"Nay, ye'll not fool me, lassie. Had six daughters of me own." Sile chuckled, the sound forcing Sarita to grin because it reminded her so much of her nanny, Lalita.

All her memories of Lalita made her heart happy. Her sweet smile. Her warm eyes. The way she'd hug Sarita tight whenever she'd been frightened.

Once Sarita had become an Amazon, she'd learned both her aunt Kamala and Lalita were Ganga's high priestesses. Despite Kamala's constant absences, Sarita's childhood had been full of joy. Thanks to Lalita. Although Sarita been an intelligent and precocious child, her nanny had tempered her with a gentle hand, using the same kind of wisdom Sile seemed to possess to keep Sarita out of trouble.

"I probably couldn't read anything in Ian's library." She tried to hide her disappointment. "They're probably all in Gaelic or English too old for me to read."

"Nay. Most are new. The laird has mastered several modern tongues."

"Then show me the books. Please."

"Well then," Sile said. "You don this bonnie blue dress, and I'll be showing ye the way to the library."

"That's blackmail."

"Aye, it is. I'm wanting ye to look your bonniest for our laird."

"Why?"

Sile tossed her an incredulous scoff. "As if ye donnae know."

"Know what?"

"Och, are ye blind, m'lady?" Sile pulled out the silky shift she always insisted Sarita wear under her gowns.

Leaving the window to go to the bed, Sarita ran her hand over the fabric of the gown. The blue would complement her dark skin.

So what? She'd be a beautiful bird that was still trapped in a cage.

Since the servant seemed intent on taking over a grandmother's role, Sarita decided to use that to her advantage. "Sile... I want to go home."

"What say you?"

"I'm so unhappy here." Her voice caught, making her voice authentically sad. She was able to work up a couple of tears. "I was kidnapped, and I'm locked away from all the people I love. I—I want to go home." Sarita sniffed hard as she bowed her head.

"*Six* daughters," Sile said again. "I'm knowin' fake tears when I see 'em."

Sarita shrugged, not at all that surprised. Gina always told her she was a terrible liar. "It was worth a try."

"That it was, but ye know the laird willnae let you go. He's quite taken with you."

"What you meant to say was that your laird *took* me. I was kidnapped, remember?"

"Och, nae truly kidnapped. 'tis fate."

"Fate?" She scoffed. "Being hit over the head and dragged away had nothing to do with fate. It was Ian's *choice*."

"'Tis fate, I tell ye. If you watch yer step, ye could one day be mistress of *dorcha àite*."

"Dor-what?"

"This clan's castle, the place you now rest your wee head at night. *Dorcha àite*."

"What's it mean?"

"A dark place."

Sarita snorted a laugh. "That's appropriate for this prison."

"'Tis a prison only if ye see it that way. Now did ye wish to see the library or nae?"

Bored enough to scream, she had no choice but to give in to the blackmail. "Fine. I'll wear the damn gown."

IAN STEPPED INTO the library, intent on reading one of his favorite tales to keep his mind off his captive. Instead of the diversion, he found temptation.

Rebecca had curled up in a chair, legs pulled under the skirts of her dress, while she read one of his most beloved books. The sunlight streamed through the window, painting her in an ethereal glow as though she were an angel sent to him as a reward for seeking justice for himself and his clan.

Did she know she moved her lips as she read? Each bat of her impossibly long lashes mesmerized him. Smiles formed from the story she savored.

As it did each time he saw her, his cock rose to attention, pitching a tent in the fabric of his black kilt. Ian adjusted the pleats to try to hide his arousal. Damn, but Artair didn't deserve a woman so devastatingly beautiful.

"Who gave you permission to come here?" he snapped. Perhaps one day he would learn not to take his frustration out on her. She hadn't set out to tempt him, but tempt him she did—as much as the devil himself.

She flinched, catching the book before it tumbled to the floor. "I didn't ask for permission."

"Ye should have."

"Why? Didn't you tell me I could come and go as I pleased?"

"Not in *my* library." He stomped over to one of the shelves lining the walls and snatched a book, not caring which one he took.

Slamming her book shut, she put it on the small table that sat beside her chair. "You made me lose my place."

"Donnae expect an apology. You trespass here."

"Sile brought me."

Not a surprise. The meddling old woman had been poking her nose into his business from the time he'd been a child. Once he became laird, Ian'd had to fend off Sile's numerous attempts at finding him a bride. She knew his habits well and had led Rebecca here. The servant had probably chosen the dress as well, knowing that shade of blue was his favorite color.

"She should know better," he mumbled.

Rebecca rose, the length of her dress swirling around her bare feet. Then she crossed the room to stand in front of him. That thought made a smile cross his lips.

"Your moods are like the wind," she said.

Her voice could charm Eden's snake to eat the apple himself. He wanted to hear that sexy voice cry out his name as passion held her in its talons—passion for him and him alone.

He frowned.

"See? Goddess, you're smiling one second and scowling the next." Wrapping her arms around her waist, she took a deep breath then blew it. "I need a bath."

"Does Sile not bring you water to wash?"

"Well, yes, but—"

Ian leaned forward to sniff at her, hoping to tease her, but he ended up breathing in her seductive smell. "You smell fine to me. Not *too* offensive, at least."

He had to will himself not to grin at her indignant gasp.

She wrinkled her nose as she sniffed the air. Then she coughed. "You could use a bath."

"What say you?" Damn it if he didn't almost lift his arm to give himself a quick sniff. He narrowed his eyes. "I bathed last eve."

"Bathed? You mean there's a tub in this pile of rocks? Where?"

"Pile of rocks? 'Tis my home you insult, lass."

"Dorcha àite."

The Gaelic from her lips was music to his ears. "Who told you those words?"

"Sile. She said that's what this place is called. A dark place. Right?"

How easily he could drop his guard around her. "You know enough now. Sile shouldn't be telling tales of the old times." He rose and walked to the archway before he took Rebecca in his arms and kissed the frown right off her lips.

She hurried after him, grabbing his upper arm. "Wait. Please."

"Yes?"

"You said you had a bath."

"Aye."

"Where's the tub?"

"No tub."

Her eyes searched his. "If there's not tub, then where—"

"The pond."

She scrunched up her forehead. "You don't mean the pond at the end of the courtyard?"

"Aye. The very same."

"Isn't it muddy?"

"Nay. 'Tis lined with rocks."

She dropped her hand. "You're pulling my leg. No way. Not in front of your entire clan. Where did you used to bathe, back when your clan lived here?"

Ian tweaked her nose. "You're a bundle of nosiness this fine day. We had a bathhouse. Does that satisfy your curiosity?"

"Where is it now?"

"Gone long ago." Done answering her questions, he tried to walk away.

She stopped him again. "Can I swim in your pond?"

His first inclination was to deny her impertinent request. The woman had somehow gotten it into her mind that she was no longer a captive. Hell, from the moment she'd arrived, she'd refused to cower to him. If she wanted something, she got it. Sile added more and more vegetables to their meals, knowing that, despite Ian's repeated orders, Rebecca wouldn't eat a single bite of meat.

He'd gone soft. In the old days, he'd have told her to go hungry if she wouldn't eat the mutton or venison he'd provided. Damn it all if *he* wasn't eating more of the funny vegetables that Sile produced. He envied the ghost's freedom to roam.

Then he saw something in Rebecca's eyes—some sadness. God forbid she learned just how easily she made him want to give her anything she desired.

He gave her an exaggerated sigh to make her think her request was exorbitant. "Fine. Ye may use the pond."

Happiness radiated from her face. "Thank you, Ian." She rose on tiptoes to brush a kiss over his cheek, hardly able to reach until he bent a little to help her span the distance.

"That's the only thanks I get?" he teased with an indignant huff. "Hardly worth the bother of the favor."

IAN HAD DELIBERATELY made something simple seem as if it had cost him a great amount of money or effort.

Figuring she could be every bit as aggravating, Sarita frowned. "It *was* a big way to say thanks. It's not like I want to kiss *you*." She swallowed hard. "Makes me nauseous just to think about it."

His scorching frown could have set a green tree aflame. "You *love* kissing me!"

Biting back a smile, she shook her head. "I'd sooner kiss a pig." She whirled to walk away.

Ian grabbed her, wrapping his arms around her waist and raising her off the stone floor until he could look her in the eye. "When I kiss you, you *melt*."

When she tried to shake her head, he stopped her by slamming his mouth against hers.

The ruse ended the moment his lips touched hers. The chemistry was instant. Consuming. His tongue swept in her mouth, and she grasped it between her teeth to give it a tug. He moaned and squeezed her tighter against him.

Sarita stroked his shoulders, marveling at the strength of the muscles rolling beneath his skin. Should he ever turn his anger on her, despite her Amazon skills, she'd be hard-pressed to defend herself. That strength didn't frighten her. Instead, it made her want to touch every part of him, to explore each hard plane, to run her tongue over every inch of his body.

He carried her to the settee in the corner and laid her out, following her until his body blanketed hers. Without his encouragement, she spread her legs wide enough he could rest between them, only her gown and his kilt between them. Had those barriers not been there, she would have welcomed him inside her body. As it was, she kept only a tenuous hold on her self-control.

Ian fumbled with her bodice, unlacing it before jerking it down to bare her breasts. She had no will to stop him as his head moved lower and the velvet surface of his tongue stroked across her nipple.

Sarita arched her back and dug her fingers into his shirt. Only her teeth biting into her lower lip kept her from crying out. He shifted to her other breast, licking and sucking until she laced her fingers through his hair, demanding he keep up the blissful torture.

"So verra beautiful," he whispered against her flesh before he took a nipple between his teeth and tugged.

She gave him a moan then, especially when his hands tugged at the skirts of her gown. It dawned on her that once he lifted her dress, there was nothing left to protect her. No panties. Sile didn't know what Sarita had been talking about when she'd tried to explain.

And weren't Scotsmen naked under their kilts?

This was quickly getting out of hand, and her body warred with her mind over what to do. Every touch was so familiar and so arousing, she couldn't stop writhing beneath him. Her core throbbed for completion, wanting him to press deep inside her and fill her the way she'd dreamed about for so long.

Yet if she surrendered to him, he'd be winning some kind of victory over her.

The truth slammed into her.

Ian didn't want *her*.

He wanted to seduce *Artair's wife*.

How could she have forgotten? Ian thought she was Rebecca MacKay, that she was Earth. Sarita had been so lost in the sensual web he'd spun in her dreams and continued with each kiss, each caress since he'd taken her prisoner, she'd completely forgotten her ruse and his ultimate goal.

Damn. Damn. Damn.

Sarita wiggled her hands between them and pushed with all her might.

Ian stopped to stare into her eyes. "What's wrong, loving?"

"Get off me! Get the hell off me!" She thrashed, trying to bring her leg up between his so she could land a blow that would get him to move.

"Nay." His hands framed her face as he used his thighs to trap hers. "Stop. Stop struggling and tell me what's wrong."

"Get off me!"

"Nay! You wanted me, lass. Don't deny it. You were as ready as I was to make love."

She refused to answer him and tried to move him again. She might as well have been trying to move the Himalayas.

"Tell me what's wrong," he said as his thumbs stroked her cheeks.

"You want Artair's *wife*."

"I don't understand."

"Oh, yes, you do. You don't want me. You've never wanted *me*!"

THE DESPAIR IN Rebecca's voice sliced through Ian's sexual haze. While they'd acknowledged she was Artair's wife, he thought he'd made it clear that what flared was about them, not about cuckolding her husband. That was Helen's game. Somewhere in the time he'd spent with Rebecca, Ian had separated his goal from Helen's. Now, he wanted her because of *who* she was, not *what* she was. "Lass, listen. Please."

For a small woman, she was damned strong. Despite his heavier weight and taller body, he had a hard time holding her down. Fearing she'd hurt herself, he pushed himself away and jumped off the settee.

She refused the hand he offered to help her to her feet. Eyes angry and wild, she faced him. "You won't touch me again."

When Ian reached out to caress her face, she jerked her head away. His hand fell to his side. "We'll speak again at dinner. Perhaps you'll have a grip on this irrational anger by then."

"I hate you, Ian." Sarita gathered her skirts in her hands, hiked them to her knees and ran from the library.

SEVEN

Sarita wanted to grab a sword and run it straight through Ian.

"Damn him."

She'd been a fool. An utter fool. How easy to forget that she was supposed to be Rebecca MacKay—Artair's wife. Sarita had lost herself in the way Ian made her body sing. She hadn't thought about how Rebecca *should* have been reacting to Ian's attempts to sleep with her. Instead, she'd acted like a teenager in the backseat of her boyfriend's car.

She'd been seduced by her own dreams.

"Goddess, damn him."

The blue dress only reminded her of Ian, so she yanked it from her body. Sile took care of the clothing or else Sarita would have either stomped on it or picked it up and tried to shred the material just to vent her anger. She considered stuffing it through the tiny window so she'd never have to see it again and be reminded of what had happened in the library.

Dressed only in the silk shift, she closed her eyes, wishing Ganga could hear her and pop her back to Avalon. Her sisters had to be searching everywhere for her, trying to reach out to sense her.

What if they needed her help? What if Marbas wasn't the only demon that had been unleashed? What if someone had let a *bunyip* loose? One of those could crawl out of a swamp and swallow a person whole. Only she could bring the evil creature back in check.

What if the Children of the Earth were stirring up trouble? While there were reports of arsons and disappearances in several large cities, police never seemed to find anything tangible to arrest any of the cult members. Priceless antiquities around the world were being targeted for vandalism—always some piece that honored one of the Ancients. As though destroying the painting or sculpture would steal away some of that Ancient's power. The Louvre in Paris. The National Gallery in London. The Uffizi in Florence. There was a plot to blow up the Parthenon—although that was blamed on terrorists, the Amazons knew better.

Families protested when their relatives joined the cult and handed over all their assets to Helen, but no one could find anything criminal in nature. It wasn't as if the Amazons could announce that magicks were involved. To the world, the Children of the Earth were just another cult bilking members of their money. Yet there were at least ten Congressmen and a couple of generals who sang Helen's praises.

Sarita felt as dry as she had back in the desert when she, Gina and Zach had faced Sekhmet. Dry to Water wasn't only uncomfortable but dangerous. Drinking the spring water and washing didn't cut it anymore. This ordeal had taken too much out of her. She needed to immerse herself in water.

That left her only one choice.

She opened the door to her room and stuck her head out to check the corridor. The torches had all been extinguished, which meant the servants weren't around. With any luck, Ian was sound asleep.

The coast was clear.

Stepping into the hall, she let her eyes adjust to the darkness. Once she could see well enough not to bounce off the walls, she worked her way down the long corridors to the exit leading to the enclosed courtyard—and the pond.

The full moon showered the grassy area with plenty of light. Seeing it made her homesick to see Avalon and the other Amazons. Gina was her closest sister, and a full moon meant Air was at her peak strength. Gina would always go a bit...*wild* those three days, and she usually needed Sarita to keep her grounded.

Of course now Gina had her husband, Zach. He would help her through. Gina didn't need Sarita. Honestly, *none* of the Amazons really needed her anymore.

And Ian only needed her for bait.

She felt about as useful as a rotary dial telephone.

Although the night was chilly, the water was warm enough to raise a light fog over its surface. The temperature didn't matter. It was water.

A quick look around declared the courtyard empty. Not that she'd expected to see anyone. Judging from the moon's rise, midnight had come and gone. How depressing to know she'd allowed herself to sulk for that long after she'd fled the library.

The rumbling in her stomach wasn't bothering her. Yet. But it reminded her she'd skipped dinner, choosing not to face Ian again. Better to be hungry than to let him gloat. Hell, she'd almost made love to a man who only wanted to use her.

She'd never felt so humiliated in her whole life. Nor so stupid. He didn't *want* her, despite what he'd said. Oh, he wanted *sex*. Didn't all men?

No, Ian wanted to make Artair's wife betray him.

Tired of the endless circles of her thoughts, Sarita pulled her shift over her head and tossed it on the grass before she ran to the water.

The pond's water was crystal clear. Now, the water beckoned her, its irresistible pull holding her fast. Taking a couple of long breaths, she inhaled once more and held the air in her lungs while she dove below the surface.

Every cell in her body sprang to life, loving the weightlessness of being in the life-giving water. Curling into a ball and holding her knees to her chest, Sarita sank until she bumped against the cold stones of the pond's deepest point.

Not as deep as she would've liked. Maybe ten feet, judging from the darkness and how long it had taken her to touch bottom. She planned on resting on the pond's floor as long as she could. *This* Water power seemed not to be affected by the castle's enchantment.

Eleven minutes was her best time underwater. By human standards, phenomenal. By Amazon standards, nothing but average. According to Ganga, one of her past Waters could stay underwater for a good thirty minutes.

Sarita wanted to give that record a try. The water worked its magic, and she never wanted to crawl out of it.

Stretching out, she explored the pond's floor, gliding her fingers along the rocks. There were no fish for her to play with—no creatures who loved and needed the water as much as she did—but at least she was free and calm for the first time since she'd arrived at *dorcha àite.*

AFTER HOURS OF tossing and turning, Ian finally tossed the blanket aside and threw himself out of bed. Sleep was impossible.

Rebecca haunted him. He could still see her eyes, dark with passion as he'd touched her. Then those eyes filled with hatred. The memory made him scowl and stomp around the room.

She had things all wrong in that wee female mind of hers. Oh, this might have started out as a way to please Helen. He would have seduced Rebecca to humiliate Artair. Stealing her love away would only have added to the sweetness of the victory.

Then the rules had changed when he wasn't paying attention.

This wasn't about Artair anymore. It had ceased to be about him the moment Ian opened himself up to the tiny, exotic woman who held him spellbound.

She'd captured his dreams, and that had been torture enough. Now that he was with her and had the chance to not only get to know her but also to touch her, to kiss the *real* woman, she haunted every minute of his existence. He could taste her against his lips. He could feel the weight of her breasts in the palms of his hands. He could sense her writhing beneath him, her passion running every bit as hot as his own. She'd become a fever in his blood.

For that one moment he'd had her beneath him, Ian had forgotten everything but Rebecca. No revenge burned through him—no need to right the wrongs committed against him so very long ago. All he knew was *her*.

Damn it all. That was what he got for thinking with his cock.

Ian grabbed his plaid, draped it around his hips and headed for his pond. A nice cold swim would help settle his nerves and, hopefully, his body. Perhaps then, he could get some sleep.

He didn't make it all the way out into the courtyard when he saw Rebecca's crumpled shift resting at the edge of the pond. His gaze searched the area as his heart sped to a rough beat. She was nowhere to be seen.

The pond.

She had to be in the pond. Below the surface, rinsing her hair perhaps?

Time passed slowly as he waited for her to appear until panic seized him. Casting aside his plaid, he jogged into the water, fearing he'd waited too long. What if she'd already breathed so much water into her lungs he couldn't save her?

He dove, trying to find her shadowy figure in the dark depths of the waters. If only he could shout her name, but all he could do was sweep his hands across the rocks and pray he'd stumble across her.

His lungs burned for want of air, and his panic grew by leaps and bounds. One horrible image stuck firm in his mind—Rebecca resting lifeless at the bottom of his pond.

Forced to surface, he gulped in a couple of breaths and dove for the rocks again. He sliced furiously through the water and cracked his forehead against a heavy stone. Dizziness made him lose track of which way was up, and he started thrashing, finding nothing but more water.

He was going to die, his new life wasted. And Rebecca—the one person who'd meant something to him besides his brother—would die anyway.

Ian suddenly felt a thin arm wrap around his waist and tug.

The moment his face broke the surface, he coughed and sputtered to drive the water from his lungs. Only when he could breathe again did he notice Rebecca kneeling on the grass, watching him with wide eyes.

He hauled himself out of the pond and flopped to his back.

"You okay now?" Her voice was whisper soft. She picked up his plaid and touched the corner to the sore spot on his forehead before letting it fall back to the grass. "At least, you're not bleeding."

"Aye, although I believe I inhaled most of the pond's water. 'Twill have to wait for a good rain to fill it again." How odd to be teasing after the terror at almost losing her and nearly dying himself. Perhaps it was the overwhelming relief that they'd both survived.

Then anger swept through him. He sat up to face her. "What were you thinking, lass? Swimming in the dark? Ye donnae know the depths of the pond."

"I'm a strong swimmer." Her reply came in a calm voice, one full of strength and control, things she'd been lacking the last time they'd met. Had she realized she was naked as she knelt beside him, she might have been more cautious.

It took all his concentration not to reach out and touch the beauty being paraded before his eyes. Her breasts were full, firm and high, graced with dark nipples that had become tight buds in the night's cold. A

V of dark curls hid her treasures, making him lick his lips in anticipation of tasting her. Her waist was slim, her legs and arms lean muscle and strikingly dark skin. Her wet hair tumbled in beautiful disarray around her shoulders.

"Strong swimmer or nae," he scolded, "you should be more careful."

"You told me I could use the pond."

"Not in the wee hours of the morning, I didnae." When she tried to rise, Ian grabbed her arm. "Promise me you'll not do something so foolish again."

Rebecca jerked her arm away. "Foolish? Seems to me I saved *your* sorry ass, Ian. You should be thanking me, not scolding me."

She had him there, not that he was ready to admit it. The terror that had gripped him when he thought he'd lost her remained so vivid... "Promise me."

Rising to her demure height, she frowned down at him. "What do you care anyway? All I am is a way for you to humiliate my...husband." The emphasis she put on the last word was strained. "I assure you, if you think I'll betray him—or my sisters—you're wrong. I'd rather drown than lure any of them here. So I'll swim whenever I want, and you can't do a damned thing about it."

Whirling on her heel, she only took a few strides before Ian got to his feet and caught her upper arm. She tried to twist away, but he wouldn't allow it. "Wait. Please, Rebecca. Wait."

She wouldn't face him, but she did stop struggling.

"I'm sorry, lass. You're right."

Glancing back, she lifted a dark eyebrow.

"I owe you my life."

"And?" she urged.

"I'll not be shaming you. That game is over. I owe you that much."

She snorted. "But you mean to kill Artair."

"He led me to my death. You cannae expect me to set that aside because you saved me from dying. I've died before. Once more is not frightening. I give you this favor—the promise not to touch you for revenge or shame. Take the boon, lass, and be satisfied."

"How?" she asked, tilting her head back and look him in the eye.

Ian had to will himself not to take his fill of looking at her body. The moonlight cast down on Rebecca, making her wet hair appear so dark as to be purple. She didn't shiver against the chill of the night, as if the swim had truly made her stronger.

Didn't she realize that he wanted her? If she'd only drop her gaze, she'd see the obvious sign of what being around her did to him.

"How, Ian?" she demanded.

"How what?"

"How did Artair lead you to being burned to death?"

"He made my clan believe I was practicing the dark arts, that I was a witch."

"A warlock," she corrected.

"Does it truly matter?"

"It does to warlocks." A smile bowed her lips before it quickly faded. "What did he do to make them think you practiced black magicks?"

The memories were painful, even after all this time. To be betrayed by someone Ian had admired and loved with his whole being would always feel like a part of his soul had been ripped away. "I don't wish to talk about it."

This time, when she tried to move away, he'd have none of it. He jerked her against him.

She gasped when her breasts brushed his chest. "I'm naked."

"Aye, so am I. Makes it convenient." His mouth swooped down to cover hers.

She bit his lip.

He let her go and swiped the back of his hand against his mouth. At least she hadn't drawn blood. "Why would you do that?"

"Because you broke your promise."

"Promise?"

Taking a step back, she narrowed her eyes. "You've forgotten already? You promised you wouldn't use me to shame Artair."

"You think that's all I want from you?"

She gave him a curt nod.

"You're wrong. I didn't break my promise. This isn't about Artair. Not anymore." Grasping her hand, he tugged her forward. "It's about us, Rebecca. Just *us*."

"You're not making any sense."

"When I make love to you, it will only be you and me. Artair will never have to know."

"And that makes it better?" She tried to take another step back, but he wouldn't let her go.

"Aye, it does. When I look at you, lass, I don't see Artair MacKay's wife. I see the woman I want above all other women."

"Yeah, *right*..."

Wrapping his arms around her waist, Ian picked her up, pulling her hard against him as her feet dangled.

The length of his erection pressed against the juncture of her thighs. "I see *you*, lass. Just *you*. Not another man's wife. Not Earth. I see the beautiful woman I desire."

This time, when he kissed her, she relaxed, letting his lips explore hers. She shocked the hell out of him when her tongue heightened the exchange, slipping past his lips to stroke across his as her arms looped around his neck.

The feel of her bare breasts flattened against his chest, the softness of the curls rubbing against his cock, the taste of her, intoxicated him. With a growl, he ripped his mouth away from hers and tucked his face against the crook of her neck, loving how she tilted her head to let him play.

Licking and nibbling along her soft skin, he worked to her ear and tickled it with his tongue. "Just us, loving. This is just *us*."

SARITA TRIED TO find the strength to push herself away, but she couldn't. He stroked her body like a talented musician mastered an instrument, and she was helpless to bring the embrace to an end.

She'd been so frightened she'd lost him and then so angry at his reaction to her pulling him from the pond, she'd forgotten she was naked until he took her into his arms. Now that they were skin to skin, she wasn't sure she'd walk away from this still a virgin.

Her stubborn pride kicked in, and despite his words to the contrary, she was sure he wanted to use her as a weapon against Artair. What man would want a woman with such a horrible scar and a shredded earlobe? "Please. No."

His face was suddenly in her vision. "No? You donnae want me?" His hands settled on her hips as he slipped his erection between her thighs and thrust across her core. "Don't deny it. You want me as much as I want you."

Heat surrounded her, enveloped her. "I *do* want you," she admitted, then wished she'd bitten her tongue.

"Then let me make love to you, here in the moonlight."

He doesn't want you. He wants revenge.

"I—I can't. Artair—"

Ian released her, giving her only a moment to steady herself on shaky legs before he groaned and stepped away. He snatched his plaid from the ground and tossed her a scowl as he wrapped it around his hips. "I told you, this isn't about your bloody husband!"

No longer caring if she was naked, she faced him, hands clenched at her side. "How can it *not* be about Artair?"

He just shook his head and marched toward the door.

"Ian!"

No response.

Goddess, she wanted her powers! She'd freeze the dew in the grass and make him stop and listen—as well as explain. There was so much he needed to know. "Ian!"

Stopping at the archway, he turned back to her. "This isn't about your husband. This is about *you*."

"What's that supposed to mean?"

This man who had been nothing but cocky arrogance from the moment she'd met him now appeared vulnerable. He gave his head a shake.

"What do you mean, Ian?"

"I care for you, loving. That's what it means."

On that puzzling pronouncement, he slipped inside the castle.

EIGHT

THIS BATTLE WAS the hardest Sarita had ever fought. If only she could take up her sword and attack this demon the same way she'd faced Marbas, she would feel as if she had some control over the situation. Alas, this enemy she couldn't face on a battlefield.

Hard to fight myself with a sword.

Her pride warred with the passion Ian inspired. She kept seeing his naked body, slick with water and glowing in the moonlight. The man was a mountain of muscle, his arms and shoulders sculpted as though Michelangelo himself had created him from a block of pristine marble. His face was sharp angles and his cheeks were covered with reddish beard stubble that made her fingertips itch to trace each line and rub against the roughness. His erection had stood away from his body, bobbing with his movements. Firm, thick and long, seeing it in all its glory had sent fire sweeping between her legs.

I'm an idiot.

At least she was if she planned to follow through with the scheme her mind was forming. Everything inside her screamed to steal away his power by going to him and consciously making the choice to sleep with him.

But if *she* went to *him*, she'd also be taking him at his word, that this was no longer about making a fool out of Artair—or her, for that matter. Why should she believe Ian? He'd taken her captive as a way to lure Artair out, and no doubt the Amazons, as well. She'd yet to figure out exactly what he wanted to do with them, short of knowing his hatred for Artair ran deep. Someone else—someone powerful—was behind this mess, and whichever Ancient it was probably wanted the Amazons dead.

That god or goddess would have to take a number and get in line. The women were at the top of quite a few deities "must kill" lists. Since being called into service, the Amazons had faced more demons than Sarita could remember. As far as gods, they'd defeated Chernabog and Sekhmet, as well as a few lesser deities.

No matter how many names she tossed around in her mind this whole nightmare smacked of Helen. Only someone as vindictive as her would be on a quest against Artair. To research his past and discover the sad history of Ian's death had to require years of dedication.

Just like the first time she'd stirred up trouble, Helen was bringing the fight straight to the Amazons.

"That *bitch*."

Helen hated Rebecca more than any of the other Amazons since Earth had denied her what she wanted most—a partnership of sister Earths to rule the world. It *had* to be Helen who'd ordered Ian to set Marbas loose so he could capture Rebecca.

The whole puzzle fell neatly into place. Helen had enjoyed quite a bit of time to master her powers since she'd ascended to become an Ancient. Because she was a daughter of Gaia—the mother of all creation—she could learn how to master Seior. Especially its greatest power—to resurrect the dead. That was how she brought Ian back. Sarita had no doubt she'd uncover Helen's connection if she could get him to open up and talk about what had happened so long ago.

And there was a good way to coax him into that kind of trust...

Oh, Goddess.

She was actually becoming as bad as he was, thinking of seducing him just so she could find the connection between Artair and Ian's clan.

No.

That was an excuse to justify going to him so she wouldn't have to take responsibility for her own feelings. What flared between them had gone much, much further than either had expected. She didn't want to sleep with him to force him let his guard down any more than he wanted to use her to punish Artair.

Something had bonded them in a way she wasn't able to fight. But if she let Ian seduce her, she would be the one who was conquered by her own desire for the frustrating Highlander.

Ah, but if *she* went to *him* first?

All's fair in love.

And war.

With a smile on her face, Sarita headed to the door.

THAT BITCH HELEN was playing games with him, sending Rebecca to haunt his sleep again.

He'd just drifted off when he sank into the familiar world of his erotic dreams. Rebecca slid between his sheets, her hands stroking up his chest as she feathered kisses across his shoulders. She was naked, her skin burning him each place it met his.

He dug his fingers into her hair, wondering at how the thickness held a bit of dampness... From her swim.

This was no dream.

Gripping her shoulders, he sat up, holding her away from him. "What are you doing, lass?"

"I'd think that was obvious." With no warning, her fingers encircled his stiff shaft.

Something between a groan and a gasp fell from his lips. "But ye said—"

Her hand slid up and down his length. "I want you, Ian."

While he might damn himself for his reaction, the shreds that remained of his honor wouldn't let him take her until things were straightened out between them. He'd promised not to make love to her out of revenge. He needed to know what purpose she had in coming to him like a wraith in the night.

"Why?" he asked.

Instead of answering, she released his erection and straddled his hips. In a tantalizingly slow pace, she set herself down on his groin and rubbed against him. "I want to make love with you."

Before he could ask another question, she put her palms on his shoulders and pushed his back to the mattress.

"But why would you—"

"Shut up, *jaanu*." The sparkle in her eyes took the sting out of her command.

"Jaanu?"

She didn't explain the endearment. "This is *my* choice. I want you, and I don't give a damn about anyone else right now except you and me."

"Are you sure, loving?"

"Shut up, *jaanu*," she said again, "and kiss me."

Her smile intoxicated him, her skin iridescent as it glowed in the light of the fire in his hearth. He'd never seen anything half as beautiful.

"Yes, m'lady. Anything you ask that I can give you is yours."

"You. I want *you*."

"With pleasure."

Cupping her neck, he pulled Rebecca down until he could kiss her. Not a gentle kiss, but one to tell her he'd passed the point of letting her walk away.

His tongue caressed hers as he smoothed his hands up her arms and across her collarbone. Her breasts beckoned him. He savored the press of them against his palms. Soon it wasn't enough to touch, he had to taste her.

He sat up and grabbed her waist to set her higher on his lap so her damp heat nestled his erection. Then he ran his tongue across one distended nipple.

Rebecca arched her back, laced her fingers through his hair and tugged.

He drew the tip into his mouth, applying suction while she moved against him. Since she seemed so receptive to his touch, he shifted to the other breast, laving and teasing until she pulled his hair rough enough to sting.

IAN'S TOUCH, THE feel of his tongue, his lips, threw her mind into a riot of emotions. Her skin was on fire, her breasts heavy and sensitive as she held him right where he was, demanding he continue the exquisite torture.

Jaanu. The Hindi endearment repeated in her mind, over and over in a chant. *Jaanu. Jaanu.*

My life and my heart.

She needed more, wanting to praise his body the same way he worshipped hers. Pushing her palms against his shoulders, she tried to separate from him.

He wouldn't allow it, drawing her back to him by holding her nipple between his teeth.

She pushed harder, loving the mix of pain and pleasure, until he released her and let her have her way. Burying her face against his neck, she nipped at his skin, soothing each bite with a loving lick. His neck. His shoulder. Moving to his chest, where she rubbed her nose in the crispy hair that spread across his pecs, tapering as she followed the trail down to his stomach.

Her tongue circled his navel, making his abs quiver. Sarita smiled as she put her hand on his erection.

"Lass, ye donnae have to—"

Stopping only long enough to throw him a smile, she indulged herself in the one thing she'd always been afraid she wouldn't have the nerve to try. She licked him from root to tip.

With a sharp inhale, Ian raked his fingers through her hair.

Sarita found that not only did she have the courage, she loved taking him into her mouth, learning his taste and his shape. She trailed one hand up his inner thigh until she could cradle his soft sac in the palm of her hand. Everything about his body was so new, so exciting to her. Touching him in such an intimate way made her insides burn. When she gently squeezed him, he groaned.

"I cannae take much more, loving."

Releasing him, she kissed her way up his body until she straddled his hips again. "Neither can I."

"Take me inside you, Rebecca. I need to feel you around me."

The name grated on her, but she brushed it aside. It was the only name he knew for her, and no matter how she wanted to hear her name spill from his lips, that just couldn't happen.

She loved that he let her make the choice, somehow it made everything between them equal again. He'd handed her his need for revenge, letting her know this wasn't about Artair any longer. This was a man and woman, lost in desire, coming together in passion that had been nurtured for so long it had become far too strong to deny.

Rubbing the tip of his cock against her, she shifted until he slid inside her body.

He gasped.

She whimpered, letting the fleeting pain of losing her virginity pass and praying Ian wouldn't notice.

IAN HAD NEVER felt anything as wonderful as her tight heat surrounding him, squeezing the breath from his body. But his entrance had been less than smooth. He dug his fingers into her hips and gaped at her.

No. It wasn't possible. She was Artair's *wife.* He shouldn't have had to push past the barrier he'd just plunged through with all the finesse of a battering ram.

"How can you be a virgin?" he demanded.

His thoughts tumbled and twisted. Why would Artair MacKay marry a woman as beautiful as Rebecca and not take her to his bed?

"How can this be?"

She shook of her head, sending her glorious mane of hair spilling over her shoulders.

"But—"

She took his words away with a heartfelt kiss.

"Not now, Ian," she whispered before pressing herself down hard against him. "Make love to me."

"But—"

She leaned forward and captured his lips for a kiss that robbed his every thought, especially when her tongue caressed his at the same time she lifted her hips and then pushed down again.

Ian was lost. Keeping his grip on her, he rocked up, planting himself deeper inside her.

"Goddess," she said in a breathy sigh, "that feels good."

"It feels a whole lot more than *good*, loving. 'Tis heaven."

Something primitive surged forward from deep inside him. He was the first man to possess her, and damn, if that didn't thrill him.

Her eyes were full of desire. "Aye," she said, imitating his brogue. "'Tis heaven, indeed, for this lass."

"Ah, my love—you do please me." Sitting up enough to slip his palm behind her head, he pulled her down, capturing her lips in a searing kiss.

There was no more talk, only the feel of her breasts against his chest, the slide of her tongue across his and the rhythm of her body meeting each of his thrusts. He'd be damned if he'd find fulfillment before her, especially after she'd gifted him with her precious virginity. But each time he moved within her, another thread of his control snapped.

Just when he feared he'd lose his battle, she took her lips away from his, panting for air before a cry of ecstasy escaped. In that moment where her muscles squeezed him tight, he found his own release. He called her name as he thrust into her one more time and let his climax take hold.

Sunlight trickled through the window, its warmth making Sarita stretch like a contented, lazy cat. She arched and raised her arms above her head to ease the tightness in her muscles.

A strong hand captured her wrists, trapping her arms. Ian's body blanketed hers. He brushed his beard-stubbled cheek against the spot where her neck met her shoulder, adding nibbling kisses as he rubbed his naked body against hers. There was no doubt he'd woken up hungry for her—as hungry as she was for him.

"Such a nice way to wake up," she murmured.

Instead of speaking, he put his lips to hers, his tongue sliding inside her mouth to stroke and tease and tempt.

She replied by wrapping her legs around his hips, loving how he moaned against her lips. Damn, if she wasn't wishing he'd leave the teasing behind. Her desire was already soaring, and she wasn't sure how much taunting she could take before she'd resort to begging. She needed him inside her. Now. Squeezing her thighs tightly, she tried to pull her arms free.

He wouldn't let her. Instead, he pinned her wrists to the sheets with one hand while the other squeezed between their bodies. Without so much as a word, he grabbed his erection and slid into her body.

Sarita gasped, closing her eyes and surrendering to the riot of feelings racing through her.

Ian had awakened with the taste of her still on his lips, and he could think of nothing more than making love to her again. He was probably moving things along far too quickly. She'd need time for the tenderness of losing her innocence to leave. Finesse hadn't entered this interlude, but the need to be the aggressor this time was more than he could control. Now that he was deep inside her, he almost breathed a relieved sigh. Her passion matched his perfectly. She was wet and ready.

And she belonged to him now.

When he moved, pulling back before thrusting inside her again, she moaned against his mouth, the sound driving his desire for her higher and higher.

Ian released her wrists, and her hands moved to his shoulders, where she dug her fingernails into his skin and raked deep furrows. The sting made him speed the rhythm.

That's it, loving. Mark me as yours.

The race for fulfillment was on, and she met each of his strokes with her hips. Afraid her uninhibited response would force his own orgasm first, he was ready to reach between their bodies and stroke her to release. But she drew her knees up and tightened around him. Her back arched as she ripped her lips away from his and called his name.

He joined her a heartbeat later, his climax so strong, he could barely hold himself up so he wouldn't crush her with his weight.

Long moments passed, the only sound in the bed-chamber the breaths each gulped. He'd never known the type of contentment he felt at that moment, and with that realization came fear.

Ian rolled away from her.

Rebecca followed, draping her slender thigh over his legs while her fingers toyed with his chest. "Good morning."

His thoughts were so tangled, all he could do was grunt in response.

Pushing up on an elbow, she stared at him. Her hair had fallen in beautiful disarray around her shoulders and her face. He combed through the heavy locks with his fingers, brushing it back over her shoulder. Then he traced the length of her scar with his fingertip. The mark grounded him, making him realize she wasn't as perfect as the image he'd created of her.

Rebecca pushed his hand away and pulled some tresses back to cover her ear and the side of her face. "I know. It's unsightly."

"Nothing about you could be unsightly. How did you come by the mark?"

"It was a gift from a goddess who hated me and my sisters."

"A goddess?"

She tried move, but he grabbed her wrist. She frowned. "I don't want to talk about it, Ian."

"Fine. We have other matters to discuss."

"Discuss? Like what?"

"The weather in the Highlands?" He scoffed. "You were a virgin, woman! How is it yer married and have never been bedded?"

"The last thing I want to do right now is talk about *any* of this. Besides, there's nothing to talk about. What happened—or didn't happen—between Artair and me is none of your business."

Jerking her wrist from his grasp, she threw herself from the bed. She picked her shift up off the floor and donned it. "I'm going for a bath in the pond."

Without waiting for him to say a word, she hurried to the door and left.

She had it all wrong. There was *plenty* to talk about.

In the act of loving her, his whole world had been flipped upside down.

When he'd been making love to her, he hadn't been thinking about Artair MacKay or Helen or the Amazons. For those precious moments, the only two people who existed were him and his beautiful captive. Once he'd claimed her virginity, all his plans were thrown in disarray.

The need for revenge was a dying fire. In loving Rebecca, those flames had dimmed, growing fainter until all that remained was her.

He couldn't use her anymore. And no matter how much he wanted to, there was no way he could keep her, either. There was only one choice remaining.

The time had come to send her back to the world—to her sisters.

Knowing she'd return to Artair killed Ian inside. The notion of another man touching her, even if that man was her wedded husband, turned his stomach. But to know she was safe was more important than worrying about her sharing her husband's bed.

Ah, but she *hadn't* shared Artair's bed. Ian had been the first to claim her, a victory no one could take away from him and a memory he'd cherish forever.

Yet Ian couldn't keep her. Nor could he ever allow Helen to harm her. The safest place for her was with her sisters.

How could he get Rebecca home?

Helen couldn't harm her so long as the magicks stayed spun around *dorcha àite*. No doubt she'd try to end the spell when Ian refused to hand over Earth. Yet the instant the spell fell, the Amazons would be able to sense Rebecca and transport her back to Avalon.

Once she was home, then Helen could do her worst. He almost smiled as he pictured the divine tantrum the goddess would throw. He'd witness quite a show before she punished him.

Until Helen returned, he would sate himself with the tiny woman who'd captured him with the stealth and skill of the best reiver. Just like a thief, she'd stolen the only thing he had left.

His heart.

NINE

AFTER THREE GLORIOUS days of acting like newlyweds, Sarita wanted to pretend this was forever. That she wasn't an Amazon. That Ian didn't hate Artair.

Every time Ian tried to bring up why she'd been a virgin or discuss the future, she distracted him—usually through seduction. Amazed at the greed she possessed for him, she cut loose any binding she'd held on her passion. Although she'd never considered herself a prude, she'd also never experienced the kind of freedom her love for Ian gave her. Nor had her sisters warned her how terrifying being in love could be—how she'd lose herself in making love, feeling as if her soul joined with Ian's each time they came together.

They swam nude, bathing each other, and she didn't try to hide her body from him. They slept naked, something that seemed decadent. But she enjoyed the feel of his hot skin against hers. Without his touch, she wasn't able to rest at night. They made love so many times, she lost count.

For as long as she was in this place, she'd act on every fantasy and fulfill all of his.

Not that she wasn't forming a few plans...

Even though Ian had never slipped and told her that Helen was behind this, in her heart, Sarita knew. What she didn't know was how they could come out of this mess without her losing Ian and still being able to protect Artair from his wrath.

Turning idea after idea around, she came to one stark and scary conclusion—if she could get Ian to Avalon, he would never stay for the simple fact Artair was there. Nor could Sarita leave her home and her sisters to be with Ian. She was, above all things, the Water Amazon. She owed her allegiance to Ganga and the Amazons. Although she loved Ian more and more with every passing minute, she wouldn't walk away from her duties or her sisters to be with him.

Goddess, this whole thing's a nightmare.

Before she could decide on a plan, the world intruded on *dorcha àite.*

Sarita looked up from her meal when someone pounded on the heavy oak door. She'd wondered how long it'd be before Ian's benefactor came for a visit. No doubt, Helen would be the Ancient who walked in when Old Ewan finally made his way over to the door.

She glanced to Ian, who'd dropped his spoon into his stew. "It would appear you have a visitor."

"Aye." His gaze went from the door to her. "Ye best take yourself to our bedchamber, loving." The legs of his chair scraped across the stone floor as he got to his feet.

It warmed her heart to hear him refer to his bedroom as belonging to both of them, yet she knew who'd come knocking. The time had come to face her enemy. "I'm not hiding."

"It wouldnae be hiding—"

"The hell it wouldn't."

"I'm trying to protect you."

She scooted her chair back and stood. "Rule number

one for dealing with an Amazon—*don't protect her.* She can damn well protect herself."

"Are you sure?"

She tossed him a brusque nod. "Let me be a surprise."

"You were certainly a surprise to me, especially the first time you came to my bed."

She ignored his cheeky remark.

By letting Helen see that Ian had captured Water instead of Earth, Sarita might be able to use the element of surprise to her advantage. Since *dorcha àite* was shielded from magicks, she could provoke a confrontation. While she might have lost a fight in the real world because Helen was a goddess, their powers weren't in play here. Helen couldn't blast things or toss Sarita aside with nothing but the swipe of her hand. There would be no revenants.

Sarita was fast and a master of hand-to-hand combat. She just might have a shot now that the playing field had been leveled.

How would Ian react when her secret came out? He already knew she'd been a virgin, but from what he'd said, he'd "blamed" that on Artair. Ian took great delight in insulting Artair's virility.

Now, the time had come to show all her cards. "I'm sure Helen will be *really* glad to see me."

He clenched his jaw. "I didnae say it was her."

"Aw, c'mon. It wasn't tough to figure out. Helen's hated Earth from the day she became an Ancient. Each new defeat the Amazons hand her only makes her more rabid to kill us all. What I need to know is why she chose *you*. What's the ace you're holding up your sleeve that made her bring you back to the world of the living? 'Cause I know it's more than just what your clan did to you—what you think Artair made them do."

"Rebecca, please…"

"Are you going to tell me?" she demanded. "Or are you going to let Helen spill the beans?"

"Loving, I—"

"Ian!" Helen's distinctive voice echoed from the foyer. "Where are you? I have news!"

"Please. Go upstairs. *Now.* Let me handle this. Maybe I can reason with her."

At least he wasn't lying by denying that he'd been used by Helen. A fair start to a new beginning for them.

"I'm not leaving, Ian. The game ends tonight. One way or another, I'm done playing by that bitch's rules." She headed into the shadows to wait for the right moment.

OLD EWAN LED Helen into the dining hall. As slowly as he shuffled across the floor, he acted as though he were being led to his own execution.

She swept past him, shoving the servant out of the way, the train of her forest-green gown dragging behind her.

"My plan is finally falling into place," she announced as she strode over to Ian. "It won't be long before I can call them out!"

"Who?" Ian couldn't make himself care.

He watched her, his heart pounding, as he waited for Rebecca to make her move. There was normally no way someone that tiny could take a woman of Helen's size, especially a goddess.

Ah, but the rules were different at *dorcha àite*, and Helen had been the one who changed them.

He tried to contain a grin. If hard-pressed, who knew what Rebecca was capable of doing? She might not be able to use her vines or shake the ground, but Helen wouldn't be able to throw energy or stop her with force fields. Nor would the old Earth be able to stop the new one with any of the killing spells the Ancients possessed.

Since Rebecca had retreated—probably to use the element of surprise—he would give her the chance to make the odds as even as possible.

This would be a fair fight.

His chance for justice might be forever lost. Without Helen's backing, how would he be able to face Artair MacKay?

No.

Ian had made his decision. Rebecca was more important than revenge. He only hoped Helen wouldn't kill him when Rebecca escaped.

"The game ends tonight," he whispered.

"What did you say?" Helen demanded as she came to stand at his side.

He shook his head. "To what do I owe this pleasure, *m'lady*?"

"I told you, I have news."

"Well then, share your news and be gone. As you see, I'm in the middle of my meal and wish to finish it before my meat grows cold." When he looked down at what remained of their dinners, he noticed Rebecca's knife was missing.

What a smart woman she was, and damn, if he'd never considered that she could use it against him. In that moment of recognition, he knew she cared for him.

She could have easily slit his throat. After kidnapping her, it would be no less than he deserved.

Helen clucked her tongue. "Ever disrespectful, aren't you, Ian? After all I offer you—"

He snorted, a habit he shared with Rebecca. Seemed whenever she laughed, a small snort would slip out. Worse, whenever she wanted to let him know just how displeased she was with him, she'd do the same.

Such a strange sound from such a beautiful woman.

Helen knit her brows. "What's wrong with you? It's like you're not hearing a word I say."

"Oh, I heard. I'm supposed to be grateful for all you offer me." He gave his head a small shake. "I've yet to see any of these *offerings*."

"You're alive. You're in your own castle and holding Rebecca hostage." A sly smile crossed her face. "Have you seduced her yet, Ian? Have you cuckolded your enemy? Better yet, have you stolen her away from her husband? I want him to know true pain before he dies."

Ian caught Rebecca's movements and tried to distract Helen. "Nay. The lass will not be seduced."

"Then try harder—rape her if you have to. I want Artair MacKay to suffer. I want Rebecca to suffer, too."

"Too bad you got the wrong Amazon." The knife was pressed between Helen's shoulder blades before the goddess had a chance to react.

"Wrong Amazon?" Ian's thoughts spun. "What are you talking about?"

The woman he'd thought was Rebecca marched Helen toward one of the chairs. She had to know she couldn't kill Helen, but that knife could do a lot of temporary damage.

He couldn't make himself move. His mind was in turmoil. "You're not Rebecca MacKay?"

"Get me something to tie her up with," she replied.

"Answer me!" His voice echoed off the tall walls.

This woman he cared for—the one he was risking everything for—had lied to him. His conscience shouted that she'd had every right to fool him, yet his heart felt betrayed.

He should have known the moment he'd realized she'd been a virgin. A man like Artair MacKay would never have left his wife unbedded.

"Are you Artair MacKay's wife? Are you Rebecca?"

SARITA WINCED. "No, I'm not Earth, and I'm not married to Artair. I'm Sarita Neeraj, the Water Amazon."

"Why did ye nae tell me?" His brogue always got thicker when he was emotional, and right now, he was clearly spitting mad.

She'd known he might not take the news well, yet she hadn't expected to see him so red-faced. "I knew you wanted Rebecca. I was protecting myself and my sisters."

He raked his fingers through his hair. His hand trembled. "After what we shared—"

Despite being held at knifepoint, Helen laughed, long and loud. "So you *did* seduce her, didn't you?"

Ian narrowed his angry green eyes, but Sarita wasn't sure if the gesture was meant for her or Helen. His face was filled with a fury that made her heart clench.

Now wasn't the time for sentimentality. She had a job to do, damn it. Explanations, apologies and forgiveness would come later. Much later.

Sarita spared Ian having to answer. "*I seduced him.*"

"Aye, she did. Came to me like an evil succubus in the night."

That remark stung. "I'm a succubus? You're the one who started this damned game. *You* kidnapped *me*. You told me you wanted Artair dead. Then you wanted me to betray Artair and you wanted to let this bitch get my sisters. And you're calling *me* names?"

"Hard to betray a husband you don't have!"

Good goddess, this was a stupid argument. There were bigger things at stake here than either of their feelings. "We'll talk about everything later. Just get me something to tie Helen up. I'd like nothing better than to kill her, but we all know I can't." She sighed and tried to find some control. "We're getting out of here before she can hurt you."

"*We?* Why would I go with you?" he snapped.

"Don't be stupid. I'm not leaving you here with her. Let me protect you."

"He can't leave," Helen said, her voice arrogant. "He's pledged his loyalty to me. He has nowhere to go. Nor can you leave this castle."

"I'll find a way out, and I'll take him to Avalon," Sarita insisted. "The Amazons can protect him. *I'll* protect him." Tired of waiting, she gave Ian one last chance, using the tone her Sentinels always employed when they wanted no refusal. "I need some rope. *Now.*"

"Leave," he said, his voice a command. "While you've got the chance, just go."

"No. I'm getting you to my home, then I'm bringing my sisters back here so we can finally take care of Helen."

"Go! Now!" Ian moved to her side and reached for her knife.

The blow was landed against her temple so quickly, Sarita never saw it coming. Lights flashed through her head as her knees buckled.

She sank against the cold stone, the knife clattering across the floor and out of her reach.

IAN BELLOWED HIS outrage when Helen whirled to slam her elbow against Rebecca's head.

No, not Rebecca.

Sarita.

When she fell, her eyes closed and she lay still as a corpse. He gave Helen a hard shove to get her away from Sarita. Never had he struck a woman, but this was no mere woman. The instant she stepped out of the protective walls of his castle, she would be a goddess—an Ancient of great power. She would be able to reduce him to dust with a blink of her elegant blue eyes.

But right now, she was vulnerable.

Fearing for Sarita, he kept his attention on Helen. Out of the corner of his eye, he saw Old Ewan move to Sarita's side and knew his love was in good hands. The old man could never stand violence against women. If Helen made a move on Sarita, she just might find a vengeful ghost launching himself at her.

"So the little bitch seduced you?" Helen pulled a jeweled dirk from the folds of her gown. "Duped you, too, I'd say."

"*You* were the one who sent her to me in the night," he sneered. "'Twas the reason I believed her to be Rebecca. I captured the same woman who'd tortured me, the one I saw defeat the demon you had me set loose to lure Earth out of Avalon. This was *your* mistake."

Despite the situation, he couldn't help smiling over the fool Sarita had made of Helen.

Until he realized she'd made a fool of him, as well.

"It was the damned Aramaic," Helen whined—something she did whenever she was trying to deflect blame for her own error. "I knew something about the spell wasn't right."

"Perhaps you'll live long enough to learn from your mistake," Ian chided.

Helen brandished her dirk. "I'll celebrate her death when I drive this into her heart. She may not be Earth, but she's an Amazon. One down, three to go."

When she took a step toward Sarita, Ian blocked her path. "Don't touch her."

"You're insane. She's an Amazon. She has to die. You knew the plan all along."

"You'll not kill her." He shoved her back hard.

After glaring at him for a few moments, she let a lazy smile fill her face. "Sweet Zeus. You fell in love with her, didn't you? That's why you're standing here, begging me not to kill her."

"Get out of my home!"

Helen's mood changed in a heartbeat, and she lashed out at him with her weapon. He blocked the blow. She slammed her other fist into his ear.

For a woman, she packed a Highlander's punch. His ear stung and a high-pitched whine drowned out most sound.

Before he could retaliate, Sile flew in from the kitchen, circling the ceiling in her ghost form. She swooped down in front of Helen, blocking her path to him. Then Sile let her true self show, screaming a banshee wail while her face aged, contorting into a grotesque corpse.

Helen didn't bat an eye, simply walked through Sile's shadowy form to face Ian again.

Ignoring both his pain and the annoying buzz in his ear, he went for the dirk Helen held. If he disarmed her he could hold her at bay until Sarita could escape.

Where he'd go after that, he had not a clue. Helen would kill him and send him to hell. Or back to limbo. Truth was, even if he survived he was a man with no country, no family and no one who cared whether he lived or died. Even Sarita had betrayed him.

Helen fought well, and she was able to keep the dirk from his grasp, inflicting several good cuts along his forearm and a particularly painful slice to his midsection. Someone had trained her well. Through the attack, she uttered words in a language he'd never heard, no doubt trying to break the Seior she'd used to shield *dorcha àite*.

Good. That would aid Sarita's escape.

He glanced to her. White lights suddenly appeared, swirling around her like tiny stars.

The magicks around the castle had been broken.

As Sarita sat up, her dark eyes locked with his. In that moment, he knew he'd give his life to protect her.

"Ian…" Her body faded as the light intensified.

Her sisters were calling her home.

TEN

THE WORLD SPUN around Sarita, making her dizzy and queasy. She recognized the feeling from when her sisters had cast a spell to bring her and Gina back from the desert where they'd faced Sekhmet. Sparks of white light filled her vision.

She looked to Ian, her heart breaking. She'd never have the chance to explain her deception. Although he held Helen back, Sarita didn't dare to hope he'd abandoned his plans for vengeance. Helen surely wasn't on his side any longer, considering he'd cost Helen her best chance to kill an Amazon.

That thought made her smile until another realization hit.

She'd probably never see Ian again.

As the world around her faded, she stretched her hand out to him. A tear slipped from the corner of her eye.

Then there was a void. For a few moments, the world didn't exist.

Cold dew touched her hands. Without opening her eyes, she tangled her fingers through the blades of grass, caressing the moisture and drawing strength from it. A familiar scent filled her nostrils.

Home.

"It worked. Thank God!" Gina said.

"Sarita? Are you okay?" Rebecca asked.

Opening her eyes, Sarita nodded. "I'm fine."

She glanced up to see her three sisters holding hands as they encircled her. The last time Megan and Rebecca used the spell, they'd come through the ordeal looking as though they'd just weathered a hurricane. Having three Amazons casting the spell was evidently less draining. All of her sisters were their normal, beautiful selves—dressed in casual clothes.

"Thanks for getting me back."

"Quite an outfit," Megan said, dropping Gina and Rebecca's hands to crouch. She ran her hand over the flowing skirt of the gown. "Where'd you get this?"

Sarita snorted at the redhead. "How much time do you have? 'Cause it's a *long* story."

Rebecca reached for Sarita and helped her up. "And we want to hear every word of it." She embraced Sarita. "I'm glad you're back, honey."

"Glad to be back, Guardian."

Gina pulled Sarita out of Rebecca's hug. She gathered Sarita in her arms and squeezed the breath right out of her. "I've been worried sick. I tried and tried to get you to answer, but—"

Sarita hugged her closest sister just as hard. "We should all talk."

"*I missed you!*" Gina's thoughts came into Sarita's mind.

"*Missed you, too, sis.*"

When Gina finally turned her loose, Megan gave her a hug, as well. Whether Sarita was the weakest Amazon or not, her sisters loved her. That love filled her and renewed her. They needed her as much as she needed them.

It was enough for now.

GODDESS, IT FELT good to wear sweats again. After a long, hot bath, Sarita had found her favorite clothes draped over her bed. Beagan and Dolan, Avalon's shapeshifting caretakers, were welcoming her home.

At least her cabin had been upgraded since her sisters married and were given houses by their patron goddesses. Sarita's humble home was expanded to include a wonderful spa tub that she used often and a shower stall. She no longer had to traipse across the compound to the old communal shower room.

Avalon was finally updated for the twenty-first century.

She sat on her mattress and let Gina brush her hair before plaiting it into a braid. Megan had sprawled over the desk chair, and Rebecca leaned against the wall with arms folded over her breasts.

For a moment, Sarita imagined they were nothing more than sorority sisters sharing gossip about what each would be doing on her weekend date. Sometimes it was easy to forget exactly why the four women had been drawn together.

"Where were you?" Megan, as usual, got right to the point. Patience wasn't a part of Fire's personality.

"Scotland," Sarita replied.

"Where in Scotland?" Megan pressed. "We had the goddesses send all of us there—even the guys—and we couldn't find hide or hair of you."

"Did you get Marbas?" Sarita asked.

"Yeah," Rebecca replied. "He's back in Tartarus. Kampe doesn't know how he got loose to begin with."

"Ian let him out."

All three of her sisters gaped at her.

"Who's Ian?" Rebecca asked.

While it might be fun to keep them hanging on her every word by drawing out the story, Sarita couldn't torture them that way. Besides, Helen had to have been busy while she was away, and the sooner they went after her, the safer things would be.

"I'm confused," Megan said, shifting her gaze between Rebecca and Sarita.

"So am I," Gina added. "How about we start at the beginning?"

"Aye. A verra good idea." Artair held the door to her cabin open.

Without waiting to be invited, he came in. Johann and Zach were right behind him. The size of the three men made the cabin suddenly seem far too small.

"We all need to hear the tale," Artair said.

Hearing his rich brogue—so much like Ian's—made Sarita's heart hurt. She knew she'd left part of herself back at *dorcha àite*, but until that moment, she hadn't recognized how deeply she'd fallen for her Scot.

Goddess, I'm a freakin' idiot.

The feeling refused to be pushed aside. No, she loved a man she could never have—a man she'd likely never see again.

Unless—

What if Ian convinced Helen to take him back under her protection? What if he remained part of whatever scheme she'd cooked up this time? What if he came after Artair as he'd planned? Sarita could easily find herself staring at him down the blade of her sword as she drove it into his heart.

Could she do that? Could she kill the man she loved to save her sisters or her Sentinels? Could she kill Ian to protect Zach or the changelings?

She needed to feel that Ganga was close, so her gaze swept the room for her sword before she remembered she'd left it behind. "My sword. Did you find my sword?"

Artair strode to the bed and frowned at her. "Yer sword? I'm asking you where you've been, and you're worried about *yer sword?*"

Sure, it was a stupid thing to ask considering they all needed answers.

She still wanted to know.

"It's at my house," Rebecca replied. She put a hand on her husband's arm. "Give her some breathing room, Artair."

Johann glanced up from his electronic table. His gaze caught hers. "Glad you're back in one piece. You did me proud."

"Thanks, Sentinel."

"She's probably been through hell," Zach chimed in.

Hell?

No.

Dorcha àite hadn't been hell. In some ways, it had been heaven.

"I found your sword," Johann said. "Gave it a good polish while we waited for news." Which translated into *I was worried about you.*

"Thanks for bringing it back."

"*Sarita, what's wrong?*" Gina's voice filled her thoughts again.

This was one of the few times Sarita considered their telepathic connection intrusive. What she'd shared with Ian should remain between her and her lover.

But that couldn't happen. She was an Amazon. Her life wasn't her own.

"Ian took me prisoner to lure out Artair. He let Marbas out to get Rebecca to come after him. He thought I was Earth. I let him keep thinking that until I could escape."

"Why couldn't we sense you?" Megan asked. "It was Seior, wasn't it?"

Sarita nodded. "Seior and Helen."

"That bitch!" Rebecca slapped her hand against the headboard. "Like she hasn't caused us enough trouble lately! She was trying to catch me?" She took a couple of breaths before her brows knit. "Wait. She'd know the difference. Once she saw you, she'd know she had the wrong Amazon."

Sarita let the whole story spill out about her capture and the time she'd spent in Ian's castle. While she held back some of the more personal aspects, her sisters—and probably the men—had to know something had happened between her and Ian. They'd be stupid not to figure it out.

"So I have no idea what happened to Ian after you called me back to Avalon," she said, completing the tale. "Helen was pretty pissed he helped me get away, but I don't think she'll kill him. At least not yet. Maybe he'll give up his stupid vendetta."

"Nay. He's a Scot," Artair replied. "If he wants me dead, he willnae give up. Ever. If he needs Helen to get his vengeance, he'll find a way to get back in her good graces."

Rebecca frowned at her husband. "What I don't get is why he thinks you helped his clan murder him. Do you remember your people burning someone at the stake for being a warlock?"

"Nay. My clan wasn't capable of that. Aye, people

were a mite superstitious of strange things back then, but cry someone a warlock?" He gave his head a shake. "Had to be another clan, perhaps one we feuded with." His gaze moved to Sarita. "He never gave you his last name or the name of his clan?"

"No."

"What color was his plaid? Perhaps if you describe it to me—"

"It was pure black. No tartan. Sorry, Artair." Trying to think back to the things Sile had let slip whenever she'd been able to get the woman to drop her guard, she found nothing that could help Artair—except perhaps Sile herself. "The servants were as old as Ian."

"Pardon?" Artair asked.

"The servants. They talked about Ian being laird. They remembered him being there from his own time. They haunt the castle."

"Were they loyal to Helen?" Artair asked.

"Not one bit. They tried to protect me from her. Their loyalty was to Ian." He'd helped her escape. That thought brought a smile to Sarita's face. He'd valued her more than Helen. "Maybe I can get back there and talk to them."

A needle in a haystack. There was no way she could find her way back to the castle, because she'd never known where it was to begin with. Her sisters and the men hadn't managed to find it when they'd searched Scotland, either.

Since no one responded, they must have thought her idea was inane.

"Helen probably punished them anyway," she finally said.

"Oh, good God." Johann interrupted them all. His fingers flew over his tablet.

"What's wrong?" Moving back to her husband's side, Megan looked at his screen.

"She's at it again. I can't fucking believe it."

When everyone tried to crowd around him, he tapped a few more commands to the screen then turned it so they could see.

Since Sarita was so damned short, she couldn't get a glimpse. "Hey. Down in front."

With a chuckle, Gina grabbed her arm and pulled her forward.

Once settled in front of Air, Sarita focused on the image. Her gasp was echoed by her sisters.

Helen stood on the stage of the enormous glass church the Children of Earth had built—the headquarters of the entire cult. Amazing how animated she could be in front of a crowd, weaving her spell with passionate words and emphatic gestures. Still beautiful despite her age, she was a commanding presence who drew people to her.

The sanctuary was packed, people standing shoulder to shoulder, staring up at her with a reverence that made Sarita nauseous. The news stations scrolled commentary, estimating how many COEs were loyal to Helen and listing some of her noteworthy followers.

Her voice filtered through the tinny speakers of the computer. "I have seen the future. We have enemies. Four women who want me dead!"

The crowd replied with a growing rumble of anger and disbelief.

With a triumphant smile, Helen pressed on. "And

now, with the powers I possess, the powers your love strengthens in me, I can give you their names. We will hunt them to the ends of the Earth. We must find these women and destroy them before they destroy us!"

"Holy shit," Megan said. "She can't be talking about us. Can she?"

Gina raked her fingers through her spiked hair as the highlights slowly changed to red—the color of her anger. "She's exposing the whole world to magicks if she does. She's not that stupid."

"Bring these women to me and you will be rewarded," Helen promised. "Greatly rewarded."

The cheers of her followers echoed through the temple until their voices joined in a chant. *Helen. Helen. Helen.*

"We are so screwed," Megan said, her gaze darting to each of the Amazons.

Everyone starting talking at once. Everyone except Artair. He continued to stare at the screen, grabbing it when Johann tried to turn it back. "Wait."

The anguish in that one word caught Sarita by surprise.

Since Rebecca edged closer to her husband, she had to have sensed it, as well. "Artair? What's wrong?"

"But his hand is nae crippled." Artair looked lost, confused. "It cannae be him."

"Artair! Talk to me!" Rebecca insisted.

Instead of answering his wife, he whirled to Sarita. His green eyes suddenly seemed so familiar that seeing them sent a shudder ripping through her. They bored holes straight to her soul.

"What was the name of the castle?" he demanded in a near roar.

"*Dorcha àite*. Sile called it *dorcha àite*," Sarita replied. His plea could mean only one thing. "You remember, don't you? You remember Ian now."

"Aye." Artair gave a ragged sigh and took his wife's hand in his. "The servant—her name was Sile? She was married to Old Ewan?"

Rebecca laced her fingers through his. "You remember him now?"

"I didnae know him as Ian. I—" He choked on whatever he was going to say as he swallowed hard.

Artair had always been a pillar of strength in Sarita's eyes—as solid as a block of marble. In all the times he'd led the Amazons into battle, he'd never once backed away, nor had he ever been anything but totally in control. Nothing could rattle Artair MacKay.

Until now.

"Who is he?" Sarita dreaded the answer enough to want to run from her own cabin. "Who's Ian?"

Artair pointed at the screen.

"I don't—"

"Look!"

Sarita stared at Helen, anger rising from deep inside her as she thought about what the goddess had done to hurt so many people. "It's Helen. I hate her, too."

"Nay." His finger moved to point out the man standing just behind Helen.

Because he wore reflective sunglasses and his hair had been cut short, he didn't look familiar. That, and his profile was to the camera. He'd slicked back his hair with gel, making it a dark reddish-brown. It wasn't until he turned to face the camera that recognition dawned on her. "Ian. Oh, my goddess, it's Ian."

"His name isnae Ian." Artair's voice was a shaky whisper. "His name is Darian—Darian MacKay. He's my brother, returned from the dead."

ELEVEN

"BUT—BUT—YOUR BROTHER didn't burn at the stake! Ian can't be Darian. He can't." Sarita's mind reeled. "We all know the story of how you became Sentinel. You begged Rhiannon to save his life."

She'd heard the tale from Rebecca so many times, it was drilled into her mind. Darian MacKay perished in the infamous Battle of Culloden Moor, where he'd fought and died at Artair's side. Artair had been so grief-stricken, he'd called out to Rhiannon, pledging his fealty to her so she'd resurrect his younger brother. As was the custom with any man who became Sentinel, Artair should have disappeared from the world, having been erased from the minds of anyone who'd known him—including his brother and his clan. Rhiannon should have seen to that task.

If Ian was truly Darian MacKay, how could Artair have been responsible for his clan burning him to death after condemning him as a warlock?

Neither Ian nor the MacKay clan should have remembered Artair existed.

Johann interrupted her thoughts as he brushed back a lock of his blond hair that had fallen over his eyes. "If that's your brother, Artair, what in the hell is he doing helping Helen?"

Megan threw her husband a scorching frown. "One question at a time, Joeman. Okay? My head's already spinning. I can't imagine how Artie's feeling right now."

"Not to mention that the Amazons were just outted by that bitch," Gina added.

Helen was the least of Sarita's worries, no matter how much her announcement had plunged the magical world into turmoil. Sarita could only think of the man she loved.

She wanted to scream in frustration. Both Ian and Artair had to feel so hurt and betrayed. It was clear there was one person—one *goddess*—to blame for the mess. "This is all Rhiannon's fault. It had to be her."

Rebecca faced Sarita. "I was thinking the same thing."

Megan and Gina nodded.

Only Zach shook his head. "Well, I'm not getting it. So maybe one of you ladies wants to explain to me how we moved from Helen being back to Ian being Artair's brother to this all being *Rhiannon's* fault?"

Zach's defense wasn't a surprise. A lover of the legend of King Arthur, he looked at the Lady of the Lake through starry eyes.

But the pieces fell into place in Sarita's mind. "Rhiannon saved Ian's life."

Artair growled low in his throat. "His name is *Darian*."

While she wanted to argue with him that the man she knew was Ian, now wasn't the time or place. Bigger battles needed to be fought. Ian had probably shortened his name for a number of reasons, least of which had to be to keep Artair in the dark.

"Fine," she said. "Rhiannon saved *Darian* just like Rebecca told us, and she sent him back to his clan."

"He shouldnae have remembered me," Artair insisted. "He'd died there on that bloody battlefield. I watched the English pig cut him down. I should've stopped him. I was his brother—his laird. I should've protected him. He was just a boy with a crippled hand." He took a deep, shuddering breath and ran his hand over his face. "'Tis why I called to Rhiannon. She was to send him back to our clan. Alive and well."

"But your clan burned him at the stake after calling him a warlock. Why would they do something like that?"

Rebecca took up the mantle. "Think about it. A man comes back from a battle where almost every other Scot died? That would be more than enough to start gossip."

"His hand…" Artair said. "His crippled hand."

"It's not crippled," Sarita couldn't help but point out.

"Nae more. He has a normal hand when he'd been a cripple—another reason to accuse him of witchcraft," Artair added. "That had to be Rhiannon's doing. She could fix the deformity."

"Oh, good God." Zach splayed his hand through his short, brown hair. "They'd think he used black magicks to heal himself, wouldn't they? That long ago… They'd freak out over something like that."

"Rhiannon!" Artair bellowed. "Rhiannon, get your arse down here!" His volume made the cabin's windows rattle.

With a scoff, Johann shook his head. "She won't come, especially when you scream at her like that. She'll know you're pissed and stay a million miles away until you've calmed down."

"I shall *never* calm down. She murdered my brother!

I gave my life to her service to save him, only for him to be murdered! All because of her!" A noise that reminded Sarita of a wounded animal bubbled up from inside him. He hurried out of the cabin, Rebecca close on his heels.

Tears stung Sarita's eyes. She wanted to cry for Artair, for the anguish he was feeling. She wanted to cry for Ian and all he'd needlessly suffered. And she wanted to cry for herself—because she'd never be able to help fix this.

Now that Ian'd put his trust back in Helen, there would be no way for her to get to him and explain about what had happened so long ago—how it wasn't Artair's fault. Not only was Ian never going to forgive Artair, he wanted his brother dead. The brothers would never be able to mend that kind of rift—not from Ian's point of view. If he couldn't come to terms with what had happened and lose his hatred for his older brother, he could never come to Avalon.

Come to Avalon?

How the hell could she *think* about bringing Ian to her home? He couldn't be a part of her life. The man was helping Helen—along with the rest of the idiots who followed her. Yes, he'd helped Sarita escape, but who knew what reasons he'd had to aid her? Perhaps he had a covert agenda—one that neither she nor Helen understood.

The man was nothing if not an enigma.

But he'd made his choice. He'd taken her love and brushed it aside, holding his need for revenge closer than her heart.

"Sarita?" Megan's voice brought her back to reality. "I'm sorry, what were you—"

"You're the only one who knows Darian as he is now, and you're the only one who's seen Helen since she was with Sekhmet."

"And?"

"What is there between them? Why would she keep him close after he helped you escape?"

A question Sarita had been asking herself from the moment she saw him. He'd hovered behind Helen, dressed in his black suit, wearing Ray-Bans as though he were the newest member of the *Men in Black* crew.

He's the enemy. Don't forget that.

Funny, but her heart didn't seem to care.

"Seior can do strange things to a person. Even make them ally with someone as evil as Helen," she said. "At least that's what we were all taught. Ian wants revenge. Desperately. He hates Artair with a passion that we can't imagine."

"But Artair's his brother," Johann pointed out. "Hell, he shouldn't *remember* him, let alone hate him."

"He blames Artair for the clan killing him."

"I think I know why," Zach said.

Everyone turned to him.

"If I'm right—"

"Which you usually are," Gina said with wifely pride, the highlights in her spiked hair shifting from the angry red to purple—her color for love.

Zach smiled, a grin of affection for his wife that sent a stab of envy through Sarita. "Rhiannon didn't do her job," he said. "Knowing her the way I do, I'd guess she forgot one important detail. She probably thought she was doing Artair a huge favor by fixing his brother's hand. But I'll bet she was so wrapped up in being benevolent, she forgot to wipe Darian's memory when she took Artair out of the memories of the rest of the clan."

"Oh, goddess." Sarita closed her eyes, following Zach's train of thought to a logical conclusion. "He not only would have come back to the clan alive and with a new hand, but they'd think he was babbling about a guy none of them had heard of before." Opening her eyes, she glanced to Gina.

"He suffered so much, Gina."

"I know. I'm sorry, sis."

"They'd think he was schizophrenic or something," Megan added. "Wasn't Culloden Moor in 1740-something?"

"1746," Johann replied without looking up as he tapped more commands against his touch screen.

"People of that era could've easily thought someone who had signs of mental illness—like talking about a person who never existed—were possessed." Megan pressed her point home.

Sarita wanted nothing more at that moment than to run to Ian, to take him into her arms and soothe away his hurt. Yet she couldn't. He was back in league with Helen, and her job now was to figure out that bitch's plans and stop them both before people got hurt.

Had Helen brainwashed him? Had she used Seior to wipe Sarita from his memory? What if he had no choice, if she'd taken his free will? Her skill with black magicks had earned her thousands of followers in the blink of an eye. She could easily force Ian to do her bidding.

"So he's with Helen, and she's after the Amazons," Zach said, turning the topic. *"Again.* Why not put her people on the attack, as well? Makes perfect sense."

Sarita nodded. "Anytime we leave Avalon to hunt down some demon, we'll be targets. Wouldn't surprise me if she turns quite a few of them loose, like she did Marbas, just to get us out in the open. Then she'll sick the Children of the Earth on us."

"Makes sense," Megan added. "I bet my bottom dollar she's got more on her plate than that."

"Fuck. Fuck. *Fuck!*" The outburst came from Johann as he slapped the back of his knuckles against his screen. "I can't believe she'd have the balls to do it. The patron goddesses will want her head on a platter."

Megan sidled up closer. "What are you talking about, Joeman?"

"She did more than just exposed the Amazons." After a few more taps, he turned his gadget for everyone to see again. "You all need to hear this."

As usual, Sarita couldn't see. Once she moved closer, she wished she hadn't bothered.

An enormous screen had been pulled down behind Helen, and a projector shone its light against it. Helen was using a laser pointer, the red dot it produced hovering as she named each face on the screen behind her. The familiar names made the bile rise in the back of Sarita's throat.

"Fuck," Megan echoed her husband.

One by one, photos of the Amazons appeared. All four of them. The unflattering mug-shot style pictures stared back from the screen.

"These women," Helen said, "are our worst enemies. Each and every one of them wants me dead." She put her hand against her chest. "Your savior, and they want to destroy me. They must be stopped! The Children of the Earth will pay a reward to anyone who can capture one or all of these traitors!"

"So much for the world never knowing we existed," Gina said.

"Where in the hell did she get those pictures?" Zach asked as his face flushed red. "I thought the goddesses wiped away all the memories of the girls existing? Those look like drivers' license photos. And how was she able to add Sarita's scar to hers?"

"Beats the shit outta me," Johann replied. "But my bet's on Seior, either to erase memories or to scour for information." A rueful chuckle slipped out. "I'm guessing you're going to pop up on that list soon. How much of a bounty do you think they'll offer for the infamous computer giant Zach Hanson, especially if he wants to kill their *savior*?"

A crooked smile crossed Zach's lips. "Hope it's not enough for my wife to turn me in and claim the reward."

Gina elbowed her husband in the ribs. "You're not getting away from me *that* easily."

He gave her a quick kiss. "Glad to hear it."

"Helen used all your maiden names—except for Rebecca. Megan Feuer, not Herrmann." Sarita interrupted them.

"And I'm Gina Himmel. She's not as up-to-date with us as we feared. But she's obviously using Seior."

"Seior is powerful stuff," Johann said. "If it's used right, it can undo all the good of white magicks. Helen's gone to the dark side. She's not hiding behind someone this time, either. No Chernabog or Sekhmet. She's hanging her ass out there."

"She has Darian," Gina pointed out.

"But he's not an Ancient," Zach replied. "From the way he's dressed, I'd say she's passing him off as her personal assistant."

"Or bodyguard." Johann's gaze grew hard, his blue eyes turning stormy, as he became the Sentinel Sarita knew so very well. "She wants a fight? Well, we'll give her a fight. In fact, we'll give her a *war*. I vote we get ourselves ready and we strike the first blow."

"And we make it a doozy," Zach added.

"We need to tell Rebecca and Artair about this." Sarita headed toward the door.

Gina followed. "If it's war, it's time to make a battle plan."

IAN TOSSED HIS sunglasses aside and grabbed the crystal container of scotch.

"Drinking again?" Helen asked. She cast off her gold robe and strode to the bar. "I should forbid you. I need you sensible, not drunk."

As if he could get drunk on the swill they called scotch. In his era…

Ah, but that was the problem. This *wasn't* his era. He was trapped in a time not his own, alone. "I want Sile and Old Ewan to come to me."

"I tire of you asking the same thing," Helen replied. "They stay at the castle until you complete your job. Once Artair is dead, I'll send you home. Then you can rot in that stupid hellhole for all I care."

Drinking the contents of the glass in one swallow, he let the whiskey burn its way down his throat. Everything about his existence seemed…wrong. Yet he couldn't understand why.

He'd been granted a reprieve when Helen rescued

him from limbo, and now his chance for revenge grew near. Helen had launched her quest to capture the Amazons, and with them came Artair MacKay.

Ian would face him—man to man—and cut him down.

So why wasn't he relishing his chance to finally avenge his death? Instead, he felt lost. Confused.

Wrong.

His brother was a formidable warrior, so the fight wouldn't be easy. Although Ian had spent so much of his life being groomed as the laird's brother—dealing with the livestock and the crops—he'd also trained with the soldiers. At least he had when the men would allow a cripple to spar with them. Then he'd become laird in his own right when Artair was gone.

Once Ian's hand had been restored, he'd tried to make up for lost time, training like a madman for near to six months until...

No wonder his clan thought him possessed.

He snorted, not sure why the sound made him smile.

When he faced Artair, Ian had a good chance of victory. They would be more evenly matched now that he was training again. Should he lose and faced death again, he was taking his brother with him, no matter what.

Helen motioned him over to the table. Spread over the surface were pictures of the four women she wanted. "You will see to any reports that the Amazons have been found. Take all the help you need, but check each viable lead."

Ian stared at the pictures. He knew the faces well, having studied them at Helen's insistence. Yet his gaze always returned to the exotic Water Amazon. *Sarita Neeraj.*

Her eyes fascinated him. Hell, *everything* about her fascinated him. He could almost hear her voice, feel the silky thickness of her hair. But he'd never met her. He hadn't personally encountered any of the Amazons. So long as they remained in their home of Avalon, he couldn't touch them. Helen was working on breaking the enchantment around the floating compound, but she wasn't quite there. Not yet.

Helen picked up a remote and flicked on the enormous television, flipping through channels until she found one discussing the destruction of art happening around the world. The reporter commented on the strangeness of each piece depicting a god or goddess from many different cultures.

Helen tilted her head back and laughed, sounding a bit crazed. "I'm winning. Do you hear me, Ian? I'm *winning.*"

"Ye truly believe all of this—" he swept his hand toward the screen, "—is necessary."

Her laughter stopped abruptly. "I've told you before—don't question me. I do what I must to ensure my power exceeds those of any other Ancient. None will be able to challenge me. Once I am ready to claim my place as the leader of this world, there will be none who can defeat me. When everyone worships me, my powers will grow as the other Ancients weaken—until I am the strongest goddess the world has ever known. Then I'll show them all that I am truly a daughter of Gaia—that I have become all I knew I could be—the savior of the earth."

Ian poured himself some more scotch, drank it down and then headed to his room. He slammed the door behind him.

Stripping out of his suit, he longed for the freedom of his plaid, although he would never wear the MacKay colors again. After spending the day with Helen and the stupid sheep she called followers, he felt dirty. Used. Was his revenge worth...*this?*

"Aye."

So why wasn't his heart consumed with revenge any longer? What had changed?

Searching his thoughts he found nothing. Worse than nothing...he felt as though something important had been lost.

He stepped in the shower and started the water, not caring that the first spray against his skin was ice cold. At least it reminded him he was alive. Closing his eyes, he let the water run over his hair, wanting to scrub out the sticky goop Helen insisted he wear. She dictated his dress, his haircut, his manners. She groomed him like some prized pony, and he was fucking tired of it.

As always happened when Ian closed his eyes, images hit him from every direction, making him dizzy. Artair kneeling at his side, screaming out for help, his palms slick with Ian's blood. The MacKay clan chanting as they tossed more wood on Ian's pyre, damning him as a witch as the flames licked at his skin. Sile and Old Ewan standing tall, refusing to denounce their laird.

And then there was a woman—an exotic woman with dark skin.

She was always there, her beautiful face and brown eyes swimming in his thoughts, pushing aside the bad memories and filling his heart and his mind in a way he couldn't understand. She would kiss him, caress him, love him.

But why? How could a woman he'd never met haunt him so?

Ian opened his eyes and slammed his fist against the tile wall. Was this some torture Helen had designed to keep her lapdog in line? Even that question raised a familiarity that chilled him to the bone.

This would all be over soon. Then Ian could return to his home.

Assuming Helen allowed that, and he had his doubts, not trusting her any further than he could toss a caber.

Only she knew the end game, so all he could do was wait.

TWELVE

"WE CAN'T JUST storm her church." Johann plopped his behind into one of the chairs in the MacKay living room. Plucking the remote from the coffee table, he hit the mute button.

Sarita was grateful. The sound of so many raised voices coupled with the droning of some news network reporter was making her grind her teeth. She longed for the silence and serenity of *dorcha àite*.

Ever since Helen's announcement, Avalon had been a flurry of noise. Between monitoring the television stations for anything about the four "most hated" women in the world, the heated discussions over what they should do about their situation and curse words being hurled about Helen, the din was maddening. It shouldn't have come as a surprise that she had so many followers in the media, but so many different stations demanding the Amazons' capture? Helen's reach extended further than they'd imagined.

Everything came back to one problem—the sisters needed to know Helen's ultimate goal. They feared they already knew what she wanted—to rule the world. Painting bull's eyes on the Amazons was distracting, but as long as they stayed in Avalon, no real harm could come to them. Yet if they remained in Avalon, Helen could do as she pleased.

Which doomed the world to conquest by the Children of the Earth in the name of their savior.

There was so much to think about, so many decisions to be made, and Sarita tried to stay focused on the mission. The problem was she couldn't get Ian out of her mind.

He was her enemy now.

Why couldn't she make her heart believe it?

"Call it what it is, lad," Artair said. "Her temple. She's an Ancient, and they have *temples.* As for taking the fight to her, aye, we *can* storm in. Although I suggest we try to find out if she's hiding anything up her sleeve first."

"A covert mission," Rebecca added. "Let's do some fact-finding to plan our strategy."

Looking to Megan, he nodded. "She can be Helen."

The way Johann was clenching his jaw spoke volumes. He didn't want his wife shape-shifting into Helen just to get someone inside her headquarters so they could dig up some information. Unfortunately, his silence meant he didn't have anything else to suggest.

"I *could*," Megan said. "Wouldn't like it much, though."

Artair frowned. "You've never backed down from a challenge before."

"You've got it wrong, Artair," Megan replied. "I'm not backing down. I'd love to get into her temple and do some snooping. I just don't want to make myself look like her. The shape would be hard to hold since I hate her so much. But you tell me to go, I'll go."

Instead of saying anything, Johann wrapped his arm around Megan's shoulder and pulled her closer. Her head dropped to his shoulder as his fingers caressed her ponytail.

"We'd have to go in really late," Zach said, scribbling out notes on a legal pad. Since he'd come to Avalon, he'd become the one who searched through every detail of any attack, using the analytical mind that had made him a technological legend to be sure all the loose ends were accounted for. "Lots of surveillance to figure out what her schedule is. And then there's Ian and the rest of her staff. Not to mention making sure there aren't many COEs around."

"The Ancients willnae approve of her making the Amazons public. But—"

Artair's words came to an abrupt halt when Bonnie came into the room.

His four-year-old daughter was dressed in pink My Little Pony pajamas. Her blond hair was out of its usual pigtails, and her blue eyes were heavy with fatigue. She took her brother's hand and dragged him to the sofa where her parents sat. "It's bedtime, Da."

Leaning forward, Artair kissed Bonnie's forehead. "Aye, my bonny lassie."

"Do I hafta go to bed, Da? I'm not sweepy." Darian dropped Bonnie's hand to rub his green eyes. The boy looked more asleep than awake as he clutched the navy blue MacKay plaid he used as a security blanket.

"Aye, laddie." He tousled his son's chestnut hair. "You do. Kiss your mum, bairns, then off to bed with the lot of you."

To Sarita, this three-year-old boy dressed in Spiderman pajamas giving his mother a kiss would always be the only "Darian." She'd held him right after Rebecca brought him into the world. His aunt Sarita had lovingly given him his first bath, swaddled him in soft blankets and set him back in his mother's waiting arms. As Rebecca cradled her precious bundle, Artair had announced that his son's name would be Darian. He'd sniffed back tears as he gave the baby the name of the younger brother he'd loved enough to spend his life in Rhiannon's service.

Ian could never be "Darian." Not to her. Darian was a boy. Ian was a man—the man she loved.

"If you'll excuse me for a minute." Artair got to his feet. He smiled at his children, grabbing Bonnie and tossing her onto his back.

Bonnie squealed in delight, wrapped her arms around her father's neck and her legs around his ribs to take a piggyback ride to bed.

Darian laughed as Artair scooped him into his arms and blew a raspberry against his belly. That laughter continued as Artair carried his children up the stairs to their rooms.

"This is killing him," Rebecca said when they were gone.

"I can't even imagine how much." With a shake of her head, Gina reached for Zach's hand.

"What can we do to help?" Zach asked.

Rebecca breathed a weighty sigh. "Just be there for him. This isn't going to get any easier, either. If we go after Helen—" Her gaze shifted to Sarita. "Well, then…"

Sarita frowned. "We'll have to face Ian, too."

Silence ruled until Artair came stomping down the stairs. "The bairns are abed."

"Mina was already asleep when Megan and I left,"

Johann said. "So were Beagan and Dolan. Shifted to rabbits and curled up on the rug in her room."

"Yeah, the kids wear them out. But they're such great nannies." Rebecca patted the sofa next to her.

Artair took a seat. "So…what's been decided?"

"Right now, nothing but surveillance," Zach replied. "We've got to find their patterns. Then we can figure out when to sneak Megan in. Once we know what Helen's got cooking, we'll make some solid plans for when to bring her down."

"'Twill not be easy," Artair said.

Sarita couldn't help but snort a laugh. "It never is. And we've got another huge problem. Everyone and their brother wants us now." Then she stated her demand, refusing to let anyone talk her out of it. "When Megan goes, I go, too."

"Sarita, no," Rebecca said. "You don't have the kind of powers that would help if you're caught."

It took all her self-control not to snap at the Guardian. "I *have* to go. If we see Ian, he'll listen to me. I might be able to help him get away from Helen's hold."

Artair wouldn't make eye contact with her.

"I'm going. End of discussion."

"People want us dead," Rebecca stated.

"If we're lucky," Gina added, "they'll try to shoot us."

Since Rhiannon had gifted the Amazons with skin that was as effective at stopping bullets as Kevlar, Sarita nodded. "Glad we're not living in the era when everyone carried swords. Probably won't have to fight any revenants this time. Too hard to keep zombies around for when you need them."

For the first time since Sarita had returned from

dorcha àite, she saw Artair smile. "'Twould be a muckle lot of smell if she did." His expression changed as he drew his lips into a grim line. "Sarita is right. She should go."

His announcement seemed to be as much a surprise to the rest of the group as it was to her. "Thank you, Artair."

"Donnae thank me, lass. What if he sees you and still wishes to fight?"

She swallowed hard. "I guess I'll do what I have to do. I'm an Amazon. I'll do my job."

"Could you kill him?" Rebecca asked. Her brown eyes were filled with concern.

"I don't know," Sarita replied in all honesty. "I just don't know."

"You 'forgot a few things'?" Sarita jogged to keep up with Megan's long strides down the corridor leading to the COE offices. "After all our planning, that's the best you could do?"

Megan—wearing Helen's face and her typical medieval gown—shrugged as she led Sarita to Helen's private office. "I learned when I was a cop that sometimes simpler is better. It got us past the guards, right?"

Flimsy, yes. But Megan was right. They'd stopped to sign in at the building's security post, and Megan told the soldier manning the desk she needed to go back to her office to retrieve a few things she'd forgotten. He'd barely blinked—Helen had probably established a pattern of popping in and out of the temple at all hours of the day and night.

Worried that the guard might recognize one of the most wanted faces in the country, Sarita had done her

best to change her usual appearance. A small glamour
spell she'd learned temporarily hid her scar and damaged earlobe. Her hair had been pulled into a tight bun,
and she donned nerdy glasses with thick black rims.
Add a heavy layer of makeup to her usually fresh face
and she came across as a stereotypical nobody who
trailed powerful people. The ruse was easy since Helen
always had a Child of the Earth following her like a
puppy dog.

Thanks to Zach's research into the church's blue-
prints and what Johann could discover about the COE,
the women knew exactly where Helen's office was.
Sarita used the Key—Gina's magical gadget about the
size of a credit card that could open any lock—and
quickly let them inside.

"Where do we start?" Megan walked over to the
ornate walnut desk and pulled out the black leather
chair. "How about…here?" She jerked on the right hand
drawer. It refused to open. "Hand me the Key, will ya?"

Sarita used it to pop open the lock on the closest file
cabinet before tossing it to Megan, who caught it and
passed it over the latch on the drawer.

"Can you fire up her computer while I go through
this stuff?" Sarita asked.

"Sure thing." Megan flipped on Helen's computer.

Rifling through the files in the top drawer, Sarita found nothing but mind-numbing love letters from
Helen's followers and copies of emails she'd printed
out. The extensive pile of praise being heaped on her
no doubt fed her power. Having so many worshippers
made her a formidable enemy.

The Amazons searched in silence for several minutes, and Sarita's hopes fell. Helen was playing her

cards close to her vest. They found no tangible clue as to what her grand plans were or how anyone beyond her converts would be affected by her slowly seizing power. Did she plan to topple governments? Did she hope to sweep aside all other forms of religion?

What in the hell did she *really* want?

"Damn it." Megan slammed the last desk drawer shut, and Sarita sensed her sister's frustration—and shared it. "You find anything?"

"Like you need to ask."

Fire shook her head as she sat down and let her fingers fly over the keyboard. "Stupid thing is password locked."

"Try the codes Zach gave you."

Jerking a small paper out of her skirt pocket, she placed it next to the keyboard and entered the commands Zach had provided to help get past any computer security system. After a few attempts, a small bit of fireworks shot from Megan's head. "Well, how about that! I'm in! Way to go, Zachary."

Megan plugged in the memory stick he'd also given her—one Zach designed himself to absorb a ridiculous amount of information—and started downloading the files on Helen's computer.

Sarita kept herself occupied searching the office for secret storage areas and looking at the objects in the office.

Helen was obviously an Earth Amazon deep down inside. Every piece of art—from the knickknacks to the paintings—was of animals or nature scenes. Even faux leather covered her office chair. Sarita lifted each frame away from the wall to assure herself no wall safe or hidden cubbyhole lay behind.

Just as she let the last painting rest against the wall again, another small burst of sparks surged from Megan's hair. "Here's a huge file labeled 'Amazons.' Damn thing's encrypted, but I'll bet Zach can get in."

"I'll take that bet," Sarita replied with a wink. She checked her watch. "Get that downloaded. We should get outta here before someone comes." Every little sound made her jump. Being on constant alert left her nerves raw. She was more than ready to let her hair down and end this charade.

"Done." The instant Megan yanked the memory stick from the computer, the door opened.

The breath caught in Sarita's throat when Ian walked into the office, leaving the door open behind him. He appeared exactly as he had on the televised press conference—dressed in a black suit and his hair again slicked back with gel. The only thing missing were the sunglasses.

Those hypnotizing green eyes moved to where Megan sat at the desk. "I dinnae know you'd returned. Can I leave?"

The moment Megan opened her mouth, Ian would know she wasn't Helen. While she could shape-shift into anyone, she couldn't change her voice. It was one thing to fool a guard, another entirely to fool a man Helen had raised from the dead.

Megan gave Ian a terse nod and flippant wave of her hand.

He shifted his gaze to Sarita, but no recognition came to his face. "Have we met?"

"You don't know me?"

"Nay, lass. Should I?" A fleeting twitch of a grin passed his lips.

Her heart plummeted, and she had to breathe deep to keep from sobbing. No wonder he worked with Helen—she'd clearly used Seior to wipe away any memory of Sarita and all they'd shared while he'd held her captive.

Holding tight to her tumbling emotions, she used the story they'd rehearsed in preparing for the mission. "I'm just a humble follower. Our Earth's savior needed help with filing her letters of adoration." She moved back to the file cabinet, opened one of the drawers and flitted through a file. "There are *so* many. I am truly blessed to work for her."

If she hadn't known him as well as she did, she might have missed the slight narrowing of his eyes that betrayed his disbelief. "Since my job is to see to Mistress Helen's safety, perhaps ye should have been introduced to me sooner."

So he *was* acting as her bodyguard. A good ruse that wouldn't raise an ounce of suspicion about why he stayed glued to Helen's side. "I'm just one of *many*."

"But one of *few* allowed in her office." Ian's eyes scanned Sarita from head to toe, and despite the fact he didn't remember her, she saw desire warm his gaze. "What's yer name, lass?"

"What's it matter?" Megan snapped. "I'm nearly done."

Holding her breath, Sarita waited to see if Ian would recognize he wasn't dealing with Helen.

After what seemed like far too long, he conceded with a nod. "Are ye ready to leave?"

Megan hesitated, and Ian took a step closer to the desk, those intense eyes no doubt attempting to pierce through her disguise.

"I need a few more minutes," she said. "You go ahead and go back."

Since he didn't say a word in response, Sarita assumed they'd avoided detection. A relieved sigh almost slipped out.

Then Ian retreated.

Sarita almost breathed a relieved sigh—until he slammed the office door shut.

He leaned back, chuckled and crossed his arms over his chest. "Since I cannae go home until you send me there, the ruse is over."

"Ruse?" Sarita quirked an eyebrow.

Megan followed suit. "What ruse?"

"I wondered when you'd come a'snooping," he added.

A burst of Megan's thoughts hit Sarita—they were going to try to bluff their way through this.

"What are you talking about?" Megan said in an authoritarian tone.

Ian moved closer, positioning himself right in the middle of Sarita's path to the door. "My mistress will be pleased I've caught Fire and Water." A small smile curved his lips. "The strongest and the weakest of the Amazons."

With a growl, Megan shoved her hands out and threw Ian back against the door.

"No!" Sarita put herself between them. "He's mine to deal with."

Megan's face shifted back to her own features as her hair tinted from blond back to red. "Fine. I won't hurt him." She glared at Ian. "Unless he gives me a reason to."

Sarita faced Ian. Having been called the weakest Amazon, she let her temper flare.

I'll show you who's the weakest Amazon.

She went on the offensive without giving Ian any warning.

He pushed away from the door, blocked the kick she threw at his midsection and laughed at her. "That's the best you've got, lass?"

IAN SAVORED THE blistering glare the beautiful Water Amazon threw his way. He had no time to enjoy it because, just as he'd hoped, his taunting words sent the tiny woman into a flurry of fists and feet.

She'd been trained well in hand-to-hand combat. It took all his concentration to block her attacks, but for some odd reason, he couldn't seem to force himself to land a few of his own. Not that she gave him much opportunity. Yet he let more than one chance to return her attack slip by.

Something niggled at the back of his mind, some recollection of having seen this woman before—and not just in erotic dreams. He hadn't meant to ask her name, and, had she answered, she'd never have told him the truth. He'd been curious what she'd call herself to pull off this masquerade.

As he parried every blow she attempted to land, he watched her closely, taking in everything about her and branding it on his memory. Her face was far too familiar, although…something was different. Missing, perhaps?

The scent of jasmine distracted him, and he let his guard down long enough for a dainty fist to connect with his stomach. And a damn fine punch it was. Doubling over, he tried to regain his lost breath when she followed the first hit with a solid uppercut to his nose.

Lights flashed behind his eyes. He pushed aside the pain, rising to his full height as he gulped a few more breaths back into his lungs.

Sarita had given him parlay, stepping back while he swiped his sleeve under his throbbing nose. He didn't have to look at his jacket to know it was smeared with blood.

"Let us through," she demanded, "and I won't kill you."

Such brave words from such a tiny creature.

Then he caught the jeweled hilt of a dagger tucked to her side in the waistband of her pants. Had she wanted to end him, she could have easily slipped the blade between his ribs already.

What was she waiting for?

Pictures hit him again, as though memories were flashing through his thoughts too rapidly for him to understand any of them. Sarita appeared in each and every image—dressed in a gown of blue. Staring out from the catwalks of *dorcha àite*. Sitting at the table in his dining hall. A scar along the length of her face was there, as well. The last of the images stole what little breath he'd recovered. The Water Amazon lay in his bed, arms wide open in welcome, her beautiful body bared to his gaze.

Fire had gotten to her feet and made her way to Sarita. Ian shoved aside the pictures and focused on his job. He'd fought too hard to come back to this world so he could seek his justice. His hatred burned stronger than what he felt for this woman.

Didn't it?

He wouldn't let some lust-filled infatuation pull him away from his goal. "I cannae let you go." After the words spilled out, he knew they were a lie. He should have called out to Helen to come to them and take the women hostage—or perhaps end their lives—but he couldn't bring himself to do so. He realized, with a touch of amusement, he was going to let them go.

And if that wasn't the height of folly...

I must be daft.

Megan yanked a dirk from a pocket in her skirt. "You're Darian MacKay."

They'd learned his name, and hearing it felt exactly like Sarita's punch to his face.

"We know you," Sarita added. "*I* know you, better than you can imagine."

He saw no reason to play games with the women, though he had no idea how they'd come to know his secret. "Aye, and you two lovely ladies are Megan Feuer and Sarita Neeraj."

"Come with us," Sarita blurted out.

"He can't—" Megan was cut off by Sarita's blazing scowl.

"Come back to our home with us," Water said again. "We can help you."

A snorted laugh slipped out, and Ian wondered for a moment why he'd done that. It hadn't been a habit before he'd died. Perhaps burning to death gave a body new customs. "Only my mistress can help me, loving."

Loving? What in the bloody hell was wrong with him?

"*We* can help," Sarita insisted. "I know you so well, Ian. I know what you've been through, and I know why you're with Helen. Don't you remember me?"

"Why would I remember you? This is the first time I've laid eyes on ye."

"I was with you at *dorcha àite*."

"How could you know of my home?"

"Helen's robbed you of your memories. You captured me after you let a demon loose to lure out Earth. You took me to your castle, *jaanu*, and we—" She stopped talking so abruptly, her teeth clicked when she shut her pretty little mouth.

A bright light flashed to Ian's left, and damn it all if Helen didn't appear. He'd been trying to reconcile what she told him with the fleeting memories that still assaulted his mind. Now he'd have no chance to get more information. Although he wasn't sure why he trusted the Amazon, his own mind gave him glimpses that she told the truth.

Helen took one look around, fisted her hands against her hips and frowned. "I'll assume, Darian, you were about to call to me to tell me you'd captured two of the Amazons."

He chose not to say anything. Anger brewed inside him. Anger at his brother for leaving him behind after setting him up to die a horrible death. Anger at the Amazons for trying to keep him from finding justice. And, despite the fact she was giving him a chance at vengeance, anger at Helen since she'd obviously done something to his thoughts.

Raising her hands, Helen said, "I'll take care of this problem now."

Before any words of a spell could fall out of Helen's mouth, Sarita shouted, "Ganga! Help us, please!"

As Helen screeched in fury, the two Amazons disappeared in a shimmer of light.

Helen grabbed his upper arms. "You let them go! How could you let them go?"

Ian shrugged her hands away. "Water called to her goddess. There was nothing I could do to—"

Thunder rumbled, no doubt her angry response as she interrupted him. "The moment you found them, you were to call to me."

"Killing two of them willnae achieve your goals. Let them work their mischief." He inclined his head at the computer. "They're sure to find the false trails and stay well away from your true plans."

Another clap of thunder, louder this time. "I want them *dead*."

"Keep your eye on the goal, m'lady. They'll die. No doubt. But not until the proper time."

While he waited for Helen to cease her tantrum Ian rubbed a sore spot on his neck Sarita had hit. Helen's goal—and his—would be harder if she'd killed Fire and Water. Had she done so, no doubt Earth and Air would hunt them with a passion that would never be stopped.

By letting them go—especially with the false information they'd taken from the computer—they'd be well-occupied until it was too late.

"I want them dead, Darian."

"I told you, I wish to be called Ian."

She dismissed him with a wave of her hand. "Check the computer. See if they took the right files."

Grateful that Helen had cast a spell to fill his mind with knowledge of this era, he sat down in the chair and put his hands on the keyboard. Although he could never quite get past the foreign feeling of using a computer, he brought up the encrypted files he'd put in place specifically for the Amazons. He'd known all

along they'd come to Helen, a feeling deep in his gut
that these women were no different than the Highland
warriors of his era. They didn't wait for a fight to come
to them—they hunted down their enemies.

A quick check told him the files had been success-
fully pilfered, so he smiled. "Aye, m'lady. The Amazons have the information."

"Good, good. Then let's go. I want to be home."
She sounded weary, a tone he'd grown accustomed to
with the long days she put in. "I need to have my own
things around me."

After he flipped off her computer, Ian went to Hel-
en's side so she could teleport them to the home she'd
acquired for them. Best he could gather, it was a great
distance away—someplace tropical. While he enjoyed
the opulence of the beach, he missed the simplicity of
his castle. Just as she needed to have her own things
near, so did he.

Picturing *dorcha àite* in his mind's eye, he was surprised that remembrances of the beautiful Water Amazon were now intertwined with memories of his home.
Each new image triggered a flare of emotions—strong
emotions—that he couldn't seem to control. Added to
what Sarita told him, it could only equal one conclusion.

Helen had erased his memories.

Confronting her would serve no purpose. He wasn't
surprised. What did bother him was what she feared.
Her confidence in her ultimate victory was absolute. So
what did she gain by messing with his mind? What had
been so important she wanted him to forget? Would
those lost memories pull him from her side?

Even if he'd spent time with the lass as she'd

claimed, he couldn't stray from his path of revenge. Especially when it was finally within his grasp. No interlude, no matter how sweet, was worth giving up his quest for justice.

Ian took Helen's hand in his and let her take them to her home.

THIRTEEN

GANGA WAS WAITING when they popped back into Avalon.

Not a surprise. Sarita had never called to her goddess for rescue before. Amazons weren't supposed to beg for help. Megan might have asked Freya to transport her from place to place, but Freya was her mother. Every now and then Rebecca would have Rhiannon send her to a mission. Even Gina asked for Ix Chel for a favor from time to time.

Sarita had never felt comfortable requesting anything from Ganga. Not that Ganga would deny her—the goddess had always been generous to a fault. Sarita just preferred to handle things without troubling her. This time, she'd had no choice. Helen wasn't a *usual* problem, and the fact she'd exposed the entire world to magicks made the stakes of this mission the highest any Amazon generation had faced. Once Helen had found them in that office, Sarita had no other options that didn't put Ian and Megan at risk.

She hurried to her goddess. "Thank you, Ganga."

The goddess frowned. "You know the other Ancients are angered at the patron goddesses. Their voices are raised in legion, their anger aimed at our hearts. I cannot come to your aid again."

"I'm sorry to have called." Not a lie. Not really. She *was* sorry to inconvenience Ganga because she was so reticent to help most of the time. But Ganga had personally sent Sarita on that first mission to capture Marbas, which told her this request wouldn't have gone unheeded. "I couldn't let Helen kill Megan," Sarita added, hoping the words didn't sound like a flimsy excuse.

The frown that had been fixed on Ganga's beautiful face faded. "I should have known you did not ask for my help for yourself." Her hand rose to brush Sarita's left cheek, tracing the familiar line of the scar, which meant the glamour had ended. "You are so pure of heart, so willing to help others."

She couldn't let Ganga believe she was being altruistic. "I needed to be saved, too."

"Ah, but you would never have asked for help for you alone." The goddess's hand fell away to smooth her yellow sari.

Since she didn't see Ganga often, Sarita couldn't help but wonder why the patron goddess who always seemed loathe to interfere with anything the Amazons did was suddenly willing to entangle herself in this problem. "Why did you send me to capture Marbas?"

"It was necessary."

Sarita wasn't going to get any more answers without prodding. "Why? *Why* was it necessary that *I* go after a demon Earth should have captured?"

"I cannot explain more. Nor can I help you again." Rebecca and Gina were jogging out to meet Sarita and Megan, and Ganga addressed them, as well. "Hear me now. Your goddesses will not be able to aid you further in this battle."

"Battle?" Megan echoed. "So there's going to be a battle?"

Ganga could throw one hell of a fierce glare when she chose to. "Heed me. The Ancients are angered to the point your patron goddesses would suffer should they interfere further."

"What makes this time any different?" Rebecca asked. "They *never* want you to help us."

The patron goddesses were such a contradiction. Creating and endowing the Amazons with one hand, and then washing the other of ever giving assistance in their fights against evil.

"They blame the four of us for creating the Amazons," Ganga replied. "We made it possible for Helen to join the ranks of the Ancients where she is unwelcome and unwanted."

Gina set her hands against her hips. "Only took them how many hundreds of years to get pissed?"

"You must remember that hundreds of years are but the blink of an eye to an Ancient," Ganga said.

Gina nodded but frowned. "Why don't they just... kick her out?"

"It is not our way. After millennia of conflict—of Ancient battling Ancient, destroying one culture after the other—we have finally learned to live in peace. Should any Ancient upset that balance by attacking another, the wrath of the legion would be unleashed. All of heaven and Earth would suffer. You shall have no help in this task."

"Bringing Helen down won't be easy without some help," Gina said. "She's using Seior. How can we stop her without divine tricks?"

"We can do it," Sarita insisted. She sensed the restlessness of her sisters and was fairly overwhelmed with the need to ease it. "We *can*. Helen's no different than any of the other rogue goddesses we've faced."

"I don't know," Gina said. "I don't think we could've brought Sekhmet down without Helen. And you know it kills me to admit that."

"Yeah," Sarita conceded, "but...when it was all said and done, it was you and Zach who kicked her ass."

At least Gina smiled at the comment. "Well, *you* were the one who locked Helen in the block of ice to get us out of there."

"Sarita's right," Megan said. "We can do this on our own."

Ganga put her hand on Sarita's shoulder. "I must go now. Trust your heart, Sarita. It will not lie to you. Trust your heart, follow its lead and all might turn out well in the end." On that peculiar pronouncement, the goddess disappeared in a dazzling light.

Sarita had bigger problems at that moment than contemplating the strangeness of the Ancients. "Megan? You okay?"

"Yeah. Wish you would've let me retaliate. A couple of good fireballs and Darian wouldn't be a problem now."

Although Megan was joking, Sarita let her temper flare. She clenched her hands into fists to keep from taking a swing at her sister.

Why couldn't they see that Ian was Helen's victim, not one of her mindless followers?

"No one's hurting Ian," she ordered. "No one!" A couple of deep breaths helped cool her anger. "Is that understood?"

Megan held up her hands. "Calm down."

"Sorry. I just—" With a shake of her head, she

changed the topic. "We need to get those files to Johann and Zach."

"Explain something to me," Megan said. "This guy set Marbas loose on the world. Then he snatches you up and holds you hostage so Helen can get to us. Then he says he wants to kill Artair. Why would it matter to you if I fried him?"

While she'd always been open and honest with her sisters before, since she'd been at *dorcha àite*, she'd guarded her thoughts and her words. The time was coming when she'd have to explain everything to them, especially if keeping things to herself meant putting Ian in danger. "It just does."

"Sarita…" Rebecca laid a hand on her arm. "What happened when you were gone?"

"I can't talk about it. Not—not yet."

The concerned stare Gina threw her way meant Air knew she was being blocked from entering Sarita's mind. "Don't forget what he's done to us all. Right now—thanks to him and Helen—every COE on the face of this planet wants us dead."

"I haven't forgotten." With a weary sigh, Sarita glanced to the mess hall. "Can we drop this for now? I need to get out of these clothes, and we need to get these files to Johann and Zach."

SARITA WAS GETTING tired for waiting for the men to finish analyzing the information.

"That was just too damned easy," Johann said as he fiddled with his laptop.

The Amazons and Sentinels had gathered in the lodge to formulate plans as they went through the information they'd captured in Helen's office. While Johann and Zach worked on the files, Artair paced the length of the aisle. The women all stood together and waited. Would they face a full-out attack or something more covert?

Helen was such an enigma, always surprising them. None of the Amazons would have expected to find themselves the most hunted women in the country. No one should have known they existed.

"I thought so, too," Zach said. He had his own laptop open. He and Johann had networked their computers so they could work on projects simultaneously. Both techno-geeks, they'd formed a fast friendship when Gina had brought Zach to Avalon.

Zach had blended in with the Amazons as though he'd always belonged to their motley crew. He'd accepted a supernatural power—the ability to "bind" and hold any magical creature—to help them fight Sekhmet. Then he'd fallen in love with Gina and decided to stay and marry her.

The man had been one of the leading names in technology before he left the everyday world, and he often enjoyed pulling up stories about his own disappearance so they could all laugh at the conspiracy theories on where he'd gone.

Sarita couldn't help but compare Zach's easing into Avalon to what would happen if she succeeded in bringing Ian back. Would he fit in with everyone here? Could he ever reconcile his estrangement from Artair? Would her sisters accept him?

What an idiot I am.

There could be no happy ending here.

Whatever relationship she'd shared with Ian back at the castle didn't exist anymore—if it had truly existed anywhere but in her mind. Helen had cast some kind of spell on him that had washed his memory. She'd somehow made him fit into this modern world, as well. Even if Sarita had the chance to talk to Ian and explain everything that Helen had blotted out of his thoughts, there was no guarantee he'd felt the same way about her she'd felt about him—the way she *still* felt about him. She might discover he'd done nothing but use her. A warm body to take advantage of in those boring days of captivity.

"This has to be a ruse." Zach slapped his palms on the table on either side of his laptop. "There's no way we should be able to get into any really important files that easily."

"Agreed," Johann said. "She *wanted* us to follow this trail."

Megan came over to put her hands on her husband's shoulders. "What trail did she want us to follow? Just because she made it obvious doesn't mean it lacks value."

"According to this, she's planning on setting this list of demons loose. She'll use them as her muscle and to force us out in hopes her COEs will catch us. Not much of a master plan. There's got to be more."

Normally, Sarita would have laughed to let everyone know she wasn't the least bit worried about the threat. But her mind was so full of Ian—her fears for what would happen to him as well as her dread that he'd never remember her—she couldn't muster any bravado.

She had to get to him before he could do anything stupid—like kill one of her sisters or his own brother. She had to straighten out all his misconceptions about Artair being the cause of the horrible things that had happened to him. Somehow, she'd have to find a way to heal his spirit.

What she needed was time alone with him—a luxury none of them could afford. Not while Helen was driving forward whatever plan she'd hatched this time.

"So she's coming after us? Like *that's* anything new," Rebecca said. "From the moment I became an Amazon, she's been a pain in my ass. The woman used the military to destroy Avalon. She rescued one of her worst enemies and plotted with him to kill all of us. And she cozied up to Sekhmet to get what she wanted while pretending to be our ally. All she's doing different this time is using demons and gullible people instead of revenants as her minions. We can handle them. If any of her people come after us and we have to take out a few, well then maybe—" She took a deep breath before continuing. "Then maybe we should."

Her husband finally stopped pacing and came to stand by the women. "There is one big difference, Becca mine. These targets wouldnae already be dead. These aren't revenants. They're living, breathing human beings."

Their eyes met, and Sarita saw how easily the couple communicated without words. She had to swallow a flare of jealousy, hoping Rebecca—and Gina and Megan—wouldn't know how much she envied what they shared with their husbands.

Why had her own stupid heart set itself on the one man she could never have?

"You're right. We'd be killing *people*," Rebecca said. "Live people. Not exactly an Amazon's job."

"Even if they're trying to kill us?" Megan shook her head.

Gina leaned back against the table, resting her bottom on the surface. "I'd do what I had to if it meant bringing Helen down."

Appalled by what she was hearing, Sarita jumped into the discussion. "Listen to yourselves! Since when do we get to make the choice over who lives and who dies? That's not what Amazons are supposed to do. We *save* lives, we don't *take* them."

She'd finally conquered her fear of revenants. How could she raise a sword to a living, breathing person?

The frown Megan shot her was downright mean. "The good of the many is a helluva lot more important than the good of one damned person who would kill any one of us in a heartbeat."

"I can't believe what I'm hearing," Sarita said. "Look, we can't just start killing people, even if they're helping Helen."

With a shrug, Gina said, "We take 'em out first, they can't help her. They can't hurt anyone else, either. Innocents are more important than COEs."

Megan joined Gina against the table. "Better to hunt *them* down than to have them hunt *us* down. Sure Helen wanted us to find that list. Good for her. If going after these demons and eliminating them means we get closer to finding that bitch, I'm all for it. Any Child of Earth who gets in the way, then...we deal with him."

While she'd always known Megan and Gina were the first to want to tangle it up in a fight, she'd never dreamed they'd be considering hurting humans—even those who probably deserved to spend the rest of their lives dressed in stripes and staring at life through a set of iron bars. "Rebecca, help me out here."

"Sarita's right," Rebecca said. It was unusual for her

to take Sarita's side, especially against Megan. "We're not superheroes. It's not our job to chase down minions, even if they're furthering Helen's cause. What did they do to deserve death? Destroy some art? Pass a few horrible laws? People make their own misery. That much has been true throughout history. Amazons are supposed to preserve the balance between good and evil, not—"

"COEs *are* evil," Megan interrupted.

"Once we turn ourselves into some kind of—of—" Rebecca struggled for the right word.

"Vigilantes?" Sarita offered.

Rebecca gave her a weak smile. "Yeah. Vigilantes. If we do that, there may be no going back."

A bright burst of yellow light announced the arrival of an Ancient. With the patron goddesses keeping their distance that could only mean it was the one god who had the guts and the ability to venture into Avalon.

"What are you doing here?" Megan asked through gritted teeth.

The god Freyjr—twin to patron goddess Freya and king of the troublemakers—smiled. "My dearest niece. An Amazon called?"

"*I* didn't call an Ancient," she replied, flipping her red ponytail over her shoulder. "And if I'd ever been weak enough to ask for help, you would be the *last* Ancient I'd look to."

He flicked at some imaginary dust on the sleeve of his dark Italian silk suit. While the other Ancients preferred to dress fitting their historical cultures, Freyjr loved modern clothing. He looked ready for a *GQ* photo shoot. His white-blond hair was slicked back, and he sported a large diamond earring in his right ear.

"The cut by family is always the deepest." He shifted his gaze to Sarita. "Hello, little one. You were the one who called to me in your time of need. You know how quickly I would come if you so much as crooked your elegant finger my way."

From the time she'd become an Amazon, Sarita had been some kind of forbidden fruit to Freyjr. He'd cajoled, flirted, propositioned—all but promised to take her to the moon. Not once had she been tempted to take him up on whatever sensual promise he was making. Only a fool got involved with deities, especially sexually. His decadent lifestyle only served to disgust her.

"*I* didn't call you, either."

She hated his far too sage smile. "Ah, but you did. I know you, little one. I know what is truly in your heart. That heart begged for me to come here, to be your hero."

Since everyone was now gaping at her, Sarita shook her head hard enough to set her braid to bouncing. "I didn't call you!"

When Freyjr tried to touch her scarred cheek, she jerked away. "You are searching for something only I can give you. You want a way to end this fight, to be able to face Helen on her own terms and defeat her. You want a way to bring Darian MacKay back to your side."

How could he possibly know so much about her thoughts? She hadn't even shared them with her sisters. "But I—I—didn't call you."

"I can give you what you want. I can give you *all* of it." He addressed the other Amazons. "Helen will destroy you. Without me, the fight will be the end of the Amazons. All of you will die at her hand. Unless, that

is, you take from me what you need to destroy her. I
must teach one of you how to use Seior."

"Doesn't matter if I face death by fighting her,"
Megan said. "Nothing you can say would make me
learn Seior. I saw what it did to Sparks. I won't let it
turn me bad."

"Ah," he purred, "that is what you fear? Losing
yourself to the black magicks? Dearest niece, you have
been misinformed if you think all Seior is used for is
evil."

"It *is* evil," Rebecca said. "It's nothing but black
magicks that bring misery to anyone who practices it."

Freyjr clucked his tongue as though scolding a
naughty child. "I assure you, beautiful lady, that *I* have
felt no misery from practicing the art."

"You're an Ancient," Megan said. "You can control it. A human can't. None of us want anything to do
with something that dangerous, Freyjr. You can just
go away now."

"Ah, but you are wrong. Each of you has already
been touched by Seior." Freyjr nodded at Megan. "Seior
is why you are here. It is what allowed your mother to
go to Beltane undetected and mate with your father." A
nod to Gina. "Seior is what gave your man the power
he needed to bind Sekhmet." And finally he inclined
his head at Rebecca. "And it gave you your son."

"My son was a gift from Rhiannon!" Rebecca's
shout echoed through the mess hall as the men came
to stand behind their wives.

"A gift given through magicks, just as you channeled the dark magicks when you were a goddess and
restored the fertility of your sisters." A chuckle slipped

through his lips. "You felt it, didn't you, Rebecca. The power. The strength."

Artair was the first to speak. "'Tis time for you to go."

The god gave Artair a disgusted scoff. "And you—the most hypocritical of them all. You would be dead, Sentinel, had Earth not channeled the power Seior gave her to bring you back to this world."

"That wasn't black magicks," Rebecca insisted. "I was able to harness the power from Gaia, from my mother. That's how I brought him back."

"Nay, 'twas Seior that gave you the strength you needed. Helen used black magicks to change herself into an Ancient as well as to cause you to ascend. You, in turn, used it to resurrect your lost...love." He badly faked a choke on the last word.

A roar of thunder filled the air, growing louder instead of dissipating. The floorboards beneath Sarita's feet vibrated, making her look to Rebecca. Before she could question why her sister caused an earthquake, a blinding flash of lightning caused a collection of gasps from everyone in the hall. Then Freya popped up next to her brother.

"So much for Ancients staying out of this," Sarita muttered.

Freya glared at her twin. "I should have known I would find you here. You meddle where you should not."

He shrugged. "I merely answered the call of the Amazon."

"I didn't call him," Sarita insisted. "I *didn't.*"

"Your desire to save the man you love sent the message as strong as a ray of sunlight, little one." The god reached for her again, but Freya smacked his hand away.

"Leave her be and explain what you hope to accomplish by coming to Avalon—other than to seduce Water."

Freyjr straightened his tie. "I might have desired her in the past, but she is flawed now. Sekhmet succeeded in making her undesirable."

Sarita's cheeks burned. Without caring what she was revealing about her insecurities, she pulled her braid forward to cover the marred side of her face.

"I came," he continued, "because Water wished she had the powers to get to the man she desires and to bring him back here. *I* can give her those powers."

FOURTEEN

SARITA WANTED TO shout a denial until she realized Freyjr had somehow read her thoughts. She'd been searching for a way—*any* way—to rescue Ian. "I didn't *really* call him."

"Nay," Freyjr admitted. "'Twas my doing. I've always taken a special interest in you, little one. I could feel your pain and wished only to end it." He bent into a condescending deep bow before raising his head to smirk. "I but came to act as the knight in shining armor to your damsel in distress. Let me teach you the tricks you need to rescue Darian MacKay. You love him, do you not?"

Her heart skipped a beat or two. To have her feelings paraded around everyone at Avalon made her feel downright naked. Sure, they might have all guessed something had happened between her and Ian. But she'd never come right out and said they'd had an intimate relationship. Instead, she'd shut them all out, as though it would be less humiliating if she kept it to herself.

Everyone gaped at her now.

Artair's stare was the most intense. "What is there between you and Darian, Sarita? What happened at *dorcha àite*?"

So much for keeping her private life private. She might be able to try hard to mask what she felt, but they knew anyway. Why bother fighting it any longer?

With a sigh, Sarita gave up her secrets. "We were close, Artair. *Very* close."

Freyjr gave her a rueful chuckle. "Yet another reason I no longer wish you in my bed. You are no longer pure."

"How could you possibly know that?" she snapped.

His laugh grated on her rapidly fraying nerves. "A true lover of women knows when a virgin has been compromised."

Artair's face mottled red. "You bedded my brother?"

Sarita couldn't help but roll her eyes. This whole conversation was ridiculous. Necessary, probably. But ridiculous, nonetheless. "First of all, I didn't know he was your brother at the time. Second, what I do in my private life is none of your business."

"Private life?" he shouted. "Yer an Amazon! Ye were his hostage!"

"Stockholm Syndrome," Megan said with a curt nod. "That's what it was. No other reason you'd fall for someone who'd follow Helen. You fell for your captor. It'll pass. Give it time and—"

They were driving Sarita insane. "It wasn't Stockholm Syndrome." She looked to Gina for some help.

"Do you love him?" Gina's expression softened, her hair losing the red highlights that had formed when Freyjr arrived.

"As if you need to ask me that," Sarita countered. "Freyjr said I did, so it *has* to be true." Now she understood how her sisters felt when their love lives were paraded around so publicly. Each courtship between the Amazons and their husbands had been embarrassingly open for their whole group.

"We need to know, Sarita," Johann said. "If we're

going to face him, we need to know the rules of engagement."

"You mean you want to know if you can kill him. I'll remind you, he's Artair's brother."

"Aye," Artair said, "but he wants me dead. He may nae give me a choice. Should he stand in our way, he will fall by my hand or no one's."

"We can't promise that, Artair," Johann countered. "In a battle, all bets are usually off."

"He's Helen's ally," Megan added. "If I have to get through him to get to her, I will. Unless… Well, unless—"

"Unless you're in love with him," Rebecca interrupted. "Then we'll try to be more careful."

"He's Artair's brother! You should be careful anyway!"

"Do you love him?" Gina asked again. "You've been keeping us at arm's length for so long—not only since you came back, but after Sekhmet hurt you. None of us knows what you're thinking anymore."

"Or what you're feeling," Rebecca added. "I'm supposed to be the Amazon Guardian, Sarita. I can't protect you if I don't know what's going on in that head of yours."

For one of the few times since Sarita's return, Gina's voice filled her mind. *Do you really love him?*

Although her temper was normally slow to ignite, Sarita's fuse had burned shorter and shorter with each of their comments. Gina's repeated question and Rebecca's asserting that Sarita needed the rest of her sisters to take care of her made the firecracker explode.

With clenched fists, she gave them what they were begging for—total honesty. "I don't need your protection! I know you all think I'm the weakest of the group, but I'm not. I have powers, too."

Gina stepped closer. "No one said anything about you being weak. No one."

Sniffing back angry tears, Sarita shouted at her sisters. "Yes, I love him! I love Ian! There. Are you all happy now? You know everything I'm feeling. I want to save him from Helen. I want him to know his brother didn't set him up to be murdered in a horrible and painful way. I want what all of you have. I want someone to love me! I want the man I love to love me in return. *Okay?*"

At least everyone had the sense to look contrite.

Everyone except Freyjr. He had his usual cocky grin. "Then you accept my help?"

What she needed was to get the hell away from everyone, to find a deep pool of water and immerse herself to shut out the rest of the world. She took a few calming breaths instead. "I didn't say that."

"Seior is the only chance you have to save him, little one."

"Brother," Freya said, the censure clear in her tone, "you must tread carefully. Seior is not for those who cannot control it properly."

"I shall give her only token magicks—the ability to move from place to place with her mind."

"That's it?" Sarita wanted to scream at him until she realized she already was. The jerk had just set her up to bare her heart to everyone for nothing more than simple teleportation—something her goddess could do with the blink of her brown eyes. "That's *all* you planned to teach me?"

"Perhaps a few more things that will aid you in your

quest, but being able to go where you will with only
your thoughts is the most important thing I can give
you. I have seen the future. I know the skill that you
will need the most."

"You saw the future?" Sarita couldn't keep the incredulous tone from her voice. In all the years she'd
been an Amazon, no one had ever told her the Ancients
could see into the future. If that was true, why wouldn't
the patron goddesses give them at least an idea about
the bad things that would be happening?

"Mother?" Megan's gaze searched Freya's. "Is that
true? You can see our future?"

When Freya busied herself with straightening her
long yellow skirt, Sarita rolled her eyes again. The
goddess might be powerful, but she'd never been able
to tell a lie without giving herself away.

Sparks shot from the crown of Megan's head. "You
can see the future, but you let me walk into danger
time and time again? I'm your *daughter*. How could
you do that to me?"

Freya straightened her spine. "Ancients cannot see
everything in the future. Only certain things, and they
sometimes come in riddles and images that are hard
to interpret. I tend to do more mischief than good by
trying to read them. 'Tis why there are oracles for the
task."

Megan crossed her arms over her chest and sent a
fiery glare at her mother. "Don't give me that load of
manure. You can see the future—you just choose not
to share it with me."

"She cannot," Freyjr said. "Ancients are forbidden
from revealing the future to humans."

"Well, isn't that funny, *uncle*?" Megan's voice had

risen to a bellow. "'Cause it seems to me you told Sarita you've seen her future."

"Nay," Freya said. "He did not tell her of her future. He only said he could help her if he gave her a few black magicks."

"That's just semantics." Johann jumped into the conversation. His next comments were directed at Sarita. "You can't learn Seior. It's like crack. Once you start down that path, you'll never be able to stop."

"Aye, he's right," Artair said. "'Tis forbidden to the Amazons." He shot a glower at Freyjr. "You have no right tempting the lass."

Freyjr seemed oblivious to the discussion. He kept his ice blue eyes fixed on Sarita.

She dismissed everyone else as easily and returned the intensity of his stare. "What happens to Ian? If I don't learn this from you, what happens to him?"

"I cannot tell you that, little one."

"Sarita," Johann said with a low growl. "Don't do this…"

Normally, his Sentinel tone cut through her the same way a drill sergeant's voice made a private stand at attention.

Not this time. Not when Ian was in danger.

"If you can't tell me what happens," she said, "then tell me why I need the ability to teleport."

"Sarita, no." This time, Artair barked the command.

"Ask him this instead," Rebecca said. "Ask him what he wants in return."

Freyjr whirled on Earth. "Have I asked anything as payment for this favor?"

Despite the anger in which the god had hurled the question at her, Rebecca stayed nonplussed. "You forgot one thing—I was Sparks's friend. I know you're the one who taught her Seior so she could find Helen. And I know exactly what you wanted for your *help*."

Standing behind his wife, Artair put his hands on her shoulders. "Seior is the wrong path, Sarita. Even if it meant I could save Darian, I'm nae sure even I would take what Freyjr offers."

Why couldn't they see how much this skill could help? Not only in saving Ian, but in their Amazon duties? Instead, they were ganging up on her.

Sarita appealed to her closest sister. "Gina?" For the first time in a long time, her sister's thoughts were as closed to her as Sarita's must have been to Gina. "What do you think?"

She answered Sarita with one of Johann's favorite sayings. "Beware Ancients bearing gifts."

They were all against her.

Her last route of appeal was blocked, because Ganga had told Sarita she couldn't help her again. By herself, this wasn't a battle she could win. She also had to admit, if only to herself, that the prospect of learning Seior was not only frightening, but more than a little exciting. Perhaps they were all correct—once she started down that path and knew that kind of power, she might have problems turning back.

Just about to concede to her sisters' wishes—something she always seemed to do—Sarita remembered the last thing Ganga told her before she left Avalon.

"Trust your heart, follow its lead, and all might turn out well in the end."

While her sisters might be scolding her that learning to teleport was a descent into black magicks, Sarita's heart screamed—in a much louder voice—that Ian needed her help.

The man had already died twice. Once, he was butchered at the Battle of Culloden Moor. Next, he was tortured to death by his own clan. If it was in her power to keep him from facing death a third time by learning one important skill, then her heart said to go right ahead.

There was only one thing left to know. "I only have one question, Freyjr."

He grinned at her, clearly sensing victory.

"What exactly *do* you want in return?"

Placing a long finger against his cheek, he hummed as though thinking through many choices. "I will make you this bargain. I give you the Seíor you need now, and I will collect on the debt later."

Rebecca was the first to scoff. "Oh, yeah, that's a *great* idea. Write an Ancient a blank check he can cash whenever he wants."

Then everyone was talking at once. The din was almost more than Sarita could bear. "Freyjr...promise me one thing."

"And what is that you wish of me, little one?"

"If—if when you ask this *favor*—if I tell you no, you'll respect that decision."

"Sarita, don't." Gina strode over to her side. "Please don't."

Her heart told her to keep going. "I have to."

The smile Freyjr gave her made her fear she'd just made a deal with the devil himself. "I accept your bargain."

Before she could react to his statement, he pressed

his hand against her forehead. Then he spoke in a language she didn't recognize.

The world swam in her mind and her stomach lurched. She almost shoved Freyjr's hand away. Only her love for Ian allowed her to endure the magicks he seemed to be pushing straight through her skull.

"You're hurting her!" Gina jumped to put herself next to Freyjr, and she reached for his arm.

Sarita found just enough strength to stop her. "No. Let him alone."

A sharp pain shot through her head, making her wonder if Freyjr had somehow driven a spike through her frontal lobe. Then, mercifully, the pain was gone.

Panting for breath, she stumbled to the closest bench and tried to stop herself from falling. Gina grabbed her elbow and helped her sit as the rest of their tribe gathered around.

"Sarita?" Johann crouched close to her and took a hold of her wrist. From the way he studied his watch, he had to be taking her pulse.

"You're white as a sheet." Rebecca pressed the back of her hand against Sarita's forehead.

"I'm fine." Yes, her heart pounded a furious tempo, but her stomach had settled and the blinding pain had disappeared.

Megan rubbed Sarita's shoulder.

It was one touch too many, and she almost screamed for everyone to give her some room. All she wanted was to go to the beautiful spa that lay deep in the woods surrounding Avalon. She needed to see Eden, the natural hot spring, because it offered peace, quiet and a chance to immerse herself in water.

Trying to hold her temper, Sarita closed her eyes

and thought about Eden. The noise began to die, as though someone was slowly turning the world's volume lower and lower.

When she opened her eyes, she was in the woods, standing on the edge of the bubbling hot spring.

Her heart, which had just begun to slow to a more normal rhythm, slammed against her ribs. "Holy shit."

Freyjr appeared at her side, arriving in a shimmer of light. "A nice ability, is it not?"

"How did I do that?"

"You must think hard of where you want to go, and you will go there. Be careful, little one. You must learn to control your thoughts or you shall find yourself in some...unusual places."

"All I have to do is think about where I want to go and I'll appear there?"

"You must do more than think of the place. You must wish to be there with all your mind. Direct your thoughts to that place, picture it, sense it, and you will go there."

She wanted to know everything about the new power. Loathe to admit it, she'd been jealous each time her sisters powers had escalated. They kept taking steps forward and growing as Amazons while she felt as if she were treading water. Now she was taking her own leap into being stronger. "Can I take someone with me?"

"So many questions." His fingers were under her chin, making her face him. "And what is my reward for answering? A kiss, perhaps?"

After giving her the ability to teleport from place to place, the guy deserved a peck on the lips. Besides, he'd promised if she said no, he would stop. For some odd and probably stupid reason, she trusted him. In all the time she'd known him, he'd never once crossed any boundary. He teased. He flirted. He loved to toss around innuendos. But he'd always kept his distance when she'd let him know he made her uncomfortable. And in the end, she found his attention flattering.

He'd given her an amazing gift—one that would save Ian. What could one kiss hurt? "Fine. One kiss. One quick, *friendly* kiss."

The god lowered his head, smiling as he drew closer. "And if you want more?"

"Trust me. I won't. I love Ian."

"We shall see." He was chuckling when he pressed his mouth to hers.

His lips were soft and warm and got no more response from her than would have happened if she'd kissed one of her Sentinels.

Freyjr pulled back enough to look into her eyes.

When he tried to kiss her again, she put her hands against his chest and gently pushed. "You got your kiss. Now answer my question."

As he stood back to full height—tall enough her head barely reached his armpit—he licked his lip in an almost obscene way. "You taste like honey. I would love to taste *all* of you."

She refused to rise to his bait. "You still haven't answered my question."

His sigh sounded far too human. "Yes. If you hold tight to a person and imagine him going with you, then he will go with you."

"Thank you, Freyjr."

"Yes, well… I shall let you know when I am ready

to claim my recompense." He snapped his fingers and disappeared.

Although the waters of Eden called to her, her sisters would be worried. Closing her eyes, she imagined herself back in the lodge. When she opened them a few second later, she was exactly where she wanted to be.

Six pairs of stern and worried eyes drilled holes right through her.

Let the inquisition begin…

FIFTEEN

IAN HAD COME to visit her in her dreams again.

Sarita sighed his name, loving the weight pressed so intimately against her when the length of his body covered hers. One of his hands took her wrists and stretched them above her head. The other hand slid up her body, tangling in the sheet, caressing her hip, her waist.

"Ian," she whispered again. "I missed you so much."

Soft, warm lips tickled across her scarred cheek and then a tongue traced the length of the defect. She pulled her hands out of his grasp and threaded her fingers through his hair to urge him on. His touch felt wonderful, but she wanted more. She needed the connection and the passion she'd felt from the first time his lips had touched hers in that first dream that seemed so long ago. "Kiss me."

He denied her, which came as a surprise. In all the intimate interludes they'd shared, he'd answered every one of her hushed pleas, fulfilled each sensual command she'd given.

Something about his touch was different. Almost predatory. His caresses became more demanding, forcing her senses to kick in and drive away the groggy haze hovering from sleep. A deep breath made her eyes fly open. The earthy masculine smell she loved so much had been replaced by a new spicy scent that could only mean one thing.

This wasn't Ian.

Didn't matter that he looked like Ian. This man wasn't him. Before she could blurt out that fact, lips covered hers. They weren't Ian's lips, but the feel was familiar nonetheless.

The Amazon in her came to life as Sarita shoved her hands between their bodies. "Freyjr, you bastard. Get off me."

She pushed hard enough he had to catch himself from falling off the bed. Then he frowned at her, the guise he'd donned to seduce her shifting to his true appearance.

In the moonlight streaming through her window, the god appeared ghostly blue. "Ah, little one. You do not mean that. I felt the desire in you. Your passion matches mine."

Her face flushed hot. Yes, she'd responded to him, but only because she'd thought he was Ian. She clutched the sheet against her chest to cover herself. Even though she was wearing a cotton nightgown, she felt far too exposed. Probably because he was naked.

She quickly shifted her gaze to his face, but not before he caught her looking.

His arrogant chuckle made her long to slap his face. Not that it would do any good. She might be agitated with him, but this was simply Freyjr being true to his nature.

Grabbing one of her pillows, she tossed it onto his lap. "I already told you no."

"Nay, my beautiful infatuation, you did not. Your body said aye, most definitely *aye*."

"I thought you were Ian."

Freyjr tilted his head as his face changed, his hair tinting darker as his face became Ian's again. "Then I shall be him if his form pleases you more than mine. Anything to know your love." He leaned in to try to kiss her again.

She dropped the sheet to put her hands against his chest again. "You might look like Ian, but you're *not* him. Besides, you said my scars were repulsive."

"I merely jested."

"It was cruel."

"'Twas said to hurt you for denying me. Let me shower your body with my apology. Why does it matter if I'm not your man? Can you not pretend for this one night that you love me? Can you not let me show you pleasures beyond your wildest imagination?"

A snorted laugh slipped out. "Typical guy. Brag, brag, brag."

Freyjr tilted his head as he watched her closely. "You confuse me, little one."

"I hear that a lot."

His hand moved to her face.

Although she shouldn't allow him to touch her, Sarita didn't fear him. As he'd promised, he'd honored her request to stop. The other Amazons—and definitely the Sentinels—didn't trust Freyjr any farther than they could toss him. Only Zach seemed to appreciate him as much as Sarita did. Yes, he came on a bit strong, and he was hedonistic. All the Ancients were. But when push came to shove, Freyjr had always come through.

He'd let them know when his twin had gone missing—kidnapped by Chernabog and Helen. He'd brought Ra to Zach to give him the binding power to stop Sekhmet. And now he'd given her teleportation so she could help Ian.

If the god wanted to stroke her face, she'd let him.

Freyjr's hand cupped her cheek as he rubbed his thumb over her bottom lip. "You are such a contradiction, Sarita Neeraj. Your heart is pure as a first snowfall, yet your body is fashioned for sinful pleasures." His fingers traced her scar and then brushed over her earlobe. "You are flawed, yet those flaws only enhance your beauty. Had Sekhmet not marked you, I fear Aphrodite might have taken notice of you and injured you herself so you would be no rival to her splendor."

Funny, but she didn't feel any sadness at his statement that she was *flawed*. Given so matter-of-factly, the words didn't bring forward the lingering hurt over having been given what she'd considered a horrid scar. Perhaps Freyjr helped her by saying she was beautiful, or perhaps knowing Ian desired her and didn't consider her hideous lessened her pain. For the first time since Sekhmet had dragged her claws across her face, Sarita didn't feel ugly.

"Thank you," she said. "I needed to hear that."

He leaned in to try to kiss her again.

"But my answer is still no."

He transformed himself back into Freyjr. "Need I remind you that I have yet to claim my reward for your new skill?"

Panic sizzled through her. She needed to be able to teleport to save Ian. Would she compromise herself— *whore* herself to this god—just to save the man she loved?

That was something she wasn't prepared to do. "You

won't take it away, will you? You won't take away my power?"

"I could demand you submit."

The panic eased. "Not after the promise you made." She was probably stupid for being so self-assured with a god of Freyjr's power. Yet she dared because she trusted him. "You won't because that means you'd still lose."

He quirked an eyebrow.

"If you can't seduce me, I win. If you rape me, that means you couldn't convince me to accept you, which means you'd lose this game we've been playing for all these years."

His scowl was scorching.

"Would it help to know I think you're a handsome devil?" She reached out to brush back a lock of hair that had fallen across his forehead.

Freyjr's frown eased.

"And if it weren't for my love for Ian, I'd actually consider it." A lie, but one his ego probably needed— exactly like he might have been telling her a sweet lie by saying she was beautiful.

"Ah, but you please me, little one. Very much." This time, when his hand came forward as though he was going to touch her breast, she pulled the sheet higher up her body. "I but mean to give you one last gift," he said, his voice raspy.

Was he testing her to see if she truly trusted him? Sarita couldn't read the look in his eyes. "What will *this* one cost me?"

"A gift freely given requires no payment."

She let him drag the sheet to her waist. Before she

could say anything about his generosity, she gasped as he pressed his palm between her breasts.

His hand glowed orange, and the heat of it was close to unbearable.

"Freyjr, what are you doing?"

"I give your heart the ability to always find Avalon. You now possess the skill of the Sentinels—to be able to find your way home."

Damn, but she hadn't thought of that. She could do something none of the other Amazons had ever been able to do. She could leave Avalon and return. Rebecca and Megan had to depend on their husbands, and Gina usually called to her goddess, Ix Chel. Only Sparks had left and then found her way back, but that was after Freyjr had given her Seior, a gift he'd now shared with Sarita.

Her task was to make sure it didn't corrupt her the way it had Sparks.

The god pulled his hand back.

"Thank you," she said.

"I want to stay. I want to show you all the wonderful ways of love. I care not that you are no longer a virgin, although I had always hoped to claim that prize as my own." His voice held a hint of sadness.

"Not happening, Freyjr. I told you no."

"You do not fear my punishing you for your refusal?"

She shook her head, and he actually grinned in response. "I see good in you, Freyjr. I always have."

A snap of his fingers saw him fully clothed in a dark suit and his arrogance back in place. He tucked her pillow behind her back. "I cannot abide by your imper-

fections any longer. I am on to find a lover who is not
so—" a shudder ripped through him "—pure of heart."

On that pronouncement of what he obviously considered her true "flaw," he disappeared in a burst of
light.

Sarita couldn't help but smile. Sure, he might present himself to everyone as the Hugh Hefner of the
Ancients, but deep down, he was nothing but a big
teddy bear.

Her thoughts shifted to Ian. She was ashamed that
her body had responded to Freyjr's touch. The moment
she'd realized he wasn't Ian, she felt as though ice water
ran through her veins.

Taking another lover simply wasn't possible. Not
only because of her love for Ian, but because she could
never be as free with anyone else. Love gave her that
freedom.

But he didn't remember her.

Closing her eyes, she sniffed back the threatening
tears, wanting nothing more than to see him again, to
be able to touch him—to love him again—if only one
more time.

Sarita tried to picture him, to see his face. A tear
slipped from the corner of her eye.

The smell of Avalon's woods faded as the aroma of
saltwater filled her nostrils. Her eyes flew open, and
she gawked.

She was on a beach, odd because that wasn't what
she'd expected since the last place she'd seen Ian was
at Helen's temple. The only thing that had filled her
thoughts when she came to this place was Ian. Checking her new surroundings, she let the roaring sound
of the waves rush through her as she dug her toes into

the wet sand, fighting the urge to jerk her nightgown over her head and sprint into the water.

A small cabana stood where the beach met the trees. It wasn't any larger than her stark cabin at Avalon, but it seemed cozy and inviting. There wasn't a door, just an entrance into what couldn't be any larger than one room.

Figuring her power brought her here for some reason, she went to see what she'd find inside. She followed a trail of footprints in the sand as they led toward the cabana. Placing a foot inside one of the prints in the damp sand, she smiled at how much larger the footprint was. Her heart suddenly knew why she'd transported herself here.

There were only three pieces of furniture in the cabana. A table with a porcelain pitcher and bowl. A small bureau. And a rather large bed upon which Ian slept.

His chest was bare to her, and a light sheet covered the lower half of his body. The moonlight eased the fierceness of his features, making all the anger in his face disappear to leave behind a man so handsome, she drew in a sharp breath. Her body flooded with heat as memories of what they'd shared filled her.

Sarita stepped closer to the bed until she could have touched him. "I love you, Ian," she whispered before she leaned down to press her lips to his.

Sarita had come to visit him in his dreams again.

Again?

Ian tried to grasp at the fragments of what had to be memories. Images hit him from every direction at the same time soft hands smoothed over his chest. The scent of jasmine seemed so familiar, as did the long braid his fingers trailed down.

His dream lover *had* come to him.

A torture designed by Helen?

Probably. She loved to work mischief, and no doubt she'd sent this nymph to tempt him.

Hell, even his thoughts seemed to be drowning in some odd déjà vu.

Warm lips caressed his neck as her tongue tickled across to his ear. Her breath was hot as she whispered, "I want you."

"I want you, too, loving." The endearment fell from his mouth with a familiarity that cleared the last remnants of sleep from his brain.

This wasn't an erotic dream. Ian opened his eyes to stare at the woman sitting on the side of his bed. Her exotic beauty stole the breath from his lungs. "I know you."

She nodded.

"You're Sarita."

"I'm Sarita."

"You broke into Helen's office."

"Yeah, I broke into Helen's office. Do you remember more than that, *jaanu*? Do you remember...*us*?"

Of course he did, but none of the recollections were tangible enough to use as the proof that he needed to confront Helen. While he was sure she'd tampered with his memories, he didn't understand the extent of her damage or her reason for doing so.

For all he knew, the bewitching creature could be using him to find Helen's weakness. "Nay, loving. I remember naught of *us*."

His words seemed to wound her. Sadness filled her

eyes and a frown bowed her lips. She tried to rise to her feet, but Ian grabbed her wrist to hold her where she was. Unable to stop himself, he snatched the tie from the end of her braid and unwound the plaits. Combing his fingers through the thick, dark hair, he let the tresses spill over her shoulders. She made no move to stop him, and he saw no reason to refuse what she offered. By keeping her close, perhaps he could find some answers to the questions that haunted him.

"Show me what we shared, Sarita," he coaxed. "What should I know?"

Sarita hesitated, her eyes holding a kind of pain that touched his heart.

He tried some honesty, not sure why he trusted her. But he did. "I want to remember, but I cannae. Every time I reach for a memory, it drifts away like smoke in the wind. I need you to show me what we felt. Then I might bring more back."

Damn, if that didn't sound like a lame attempt to lure the lass into his bed.

Sitting up, he shook his head. "Never mind. 'Tis a silly notion."

Instead of answering, she leaned in, her eyes watching his as if to give him a chance to pull away before she would kiss him.

Not only did he *want* to kiss her, he *needed* to. He met her halfway.

The first touch of her lips to his, and he was lost. *This*, he remembered. He knew her taste, just as he recognized she was some kind of fever in his blood. Her tongue slid between his lips to stroke his.

Holding her face between his palms, he returned the ferocity of her kiss. When she finally ended the kiss and pulled back, he was arrogantly pleased her breathing was every bit as choppy as his.

Without a word, Sarita rose then tugged her thin nightdress over her head. It fluttered to the floor. Her lacy panties followed.

Ian threw his legs over the side of the bed and stood. Drinking in every exquisite inch of her body, he savored the heat pulsing to his cock. His mind might hold hazy memories of this woman, but his body recognized her as his lover.

He wrapped his arms around her and held her close as he took possession of her mouth again, letting her know in no uncertain terms that he desired her as he had no other woman. Her kiss was every bit as fierce as she grasped his tongue between her teeth and pulled. A growl rose from his chest. Ending the kiss, he swept her into his arms and carried her to the bed.

Setting her on the white sheets, he smiled as more memories flooded his brain. He'd seen her, just like this, spread on his bed like a succulent feast for a starving man. Her arms opened to him in welcome. With a contented sigh, he covered her body with his and settled himself until his erection was nestled against the juncture of her thighs.

"Do you remember this?" Sarita's voice was a sultry whisper.

"I remember this...and I remember that husky voice." She stiffened under him, causing a fleeting glimpse of a similar conversation. "'Tis a beautiful voice, one meant for seduction."

"You *do* remember me."

"Aye." He had much more pleasurable things in

mind than talking about what he did or didn't recall. "I remember that in these slim arms I found paradise."

Ian kissed her again, letting his tongue lazily reclaim her mouth as he cherished the familiarity that had been out of grasp. This woman belonged to him— even though he wasn't sure how or why he knew that.

Rational thought tried to crowd its way into this world of bliss, but he banished it. Now wasn't the time to think of justice or his brother or Helen. Now was the time to indulge in the passion flowing to him from the soft and very feminine form beneath him.

Sarita's fingers flitted down his back until she palmed his buttocks, pulling him hard against her core. Her moans were music to his ears, and although he wanted nothing more than to answer her call and bury himself deep inside her, he owed her more than a quick romp.

Breaking the kiss, he smiled down at her. "Patience, loving. I want more than a tussle. I want to make love to you. I *need* to make love to you."

Her sensuous smile hit him like a punch to the stomach. "Then make love to me, Ian."

"My pleasure."

He brushed kisses down her slender neck, loving how her skin quivered at his touch. His hands covered her breasts as he licked the valley between them. Her nipples hardened, so he shifted to take one deep into his mouth, swirling his tongue around the tight bud as she arched her back and splayed her fingers through his hair. After pulling with his teeth, he shifted to the other breast.

Ian worked his way down her body with tender kisses. Another burst of remembrance came as he flicked his tongue at the gold hoop adorning her belly button. But there was one more thing he wanted to try to force his mind to work properly.

The sound Sarita made when he licked between her feminine folds was a cross between a whimper and a moan. Taking that as encouragement, he set about driving her toward climax as he relearned her taste and the musky scent of her arousal.

"Now, Ian! Please!"

He ignored her pleas, needing to be sure he helped her find her release before he took her. He was so lost in a sensuous fog, if he plunged inside her at that moment, he would have spilled his seed like some untried lad. When her orgasm tore through her, she clenched her fingers in his hair, tugging so hard his scalp stung.

Unable to wait any longer, he rose above her, spread her thighs wider with his knee and thrust inside her.

Sweet merciful Jesu, she fit him like a second skin. Tight. Wet. So damned hot. Her hips pushed up to take him more deeply inside, and Ian was lost to anything but the two of them.

Setting a rough, fast tempo, he pushed into her, again and again as she wrapped her legs around his hips and cried out his name. The feel of her body squeezing him tight pushed him over the edge. With one last thrust, he came as he shouted her name.

THE MORNING SUNLIGHT streamed through the window. The splash of the waves served as a melodic alarm clock. A light breeze brought the fresh smell of the ocean into the hut.

Yet Ian could find no beauty in any of it. For when he'd awakened and reached for Sarita, she was gone.

SIXTEEN

POPPING HERSELF BACK into her cabin, Sarita frowned when she found Gina waiting.

"You didn't come home last night," Gina said. "You left Avalon. How in the hell were you able to do that?"

Since her sister seemed intent to scold her, Sarita saw no need to keep her own tone controlled. "I just can." She let her disdain drip from her words.

"Seior, right? That's one of the things Freyjr taught you, isn't it? And I'll bet you went looking for Darian. Didn't you?" Gina stood up from where she'd been sitting on Sarita's unmade bed. "Did your black magicks help you find him?"

The sun's rise cast an orange glow through the cabin. Instead of feeling ready to face a new day, all Sarita wanted to do was crawl into her lonely bed and sleep the rest of the daylight hours away. She sure as hell wasn't up to being badgered.

Had Ian awakened yet? Did he miss her lying next to him? They'd spent the wee hours of the morning making love, catching short bursts of rest before reaching for each other in greedy abandon. They hadn't said more than a handful of words to each other. She'd been foolish to go to him, but her heart wouldn't be denied. If she could trigger his memories by being with him and reminding him of what they'd shared, it was worth the risk of being discovered.

"Answer me!" Gina's hands clenched into fists at her side.

While Sarita hated being treated like a kid who'd broken curfew, she swallowed her annoyance. It was a difficult task, her usual ability to endure in silence somehow stretched taut. Any tighter, and she'd snap. "Yes. I found him."

"God, Sarita! What were you thinking? He'll lead Helen right to us!"

About to launch into a tirade to justify why she'd left in search of him, Sarita looked at the door that had just opened. She scoffed as Megan and Rebecca came into the cabin without so much as knocking. "Gee, come right in. Not like this is *my* home or anything."

"You're finally back," Megan said. Her gaze swept Sarita from head to toe, no doubt taking in that she was in her nightgown, her hair probably a disheveled mass of tangles.

"Where'd you go?" Rebecca asked. "We were all worried sick."

"No, you weren't. You were worried that I was using my new powers—powers you're all jealous of."

"What's gotten into you?" Megan asked.

Before Sarita could answer, Gina said, "She went after Darian."

"His name's *Ian*," Sarita replied. "I don't care what Artair says. He's not the same man Artair knew."

Megan narrowed her eyes. "Damn right, he's not. Now he's a son of a bitch who wants to use you to get to us."

Sarita let her tumbling emotions loose. "You're all a bunch of hypocrites. You break the rules by falling in love with Sentinels or bringing a guy you're supposed to protect here, and *that's* fine. I go to see the man I love, a man who's done nothing wrong but has suffered like no one should suffer, and you all act like I'm doing something evil. Like you think I'm recruiting demons or torturing animals."

Rebecca leveled an accusing stare. "He's Helen's ally. She killed Sparks and tried to murder Artair. She wanted to hand Megan over to that psychopath Maksim Popov. She tried to kill Gina and Zach—*would* have if you hadn't frozen her. I could go on for hours! If she got near any of us, she'd just as soon kill us as look at us. And you want to help him help her?"

"You're putting us—and our *kids*—in danger," Megan added.

"By taking a quick trip to visit Ian?" Sarita shook her head.

"He'll lead her right to us," Gina said.

Even Gina was against her now.

Sarita jerked her bureau drawer open, grabbed a T-shirt, some workout shorts and a clean pair of panties. "I'm getting dressed, having some breakfast, then I'm training. No doubt Johann and Artair want their chance at chewing off a piece of my ass."

She slammed her bathroom door hard enough that the mirror on the wall shook.

Her temper hadn't cooled by the time she'd dressed, made some sense of her mop of hair and pulled the door open again. At least her sisters had left the cabin— probably to head to the mess hall to feed their happy little families.

Funny, but the envy that was always there, simmering right below the surface, surged forward until she was nearly blinded by it. Then she realized what *wasn't* there—she couldn't "feel" any of her sisters.

The quiet felt...*wrong*, leaving her with an emptiness in her heart. But was it her fault or theirs? Were they blocking her? Or had the Seior shut them out of her mind?

Dismissing the phenomenon as nothing more than a product of her anger, Sarita marched across the compound to the lodge. Instead of her usual oatmeal, she wished for a breakfast like she'd had back at *dorcha àite*. Sile's homemade bread, dipped in milk and egg and fried to a golden brown. Sile would smear it with thick honey and set it in front of Sarita with a smile.

Damn if she didn't miss Sile and Old Ewan.

The entire Amazon clan was already eating when Sarita went inside. Was it her imagination, or did everyone—including the children—seem to have nothing better to do than stare at her?

Her own temper rose higher in response, so she didn't offer her usual morning greeting or kiss her godchildren on their chubby cheeks.

Eating became agony because stilted silence reigned. Even Zach didn't try his usual cajoling to break the tension.

Artair ate with his typical no-nonsense approach to things, finishing first and then rising. "We should be training. We face a difficult fight, and ye lasses need to be ready."

"Yeah," Megan said. "Like kicking a few demons' asses. Maybe a few COEs while we're at it."

Rebecca slapped her palm on the table. "We're *not* killing any people."

"Unless they give us no choice." Megan shoved her plate away.

"I still think it's stupid to follow Helen's demon list," Gina added. "She's just trying to divert us."

Zach jumped into the conversation. "Probably. But I agree with Megan. I think it's a good idea we clean them out before Helen has a chance to actually use them."

"We should be searching under every rock," Johann added, "looking for Helen and trying to figure out her real agenda. She's showing her face to everyone, which has to have a purpose."

"Did you see her last night, Sarita?" Gina's quiet question almost went unnoticed.

"No," Sarita whispered.

Why couldn't Gina have asked in her thoughts instead of aloud?

Sarita wasn't in the mood to have her private life paraded around in front of everyone *again*, and a small flame of loathing ignited deep in the pit of her stomach.

For the first time since Gina had come with Johann to fetch her—to let her know she was an Amazon—Sarita hated her sister.

Although there were four Amazons who all depended on each other, Earth and Fire had trained together under Artair while Water and Air had worked with Johann. As a result, the pairs were close. Up until that moment, Sarita had never wondered if that made them a weaker group than other Amazon generations who'd trained as a foursome.

Right now, Sarita sensed no connection to *any* of her sisters. From the way they were all snarling at each other, the Amazons felt absolutely no camaraderie. Their bond had somehow been broken. So it didn't come as a surprise when the rest of the gang joined in and started to badger her about her innocent trip.

"You'll lead Helen right to us." Artair's gruff words echoed the same sentiments she'd heard from her sisters. He scowled down at her, using his intimidating height to try to make her feel guilty.

"It's the Seior," Johann said. "Just like Sparks, it's making her take risks she shouldn't to get what she wants."

"And the hell with the rest of us getting hurt in the process," Megan added.

"What were you thinking, Sarita?" Rebecca demanded. Her arm swept out toward the three children—Bonnie, Darian and Megan's daughter, Mina—who were staring at the growing hostility with wide eyes. "You're putting the kids in danger just so you can prove you're not the weakest Amazon?"

"I'm *not* the weakest Amazon. Not anymore."

Gina shook her head. "That's not it. She thinks she's in love with Darian."

"His name is *Ian*," Sarita said, resisting the urge to hiss like an angry cat.

"'Tis *Darian*," Artair insisted. "Much as it breaks my heart, I fear he's on the side of evil now."

She'd heard enough. It was one thing to attack her, another thing altogether to make a man who'd endured so much agony into a villain. "I'm heading to my cabin to get my sword. You want to keep beating me up? Do it in the freakin' sandpits."

SOMETHING WAS...DIFFERENT.

Gripping her sword, Sarita smiled. From the first time she'd been sparring with her sisters, there was a distinct pecking order. Sarita lost first. Then Rebecca. The last match to see which Amazon "won" was normally between Gina and Megan. When all was said and done, Fire usually stood as queen of the sandpits.

Today, however, Sarita was the one helping Rebecca to her feet.

"Nice job," Rebecca said, her tone one of disbelief rather than concession. She brushed the sand off her behind.

"Thanks." Instead of savoring the victory, Sarita clenched harder on the hilt of her sword and eyed Gina. While she'd beaten Air a time or two, she'd always had the feeling Gina was letting her win, probably to save Sarita's ego.

Gina was matching Megan blow for blow, both women dripping sweat but smiling. While Sarita and Rebecca approached training as a duty—sometimes a chore—Gina and Megan reveled in it. Which explained why they were the strongest fighters.

A few more clangs of swords, and Gina won the round, knocking Megan's ruby-encrusted weapon aside. Whenever one of the pair was disarmed, Fire and Air ended their match, otherwise they'd start in on hand-to-hand and would be beating on each other until both were black-and-blue and too exhausted to move. No wonder. Both of their husbands were martial arts experts, and Sarita often found the couples sparring as though their matches were some sort of odd foreplay.

"Gotcha this time," Gina said.

"Nice fight." Megan crouched to pick up her sword. She shifted her gaze to Sarita and Rebecca. "Ready to go, Sarita?"

The winners took each other on, leaving the losers to fight for the third spot. Today, for once, Sarita wouldn't be dead last. "I get Gina."

Gina blinked a few times. "You beat Rebecca?"

Sarita scowled. "You don't have to sound so damned surprised."

"She beats you more often than not, so…yeah. A little surprised."

"You fought better than usual, Sarita. Your hits were pretty strong." Rebecca smiled. "Made my hands sting almost as much as when I fight Megan."

"Glad to oblige." Sarcasm weighted every word.

"Geesh. A bit touchy, aren't you?" Megan asked.

"She's probably exhausted," Gina said. "Always makes her cranky and sensitive."

Because she loved Gina so much, Sarita tended not to get upset over the blunt things she liked to say. Gina's brazen nature made her prone to blurting out things that were true but better left unsaid. So why did anger flood Sarita, making her want to shout a battle cry and start pounding Gina into the ground?

Perhaps channeling it would help. "Are you going to fight me or not?" Sarita asked, growing impatient.

"Fine." Gina swept her arm out. "Lead the way, sis."

As she made her way to the middle of the fighting area, Sarita gave her sword a few swings. Such a beautiful weapon. Well balanced. The hilt encrusted with sapphires that sparkled in the sunlight. Everything about this day—about *her*—felt…perfect.

She let Gina make the first move, deftly parrying the blow. Damn if she couldn't help but laugh at her sister's incredulous look. With a growl, Gina came at her again.

And so they sparred, neither gaining the upper hand.

Sarita's arms ached, but she held onto that sword like a lifeline, finding a strength she'd never known. Sweat trickled down her face and soaked her shirt, but she didn't take precious time to wipe it away. This was the closest she'd come to beating Gina.

She wasn't going to waste it.

Deep inside, the flame that ignited earlier grew like a fire that spurred her forward, making Sarita attack Gina with a newfound ferocity. Focused so intently on banging the sword from her sister's hand, Sarita didn't anticipate Air using her power. One huge leap, and Gina flew over Sarita's head, landing behind her. A kick to the back of the knees and one to her shoulder blades sent Sarita face-first into the sand.

Gina came to stand over Sarita. "Wow. Not sure who you've been practicing with, but you're improving." She held her hand out to help Sarita up.

"I shoulda beat you."

"Not this time, sis."

"You used your power."

"All's fair, as Johann always says." Gina offered her hand again.

Sarita slapped it away and got to her feet. "I'm taking a shower, then catching a nap."

"Why don't we go get a caramel sundae instead?"

Although she usually enjoyed Gina's company, even when they ate in companionable silence, Sarita shook her head. Instead, she gave Gina a taste of her own blunt-to-a-fault treatment. "I'd rather not. I really don't want to spend time with you—with *any* of you—right now."

She marched away from the training ground, head

held high despite her defeat. Next time, she'd win. No matter how nasty the fight turned.

Then she'd show them who the weakest Amazon was.

SARITA BREATHED DEEPLY, treasuring the moisture in the humid tropical air. The moon was bright, bathing the beach in its pale light. Watching the waves roll in, crashing again and again against the shore became so hypnotic she could stand there for hours and be content.

The ocean called to her, the pull to enter the water almost as strong as the one that had brought her back to this island. She glanced back at Ian's cabana, wishing somehow he'd know she was here, waiting to see him.

But she needed water to recharge her spirit. Then she'd go and make love to him.

After jerking her nightgown over her head, she dragged it behind her as she walked to the ocean until her toes brushed the edge of the wet sand. Refreshing water seeped through her skin, and she tossed the gown back and ran into the waves, laughing as freely as a child.

When the water deepened, Sarita dove into a wave and swam beneath the surface. Every moment she stayed submerged allowed her to grow stronger, to absorb the power of the precious water. She no longer cared that she hadn't slept in days or that she'd eaten nothing more than what a sparrow might. Energy flowed through her, and the more strength she obtained, the more restless she grew.

She wanted to find Helen—to hunt her down and kill her. If Helen was dead, Ian would be free. Once Sarita had the chance to explain everything, he'd find a way to get past the horrible things that had happened. Then they could be together and make a life in Avalon.

Surfacing for air, she gasped her first breath when she saw Ian waiting on the shore. Naked.

Here was what she needed to keep her grounded— the man who held her heart. When she was with Ian she wasn't a warrior. She wasn't balancing the pull of Seior with her duties as an Amazon. She wasn't worrying about the greater good or saving humanity.

She was simply Sarita.

NOW THAT HE knew Sarita was the Water Amazon, Ian didn't panic when he once again found her clothing abandoned on the edge of water. His memories were slowly returning, although nothing more than vague recollections, all involved the tempting creature staring back at him from across the way.

She was gloriously nude—at least as far as he could see. The waves beat against her just above her waistline. Her breasts glistened in the moonlight, her nipples taut from chill. Or perhaps desire. Her smile was inviting.

There was a difference in her bearing, subtle, but there in the way she held herself. Whatever timidity she'd had was gone, replaced by a confidence so strong it surrounded her like an aura. Her spine was straight, her chin held at a haughty angle. Everything about her was sensual and elegant and full of poise.

Just when he was ready to run out into the water to fetch her, she ducked back into the water before standing again to smooth her long hair back. She strode toward the shore.

Her undergarment was nothing but a wet whisper

of lace around her hips. Plastered to her body, it allowed him to savor the dark *V* of curls between her thighs. Sarita gracefully peeled them off, dropping them behind her on the sand as she covered the last of the distance to reach him. She stopped before her body touched his, close enough he could have easily gathered her into his arms. Instead, she stared at him, saying nothing.

Words would ruin the interlude. Once they started talking, whatever magic they'd woven to be together again would disappear. He didn't want to think about his brother or Helen or the despicable things that had set him on this path. Sarita never tried to seek out Helen's plots or to ask for his help.

All they shared when they stole these precious meetings was a passion so hot and deep, he knew he'd never find another like it again.

Unable to see her a moment longer without touching her, Ian lifted his hand to cup her cheek. Her smile made his breath catch in his throat. She took that last step forward to press her full breasts against his chest. Rising on tiptoes, she kissed him as she stretched her arms around his neck.

Ian swept his tongue into her mouth as he enfolded her in his arms and held her close. Her taste and the feel of her against him sent fire racing downward, making his cock swell fuller. The kiss quickly became carnal, a chase of tongues from one mouth back into the other. His hands dropped to cover the gentle curve of her backside, and he lifted her. Pulling her hard against his groin, he let her feel the hunger that had gnawed at him from the moment he'd awakened to his empty bed.

He raised her body higher so he could slip his hands

down to her thighs. She got his less than subtle hint
and wrapped her legs around his hips. The damp heat
of her core rubbed against his erection, stealing all his
self-control. He carried her to where her nightgown
rested and laid her back against it before settling himself between her thighs.

Sarita reached between them, taking his cock in her
hand and guiding him to her tight sheath. He didn't
hesitate, thrusting deep inside her. The wet welcome
he found there said her need matched his.

There was no teasing, no taunting. Just a fast, furious rhythm that soon had him fighting against his own
release. Sarita must have sensed his urgency, because
she wrapped her fingers around his arms and squeezed
before tearing her lips away from his. "Wait."

Such a quiet whisper. Somewhere in his desire-laden
brain, the word registered, and he obeyed. He didn't
leave her body, but he stilled and stared into her eyes.

"My turn," she said, pushing against his chest.

"Lass?"

"On your back, *jaanu*."

Her smile was so salacious he could barely conform
fast enough. Slipping from her body, Ian rolled to his
back. "I'm yours, loving."

"Damn right, you are. All mine." Sarita straddled
him and leaned down, biting him hard on the shoulder.

His whole body jerked in response.

Pushing herself back, she wiggled against him, her
core nestling his erection.

"Loving, I cannae take much more."

"I shall give ye a wee taste before I take ye to paradise." Her imitation of his brogue brought a smile to
his face. Until she ground her pelvis against him again.

A groan rose from his chest.

Holding tight to his shaft, she gave him what he needed, impaling herself on him and taking his cock all the way inside her. The sheer pleasure of her squeezing him tight was almost enough to push him over the edge. She rode him.

Ian's blinding release came a heartbeat before Sarita cried out his name. Even after his orgasm, he needed to stay connected, pushing into her in small strokes that made her hum and smile.

She collapsed on his chest, and he held her close. "I should go," she whispered.

Although she was right, he wasn't ready to let her leave. "We should talk first."

She kissed the side of his neck before breaking their intimate connection then rolling to her back on the sand. "Instead of talking, I'd rather you just come with me." Her discarded nightgown was quickly donned as she knelt at his side.

"I cannae."

"Please, Ian. Give up this quest for vengeance. Leave Helen and be with me. I'll take you to my home."

His heart was torn, warring between going with Sarita and seeing his vendetta through to the bitter end. "I will have my justice."

"There's no justice to be had, *jaanu*. Come back with me. Let me explain everything. Once you know the truth, you'll—"

"Darian!" Helen called from a distance.

"Damn her hide for interrupting." But he was talking to no one.

Sarita had vanished, taking with her the mystery of her words.

SEVENTEEN

"STAY TOGETHER," JOHANN SAID. "No one charges in there alone."

Sarita nodded, although she had to wonder if her Sentinel's order had more to do with babysitting her rather than keeping her and Gina safe. Everyone in Avalon had been walking on eggshells around her, and she'd quickly grown tired of her sisters and Sentinels watching her as though she would spontaneously sprout horns and breathe fire.

They were in a suburb of Cincinnati, having been popped to the edge of a large community park in the wee hours of the morning by an unusually cooperative Ganga. When Sarita had called to her—at Johann's insistence—asking for a quick transport for the three to hunt down the next demon on Helen's list, the goddess hadn't batted a beautiful eyelash.

A moment later and here they were.

The place was deserted—exactly what they'd hoped and expected. Sarita could do her job then call Ganga to get them all right back out. She resented the unnecessary escort. This was a job she could easily handle alone. Only her concern that Helen might be setting a trap helped her keep her temper in check. Gina would watch *her* back.

"I could have come alone," Sarita mumbled.

Gina gave her a friendly cuff on the shoulder, although Sarita was somehow disconnected from her sister, unable to feel what she did—probably because she'd had very little sleep in far too many days. She normally slept like a baby. Perhaps the stress of worrying about Ian and keeping the Seior in check was taking its toll.

"Nah," Gina said. "This is great—like old times. Just two kick-ass Amazons and their Sentinel out on a demon hunt. I'm lovin' it."

"Enough chitchat," Johann barked. "We've got a job to do."

"See? *Exactly* like old times," Gina added with a wink to her Sentinel.

He unsheathed his sword and led the way through the park to a tall shrubbery maze. Then he followed the worn path, searching for the fountain in the center of the labyrinth. He found it in short order.

There were only two ways in or out, which would make it easy for Johann and Gina to keep watch while Sarita searched the enormous marble fountain for the demon they sought.

"When I get my hands on Helen," Johann grumbled, "she's gonna wish she'd never heard of magicks. Setting a *shabriri* loose? What was she thinking?"

"She was thinking she wants to cause us as much trouble as she can," Gina replied. "If she keeps us chasing demons we can't come for her."

"At least this is a small demon," Sarita said. "Not like that dragon Megan and Rebecca had to catch the other day." She held up the jar she'd brought along to toss the water demon into so she could transport it out to the middle of the ocean. "This is all I'll need."

She opened the lid and set the jar down on the fountain. "*Shabriris* are pretty harmless."

"*Harmless?*" Johann gaped at her. "We'll be lucky if this whole town isn't quarantined by the CDC while they search for what caused an epidemic."

"At least when I catch the demon, that'll be one more off her damn list," Sarita said.

She sat herself down on the edge of the big stone fountain, keeping the open jar within reach. Skimming her fingertips over the surface of the water, she searched for the *shabriri*. She didn't find one.

She found four.

The creatures were there, waiting on the far side of the fountain for victims to inhabit. Once those four were sure there would be plenty of human victims, they'd be calling their whole tribe. If she didn't catch them, everyone in this town would eventually be infected. Then the Amazons would find themselves battling more than pesky *shabriris*—they'd be fighting blind and delirious humans.

Her first instinct was to snatch the demons up and squash them all like bugs. A bit bloodthirsty, yet horribly appealing. What she'd done the last time she captured one—just a year ago—was have Ganga send her to the ocean to set it loose. The creature was so small it would take him decades to find his way back to civilization.

She'd never enjoyed the kill—one of the reasons it took her so long to get used to beheading revenants. After so many battles, she'd shed the fear because she kept reminding herself those zombies were already dead. Megan might talk about killing a Child of the Earth, but Sarita didn't have it in her.

So why was she so willing just to stomp these *shab-riris* under her boot heel?

"Did you find it?" Johann lowered his sword tip toward the water.

"Don't!" Sarita swept her hand out, thinking to spare Johann from being infected. A shabriri could run right up his sword and burrow under his skin before he could do anything to stop it.

Instead of stopping him, she somehow "pushed" him with her mind. He fell on his ass and then turned a backward somersault.

Gina was at his side in a heartbeat. She knelt next to him, trying to help him to his feet. "What in the hell happened?"

Johann ran his hand over his face before leveling a hard stare at Sarita. "Ask *her*."

Sarita stared at them, unblinking. Since Freyjr had given her Seior, she'd only used it for one purpose—to visit Ian. Had her new powers evolved beyond simple teleportation? Would she eventually be able to master telekinesis like Megan?

Or would she be *stronger* than Megan?

A happy giggle bubbled up—one Sarita quickly squashed when Johann threw a Sentinel scowl at her.

"You're laughing at me?" Johann shoved his sword into its scabbard and fisted his hands at his sides.

"No, no... I just... I can't believe I was able to do that."

Gina only took one jump to get to her. She grabbed her upper arm and forced Sarita to face her. "What did you do?"

A spark of anger ignited, pushing aside her pleasure at having a new power. "I guess I moved him.

He was reaching right for a *shabriri*. I didn't want it crawling into him."

"You *moved* him? How?"

"Seior," Johann said. "She's infected with it."

"Infected?" Sarita shook her head, trying to swallow her growing annoyance at their badgering. She'd saved Johann. Why did it matter how? "It's not a *disease*, Johann. I learned a couple of tricks from Freyjr. So what? You're overreacting."

One of the *shabriris* jumped from the water, casting a quick look around and locking eyes with Sarita. Before it splashed back into the fountain, it showed her its ass—the *shabriri* equivalent of flipping her the bird.

Her temper rose to boiling. She jerked her arm from Gina's grasp and strode to the other side of the fountain. She stuck her hand into the water and grabbed the demon.

It bit her.

She jerked her hand back. "Sonofabitch." She slapped her palms against the water, instantly freezing it.

"You'll kill it." Johann moved to her side.

"Not it—*them*."

"How many are there?" Gina asked.

"Four. So what?"

"Quit saying 'so what,'" Johann ordered.

Gina's gaze searched Sarita's face. "What in the hell's gotten into you?"

"The little fucker *bit* me!"

"Sarita…" Johann shook his head. "You're out of control."

"Don't start with me, Johann. These are water demons—my domain." She thumped her chest with her thumb. "*Mine!* You never tell Megan or Rebecca how to do their jobs. You don't boss Gina around like you do me. You always treat me like a child, and I'm fucking sick of it!"

Thrusting her hand directly into the ice—another new ability—she grabbed each of the *shabriris*, plucking them like ice cubes from the fountain. After sticking them in the jar she'd brought along, she screwed on the lid.

Before she could tell Johann she was heading to dump the demons in the ocean, she stopped, listening hard. Something—or *someone*—was coming.

The stench hit her.

"Revenants!" Sarita shouted, setting aside the jar and unsheathing her sword.

Gina looked between the two entrances to the courtyard. "I don't sense—"

From the entrance closest to Sarita, the first zombie charged. With a snarl, he ran right at her. His flesh hadn't begun to decompose—marking him as a class one, fresh for the kill.

Sarita blocked his first attempt at grabbing her by slicing off his right arm at the wrist. He let out a howl and took a couple of stumbling steps back. Then he let out a blood-chilling wail and charged her.

She went on the attack, wishing she could behead him. Unfortunately he was far too tall for her to get the leverage she needed. So she plucked her dagger from where it was strapped to the small of her back and drove it into the revenant's chest.

"What the hell?" She pulled back the dagger—and her entire hand—from where it sank into the zombie's empty chest cavity.

The revenant didn't give her time to process why he had no heart before he came at her again.

A quick front sweep and Sarita knocked the zombie to his knees. With one clean swing, she lopped off his head.

She whirled to ask Johann and Gina why someone had cut out the zombie's heart. Before a word could spill from her lips, another revenant came lumbering from the entrance—every bit as fresh as the one she'd just destroyed.

"Heads up. More on the way," Johann rushed the second zombie. He tripped it as Gina hurried behind him to remove the creature's head.

"Shit. Why didn't I sense them?" Gina stared down at the body. "What the hell happened to her?"

"Let me guess," Sarita said. "Someone cut out her heart."

"That's what it looks like."

"Why?" Sarita asked. "Why would someone do that?"

Johann sheathed his sword. "I think I know, but that's why you couldn't sense them."

When he didn't immediately explain what he meant, what few threads of control Sarita had over her anger snapped. A low growl rumbled from her chest, and she had to clench her hands at her sides not to move Johann with her mind and toss him right into the fountain.

At least he could take a hint. "These revenants weren't sent here to kill us. They were a message from Helen."

"And what exactly was that message?" Sarita asked.

"That she's taking things to a new level."

"Meaning?"

"These were human sacrifices."

"Sacrifices?" Gina looked as confused as Sarita felt. "To whom?"

Johann drew his lips into a grim line. "To Helen by the Children of the Earth."

SARITA WAS SICK of staring at the beheaded zombies. Everything inside her screamed to get to Ian. Dawn was only an hour away, which meant she'd lose her chance to find him on his island. Her insides churned, both with fear and longing.

Helen had upped the ante—big time. Human sacrifices?

It's time to bring Ian to Avalon.

Now she just had to convince her sisters and Sentinels.

Artair stared at the bodies sprawled on the grass. The heads rested only inches away from the torsos of their owners. Ganga had sent them back to Avalon at Johann's request. Why he wanted to keep the disgusting revenants was beyond her until he stripped them of their shirts. There were symbols scrawled on their arms and stomachs. Artair had immediately sent Zach to find those symbols in the library on ancient texts Zach had scanned into digital copies.

Zach came jogging across the compound, electronic tablet in hand. "Got it!" he called as he drew near.

Johann held out his hand, but Zach rebuffed him with a quick shake of his head.

"Let me show you." Zach skidded to a stop and started tapping away at his tablet. "They're Sumerian, just like Artair thought."

Sarita didn't give a shit what Zach wanted to show them or what civilization the symbols came from. All she could do was worry about Ian. Figuring any excuse would work, she tugged on Rebecca's sleeve. "I need to release the *shabriris*. I'm heading out."

"Later." Rebecca snapped the command while she concentrated on the ancient text Zach had pulled up. "You're sure?"

Zach nodded. "She was going for ultimate power—all the elements at her beck and call. A few more sacrifices and she'd have it. But thankfully, they're spread out—timed by moon cycles. We've got to stop her soon or we might never be able to stop her at all."

"Then why in the hell would she let us know that's what she's doing?" Rebecca asked.

"She's taunting us," Artair replied. "Especially me. She cannae help herself from showing her Sentinel and her goddess what she's become."

"Twenty hearts," Johann read from the tablet Zach held for them both to see. "That's the right spell, Zach."

"Yeah, but in this case I didn't want to be right," Zach replied.

"So she really had the COEs cut the hearts out of these people?" Gina asked.

"Yeah. No heart, no ability for you to sense the person the revenant used to be."

"How could the other Ancients allow something this—this *heinous*? Ix Chel would never—"

Sarita laughed loud enough everyone in the group stopped and stared. "You think any of our goddesses give a shit? They've written us off. An Amazon created this problem, so it's up to us to fix it." She snatched up the jar of *shabriris*. The best approach was always the direct route, so she announced her plans. "I'm getting rid of these, then I'm getting Ian and bringing him back here. I want him away from that bitch. *Now*."

"Are you insane?" Megan asked. "He's on her side!"

"No…no, he's not." But Sarita wasn't positive. Sure, he made love to her, letting her come to him in the night. And he'd never once told Helen about her visits.

At least that's what she hoped.

"Funny," Megan countered, "but I remember him getting ready to hand us over to Helen."

"We don't know what he would've done," Sarita said. "I had Ganga get us out of there before he could decide. I'm going for him and I'm bringing him back here. End of story."

Gina came to stand at her side. "Not alone, you're not. If you want to get Ian, it's not going to be easy. You'll need help."

Sarita stared up at her sister, wanting to know if Gina truly understood and still gave Sarita her loyalty. But again, her feelings were closed to Sarita. Rebecca and Megan were every bit as blocked.

Seior?

Perhaps.

Didn't matter. She needed the magicks to get Ian. Then she might give closer examination to whether she would keep the powers Freyjr had given her.

Artair leveled a hard stare. "'Twould be bringing our enemy into the heart of the Amazons."

"*Ian* isn't the enemy. *Helen* is."

"Aye, but my brother serves as her right hand."

"I'm not going to stand here and argue with you," Sarita insisted. About to close her eyes and wish herself to the middle of the Pacific Ocean so she could dump the *shabriris*, she gasped when a hand settled on her shoulder.

"Your sisters are with you," Megan said.

Rebecca shifted her gaze between Artair and Sarita before moving to stand with her sisters. "All for one..."

Sarita smiled. "And one for all." Her sisters' thought flickered in her mind, but only for a moment. Then they were gone.

The men didn't look convinced.

She figured her Sentinel—the man who'd known her from the day he came to reveal her destiny—was the best place to start. Johann had always supported her, encouraged her and believed in her. While he listened to reason, he wasn't immune to an emotional appeal. "Johann...please. You know Helen's eventually going to turn on Ian. Soon. She brought him back to hurt Artair. There's only one way that can end, and you and I and everyone else here knows it. *Please*. Let me go get him."

Megan gave Sarita's shoulder a squeeze. "Look at it this way, Joeman... Worst case scenario, we capture him, bring him back here and interrogate the hell out of him."

"We really don't have anything to lose," Rebecca added.

"Aye, you do," Artair said. "Yer lives."

Sarita rolled her eyes, pleased to see her sisters doing the same. "We can handle ourselves fine—especially now that I have a few dirty tricks up my sleeve."

Not that she needed Artair's approval, but she wanted it. This mission could easily end up being a battle if Helen somehow knew what Ian meant to Sarita or somehow figured out she was coming for him.

But the longer they waited—even if only another day or two—the more power Helen gained.

"Please, Artair. Let me bring Ian home."

He thought it over a good, long while—long enough to make Sarita fear she'd have to just pop out without his blessing. Then he nodded.

"I'll be back soon," she promised.

EIGHTEEN

IAN SHED HIS suit jacket and dropped it on the bed. The sweltering heat of the tropics was welcome, but not when he was wearing the cumbersome clothing Helen demanded he don whenever she teleported them to her temple. The many layers made him hot and left him feeling trapped. He missed his plaid and its freedom. Modern undergarments were far too...*confining*.

He hated the city, too. *Dallas*. In a place called Texas.

So many people. Buildings everywhere. Cars zipping around. Only when he was back here on the island could he breathe. Although much warmer and with a different landscape, the place was as calm and peaceful as *dorcha àite*. Only his friends were missing. Perhaps Helen would soon follow through with her promise to bring Old Ewan and Sile to him.

Right now, he needed tranquility. He had some serious thinking to do.

Sarita's last visit weighed heavily on his mind. His memories of her were returning, but only of the heated moments they'd shared. He still wasn't sure how she knew of the castle or what made her believe his brother wasn't responsible for his death.

If only Helen hadn't interrupted some of the mysteries haunting him might have been solved.

Today, Helen had revealed more of her grand scheme. When they'd returned to the city, she made a "big announcement," placing a bounty on the heads of the Amazons. Ian's job was to protect her—at least that was what she told everyone when she introduced him as her bodyguard.

His true purpose was to look for any magical opposition to her plans.

Helen had packed his mind full of information on everything from demons to demigods who might try to act as white knights. Should he detect anyone or anything launching an attack, he was trained to kill it. Swiftly.

Especially any Amazon.

What if Sarita decided to be one of the white knights? Could he drive his blade through her heart? Could he kill her and the other Amazons as Helen planned?

Helen had returned in a fine mood, although she wouldn't tell him what made her laugh so freely. There had been some "ceremony" scheduled at her temple— one of many—but she hadn't let him attend any of them. Whatever she was up to, he was better off not knowing. The more he learned about Helen and her plans, the more he wished he'd stayed in limbo.

Ah, but then he never would have known Sarita...

After he kicked off his shoes and socks, he walked out of the hut, heading to the beach. The smell of the salty breeze reminded him of Sarita, and he smiled when he remembered how beautiful and confident she'd been when she came striding out of the waves and into his arms. Something about her had been different. Not in a bad way. But different nonetheless.

Her vulnerability had vanished.

While he loved her taking the reins of their lovemaking, he mourned the innocence she seemed to have lost. He wanted time to talk to her, to have her explain everything she knew that he obviously didn't. Perhaps she could fill in the gaps of his memory. Just being with her eased the ache in his heart, the burning hatred that had driven him for so long. When he thought of Sarita, Ian was able to sweep aside the destructive anger and revel in all he felt for her.

How had she managed to capture his heart so completely? In such a short time?

And what did *she* feel for *him*?

She touched him as though she knew her way around a man's body, with the skill of an experienced lover. Just the thought of another man touching her made rage roar inside him, a primitive, possessive need to run his sword through any man who tried to take what belonged to him.

Then he remembered claiming her innocence. He was convinced she'd taken no other man to her bed since then.

No matter what angle he used to look at this situation, it could never end well. Sarita was an Amazon, and by pledging himself to Helen, Ian had made himself her enemy. When they faced each other again, it wouldn't be to make love—it would be for one of them to destroy the other.

This bargain he made with Helen no longer seemed to be the answer to his prayers.

He tried to remind himself of all he'd suffered. His clan had shunned him when he'd wanted to be a good laird and help them survive the horror the Sassenachs inflicted after Culloden Moor.

They'd tied him to a stake and burned him to death.

They'd also murdered Sile and Old Ewan, the only clan members who supported him once he'd been cried a witch.

"It's warlock, not witch." Sarita's voice filled his mind.

None of his past fired the rage any longer. His love for Sarita smothered it.

Love? Did he truly love this woman—this Amazon who might be the one to send him to his death?

"Ian!" Helen stood next to his hut. "Come along, I want to eat some supper. You will join me."

No closer to the answers he needed, Ian sighed and nodded, wondering how long he'd have to wait before he could end this devil's bargain.

"I'm ready," Sarita said. "Let's get this show on the road."

Had she been Fire, no doubt sparks would have flown from her fingers and her hair. She was antsy, raring to get to Ian and bring him to safety. It had been agony to wait until after midnight, and she'd watched every minute of every hour tick by in agonizing slowness, not giving herself a chance to sleep. Not that she could have as wound up as she was.

The time had finally arrived, and she wasn't about to wait a minute more.

"Calm down." Rebecca slid her diamond-hilted sword into its scabbard.

"Don't tell me to calm down." Adjusting her own sword, Sarita resisted the urge to close her eyes and go to Ian without waiting for her sisters.

Zach flexed his fingers and then shook his hands out. "I'm ready. If Helen interferes, I'll bind her good and tight."

His binding powers were needed on this mission. Should Helen be there, he could control her until they could all escape. All Sarita cared was that Zach represented a better chance of rescuing Ian.

"I've got your back," Gina said.

"Artair?" Rebecca looked to her husband. "Are you sure I shouldn't take my bow and arrows? Rhiannon blessed them and if Zach can hold Helen—"

Artair shook his head. "'Tis tempting, but nay. You have no idea where Darian is and—"

"Ian," Sarita said through gritted teeth.

"—if there are revenants, you'll have to fight. I doubt she'd let you get a shot off. If we're going to kill Helen, it must be better planned."

"It's a rescue," Johann added. "A grab and run." He brushed a kiss over Megan's mouth. "Be careful."

She nodded. "Are you sure you can take all of us, Sarita?"

Since the other Amazons and Zach were heading on this mission, it wouldn't be easy. Yet Sarita had no doubt her powers had grown enough to take them all along for the ride.

"I can do it." She started pacing, turning tight circles in her impatience to leave.

Artair and Johann retreated a few steps back, both frowning. She could almost hear their thoughts, their worries about how the Seior was affecting her. The furtive glances between the Sentinels were as powerful as spoken words.

"Stop worrying about me. I've had enough of your babysitting." Yes, it was changing her, but for the better. She hadn't turned into a rabid demon.

"Settle down, Sarita," Gina said. "I've never seen you like this."

Her temper snapped. "I'm fucking done waiting for all of you to decide whether I'm dangerous enough for Zach to bind me. You can all stop wigging out. I'm fine." She made up her mind not to wait a moment longer. "Ready or not, we're going." Sarita held out her hand. "Put your hands together and I'll get you there. Otherwise, *sayonara*."

"Remember," Artair said, his tone somber, "that this is a *rescue*, nae a *battle*. Fight only if you have to."

"Get Darian," Johann added, "and get out. Don't give Helen a chance to catch you."

Sarita scoffed. "If *Ian's* in her temple, we'll probably have to tangle with a few COEs. They try to hurt Ian, they're dead."

"This late at night?" Artair shook his head.

"I told you, I only picture Ian. I don't know where he'll be when I take us to him."

"If they're in the temple, 'twill be empty of her people. With a little luck, he'll be in his bed on the island. Ye can sneak in and talk to him, get him to agree to come with you and then get everyone back before anyone knows we've been there."

"Fine, fine. We'll do it your way." Sarita's nerves were stretched taut, and she was sick and tired of their patronizing her. "Let's go." She thrust her hand out again as the Amazons and Zach pulled into a tight circle.

One by one, they stacked their hands over hers.

"Here we go." Closing her eyes, Sarita pictured Ian and wished the group could find him.

The smell of salt water announced where she'd arrived. Her sisters and Zach were there with her when she opened her eyes to look out at the familiar stretch of beach.

"I'm going for Ian." She pointed to his hut. "Watch my back."

"Hurry," Gina said. "I don't like this one bit."

"Me, either," Megan added. "Too damned easy. Too much like a trap."

"Oh, for the love of—" Sarita fisted her hands at her sides. "It's a deserted island. There's no one here but Ian." She stomped away before she totally lost her temper.

The hut was empty. Her heart slammed in her chest. She should have gone right to where he was. "Ian?"

Something was wrong. "Ian? Where are you?"

"Sarita!" Hearing him shout her name, she sprinted back to the beach.

She skidded to a stop and gaped.

Her sisters had unsheathed their swords and were all facing Ian as he walked out of the ocean. At least he wore boxers, although they were clinging to his hips and upper thighs.

She ran to him then threw herself between Ian and the blades, glaring at her sisters. "That's Ian. Put your swords down."

They obeyed but kept wary gazes on him.

"You're really Darian MacKay?" Rebecca asked.

"His name's *Ian*," Sarita replied, not giving him the chance.

"Then get us out of here," Megan insisted.

"I know who you all are, and I want you to leave. Now." He stepped around Sarita and marched up the beach toward his hut. "Ye can get the hell off my island. I'm not going anywhere with the likes of you."

"Ian...wait!" Sarita jogged after him. "I came for you."

Not even a faltering step to acknowledge he'd heard her.

"I want you to come back to my home with me." She followed him into his hut.

"Is my brother there?"

"Of course he is."

"Should I go with ye, loving, I'll kill him." He shed his boxers and grabbed the dry pair resting on his bed. He donned them and jerked on a blue T-shirt. "Are ye sure you want to take me there?"

She wrapped her fingers around his upper arm. "I have so much to explain to you, especially about Artair. Nothing is what you think it is. Please, *jaanu*, come with me. Let me have a chance to make this right."

All she had to do was close her eyes, and they'd both be back in Avalon. But she couldn't do that to him. His choices had always been taken away, and she wouldn't add to his grief. She wanted him to *want* to come back with her.

"It wasn't Artair's fault."

He snorted.

"Come back with me. Give me time to explain everything. Helen's evil, Ian. She's—"

"You think I don't know that?"

"Then why? Why won't you just listen?"

Before he could reply, the breeze shifted, bringing with it the stench of piss and decay—the smell of danger.

"Revenants." Pulling her sword free, Sarita ran back to the beach. "Revenants!"

Gina's shout followed Sarita's. "She's right! Revenants incoming soon!"

Helen's laugh rang through the air, her voice booming as if through a loud speaker. "I knew you'd come right to me."

Zach was the first to react. Palms out, he turned this way and that, clearly unable to figure out which way to send his invisible tethers.

The Amazons stood ready as well, four swords prepared to face any threat. If only they could see one...

Helen laughed again, the sound making Sarita see red. "My dear, Sarita. We meet again. After chasing you for so long, you're here, in my grasp. And so easily. After targeting the stronger Amazons, I never imagined to destroy you all through the weakest of this generation's warriors."

"Show yourself, you bitch!" Sarita screamed.

Gina put her hand on Sarita's shoulder. "Easy. Don't rise to her bait."

Sarita shrugged away Gina's touch, seething with rage over Helen's insult. Seior had taken the reins, but she didn't care. The magicks flowing through her heart and her mind made her strong, and right now, strength was exactly what she needed.

It was time for Sarita to show Helen her strength. "I mean it, Helen! Show yourself! Then you'll see who's the weakest Amazon!"

The stench grew as revenants poured from the trees, their sing-song moans filling the air.

"Helen, you chicken shit! Come out and fight me instead of sending your stupid minions!"

The only sound was the groaning of the approaching zombies who lumbered onto the beach in a steady stream.

Megan was the first to shout a battle cry as she charged the revenant leading the pack, beheading it in a single swing of her sword. Gina and Rebecca attacked as well, leaving Sarita—as usual—to guard their backs.

Fuck that.

Power surged inside her and she sprinted past her sisters, throwing herself in the thick of the revenants.

IAN WATCHED THE tiny woman he loved charge into the fray and reached for his own sword—only to remember it was back at his castle.

His heart pounded, and he tasted fear. Until he saw her rush toward the hideous creatures spilling onto the beach, he'd lied to himself that she was nothing but an infatuation—a woman who might have captured his heart but meant nothing more than a few pleasant interludes.

Revenge had driven his soul for so long, he hadn't recognized the depth of what he felt for Sarita. Now, justice seemed unimportant when he compared to the devastating loss he'd experience should Sarita die now.

Running from his hut, Ian went to the man who'd arrived with Sarita, the one whose gaze scanned the area, no doubt looking for Helen. The man hung back, letting the women take on the creatures—the undead— that smelled worse than they looked.

"I need a weapon," Ian told him.

"So you can kill me?" The man shook his head.

"To help the women!" Ian insisted. "I need to protect Sarita!"

"Swear it."

Anything for Sarita. "I swear!"

Without taking his eyes away from his task, the man yanked a dagger from his belt. "Stab them in the head and don't let any of them bite you."

"What *are* they?"

"Revenants. Zombies. Dead people brought back for one purpose—they want to kill you and eat you. Don't let them."

Ironic, but when he joined the fight against these dead people, Ian felt more alive than he had in a long, long time. He ran after Sarita, ready and willing to attack anything that kept him from her. He might have been the laird's younger brother, more concerned with keeping the clan fed than fighting, but he'd been trained as a warrior—at least when Artair wasn't babying him for his crippled hand.

Artair. Should Ian follow Sarita to her home, he'd finally face his brother—and only God knew what would happen when they finally met again. Could Ian truly kill the man who'd raised him? That man who'd fought at his side at Culloden Moor?

The man who'd so callously left him to die an agonizing death?

Letting a battle cry spill from his lungs, he channeled all his anger into killing the undead.

The first creature he attacked had a fragile skull that cracked and split as Ian drove the weapon deep into its brain. Damn, but he wanted his sword. Getting close to the revenants brought a stench that rivaled any other. What had once been a man collapsed to his knees and planted his face in the sand. Ian moved onto the next one, keeping his eyes open for Sarita.

He had to kill three more revenants before he found her. Three creatures had encircled her, and her sword was embedded in the neck of one she'd felled. Before she could jerk her weapon free, a female zombie jumped on her back and dragged Sarita to the ground. Hands clenched in Sarita's hair, the revenant yanked her head back and opened her mouth, ready to take a fatal bite.

NINETEEN

"NAY!"

The cry of warning rose from Ian's chest until it became a roar. His strength surged, and he shoved aside the zombies blocking his path. When he reached Sarita's attacker, he never got the chance to touch her.

A shout sounded from under the zombie, and Sarita rose to toss it from her back. She grabbed the hilt of her sword, put her foot against the zombie she'd been trying to decapitate and jerked the weapon free. Then she finished the job before whirling and slamming her sword down to behead the one that had been on her back.

Ian gasped when she faced him, holding her sword high as though she'd split him open. She barely stopped the swing of her weapon before delivering what he had no doubt would have been a fatal blow.

"Ian!"

"Aye." His gaze scanned her from head to toe. "You're well?"

She didn't *look* well. She panted for breath, and her eyes were no longer a warm brown, but had shifted to black orbs.

"Where's Helen?" she demanded.

"I'm nae sure. Her home's on the other side of the island, and though I hear her, I cannae see her."

More of the revenants surrounded them. Ian and Sarita turned their backs to each other and faced the threat.

SARITA SWALLOWED HARD, worried that Ian was caught up in a fight against creatures he probably never knew existed. Although he brandished a dagger, he wouldn't know how to use it properly to take out a revenant.

She'd just opened her mouth to explain when a male zombie—fresh enough to be a class one—lunged at Ian. Before she could shout instructions, he'd buried his blade deep in the top of revenant's skull and sliced down hard enough to split the creature's nose.

The battle was on. Swinging her sword and using sweeps and kicks to bring down the zombies, Sarita tried to cull the herd. Seemed the more she eliminated, the more appeared.

Anger ripped through her and she shouted, not caring who heard. "Where in the fuck is she getting all these dead bodies?"

"Sarita!" Gina's desperate tone cut through Sarita's rage.

Her sister was in trouble.

How could she not have felt it? In every fight, the women were connected by their bond, a tie so strong they could work together and—

But they weren't working *together*. She hadn't been helping her sisters. Instead, she'd let the Seior blind her and set her out to hunt Helen instead of doing her job.

Sarita screamed her frustration as she kicked aside two attacking revenants. Then she sprinted over the bodies littering the beach to get to Gina.

Air was down, an obese male revenant pinning her to the sand. He knelt on her sword arm and had his mouth wide open, ready to take a bite while Gina struggled to hold him back with her free hand.

"Get off her!" Sarita's flying kick sent the zombie

flopping to his side. She lopped off his head while Gina scrambled to her feet.

There wasn't time to exchange a word. Revenants were on them again.

In her mind's eye, Sarita suddenly saw her sisters, Zach and Ian, sprawled on the sand—bleeding and broken.

They were going to lose this fight if she didn't do something. *Now.*

Her hand shot out to touch Gina, and in the blink of an eye, they were both back in Avalon. Another blink, and Sarita returned to the island.

Ian was nowhere in sight, so she hurried to Zach's side and flashed him back to Avalon as well.

The next round, she popped up between Rebecca and Megan and had them both home before either could protest. She dropped her hands, ready to go get Ian when Rebecca grabbed her arm.

"You can't go back," she ordered.

"Ian's there." Sarita shrugged Rebecca's hand away.

"Helen will protect him. He's on her side, *remember*?"

"I'm not leaving him there!" When she tried to jerk her arm free, Rebecca squeezed harder. "Let me go!"

About to close her eyes, she sensed Megan's telekinetic power before Megan used it. Sarita held out her hand and "caught" the energy that would have sent her sprawling at Rebecca's side. She crushed it in her fist, absorbing the power into her own body.

"Nice try, Megan." Narrowing her eyes, she growled before saying, "Don't try that again or it'll be the last thing you do."

Rebecca tugged on Sarita's arm to pull her closer.

"You're playing with danger, and there's no way I'm letting you leave."

With nothing but a sweep of her arm, Sarita used Megan's energy to send Rebecca flying. Earth landed on her butt in the grass.

"I *told* you. I'm going back for Ian. None of you are going to stop me—or *I'll* stop *you*."

"Sarita, what are you saying?" Gina asked before gasping. "Your eyes. What in the hell happened to your eyes?"

"What are you talking about?"

"They're black."

Rebecca was on her feet and striding back to the Amazons. "Just like Sparks. You've got to get rid of the Seior. It's going to destroy you."

The ground beside her split as Rebecca's kudzu came hurtling at Sarita. The moment the vines wrapped around her wrists, she jerked hard, breaking what were supposed to be unbreakable bonds. The plants slithered back into the grass and the splits sealed.

"Another nice try." Sarita dropped the remnants of the now brown vines to the ground. "Actually, *lame* try. Is that the best you two can do?"

With one jump, Gina was behind Sarita, wrapping her arms around her. "I'm not letting you go without me. Can't you see what this is doing to you?"

Sarita laughed as she bent forward and flipped Gina over her back. The power growing inside her was incredible. Intoxicating. There was an almost over-whelming urge to kick Gina while she was down.

Instead, she thought of Ian. He needed her.

Since this discussion and her sisters' pathetic at-tempts to show they were more powerful were getting her nowhere, Sarita closed her eyes and took herself back to the island.

Beheaded revenants were scattered across the beach, their stench almost unbearable. Several zombies milled around, stumbling blindly as though having no true destination. Ian was nowhere to be seen.

She had to resist the urge to shout his name because it would alert the last of the revenants to her return. Instead, she stepped lightly over bodies and heads, ignoring the macabre litter. When she had a clear shot to his hut, she sprinted.

Snarls rose behind her, making her speed her pace.

"Ian! Where are you?"

The hut was empty.

"Ian!"

"I have what you're looking for." Helen's voice boomed through the hut.

"Come out and fight!"

Ian's voice came from the beach. "Sarita, leave! Now!"

Sarita beheaded two revenants that had made their way inside the hut. Two more fell to her sword before she had a clear view of Helen standing ankle-deep in the ocean with Ian kneeling in front of her, hands bound.

She had her fingers tangled in his hair and held a dagger to his throat.

From deep inside Sarita, a fire exploded into an inferno. She dropped her sword as her hands burst into flames, although she felt no pain. When the revenants closed in around her, she unleashed her new power on them.

Fireballs erupted from her palms as if fired from a

machine gun. One after another, the revenants were hit by the fireballs and burst into flames, collapsing to the ground. Only when the last zombie fell did Sarita close her hands into fists and smother the blaze.

"Impressive," Helen had a rather calm tone considering the situation. "You've managed to do something I never had the chance to do. Bravo, my dear."

Marching away from the smoldering, fetid corpses, Sarita headed toward Helen. "Let him go, and I *might* not kill you."

"Leave, and I *might* not kill him—or you."

Sarita sprang into the air and across the sand, halving the distance between them.

"*Another* power you borrowed. Oh, how I wish I'd had the chance to feel the strength of my sisters' abilities as you do." Her words were wistful, but her commanding voice revealed how much she believed she held the upper hand. "Now, you need to tell me exactly what you plan to do with them." Helen pushed the tip of the blade against Ian's skin, drawing a bead of blood.

"Don't touch him again!" The ground beneath Sarita rumbled in response to her rage. After a few moments, the quake subsided and her steps faltered. Every ounce of her energy evaporated, and she sank to her knees.

Helen clucked her tongue. "I should have warned you. Seior might let you steal powers, but it comes with a cost. You must pay for it in body and blood."

Body and blood.

Using her new abilities had cost her, all right. She didn't have the strength to fight off a trout. What good was Seior if she couldn't use it to help the man she loved?

"You surprise me, Sarita. Of all your generation, I

never would have thought you'd be the one who'd turn out to be the strongest."

Strongest? Hard to feel that way as she knelt on the wet sand, unable to launch any kind of attack to save Ian.

"But here you are, wielding black magicks and stealing your sisters' powers."

"I didn't steal my—" The words froze in Sarita's throat.

Helen was right.

Back in Avalon, Sarita had absorbed each of the Amazons' attempts to stop her. And each time, she'd grown stronger.

"Now," Helen continued, "you'll have a chance to do what Rebecca was too afraid to."

"Get out of here, Sarita!" Ian was rewarded for his shout with a brutal yank on his hair.

Sarita couldn't stand to see him suffer. "Let him go."

Helen shook her head. "Not until I know where we stand."

"What are you talking about?"

"Do you enjoy being so strong?"

How could she possibly deny it? She gave Helen a nod.

"Then I can make you *stronger.*"

Although she wasn't sure what Helen was babbling about, she kept an open mind. Whispers filled her thoughts, tempting words of the power and control she could enjoy. She shoved them aside.

"Let Ian go," Sarita suggested, "and I'll stay. We can talk. Just the two of us." At least her energy was returning, and her words no longer sounded breathless. If only she could have made it all the way to the water,

SANDY JAMES 247

she could have recharged her batteries. Then Helen would see what magicks she could wield.

"Nay," Ian said. "Donnae do this. Go back to your home. Keep up the fight."

With a growl, Helen jerked his head back and dragged the tip of her knife down his cheek.

Déjà vu swept over Sarita, and she was back in the desert. Sekhmet, the lion goddess—the Destructor—was scoring Sarita's face with one long claw.

She'd been aware of what was happening, although she'd never told Gina. Her sister had remarked once that it was a blessing Sarita had been unconscious when Sekhmet attacked her.

No, she'd felt every bit of the searing pain as that claw dug into her flesh and drew a jagged line from her eye to her chin.

Shaking her head to dismiss the haunting memories, Sarita glanced back to Ian. Blood seeped from the cut.

"Let him go!" A burst of energy propelled her back to her feet, and she clenched her sword in her fist.

"Bravo," Helen said. "That's exactly the way to make Seior work for you. Find that anger. Use it. Let it flow through you. Focus all your energy on what you hate. Only then can you use it for your purpose."

How odd. Sarita was trying to destroy this bitch, and Helen was giving her lessons in using black magicks.

"Let me show you all you can do once you set the rage free." With a chilling smile, Helen raised her dagger high.

"No!"

Every ounce of her fear and anger pooled inside Sarita's chest. She dropped her sword and raised her hands. Two balls of white flames formed against her palms, and with a cry, she shoved them forward. They joined into one sphere that flew across the beach at Helen.

Helen shoved Ian to the side and raised her left hand. When the flaming orb reached her, she swept it aside. It landed in the ocean and fizzled out.

"Good, Sarita. Good. You're using Megan's power well."

"Then you'll *love* this."

Seaweed sprung from the water on either side of Helen, twining around her wrists and forearms.

With nothing but the blink of her eyes, Helen made them wither and die before they snaked back into the waves. She blinked again and disappeared.

Sarita hurried to Ian. He'd sat up and was struggling to remove the binding on his ankles.

Instead of helping him, she laid her hand on his arm and closed her eyes, wishing them both back to Avalon.

Nothing happened.

"We should go, loving. *Now.*"

"I'm trying!" She wished again, imagining the beauty of her home and trying to sense the love of her sisters.

"The powers will return," Helen called from where Sarita had stood moments before. "You lost your anger, which took away your true strength."

"Then I'm in luck," Sarita replied, "'Cause just seeing you stirs my rage right back up."

"I like your spirit. Are you brave enough to do what your sister couldn't?"

"What are you talking about?"

"Can you see more than the black and white most Amazons limit themselves to seeing?"

Since Ian was making good progress on getting

himself free, Sarita focused on her enemy. If she could keep Helen occupied, perhaps her own energy would revive enough that she could teleport herself and Ian out of this place. "What are you talking about?"

"Do you see yourself as something more than cannon fodder in the war between good and evil?"

"You know what? If I hadn't known you were an Ancient, I would now. 'Cause you all like to ask stupid questions that have no answers. Wanna move on to knock-knock jokes now?"

Helen's eyes flashed red. "I'm offering you a chance, Sarita."

"To do what?"

"To join me. To let me help you gain more powers and to sit at my right hand."

She couldn't believe what she was hearing. "Join you? Are you insane?"

"I assure you, I'm nothing but serious. I need your strength. Join me. Become something more than an Amazon."

"When pigs fly, you crazy bitch."

"So be it."

One moment, Sarita was standing on the sand. The next, she was submerged in water.

Swimming hard, she took a long time to reach the surface. She scanned the beach, barely able to see Ian's form in the moonlight. He was on his feet, looking out over the waves. Helen had vanished. Who knew how long she'd be gone this time?

As Sarita made her way back to the shore, she let the water refresh her. Her strength returned, increasing her speed. When she reached Ian, she'd get them both out of there and back to Avalon.

As soon as Ian was safe, she was giving up the Seior. *For good.*

How would she ever get her sisters to forgive her for her betrayal? Until Helen had made her ridiculous proposal, Sarita had been blind to what she'd done to them.

Ian waited for her, hands on his hips and legs braced apart. At least he'd freed himself.

"Are you well?" he asked when she walked from the surf back to the sand.

She nodded. "Let's get the hell out of here."

When Sarita drew closer, almost close enough to touch him, she smiled and sighed in relief.

A pop sounded behind her.

Ian grabbed her upper arms and whirled her around as though they were caught in a dance. Then his eyes widened and his mouth opened in a gasp of surprise. Pain washed over his face and his body trembled.

"Ian? What's wrong?"

Only when he dropped his gaze to his chest did she see the tip of the sword protruding and hear Helen's laughter.

TWENTY

HELEN JERKED HER sword back, and Ian fell forward, his knees giving way.

Sarita caught him. "I'll kill you for this."

Then other words formed in her mind, born of her hatred and coming from her heart in a plea for justice that made her stomach lurch and her head burn. "Your rancid soul hides behind a beautiful face. I wish the world to see you as you *truly* are."

With a blink of the eye, Sarita and Ian were in Avalon. Funny, but she thought she'd heard Helen's scream echo behind them.

He was too heavy for Sarita to hold, so she eased him down to the ground. His soft cry when his back hit the grass made her whimper. She threw his plaid off his shoulder and tugged the ripped shirt open wider, wincing at the stab wound. Blood seeped at an alarming rate. No doubt the wound to his back was worse.

Ian's going to die.

"Sarita," he rasped out. His shaky hand rose to touch her cheek before it fell away. Each shallow breath he took was agony to watch.

"Don't you dare leave me, Ian. Don't you *dare*."

Her sisters came running from the lodge. Gina gasped, a sound echoed by Rebecca and Megan.

"Oh, my God." Gina shouted at Zach. "Go get Beagan and Dolan! Now!"

Her husband ran for the mess hall as though the devil himself were on his tail.

Avalon's caretakers couldn't fix a lethal wound. Ian was dying, and the shape-shifters wouldn't be able to stop him from slipping away.

Sarita was Water, and Water could heal—but only her sisters.

To hell with that.

She wasn't giving her man up without a fight.

A tear spilled over her lashes. She couldn't lose him. Not now that she'd finally found love. He'd taken the blade to protect her.

"I love you," she whispered.

Then she focused on the energy that had sizzled inside her back on the island, the energy that had allowed her to channel the powers she'd stolen from her sisters.

Please let me save him the way he saved me.

The heat burst in her chest, hot and fast enough she struggled to control it—to channel it. Ethereal flames spread down her arms, burning a white fire that reached her hands and enveloped her palms. She settled her shimmering hands on Ian's chest, framing the sword cut with her fingers and thumbs.

His wound knit before her eyes until the skin closed, leaving behind a red scar.

Whether the power came from being the Water Amazon or from the Seior, she didn't care. Ian wasn't going to die. That was all that really mattered.

But…damn. For that moment she'd wielded the power of life and death—just like an Ancient.

She didn't stop until the trail left through Ian's body by Helen's sword closed, seeing each piece of him in her mind as it rejoined and strengthened. He was whole again.

With a gulping breath, Ian sat up.

Hands glowing, she traced the length of the cut Helen had made to his cheek, sealing the wound and coming close to tears that his handsome face now bore a scar much like her own.

Then she righted her other wrongs. Three orbs of light burst from her palms, hitting each of her sisters in their chests.

The brilliant light coming from her palms faded, leaving Sarita dizzy and exhausted. Her heart was slamming inside her chest, and she couldn't seem to catch a decent breath. While healing her sisters had often left her tired, this experience—bringing Ian back from the brink of death—had taken every last ounce of energy she had to give.

She fought against the blackness, an undertow that threatened to pull her away.

IAN CAUGHT SARITA as she collapsed against him. Everything that had happened in the last few minutes was hazy, but all the memories that had been blocked, the ones lost to Helen's meddling, returned. The force of the emotions behind those recollections made him tremble.

He was in Avalon. The home of the Amazons and the Sentinels—most especially Artair MacKay.

Ian's time of vengeance was finally at hand—the moment he'd waited and planned for from when the first flame licked his skin.

As he'd burned, he'd cursed his brother, blaming him that no one in the clan believed Ian had ever had a brother or that his crippled hand had been healed. Instead, his brother had abandoned him to face the wrath of a clan that had no memory of Artair MacKay—a clan who then cried Ian a witch.

He should take up Sarita's sword, hunt down Artair and end his brother's life. This was what he'd lived for, the one thing that forced Ian to forfeit his soul and ally with Helen.

Yet right behind the rage came worry. Not about Artair.

About Sarita.

What had she sacrificed to bring him back to her?

And what had she just sacrificed to save him?

Her hair had changed to white when she'd touched him. He combed his fingers through the tresses, marveling as it slowly tinted back to black again.

What had she done? How had she saved him? Because he was pretty sure he'd been near death. Again. His soul had been breaking free, trying to escape his wounded body.

Ian raked his fingers through her silky hair one more time, unsure as to what she'd done—or what she'd *become*. He wasn't sure how she'd brought him back. Hell, he wasn't sure *why*—not after everything he'd done.

He lifted a limp Sarita until he could cradle her against him, holding her in his lap as he sat on the grass in the middle of this place he knew but didn't recognize. She let out a small moan as she cuddled closer. "I've got you now, loving. We'll make you well again."

There were three women gaping at them, three women he knew well, thanks to Helen. She'd drilled him, making him learn each of the Amazons so there

would be no more mistakes like he'd made assuming
Sarita was Rebecca.

A tall man with blond hair strode forward. "What in
the hell just happened?" His gaze drilled through Ian.

Not sure what purpose this man played in Sarita's
life, Ian fired back a question of his own. "This is
Avalon? Aye?"

"Yes," the man replied. "What happened to Sarita?"

"I'm nae sure."

Rebecca replied, "I'm Rebecca MacKay."

"I know who you are." He let his gaze settle on each
of the Amazons. "I know all of ye."

"You're Darian," Rebecca said.

"So have you given up following Helen?" the blond
asked.

"Who are ye?"

"Johann Hermann. I'm Sarita's Sentinel. What happened?" He ran his trembling hand over Sarita's shoulder. "Is she injured?"

Ian nodded at the precious bundle he held in his
arms. "Let me tend to the lass first. Then I'll answer
your questions best I can. Where can I take her so I
may see what ails her?"

"Beagan and Dolan are coming," Megan replied,
her voice unsteady although her gaze was intense. She
glanced to Ian's left.

"Beagan and Dolan? Who are they?" All he saw
were two brown rabbits hopping at a furious pace toward the group.

So odd that the animals showed no fear. They drew
closer, stopping only when they reached Ian. About to
shoo them away, the words stuck in his throat when a

light glowed around each animal. The rabbits changed into small men.

"What *are* they?" he asked Rebecca.

"Changelings," she replied. "The redhead is Beagan. The brunet is Dolan. They're caretakers here. Let them help Sarita. They'll know what to do."

"Nay." Ian turned away when Beagan tried to reach out and touch Sarita. "I'll tend her myself."

"Please, sir," Dolan said, "let us help. She is merely exhausted from using her new power."

The changeling obviously knew a lot more about Sarita than he did. He resisted the urge to ask what they meant about her healing him being something new. This whole situation was a tangle he wasn't sure would ever be unraveled.

Sarita groaned, opened her eyes and gave him a wan smile.

"Your eyes are blue," he said, his voice quavering. He was so relieved, he nearly unmanned himself with tears.

"Blue? No...they're brown."

"Nay, loving. Blue."

"I'm too sleepy to care," she murmured. Then her eyes drifted shut again.

Ian took heart that she didn't seem injured, merely exhausted. Just as Dolan had said. "Where can she rest?" he asked again as the tightness in his chest began to ease.

"If you will follow us," Beagan said, "we shall lead you to her new home. You may both rest there."

Both?

Presumptuous little changelings. Not that he wanted

to argue. He had no plans to leave Sarita's side, at least until she was well.

Ian let Gina, the tallest of the sisters, help him to his feet. Tightening his grip on Sarita, he nodded his thanks.

Her short brown hair held streaks of lighter color, but not blond. The ends were *yellow*. Bright yellow— although the color seemed to be fading right before his eyes. "I'll show you to Sarita's place. Beagan and Dolan can follow us."

Before he could thank her, Ian's attention was drawn to the man marching toward them from the big wooden building. What drew his notice first was the plaid the man wore. With a hard swallow, Ian forced himself to look to his face.

"Artair MacKay." His words were a whisper.

After hundreds of years of hating and waiting and planning and plotting, the moment of facing his enemy had finally arrived.

While Ian wanted to draw a sword and march out to meet Artair, his concern for Sarita trumped his desire for revenge. His time would come, and justice would prevail.

He turned his back to Artair, hoping to slip away before any kind of confrontation could begin.

"Take me to her home," Ian snapped at Beagan and Dolan.

The changelings exchanged a worried glance, but Beagan beckoned with his hand for Ian to follow.

"Wait!" Artair bellowed.

"He'll want to see Sarita," Gina said softly. She stepped over to smooth Sarita's tangled hair away from her face.

"I should take her now. He can see her later." Ian tried to step around her.

She moved to block him.

A heavy hand settled on Ian's shoulder. "Let me see the lass, Darian."

Bowing his head, Ian spun around, trying hard to tamp down the rage that was rising to a fast boil. His heart pounded loud enough to echo in his ears. The only thing keeping him from striking out was the woman he held close to his body. Artair had no idea how lucky he was that Sarita acted as his shield.

SARITA MIGHT HAVE been weak, but she was aware of every bit of what was happening around her, despite barely being able to keep her eyes open.

Ian's body trembled, something she wondered if anyone else noticed. If she had any strength whatsoever, she would have tried to get Ian and Artair to talk out their problems. Instead, she sagged against Ian, letting the drama around her unfold without being a participant.

"I need to take care of Sarita," Ian said. His flat tone masked the rage she felt flowing through his body.

Artair took a step closer, his arms raised as though he wanted to embrace his brother. "I'm happy to see you."

Ian turned his back. "Lead the way, Dolan."

Dolan obeyed, falling into step behind Beagan. Ian readjusted Sarita in his arms and followed.

"Darian?" Artair called after him. "Let the changelings tend to her. We need to talk. Please."

The anguish in Artair's voice pierced the sleepy

haze in Sarita's mind. "*Jaanu*, he didn't cause what happened to you. He didn't know."

Damn, even thinking and uttering a few words sucked up what little energy she had left. Her eyelids were so heavy, it took supreme concentration to keep them open. But this situation was too important for her to rest.

Not yet. Not while she'd led a man who wanted Artair MacKay dead right to his doorstep. She wouldn't let Ian hurt her Sentinel—nor would she let anyone hurt Ian again.

Ian shook his head, saying nothing.

Since her cheek rested against his chest, she couldn't see if her sisters, the Sentinels and Zach were following them across the compound. "Tell me what happened before you…died."

"Later."

Beagan and Dolan took them to a house she'd never seen before.

While the other Amazons and their husbands lived in large homes their patron goddesses had created for them, Sarita had chosen to remain in her austere cabin, somehow feeling its starkness matched her circumstances.

After all, she was the only Amazon with no mate, and with her scarred face, she'd thought she would always be alone.

This house was beautiful, the design traditional Indian. The changelings led them through an open foyer with tall, carved wooden columns that were stained a warm and inviting shade of brown. They passed through a landscaped courtyard that held a fountain— the marble pool surrounding it large enough to swim in.

Then they entered an ornate bedroom suite. Her things were all neatly placed on new teakwood furniture. Her twin mattress was gone—replaced by a king-size bed with an embroidered canopy.

Ganga had been very generous.

So much for the patron goddess keeping her distance.

Ian laid her on the silk spread covering the bed and sat at her side. Before he could ask for anything, Dolan handed him a cloth.

Gently wiping the damp material against her forehead and her cheeks, Ian stared down at her. His hands had stopped shaking, but his green eyes were full of turmoil. She caressed his cheek before letting her hand drop away.

Footsteps slapped against the marble floor, so many it sounded as if a herd of animals might have been heading their way. Her sisters spilled into the room, followed by Artair, Johann and Zach.

She wished she had the strength to introduce them all. Instead, she looked to Gina. At least Air's hair had changed from yellow highlights to blue, which meant she was no longer afraid for Sarita. Blue was the color of control.

Sarita reached out to Gina's thoughts. Perhaps now that she gave back the powers she'd stolen from her sisters, the breach in the Amazons would heal.

"I need your help, sis. Welcome Ian to Avalon. Please...he's feeling so lost right now."

Gina didn't reply, although she scrunched up her nose as if lost in thought. She stepped to the side of the bed and put her hand on Ian's shoulder. "Welcome to Avalon, Ian. I think you know everyone except my husband Zach."

Ian just grunted as he dipped the cloth into a basin Dolan held out to him. He wrung the cloth out and pressed it against Sarita's forehead.

Gina tried again. "You're Darian MacKay."

"My name is *Ian*."

"Nay," Artair insisted. "You're *Darian* MacKay."

"Nay! Darian MacKay is dead!"

Sarita reached for Ian's hand. His fingers wrapped around hers as he let their joined hands rest on her stomach. "Talk to him, *jaanu*."

"You don't understand, loving…"

Goddess, she needed to know what was going through Ian's mind, but all she could think about was sleeping for the next three days. "Help me understand."

IAN'S HEART ACHED as if Helen's sword still rested in his body. Seeing his older brother hurt so much more than he'd anticipated. The anger and thirst for justice that had always bolstered him against any sentimentality when he'd thought of Artair had disappeared. The instant Ian saw the joy in his brother's eyes, Ian's rage fled.

He'd forgotten what had brought him back from limbo—the need for revenge and to repay the hurt and insult that had been done to him. All Ian had known was the overwhelming love a younger brother held for the older brother who'd raised him from bairn to man. Images of what they'd shared—the hunts, the training, the good times with their clan—assaulted Ian, fighting with the hurt and pain that seemed as vivid as if he was still tied to that stake.

He closed his eyes as he recalled the flames lashing his skin, the smoke filling his lungs. A shudder ripped through him.

Sarita squeezed his hand. Her hair was entirely black again, although her eyes were ice blue.

"I donnae wish to talk now!" Ian exploded, letting his tumultuous emotions take the reins. He'd never liked to be in crowds, and at that moment, Sarita's bedchamber was as busy as a marketplace. "Leave us!"

Gina stared hard at Sarita. While the other two women seemed concerned, it was Gina who'd needed to touch Sarita with her own hands. The link between them was so strong, he could almost see the threads tying their thoughts.

Gina gave him a brisk nod. "There's plenty of time to straighten this out later. Let's give Sarita and Darian...um... *Ian* some space. She's exhausted."

"I'll not leave my brother," Artair insisted. "Not until I have some answers, damn it."

"I have no brother," Ian whispered in return.

Rebecca took her husband's hand in hers. "Artair... not now. We'll figure this all out, just not now. The kids need us."

"Bairns? You have bairns?" Ian damned himself for asking, but Helen had never given him information about children being in Avalon. He knew about each and every Amazon, but nothing of their families.

"Aye," Artair replied. "Two—Bonnie and Darian. I named my son for you."

Would the pain never end? Artair had moved on, creating a new life for himself while Ian had suffered. He couldn't acknowledge the honor Artair had given him.

But Ian couldn't forget, nor could he forgive. Not yet.

"Let's go." Gina shooed everyone away with the back of her hand. She glanced back. "I'll be back later to check on Sarita."

"We donnae need any help."

She pulled her lips into a thin line. "Fine. Why don't you both join us for a late lunch tomorrow at my house?"

Zach chuckled. "Gina's going to cook? God help us all." His jest fell flat, not a single person laughing.

Gina punched him lightly on the shoulder. "Come to our house tomorrow, Ian. That'll give you both a chance to rest and get comfortable."

Sarita was the one to reply. "We'll be there."

"Only if you're ready, sis."

"I will be."

Alone at last, Ian stared down at Sarita. In a matter of seconds, her breathing grew deep and even, and the worry lines around the corners of her eyes disappeared.

He was torn between being grateful she was getting the rest she needed and his own need to talk to her. This woman who was supposed to have been nothing but a tool in his revenge now represented so much more. He wanted to share his tumbling emotions with her, knowing her touch would soothe away much of the hurt.

He owed Sarita a life-debt. Since her powers had been curbed back at the castle, he'd never known the extent of what she was capable of doing. Biting back the questions swirling in his head, he jerked off his boots and let out an extended yawn.

Perhaps nearly dying was almost as tiring as saving someone from that dire fate.

He removed Sarita's shoes and socks. Then he peeled down her bloody pants and pulled off her stained shirt.

Ian lifted Sarita, holding her against him as he pulled back the covers.

After he got her settled, he ripped off his tattered and blood-soaked shirt and let his black plaid fall to the floor.

He needed to be skin to skin with her. Sliding between the silk sheets, he gathered her sleeping form into his arms. She sighed and cuddled closer, allowing him to roll to his side and throw a thigh over her legs.

Having her near calmed him. Since her head was tucked against his shoulder, he buried his nose in her hair. Her scent filled his nostrils, and he sighed.

His world was upside down. Everything he'd assumed about what had happened so very long ago was wrong. At least he *thought* it was wrong.

Artair hadn't caused Ian's death by fire—that much was apparent. His brother's greeting had held nothing but genuine affection and surprise. Not even the wariness he'd expect, considering Artair knew Ian had allied with Helen.

Now, Ian needed to find a way to let go of the hatred he'd held for so long if he was going to get any answers about what had really happened. Perhaps those answers would come when he and Sarita dined with the Amazon clan on the morrow.

One thing was damn sure—he wasn't going to get any answers tonight. Besides, he needed to hold Sarita, to know she was all right.

Sarita whispered his name in her sleep.

He kissed the top of her head.

Once she'd recovered, they could wed. Honor demanded that he make her his wife since she'd given him her innocence. Surely she'd see the rightness of marrying him.

Where would they live? He could probably never go back to *dorcha àite*. Helen had seen to that.

Helen. She'd have to be brought to heel, although he wasn't sure how since she was a goddess—an Ancient of great power who feared nothing and no one.

The Amazons. She'd feared the Amazons or else she'd never have resorted to kidnapping one of them to lure the rest into a trap. She also feared Artair MacKay. Oh, she might have told Ian her plans were to punish all of them before she destroyed them, but he knew better now.

She *couldn't* destroy them so long as they possessed the powers of Water, Air, Earth and Fire, or else she would have done so by now.

Aye, Helen feared the Amazons.

So where did he go from here?

TWENTY-ONE

"IAN, WAKE UP." Sarita tickled his ear with her tongue.

As exhausted as she'd been after she'd healed him, it was amazing that she'd awakened first. Sleep had done her a world of good, and she woke up with her mind full of the man who'd captured her heart. She'd risked all to bring him to Avalon and had somehow gained a power she wasn't sure she was ready to handle.

She and Ian needed to talk. Eventually.

Right now she had other things—more pleasurable things—in mind. She slipped off her panties and bra.

Soft snores were slipping from between Ian's lips as he lay sprawled on his back. The red silk sheets were tangled around them both, but there was a telltale bump that told her the sun wasn't the only thing that had risen this morning. She'd just have to try harder to wake him.

She rubbed her nose against the bristly beard stubble on his chin and cheeks, nudging his face over so she could touch her lips to his neck. After a few kisses, she licked her way down his neck to his chest, circling one of his nipples until it hardened into a tight pebble. His snoring ceased.

With a groan, Ian threaded his fingers through her hair. The long tresses were probably a mass of snarls since she hadn't braided it before she fell asleep. Because it was so coarse and thick, her hair tended to have a mind of its own.

"Sweet mercy, yer a beautiful woman."

"I'm a mess."

"Come here, lass."

She pressed her breasts against his chest. Not entirely sure how she'd ended up sleeping nearly naked, she didn't care. Ian was naked, too. They were alone in her beautiful new home. It seemed only right to make love to him to christen the place.

"Good morning," she said.

He smiled before he kissed her.

The man could make her crazy with his kisses. Sarita returned his ferocity with her own, rubbing her tongue across his when it swept inside her mouth. Fire rushed through her, racing down her skin. A delightful tingle formed deep inside her, becoming an intense burst of pleasure that made her gasp.

Ian pulled back to give her quizzical stare. "What?"

She couldn't bring herself to tell him that he excited her so much, she could probably climax solely from his kisses. Her cheeks flushed warm. "Kiss me again," she murmured. "I missed you so much."

"Your voice could tempt a saint."

"We're back to my voice?"

"'Tis a tempting sound, loving." He led her hand to his erection. "This is what the sweet sound does to me."

"Liar. You were like *that* before I said a word." Stroking his length, she licked her lips, anticipating the pleasure she knew he could bring her.

Damn, but the man could move fast. He'd grabbed her around the waist and flipped her to her back in a heartbeat. Hovering over her, his weight supported on his elbows, he smiled. His red-brown hair was also in disarray, making him a temptation she'd never be able to resist.

"Well, then," he said, "perhaps I need to show you how much I want you in another way."

Although she'd never understand why he thought her voice was so wonderful, she obliged him by letting him hear it. "Oh? And how exactly would you do *that*?"

INSTEAD OF ANSWERING HER, Ian decided to show her. Covering her breasts with his palms, he kissed the deep valley between them. *Such beautiful breasts.* Round and firm with responsive nipples. Then he moved to take one of the hard nubs between his lips, suckling and loving how Sarita writhed beneath him.

One thing drove him on as he moved down her body, kissing her stomach and swirling his tongue around the gold hoop with the small sapphire that pierced her navel. Such an odd piece of jewelry, but against her dark skin, it was very appealing. Yet he had a different goal. He needed to know *all* of her—to taste her arousal.

Ian kissed the raven curls crowning her mound as he eased her thighs apart.

"Ian?"

"Hush." Then he was licking the core of her.

Her fingers laced through his hair as she let out a ragged groan that made his cock twitch. She squirmed and he held fast to her hips as he loved her with his mouth, tickling and teasing with his tongue until she cried out, "Now, *jaanu!*"

"Nay, loving. Come for me like this."

"Ian...please."

He doubled his efforts, finding the bud of flesh he

knew would push her over the edge and drawing it between his lips to suck gently.

She nearly bucked off the bed. Her husky voice shouted his name loud enough to echo through the huge bedchamber.

Knowing he'd brought her to release pushed him past what remained of the control over his desire. Rising over her, he nudged his erection against her entrance. "Loving?"

She spread her thighs farther apart. "Come to me, Ian."

With a growl, Ian drove inside her, wishing he had the willpower to simply enjoy the feel of her wet heat surrounding him. His body wasn't that patient. Pulling back, he thrust into her again.

Sarita wrapped her slender legs around his hips and met each lunge, her breathing as ragged and choppy as his. Just when he thought he'd die from the sensations, she dug her fingernails into his shoulders and tightened around him.

His orgasm seemed to last forever, his essence pouring into her as his heart beat furiously. So long as he was in her arms, buried deep in her body, the rest of the world didn't matter.

He never wanted to leave her embrace.

She drummed her fingers against his back. "You're crushing me."

With a resigned sigh, he fell to her side. Patting his chest, he said, "Lie with me for a moment."

"Gladly." Snuggling up against him, she rubbed her cheek against his shoulder.

The day he faced would be daunting. He'd have to open himself up to reliving all the horrible things that had led him here. He'd have to put aside his anger, although he admitted much of it had lessened.

A bit of a surprise that love for Artair was there, hiding right below the surface.

Perhaps his hatred burned so brightly because the betrayal cut deep—all the way to his soul. He'd loved his brother with all his heart, yet Artair had abandoned him to a horrifying fate.

He wasn't sure he'd never belong here—or anywhere. The whole world was confusing. Everything he'd assumed and believed had been tossed aside like so much rubbish. While Helen had gifted him with a new life, he'd never expected to use it for anything but seeking justice. How was he supposed to become a part of Sarita's life? How was he ever going to with this clan?

Where did he go from here?

"I'm going to take a shower." Her smile was saucy. "Care to join me?"

He wasn't sure he'd adapt to this modern world, preferring to bathe in a pond.

"Ian? What's wrong?"

"'Tis not my world anymore. Back at *dorcha àite*, I felt at home. And the island was nice." His gaze swept her opulent bedchamber. "This is so…different. Perhaps *too* different for my old soul."

"This place is as new to me as it is to you."

"Pardon?"

"This house wasn't here last time I was in Avalon. All I had was a cabin every bit as old as your castle."

"Then why did this home appear?"

Sarita shrugged. "Maybe Ganga thought it was time for me to have a nice house. The other Amazons were given houses when they married. Maybe Ganga figured out that I'll be alone the rest of my life and—"

"Yer not alone, loving." Since she'd brought up the topic, he decided perhaps now was the proper time to let her know his intentions. "Perhaps the home was given to you because 'tis time to take a husband."

"What are you talking about?"

"Perhaps you're supposed to marry me."

She blinked, saying nothing. Her expression was unreadable.

"Marry me, Sarita."

"Have you lost your mind?"

It wasn't what she'd said but the incredulous tone that fired Ian's temper. "I took you to my bed, Sarita. I claimed your innocence. The honorable thing is to make you my wife." He'd chosen his words carefully, afraid of betraying his deeper feelings. He wanted nothing more than to secure a permanent place in her life. Not only did he love her, but he needed an anchor to ground him against the coming storm he'd have to weather. Sarita was his heart's anchor.

"Marry me, lass. Let me make this right."

She tossed the sheets aside and scrambled off the bed. "I'm taking a shower."

SARITA TOOK ONE look at the enormous shower stall and reluctantly laughed. She'd never seen anything like it before. There wasn't a showerhead. Instead, there were panels—eight of them—spread throughout the tiled enclosure. She wasn't sure how to turn the damned thing on.

Fumbling with the buttons, she finally found one that made the shower spring to life. In a matter of moments, steaming water—a little over a hundred degrees, according to the control panel—was blasting from all the sprayers.

The Water Amazon was in heaven.

One moment basking in the shower was all it took for Sarita to fall in love with her new bathroom. This was a luxury she'd gratefully accept from Ganga and not feel guilty for using it.

She grabbed the bottle of jasmine shampoo and worked it through the mess of her hair. After she rinsed the suds away, she added conditioner, letting it work its magic on her hair while the water worked its magic on her body. She was rinsing the last of the conditioner out when the glass door to the shower stall opened and closed.

Ian was behind her, pulling her back against him while he nibbled kisses against the tender flesh of her neck.

"I—I'm almost done." She hated the catch in voice, but all the man had to do was touch her to turn her brain to oatmeal.

"I'd hoped to wash ye."

"Too late." Moving out of his arms, she reached for the door handle.

"Wait. Please. We need to talk."

She shook her head, not ready to think about, let alone *discuss*, his proposal. She'd be damned if she'd take him as her husband when the only thing forcing the marriage was his stupid honor.

She'd been a virgin. *So what?* It was her body, her choice.

Goddess, she wanted to scream in frustration. Why did he have to think about something as archaic as *honor?* Why couldn't he want to marry her because he loved her?

"Take your shower," she said. "I'm going to get dressed."

Sarita let herself out of the shower and cocooned herself in a towel. Then, like a coward, she fled the bathroom.

IAN HESITATED WHEN they were at the front door of Gina's strange house. He'd never seen the like before—nothing but sharp angles and various textures of stone and wood. While it was attractive, the home reminded him of the wooden blocks he'd seen children of his clan stack as they played. And so much glass—something his clan had never been able to afford for any of their homes. A decadence, really. Just like Helen's temple with its glass walls and ceiling.

Helen might have given him some rudimentary ideas about this era, but she'd left out far too many details, leaving him feeling ignorant now that she no longer acted as his guide. He was a man adrift in time, afraid of looking the fool by saying or doing the wrong thing.

Sarita would think he was witless if he needed her help to make his way in her world.

The other two homes in Avalon were different. Identical, tall, two stories—nothing like this home. Both had windows jutting from the top floor and shutters that seemed more for decoration rather than protection from storms. Only the colors of the homes were different—one white with shutters of dark green and one gray with bright red accents.

None of the Amazons' homes were as beautiful as Sarita's new palace.

Ian stared at the door, his hand poised to knock.

"It'll be okay, Ian," Sarita said. She put her hand on his arm and forced it down. Then she pushed a small, round button.

The sound of chimes echoed through the home. His eyes widened.

"It's a doorbell," she explained. "Boy, we've got a lot of educating to do with you to bring you into the twenty-first century."

The sweet understanding in her voice dulled the sting of the words. "Aye. I am a stranger in this world."

"Don't worry, *jaanu*. I'll teach you."

He wanted to ask her if she'd decided to accept his proposal, but since she'd fled the shower, they'd resorted to nothing but chitchat. While he had every intention of pushing her for an answer, now wasn't the time. They'd have privacy later, and then he could tell her what he expected—that she *would* marry him.

He also wanted to know exactly what *jaanu* meant. She used it often, and he loved hearing the exotic word fall from her lips, especially when it always seemed to be heartfelt.

The door opened before he could ask.

"Welcome," Zach said, opening the door wide. "Come on in."

Sarita gave Ian a hesitant smile, took his hand and led him inside.

The interior of the house was as inviting as the exterior—full of color, polished metal and stained wood.

"You have a beautiful home," Ian said to Zach. He'd never been one to enjoy conversations, especially with many people around. Talking to Zach felt…awkward. Knowing the others were probably waiting only made him want to head back to the peace and quiet of Sarita's home.

"Thanks. We modeled it after a Bob Burnett design. The guy's brilliant."

Since Ian had never heard of that craftsman, he shrugged.

Zach led them to a large gathering room. The furniture was dark brown fabric and appeared comfortable. A long settee and four chairs of different shapes gathered around a large hearth of rough stone.

The people in the Amazon clan had already gathered. Had Helen not educated him about the Amazons, Ian still would have remembered their introductions. He had a knack for remembering names, something he'd needed as brother to the laird and then laird of Clan MacKay. It was important to show your clan members they were valued by using their names. Thinking about the past no longer made him remember the pain of his death. The memories were better, comforting.

Sarita dragged him to the large settee and sat, pulling him down next to him.

Artair crossed the room to stand closer. He hadn't donned the MacKay plaid. Instead, he wore modern clothes like the ones Helen had given Ian—khakis and a polo shirt.

Artair stared down at him, uncertainty in his expression. "I need to know all, Darian."

"I prefer Ian now." There was a bite to his voice, but Ian tried to curb it. "If you wouldnae mind."

"Of course," his brother replied. "*Ian*. Might take a

bit of time for that to stick in my mind." Artair sat in the closest chair.

"How is it you remember Artair?" Rebecca asked as she came to sit on the arm of her husband's chair.

"Should I not?" Ian asked. He was every bit as anxious as the others to figure this whole mess out.

"No," Sarita replied. "You shouldn't. When you died at Culloden Moor—"

"But I dinnae die at Culloden Moor."

"Aye," Artair said. "You *did*, at the hands of a Sassenach sword."

"Nay. I was badly wounded, but I recovered to return to our clan. 'Twas when all went sour."

Rebecca knit her brows. "Ian, what do you know about Artair being a Sentinel?"

While some of the story would always be like a faded dream, there was one thing he understood, one thing Helen had affirmed. "Artair became the trainer of the Amazons in exchange for the gift of immortality. He abandoned our clan to serve Rhiannon so he would never die."

"Nay! 'Tis not true!" Artair tried to scramble to his feet, but Rebecca's hand on his shoulder held him down.

Sarita nudged the edge of Ian's plaid up and put her hand on his bare knee. "Artair didn't become Sentinel to earn immortality. He called out to Rhiannon because you'd died and he wanted to save your life."

"But… Helen said—"

"You shouldn't believe a single word out of that bitch's mouth." For such a beautiful woman, Rebecca could make a frightening scowl. "Did you know she killed Artair?"

Ian rubbed his hand over his face, wondering if he'd ever understand everything that had happened. "How could she kill a man who is immortal?"

Johann jumped into the conversation. "A Sentinel has one weakness. He can be killed if a blade pierces his heart."

Rebecca took up the story. "She stabbed him as a sacrifice to make me a goddess."

"Yer a goddess?"

"Not anymore. I gave the powers back. Helen didn't. She killed her Fire sister to become a goddess."

"Rebecca surrendered her powers after she restored my life," Artair added. "I only called out to Rhiannon because of you, Ian. At Culloden Moor, after I pledged to train her Amazons, she gave you back your life."

Perhaps everything wasn't as cut and dried as Ian had always assumed. "Let me start from the beginning... When I returned from the battle, I told the clan you'd left to become a servant of Rhiannon."

"How did you know?" Artair asked. "Rhiannon should have removed me from your memory—from the clan's memories, as well."

"Oh, she did pluck you from the *clan's* minds. But she dinnae pull you from *mine*. I saw you pledge yourself to her service, and she touched my hand before the two of you disappeared. When I spoke to our people of my brother who was gone to be with a goddess and how I was now laird, they thought my mind had broken in battle. All they remembered was me as laird—they knew no Artair MacKay."

Megan nodded. "That's what we assumed. That they thought you were crazy because you remembered someone they'd never known existed."

"Aye. Then there was my bloody hand. They remembered me being crippled. They dinnae believe my story that Rhiannon healed me. Seeing it useful raised whispers of witchcraft. Those whispers soon became shouts."

Artair rested his elbows on his knees and dropped his head to his hands. "Nay."

"Och, aye. Then the English moved against us, destroying most of the cottages and killing all the livestock. Only *dorcha àite's* keep was spared. The clan believed I'd made a pact with the devil to spare it and heal my hand. They thought I was a witch." He choked on the last word as the memories of his execution flooded his thoughts.

Would he ever be able to push the pain away and assign the experience to being nothing but a faded memory of a horror long past?

Death by fire—a painful, torturous death. To be tied to that stake and set afire by people who'd worked at his side made it more horrendous. The final monstrosity was to be forced to watch the only two in the clan who supported him—Old Ewan and Sile—executed.

Would they be able to come to Avalon? Perhaps Sarita could find out. He hated the thought of them being trapped at *dorcha àite*, haunting a keep that would probably never be inhabited again.

Sarita leaned over and wrapped her arm around his shoulders. Mercifully, she finished the tale. "Like I told you all, they burned him at the stake."

Silence descended on the room.

"How did you come to follow Helen?" Artair asked. "Didn't you know she was evil?"

Ian gave it a great deal of thought before he spoke.

"I didnae know right away. She promised me justice. 'Twas all I cared about."

"Justice?" Gina asked.

"To avenge my death. I wanted my brother to suffer the way I'd suffered."

How cruel it all sounded now, and how naïve he'd been to think he'd could right the wrongs. Especially now that things weren't as black and white as they'd seemed when he'd walked endlessly in limbo.

Megan's stare showed no consolation, only suspicion. "How can we trust you after you worked for Helen?"

"You can trust him," Sarita said, her voice hard.

Megan narrowed her eyes. "Of course *you'd* say that. You love the guy."

His head whipped around to stare at Sarita. "You love me?"

He hadn't dared to hope. Yes, her actions screamed she cared, but he'd never been sure whether she acted out of affection for him or the desire to destroy Helen.

Ice blue eyes stared back at him, and she pulled her arm back to drop her hands onto her lap. A high blush rose on her cheeks. "Can we talk about this later?"

"There are more important things to discuss," Artair said.

"What's more important than love?" Gina asked, sounding amused.

Dropping her gaze to her lap, Sarita shook her head. "Not now."

Ian put his hand over hers. "Later, loving."

"How about fixing this mess first?" Rebecca hopped to her feet, her hands clenched into fists. "Rhiannon! Enough hiding. We need to straighten this out. *Now!*"

A bright flash and a loud pop brought the goddess into the middle of the room. Dressed in a gown of silver trimmed with sable, she stood as tall as Gina. Smoothing her fingers over her elegant dress, she lifted her chin, setting her long, blond hair bouncing around her shoulders. She looked no different than she had so very long ago.

"Rebecca MacKay. You called?"

TWENTY-TWO

SARITA ALMOST LAUNCHED herself at the haughty Lady of the Lake so she could pummel some bruises on her pretty face. Instead, she held tight to Ian as Artair and Johann rose to their feet, fisted their right hands and thumped their chests over their hearts in salute. Zach also stood, but he inclined his head, a gesture that brought a smile to the goddess's face.

"What do you wish of me?" Rhiannon asked as she nodded to acknowledge each of the men. Then her gaze settled on Ian. "There is a guest in Avalon? Why was I not informed? Better yet, why was my approval not sought?"

A growl rose from Sarita's chest. This whole disaster was Rhiannon's fault. If the goddess had only taken the time to wipe Ian's memory of Artair—as she was *supposed* to—so much suffering could have been avoided.

If Sarita opened her mouth to speak, a string of profanities would spill out. She looked over to Rebecca, hoping her sister understood.

Rebecca gave her a curt nod before glancing back to Rhiannon. "Don't you recognize him, m'lady?"

Ian stared at the goddess with such a ferocious frown on his face Rhiannon would probably feel the need to punish him.

"Nay," Rhiannon replied. "An unhappy looking fellow, is he not? Should he be familiar to me?"

"Aye," Ian said. "I should."

She lifted her elegant nose in the air. "A gentleman should rise in the presence of a lady, especially when that lady is an Ancient of extreme power. Do you not realize I am the Lady of the Lake, the guardian of Excalibur, the Goddess of the Isle? I am the Divine Queen and the patroness of the great King Arthur. I am the—"

Ian heaved a weary sigh. "I *know* who you are."

Rhiannon ignored him and kept right on in her litany of titles. "—protectorate of Avalon. Perhaps you did not realize my importance, so I will forgive your insolence."

Sarita rolled her eyes and stood, pulling Ian up with her. "So you don't remember his face?"

"Nay, I do not."

"I am Darian MacKay."

"Darian MacKay?" Rhiannon tilted her head, staring at him. Then her blue eyes widened. She gaped at Artair. "How has your brother come back from the other side?" She walked over and pinched Ian's upper arm. "Why is he not a ghost?"

Ian shrugged away from her. "I am no ghost."

"Then how do you come to be here? You should be naught but dust."

Artair strode to stand in front of Rhiannon. "Had you answered my earlier calls—"

"I would not come to such rude requests."

Artair's glare could've scared the paint off the walls. "Helen brought him back."

Rhiannon walked back to the middle of the room, as though she were holding court over all of them. "I tire of her interference. Why have you not killed her yet? I *demand* you kill her."

"Oh, I will," Rebecca said. "I promise."

"You will *not*," Sarita retorted. "That bitch is mine."

"We all want a piece of her," Megan added.

"Damn straight," Gina chimed in. "Every one of us owes her some payback."

"But we have another problem to deal with first," Rebecca said.

Rhiannon huffed at her. "More important than bringing a rogue goddess to justice? That is your job, Rebecca MacKay. You are my Amazon."

"I *know* my job. And I promise you, I'll take out Helen. Soon. But please, can we solve Sarita's problem first?"

"I suppose… What is it you wish to know?"

"Do you remember the day Artair became Sentinel?"

"Aye." The goddess smiled. "Such a brave man and so willing to serve me." A glance over to Ian. "As I recall, he came to my service to save your life."

"He wanted to save me?"

"Aye, he did. He was so full of grief, so angry that I heard his cry and went to him. He gave up life as he knew it to save yours."

"Why did you mend my hand?" Ian's voice was raw.

"How wonderful of you to remember!" Her face glowed. "I was so pleased to have a man like the MacKay come to train my Amazons, I offered one more reward in addition to your resurrection." She held out her hand, turning her palm up. "Since your hand was near to useless, I gave you a useful one." With a flourish, she raised a small cloud of sparkles. "Yet you do not need to thank me for such a generous gift."

Ah, but the goddess loved having all the attention focused on her.

"Gift?" Sarita growled again. "That's not how his clan saw it."

Rhiannon always reminded Sarita of a curious child, having little understanding of humans and appearing confused at most of the things they said.

"You do not see it as a gift?" Rhiannon asked. She cocked her head, drawing her brows together. "Did I not make him better than he was before?"

"You fixed his hand," Artair said. "But you didnae fix his memory."

"His memory?"

"You should have taken any remembrance of me away. Nae only from him, but from my entire clan," Artair explained with far more patience than Sarita could muster.

Rhiannon blinked, her confusion plain. "But I *did* deal with your people. They lived their lives as though you had never known them."

"Then why didn't you do the same for my brother?" Artair asked.

Rhiannon thought it over for a moment. "Perhaps I forgot?"

"Forgot? You *forgot*?" Sarita threw her hands in the air. "You ruin his life and all you can say for yourself is you *forgot*? Damn you!"

"Insolent!" Rhiannon pointed an accusing finger. "I will not tolerate your impertinence!"

"She has good reason to be angry, m'lady," Artair said. "She knows what Darian suffered. When my brother returned to our clan, he was cried a witch."

"A witch? Why would your clan believe him to be a witch?"

The goddess was truly clueless. "Because," Sarita drawled, "he remembered a person they'd never heard of. They thought he'd lost his mind and that the devil fixed his hand."

Rhiannon dismissed them with a flippant wave of her hand, her usual way of letting everyone know their concerns were petty in her eyes. "Such superstition and nonsense. I will never understand the ignorance of humans."

"'Twas not nonsense to them!" Ian clenched his hands into fists. "They burned me to death!"

She focused on Ian. "You should have explained your healing was a gift from the Lady of the Lake, the guardian of Excalibur, the—"

"I *did*," he replied. "Just another reason they thought me possessed."

"This is all *your* fault, Rhiannon." Rebecca had put her hands on her hips, and Sarita wasn't at all surprised when a small earthquake rocked the area. Since Rebecca was endowed with her powers by Rhiannon, she was the only Amazon who could get away with scolding her.

Rhiannon put her hand against her chest. "*My* fault? I but offered precious gifts to my new Sentinel. I meant no mischief. 'Tis not my doing that the clan misinterpreted my goodwill offering because of their ignorance." She tilted her head in thought. "How was he able to be in Avalon without my permission?"

"I brought him here," Sarita replied.

"You? But you do not possess such a power." She

delicately sniffed the air before wagging a finger at her. "Seior! You have Seior! How is this possible?"

A loud pop brought Freyjr into the middle of the room. "You called, little one?"

If every thought she had of Freyjr brought him to her, Sarita was in a world of trouble. All she'd done was remember Freyjr's visit, and here he was.

"I *thought* about you, but I sure didn't *call* you. Stop reading my mind."

The smile could only mean he was here to cause trouble. As usual. "But your mind is filled with such… intriguing thoughts as of late." He shifted his gaze to Ian. "I see you have used your new powers well."

Rhiannon crossed her arms under her breasts. "I should have known 'twas you making mischief. Seior is forbidden to Amazons."

"Nay," Freyjr said. "Only *your* Amazon. My sister and your compatriots have no such restrictions."

For a few long moments, the goddess stared at Sarita. Then her eyes flew wide and she pointed. "Your eyes!"

"What are you talking about?" Sarita asked.

"They're blue, loving."

"Blue? But—but my eyes are brown." The mirrors in the bathroom had been fogged over after the showers they'd taken, so she hadn't seen her own reflection. It wasn't like she fussed with makeup anyway. Not since the scar. Her memory of Ian telling her she had blue eyes had been dismissed as a faulty recollection from when she'd been exhausted. "How could they be blue?"

Ganga arrived in a shimmer of light.

The Sentinels immediately saluted her. After smiling at the men, she went to Sarita.

The goddess stroked Sarita's hair. "I am so glad to see you, my child." After studying Sarita's face, Ganga smiled. "You have changed. Just as I had hoped."

"Changed?" Funny, but she didn't *feel* any different.

"'Twas the Seior," Freyjr butted in.

"That's what I'd assumed, too, but… I didn't know it *changed* me."

"He is correct," Ganga said. "To a point. You made a choice—one I knew you would make."

"I made a choice?" Despite all of the training she'd had when she'd become an Amazon, there was so much about the world of the Ancients that confused her. "I don't remember making a choice."

"You stole your sisters' powers," Ganga explained.

Sarita hung her head, still angry at herself for that sin. Yet another reason she was ready to give up the infecting power. "I'm so sorry I disappointed you."

Ganga put a finger under her chin and nudged her face back up. "You could never disappoint me. You used the combined power of the Amazons and the Seior to prevent a soul from being taken before his time."

"You mean Ian?"

"Of course. You used all the good inside you to make the strength of what can be evil into something wonderful. Then you gave the borrowed powers—"

"*Stolen* powers," Rhiannon retorted.

"Borrowed," Ganga replied. "They were merely *borrowed*."

"Few can accomplish such feats," Freyjr added. "'Tis why I gave you the Seior. I knew it would not corrupt such a pure heart and would only be for good."

When Artair, Johann and Ian all scoffed, Freyjr shot them a scorching glare.

This whole conversation only served to confuse Sarita more. "Then I'm not infected by Seior?"

"Nay, little one," Freyjr replied.

"I don't have to give it back?" This time, she directed the question to her goddess.

Ganga's face lit with a warm smile. "You do not have to give it back. Should you do so, the fight you face would surely be lost. Did you not feel the way you controlled the magicks? They no longer control you."

Sarita thought about it before a smile blossomed. "I did control them, didn't I? But what does all this have to do with the color of my eyes changing?"

When Freyjr opened his mouth, Ganga stopped him with a slash of her hand. "You trespass here, Freyjr."

"Trespass?" He pointed a manicured finger at Ian. "*I* gave her the magicks she needed to save that man. *I* gave her the magicks to—"

"Nay!" Rhiannon's angry shout echoed through the house and tree branches slapped against the windows. "You may not speak!"

"It's okay," Sarita said. "He'd already let it slip that I needed Seior to save Ian. He's not telling me something I don't already know."

All emotion left the goddesses' expressions.

Sarita's stomach tightened into a painful knot. "There's another reason, isn't there?"

No one answered her, but her sisters' agreeing thoughts filled her mind.

"So you won't tell me why I need to keep it, will you?" Sarita asked Ganga.

"I cannot," Ganga insisted, her expression stern.

"You *can*. You just *won't*."

Rebecca leaped into the discussion. "All of you let us run around blindfolded."

"So far, we've been lucky," Gina added. "We've stumbled onto plots and plans we needed to end."

"This time," Megan added, "Helen is kicking our asses. If you could help us—"

"Nay," Rhiannon said with a shake of her head. "We cannot."

Sarita appealed to Freyjr. "How about you? Will you tell me?"

"Freyjr…" Ganga glared at him. "Do not do this."

Rhiannon wasn't nearly as nice. "Leave my Avalon. *Now*."

Sarita tried again. "Freyjr? Please?"

"Nay, my beautiful Sarita. I would anger many Ancients should I spill the truth." Adjusting his jacket, he gave her a cool smile. Then he scowled at Rhiannon. "It would seem my assistance in this endeavor is not appreciated."

"*I* appreciate you," Sarita said.

"Then will you finally repay me for all I did to help you?"

Although it wasn't wise, she nodded, knowing she owed him some kind of reward for helping her save Ian. "What do you want this time?"

"*This* time?" Ian was suddenly at her side. "You have seen this man—"

"Man?" Freyjr narrowed his eyes. "I am an Ancient, you pathetic human." He raised his hand.

Sarita put a restraining hand on Freyjr's arm to keep him from punishing what he had to have seen as Ian's disrespect. "No. Please."

Blue eyes drilled through her. "You think to constantly ask for my favors and never repay me?"

"I owe you, Freyjr. I know that. What can I do to thank you?"

He grasped her hand and led her across the room. She didn't resist. Everyone could see them, so she didn't have to worry. Her sisters would have her back.

Then it dawned on her Ian had been jealous.

She didn't have time to think about that development long, because Freyjr leaned in to whisper in her ear. "What I ask, little one, is a kiss."

"That's it? Just a kiss?" She kept her tone every bit as hushed, hoping to spare herself some embarrassment. While she might have pushed aside the night Freyjr had come to her, she didn't want to trot the episode out for all to hear.

"Aye. A kiss. Just one kiss."

Sounded harmless enough. "Fine." Rising on tiptoes, she pursed her lips.

He put his hands on her shoulders to push her back down. "Nay."

"But you said you wanted a kiss."

"What I want is a kiss freely given."

"It *is* freely given."

"I want a real kiss, Sarita Neeraj—freely given from your heart as if you were kissing the man you did so much to save. It must be heartfelt and as full of love as the ones you give to him. Elsewise, I shall consider you in forfeit and will take back the gift I have given."

Had he made the same threat only a few moments ago, Sarita would have laughed and told him to go right ahead and take it back. She didn't need magicks anymore.

Things had changed. It was clear those magicks would be needed for something important, and her guess was without Seior, they'd never defeat Helen.

She had no choice. At least she would owe him nothing else once it ended. "Fine. I'll kiss you."

"You agree?"

"Do I have a choice?"

"Aye. You do. The kiss must be yours to give, not one stolen."

"Why?" She couldn't figure out why he wanted this from her. She'd made it crystal clear she had no romantic interest in him. What was he trying to prove? "Why are you always after me?"

He sighed, sounding far more human than she'd expected. "You are a bright light in a dark world, little one. To know—just this once—the healing power of your love? For that I would risk anything—even angering the other Ancients by granting you what you should not possess."

She was speechless. "You win, Freyjr."

Freyjr opened his arms wide. "Then come to me."

TWENTY-THREE

IAN COULDN'T BELIEVE what was right before his eyes.

The god—the one who watched Sarita the way a wolf eyed a fat sheep—was leaning in as if he would kiss her. Expecting her to rebuff him, Ian could only gape when Sarita rose on tiptoes to meet him halfway. Then she looped her arms around his neck as Freyjr embraced her, lifting until her feet dangled.

Had his sword been handy, Ian would have grabbed it and marched over to the couple. After jerking Sarita from Freyjr's arms, he'd have gutted him—god, though he might be—because he dared touch her, especially so intimately.

But his sword wasn't nearby, and to Ian's dismay, Sarita was not only allowing the kiss, she kissed Freyjr back. Passionately.

His heart shattered.

After what seemed like an eternity, Freyjr eased her back to the ground as she back. Once on her feet, Sarita stared at him, confusion plain on her face.

"Ah, little one." He caressed her cheek with the back of his knuckles. "Such a temptation you are. Would that I could take you back to *Alfheim* with me. I would treat you as a queen. I would shower you with riches and have servants grant your every wish."

Sarita shook her head and backed up a step. "You've

been properly thanked, but that's as far as this goes."
She glanced at Ian.

Having been taught by Artair long ago that a warrior should hide anything he felt, Ian kept his expression calm. His insides churned with anger and hurt, but he wouldn't hand the smug god victory by letting him see any of the strong emotions running roughshod over him.

She approached Ian in hesitant steps, her new and startling eyes studying him. "Please don't be mad, *jaanu*."

"You kissed him." Damn, he hadn't meant to say a word.

"It was what Freyjr wanted as payment for giving me my new power."

"'Twould seem you paid him back quite well. One might think you love him after an embrace such as that."

"Love?" She snorted. "Hardly. I had no choice. He wanted—"

"I *know* what he wanted."

"Sarita?" Rebecca asked. "Are you okay?"

"I'm fine," she insisted, although she rubbed the back of her hand across her mouth.

"He didn't force you?"

"It was just a stupid kiss. That's all. One stupid kiss so I don't owe him anything anymore."

"Nay," Freyjr said, his eyes never leaving her. "'Twas only a beginning."

"No, Freyjr," Sarita replied. "It wasn't. I gave you what you wanted, just like I promised. And I appreciate you giving me the magicks that helped save Ian. But that's it. There's nothing else between us."

Ian had heard quite a few things lately that he didn't understand. Helen had given him an education about the Amazons—mostly what he needed to know about their weaknesses and how to exploit them. She'd obviously left out a few important things. Added to the fact that everyone in the room shared a history he knew nothing about, he found himself at a disadvantage.

One thing, however, he now understood, having caught it being discussed more than once. Sarita had put herself at risk to gain powers, and she'd done something that perilous to save him.

His anger eased. When she held out her hand to him, he grasped it and pulled her closer.

"You may go now, Freyjr," Rhiannon ordered.

The god hadn't stopped ogling Sarita. "My beautiful Sarita, fare thee well 'til we meet again." He snapped his fingers and disappeared.

SARITA HEAVED A sigh of relief. Who knew what Ian thought when she'd given Freyjr the kiss he demanded? She hadn't enjoyed it, feeling nothing but relief that was all he'd demanded as payment. To force herself to kiss him, she had to picture Ian and try to pretend his lips were the ones touching hers. When she'd pulled away from Freyjr and seen the hurt on Ian's face, she'd wanted to cry.

The man had been hurt so much in so many ways, and she'd made that pain worse. "I didn't mean to hurt you. It was just a stupid kiss. Honest."

He squeezed her hand, which she tried to take as a good sign.

"'Tis time for *him* to leave, as well," Rhiannon said.

Sarita narrowed her eyes. "Ian's not going any-where."

Ganga strode over to Ian and set her hand on his shoulder. "He will stay here." She patted Ian. "You have a new life now, but no one can make up for your suffering at the hands of your people." She tossed a fierce frown at Rhiannon. "My Amazon is correct—this *is* your fault. You should have wiped the man's memory. The rules were put in place to prevent this kind of mishap."

"I merely forgot," Rhiannon said with a huff.

Sarita sensed the rage and pain flowing through Ian, but there was no true way to fix his past. All she could do was guarantee his future was full of love—if only he could love her in return.

Only time would tell, and there was no guarantee she was anything more to him than an obligation.

Ganga glared at Rhiannon. "This man shall be wel-come in Avalon."

"I should have been asked!" Rhiannon insisted.

"I believe you owe him this much and more."

"Oh, aye, *you* would believe so. Your Water is bed-ding him."

Sarita's cheeks burned. There were never any se-crets in Avalon. Now that their bond had returned, her sisters had to know how happy Ian made her and how much he pleased her when they made love. When they got her alone, there'd be a world of questions to answer.

One problem at a time.

"And," Rhiannon added, "you have the audacity to erect a home for her in *my* sanctuary without asking *my* permission or *my* blessing." Ever the histrionic, she closed her eyes and dragged the back of her hand across her forehead. "Will the insults never cease?"

"She is *my* Amazon. I shall see to her comforts as *I* see fit. Now, you must make this right for Ian."

The Lady of the Lake blinked a couple of times. "Who is Ian? Were we not speaking of Darian MacKay?"

Ganga's growl sounded so much like her own, Sarita almost smiled. "Do not try my patience further, Rhiannon. Ian MacKay is welcome in Avalon, and you will grant him a boon."

Rhiannon arched a blond eyebrow. "And exactly which boon shall I give *Ian?*"

"The same you offered to his brother when Rebecca restored his life as Sarita restored Ian's. You will make his life match that of his savior, his mate."

Rebecca was the first to smile, clearly understanding something that escaped Sarita. "Perfect solution, Ganga."

"Thank you." The goddesses smirked at Rhiannon. "I thought so, as well."

Sarita had only heard and understood one word. *Mate.*

"Ganga, no." She tugged on her goddess's golden sari. "He's not—I can't—"

"What is wrong, my child?"

"Ian's not—I mean—we might have slept together, but he's not…"

The goddess had a wonderful dimple in her right cheek when she smiled. "This is not simply for you, Sarita." She glanced to Ian. "You, sir, have given your life three times—"

"Three?" Artair asked. He stared at his brother. "I

only know of one." His head bowed. "Now, two. After what our clan did…" He swallowed hard. "Two deaths."

"There were three, Sentinel," Ganga replied. "Sarita was granted the power to heal all people when Ian's life was slipping away here in Avalon. She saved him before he slipped to the other side."

"Aye," Ian said. "She did. I owe her a life-debt."

Sarita shook her head. "You don't owe me anything, Ian. You took that sword for me or you wouldn't have needed saving. I'd say we're even."

The goddess's hand cupped Sarita's cheek. "Few have been worthy to receive this power. Your heart is pure." Her other hand traced the scar running down the right side of Sarita's face.

It took every ounce of Sarita's strength not to drag her hair over the mark.

"No matter what befalls you, you put the happiness of others before yourself. Never once have you vainly begged me to remove the mark Sekhmet left. And you used the power of Seior—a power that can turn a person to evil—to save an innocent man."

"Does that have something to do with the color of her eyes?" Gina asked. "Why they're not brown now?"

Ganga nodded. "She now practices Seior as white magicks."

"That's why her hair was white, as well?" Ian asked.

Sarita gasped. "My hair was white?"

"Aye," Ian replied. "White as snow when I first came back. As the glow on your hands faded, it returned to black."

Sarita's gaze searched Ganga's. "What does all this mean, Ganga?"

"It means you are a *benandanta*—a practitioner of

white magicks. It means your powers are greater now than you could have imagined. Since you are my Water Amazon, you have taken all that I endowed in you and expanded them. You may now heal *all* people, as you did Ian."

"What about the Seior? It's gone?"

"Nay," Rhiannon chimed in. "You shall retain those powers, as well. I suggest you use them wisely, for you are still in danger."

"Danger?" Ian asked. "What kind of danger?"

"The danger that should her heart harden," Rhiannon cautioned, "she will no longer be a *benandanta* but a witch of powerful black magicks—a force of evil in the world. She would be a creature much like Helen, though lacking some of the powers only given an Ancient."

"Sarita will never change. Her heart has always been pure," Ganga insisted. "So, Rhiannon—will you do what you must to make this right?"

"Not yet," Sarita insisted. "Ian should have time to think about all of this. We're rushing him into things."

The man's entire world had changed, and he was never given time to figure out what he wanted from the future. What if his heart wasn't nearly as entangled as her own? He'd be stuck with her—a woman he didn't love—for the rest of his time on this Earth.

Not only that, but should Sarita die in any of her battles as an Amazon—including the one they faced against Helen—his life would end, as well.

Ian needed to understand exactly what he was choosing.

"He is your mate," Ganga insisted.

"Yeah, well…" Sarita nibbled on her lower lip.

"Maybe *he* doesn't think so. What if he wants to be a mortal? What if he doesn't want to be involved in this crazy world?"

Zach jumped in. "Why wouldn't he? I've loved every minute of this life."

"Trust us, Ian," Johann said. "You'll never regret it."

"Stop it!" Resisting the urge to stomp her foot, Sarita scowled at the men. "He hasn't had time to decide anything, and it's not fair if you guys pressure him. He's lived through hell. Literally."

"Nae hell, actually," Ian murmured. "More like limbo."

"Like that's any better," Sarita said. "You've been given a new life, one where you can be anything you want to be and go anywhere you want to go."

"Not really," Rebecca said.

Sarita whipped her head around to face the Guardian. "What do you mean?"

"In theory, he *could* do anything he wants to. But you're forgetting Helen. In her eyes, Ian betrayed her. She'll hunt him down without our protection."

Artair nodded. "What she'd do to him would make all he's suffered seem kind. His best chance—and best choice—is to stay here with all of us."

"With *you*," Rebecca added.

"Might I remind you," Rhiannon butted in, "that he was ally to Helen in her schemes and plans."

"Only because she offered him a chance at revenge," Sarita replied. "He thought his own brother betrayed him. Might I remind *you*, when he had to make a choice, he put himself between me and Helen's sword. He saved my life."

"He is safe in Avalon," Ganga insisted. "Sarita will love and protect him."

Artair nodded again. "We will *all* protect him."

A tear slipped down Sarita's cheek. How unfair this was to Ian! All she'd wanted was make things right for him, but the world constantly turned against him. Not only that, but everyone was arguing as if Ian wasn't standing right there.

He was a man, not a child. He should be able to make his own choices. He shouldn't be burdened with a wife he didn't want.

"Ian...what do *you* want?" she asked, her voice trembling.

IAN STARED AT SARITA, astounded.

How could she not know his answer? After all they'd shared—the times he'd made love to her—how could she not understand what he felt for her?

Her goddess claimed he was her mate. He whole-heartedly agreed. Had he been able to state his wishes before he'd seen Sarita kiss Freyjr, he might have blurted out how much he loved her. Even the jealousy of that was swept away by the love he held for her.

Now he was being given a choice—to stay at her side or to remain a mortal and live in the real world. If only he knew what Sarita wanted, the choice would be plain.

But there was that kiss, and she spoke only of protecting him, not of love.

Yet hadn't her actions screamed love each step of the way?

She'd given Ian her innocence. She'd taken on dangerous powers because she thought she needed them to save him. And she'd put herself in mortal danger to come and take him away from Helen.

So why did he want to hear it from her own lips?

God, help me, I need the words.

"Do you love me, lass?"

Her eyes widened and she tugged her braid over her shoulder, running her fingers down the length. "That's—that's not important."

"Och, aye. 'Tis verra important."

Her chin dropped. "You should be deciding what you want for your future without thinking about me. It's your choice. Your life."

"'Twould be a bleak one without you. Do you nae remember my proposal?"

"He proposed?" Gina asked, her tone more happy than curious.

"Aye," Ian replied. "I did."

"That was just because—because...you know. Because of what we did." Sarita's last words were a whisper.

He didn't feel any such constraints. One thing about Avalon was crystal clear—there were no secrets between the people who called it home. "I was your first. I took your virgini—"

"Ian!" Sarita hurried to put her hand over his mouth. "Not here!"

He smiled against her palm then gave it a reverent kiss. She was obviously feeling every bit as vulnerable as he was, which only meant one thing.

Sarita loved him. Just as he loved her.

"Why not here?" Ian asked. "These are you friends, your *family*. Your goddess is here, as well. What better time to ask for your hand in marriage?"

"You really want to marry me?

"I love you, Sarita."

Her chin trembled. "I love you, too."

"Donnae cry, loving. Will you be my wife?"

After a ragged breath and a couple of sniffles, she smiled. "Yes. I'll be your wife."

"Then it is settled." Rhiannon butted in on the magical moment. "The vows have been exchanged." Pushing between Ian and Sarita, she pressed her hand against each of their chests. Her hands glowed orange.

Fire shot through Ian, sending tingles racing from his head to his toes. He struggled to draw a breath and glanced at Sarita to see if she was having the same difficulty.

Her hair was white again, the same ethereal glow from Rhiannon's hands shone from Sarita's eyes.

Then all was as it was before.

"'Tis done." Stepping back, Rhiannon glanced at Ganga. "We should leave now. We anger many of our kind by lingering here."

"First," Ganga replied, "I must congratulate the bride." She put her hands on Sarita's shoulders and kissed her cheeks.

"Bride?" Sarita's indignation mirrored what Ian felt.

Could it all be over and done so quickly? *That* was our wedding?"

"Aye," Rhiannon said. "You both pledged your love and I joined your life forces. 'Tis done."

TWENTY-FOUR

THE FOUNTAIN IN the courtyard of her new home calmed her. Watching the water stream from the mouths of the marble fish did Sarita good. Soothing her. Pacifying her.

She plunged her hand into the water.

Koi swam closer, touching her skin with nibbling kisses. Such beautiful fish, their white and orange scales shining in the moonlight.

Her heart was never going to settle into a normal rhythm again. All she'd done was tell Ian she loved him in front of witnesses after he confessed his feelings, and—*whamo!*—she was a married woman. Not only that, but her husband was now tied to her in every possible way.

The day she died, he would follow right after.

Part of her wanted to crawl on the roof and shout her happiness. Ian was truly hers. But another part wanted to weep—he was in danger each time she picked up her sword. Although she had faith in her abilities, especially now that she was a—what was the word?—*benandanta*, she'd not only risk her own life. She'd risk Ian's, as well.

Sarita let the water trickle through her fingers, tempted to throw off her workout clothes and jump in. Ganga had made the fountain big enough to swim in, after all.

There was too much to talk about first.

I'm married. To Ian.

Wow. Just...wow.

"What are you thinking, loving?"

Closing her eyes, she let his brogue wash over her like healing water. Ian might have had other plans for his life, but the Fates had brought him here. To her.

And now he was her husband.

As she opened her eyes, she smiled. "Sit. We should talk." She patted the marble ledge.

He sat close enough, their thighs rubbed. "What is there to talk about?"

"Um, I don't know. The queen of England? What do you *think* we should talk about?"

"What's done is done, Sarita. Leave it be. 'Tis what I wanted." His hand covered hers where they were clasped on her lap. "Is it not what you wanted, as well?"

"Yes, of course. But—"

"There is no *but*. You're my wife now, as you should be. Not only do I love you, but I claimed your innocence." Ian nudged her face toward him. "And I do love you, Sarita MacKay. Now tell me again."

"Tell you what?" She couldn't ask the question with a straight face. Pretending had never been her strong suit, which made it next to amazing she'd been able to keep up the ruse of being Earth. "I love you, Ian. I should have told you sooner."

"When did you first know?" The vulnerability in the question was endearing.

"A lot longer than I was willing to admit—all the way back to when we were together at *dorcha àite*."

Ian leaned in and gave her a quick kiss. "If only

things had been different. I could have courted you properly, in my clan's way."

"I don't know about that… From the stories Artair's told us, if a Highlander wanted a woman, he didn't court her. He just *took* her. Isn't that what you did? Took me?"

He chuckled. "Aye. I wish I could tell you I've loved you that long, but it took my wee mind a bit longer to discover all I felt."

She pressed her palms against his cheeks. "As long as you know now. So do you think you can handle being married to an Amazon warrior?"

"Nae just a warrior now, lass. Yer a white witch, as well."

The word *witch* made her frown. "It's not fair."

His brow knit. "What's not fair? I thought I told you, I wanted to marry you and—"

"Not *that*. It's not fair that I'm a witch and it's a good thing. But your clan punished you when you weren't a warlock."

Every time they'd talked about his death at the hands of his clan, Ian had been so angry, his body stiffened in response. But as they spoke about it now, he stayed relaxed.

It was a good start.

"As I said—what's done is done." His hands covered hers, then he frowned. "You have no ring."

"Neither do you. Does it really matter?"

"Aye, it matters. I will get ye a ring of gold. I promise. And I'll be a good husband, loving."

She rested her forehead against his. "And I'll be a good wife."

Ian stood, pulling Sarita up, as well. "Then 'tis time

to begin our honeymoon." He marched toward the bedroom, taking her with him.

With Helen's threat looming large, there was no way they could have a true honeymoon. So if Ian wanted to call going to bed a honeymoon, who was she to argue?

When they reached the archway to her room, he swept her into his arms and carried her to the bed. After setting her back on her feet, he pushed her hands away when she tried to pull her shirt over her head.

Married in a T-shirt and yoga pants.

How romantic.

"Let me," he said. His sensuous voice made her breath catch.

Ian peeled off her shirt, moving in quickly while her arms were raised to brush his lips against her collarbone. He removed her bra. Casting it aside, he ran his hands up her stomach to her breasts and covered them with his palms.

Sarita wanted more of his magical touch. He ignited a fire deep inside her that started in her core and fanned through her limbs.

With no warning, he dropped to his knees. Wrapping his arms around her waist, he pulled her forward until he could rest his cheek against her stomach. "You're really mine now. 'Tis so hard to believe."

"I'm really yours." Tears burned her eyes as she combed his hair with her fingers, hoping he'd grow it back out. She missed it being long. "I'll always be yours."

He looked up at her, his green eyes sparkling. "Then let me make you my wife in truth." He dragged her pants down and tossed them aside. Her panties followed right behind. Before she could undress him, he scooped her up and put her on the bed. With nothing more than a couple of tugs, his plaid hit the floor. His impatience was clear when he jerked his shirt open, sending the buttons flying.

Goddess, but he was a handsome man. Not an ounce of fat. Tan skin over rippling muscle. Firm, hair-roughened thighs. She could look at him all day and never want to tear her gaze away.

His heart and soul were every bit as handsome. Even though he had little memory of all they'd shared at the castle, probably thinking of her as nothing more than a woman who'd come to share some heated memories with him in the night, he'd put himself between her heart and Helen's sword.

With a smile, she opened her arms to her new husband—the man she loved more than life itself.

His body blanketed hers. The heat was incredible, seeping into her and spreading like wildfire through her veins. The length of his erection pressed against her thigh at the same time his lips captured hers.

There was no teasing, just desire flaring between them. Ian's tongue swept into her mouth, rubbing against hers as she whimpered in impatience.

Stroking up his back, Sarita resisted the urge to drag her nails across his skin. The last time they'd made love, she hadn't realized she'd left long furrows across his shoulders. When she'd seen the marks, she'd been shocked. Her only excuse was that whenever Ian touched her, she went crazy.

IAN SHIFTED TO press his lips to Sarita's slender neck. Her skin was silken soft, and he breathed in her jasmine scent, thinking this was about as wonderful as life could get.

Damn, but he was having a hard time accepting that she belonged to him. After his memories had returned, he'd feared he might have put too many obstacles between them to be able to find himself back at her side.

From her perspective, she must have believed he'd done nothing but use her to sate his lust then cast her aside to follow Helen. Yet here she was, his wife, reaching for him, love alight in her eyes. He never would have been so merciful.

Sarita had not only forgiven him, she'd come searching for him to offer a way out before saving him from sure death.

"You really do love me," Ian whispered in her ear.

He didn't give her time to confirm what he already knew, capturing her mouth for another deep kiss.

Her breasts branded his chest, drawing him down her body. He nipped at the swell of one and soothed it with a lick. Giving her no warning, he drew her taut nipple into his mouth and suckled.

Sarita dug her nails into his shoulders, the sting adding to his pleasure because it meant she was letting go and feeling without guarding her reactions. She'd come so far so quickly as he'd taught her about making love. He wanted to make her forget everything except his touch, his love.

After he laved her other breast, savoring her passionate moans, Ian rose above her, staring down into her eyes. They'd darkened with passion—the color of a stormy sea. Without breaking her gaze, he used his knee to spread her thighs and rubbed his cock against her entrance.

She opened up, lifting her hips and offering herself to him.

"Now, you belong to me." Clutching her hips, he thrust deep inside.

Sarita gasped and closed her eyes. "Oh, my goddess—"

Ian smothered any other words with a kiss, pushing his tongue into her mouth. She replied by wrapping her legs around his hips and sucking hard on his tongue.

Again and again, he pushed into her as her body rose to meet his thrusts. Release was in his grasp, but he wouldn't leave her behind. Ian tore his mouth away, stared hard into her eyes and whispered. "Come with me, loving."

Her eyes widened and then closed. Her thighs squeezed him tight. "Ian... So close... I'm so close."

"Come with me."

In that moment, where their hearts beat as one, she tightened around him as he found his own fulfillment in a blazing orgasm.

Long minutes passed, and Ian was content to let them slip away while his rapid heartbeat roared in his ears. The scent of their lovemaking filled the air, and he wanted nothing more than to stay in her arms forever. Nothing could make the moment better.

"I love you, Ian."

He'd been wrong.

Those four words made his life perfect.

GINA GREETED SARITA when she walked into the lodge for supper the next evening. "Wait. We've got something special planned for you and Ian."

"Special?" Sarita asked as Gina placed a wreath of flowers on her head.

The day had already been heavenly. She'd awakened to Ian kissing her breasts, and he'd made her come twice before he'd let her leave their bed. They'd spent the afternoon in Eden, sharing a picnic lunch the changelings had left for them.

Now, it appeared her sisters were going to make this day more memorable. No wonder the only clothing she could find to wear to supper was a silk sari. Ian wore the MacKay plaid for the first time since she'd met him, which spoke volumes for how far he'd come from the pain of his past.

"*Very* special." Gina swept her arm out. "Welcome to your wedding feast."

"What are you talking—" The question died in Sarita's throat when she saw the decorations inside the cavernous room.

Garlands of flowers hung from the wooden rafters. Candles burned on the tables and the mantel of the stone fireplace. Delicious-smelling food was piled on the main table, which had been set with white plates and sparkling silverware. Several bottles of champagne chilled in ice buckets. A three-tiered cake waited for dessert.

Her sisters had been very busy, no doubt with the help of Beagan and Dolan. Both changelings were dressed in green velvet vests and looked so much like leprechauns, Sarita had to suppress a giggle.

When she and Gina first arrived at Avalon, Beagan and Dolan kept their distance. While they'd always made sure the Amazons had everything they needed, the changelings tended to show themselves only to Rebecca. Over time, they'd turned up more and more, and once the children arrived, Beagan and Dolan became an active part of the Amazon family, serving not only as nannies but as homeopathic doctors. The only time they shifted into rabbits and disappeared anymore was when someone yelled at them, which wasn't often.

Tears stung Sarita's eyes. After having only her distant aunt Kamala and Lalita in her life, she was overwhelmed by the love she felt flowing to her from these people—her *true* family.

Gina smiled. "Since you had such a fast wedding—"

"*Fast* being an understatement," Rebecca added.

"—we wanted to have a celebration to mark you and Ian being married."

"Thank you," Sarita choked out, but the words were barely audible.

Ian took her hand in his. "My wife and I thank you kindly."

Artair stepped forward, his gaze focused on the MacKay plaid. He cleared his throat twice before he spoke. "I want to welcome you to Avalon, Ian. I hope we can sit and talk sometime so we can put aside the past. You were wronged in so many ways…" He swallowed hard.

"Aye," Ian replied. "We should talk."

"'Tis good to see you wear the plaid I sent to you."

"Thank you for that kindness."

Ian's hand was squeezing hers tight enough to cut off her circulation.

While she wanted to butt in and demand the brothers patch up their differences *now*, she didn't. Only time and understanding would bring Ian and Artair back together, although they'd made a good beginning.

She saw both sides of the story, which neither of them could probably manage yet.

If only she could heal them.

Bonnie and Darian drew closer, and Artair crooked his finger at them. They grinned and hurried to his side.

"This is my daughter, Bonnie," Artair said, laying a hand on her shoulder.

"'Tis good to meet you." Ian bowed to her.

She studied him with her big, blue eyes while her hands clutched her pink skirt. "You're my uncle Ian, right? Like Uncle Johann and Uncle Zach?"

"Aye, lassie. Except I'm yer father's blood brother."

"I'm Darian." The redhead, dressed in his own MacKay kilt, thumped his chest with his thumb before shoving his hand at Ian.

"I'm Ian." He shook the boy's hand.

Bonnie stared at him, but she also took a step closer, which boded well. "Da says we should love you, so we'll try."

"As I shall try to love you, lassie." His tone might've been solemn, but a smile lit his face.

"And me?" Darian asked.

Ian tousled Darian's red curls. "And you, laddie."

"Go to yer Ma," Artair said. "'Tis time to eat."

Both children moved at their father's command, but they kept glancing back at Ian, clearly fascinated with the newest person in Avalon. They sat at a small table with Megan's daughter, Mina, and were soon talking and laughing.

The brothers bowed to each other, a formal greeting they'd no doubt kept from days long gone. Then Artair ushered Rebecca to their places while Ian led Sarita to the empty place settings at the middle of the table.

Tucking the train of her blue sari out of the way, Sarita let Ian help her into her chair. He sat at her side—the happy bride and groom.

As everyone else took their seats, Beagan and Dolan hurried to fill champagne glasses and pass the platters of food around. Once everyone was eating, they piled their own plates high and sat at the table with the children.

After the feast—which left Sarita so full she feared her waistband would pop—Rebecca tapped her spoon against her full champagne flute.

The jovial conversation came to a sputtering halt.

"I have a toast." She raised her glass as everyone followed suit. "To Ian and Sarita. May you live long lives and be blessed with a house full of mischievous children." She drank, as did the others.

Beagan and Dolan approached cautiously, each hiding something behind his back.

Sarita crooked her finger at them. They smiled and drew closer.

"We have gifts," Beagan announced.

"For both of you," Dolan added.

"You've done so much already," she replied. To Ian she said, "This is Beagan, and this is Dolan."

"We've met."

"Oh, yeah… When we arrived. I imagine my sisters did most of the decorating. But the food? *That* was all these two miracle workers."

Leaning down, Sarita grabbed Dolan's face and kissed his forehead before giving the same tribute to

Beagan. The changelings blushed furiously and stared at their shoes.

"'Twas a wondrous feast," Ian said. "One of the best I've eaten. Thank you for honoring us on our wedding day." He bowed low to the little men.

They shoved their boxes at the couple.

Sarita opened her lid. "How beautiful!"

She lifted a white gold ring from the box just as Ian did the same.

"Such miracle workers." Ian nodded at the changelings. "Thank ye for answering my wish."

He took Sarita's left hand and slid the ring on her finger.

Smiling in happiness, she returned the favor. Then she crouched to hug first Dolan and then Beagan as Ian patted their shoulders.

Both changelings shifted into rabbits and hopped out of the lodge.

Sarita laughed, the sound quickly echoed by her sisters.

"Did I frighten them?" he asked.

"No. More like embarrassed them. They don't take compliments well."

His gaze followed the path they'd taken. "Donnae they need protection? Are there predators near? Wolves, perhaps?"

Taking his hand, she led him back to their seats. "Not in Avalon. They're safe here."

Megan carried over a plate with a large slice of cake and set it down in front of Ian. "Time for a few wedding rituals." She glanced back. "Everyone, bring your glasses. Joeman? Can you please grab that bottle of champagne?"

"If I drink anymore champagne, I'm going to need help getting home," Gina said. "Zach and I finished the better part of a bottle already."

Zach wrapped his arms around her waist and pulled her against him. Then he planted a kiss on her lips that was probably too passionate, considering their company.

When he pulled back, he smiled. "Don't worry, love. I'll make sure you get home safely."

Sarita laughed, feeling Gina's happiness—the same happiness radiating from Rebecca and Megan—a contentment Sarita now shared in her own life instead of vicariously.

Johann refilled all the glasses then put the bottle aside. Megan raised her glass.

"And now," she said, "our wedding wishes to you both. To the happy couple—I wish you more smiles than tears."

"I wish you both long life," Rebecca added, tipping her glass to the couple.

Then Gina offered her toast. "And my wish is for you to always be as in love as you are today."

The clink of glasses was followed by a deafening explosion from the courtyard that shattered the windows of the lodge, sending glass raining to the floor.

"Sarita Neeraj!" A familiar voice screamed.

Helen.

"Come to me or everyone in Avalon dies!"

TWENTY-FIVE

SARITA'S FIRST REACTION was to grab Ian by the arm and drag him to the floor, where she threw herself on top of him.

The MacKays and Hermanns had hurried to the children, who had been taught long ago to be as quiet as mice whenever Avalon was under attack. Silence was the first rule for everyone until they knew the nature of the threat.

Gina and Zach had hit the deck too far down the aisle for Sarita to talk to her sister. Her mental calls when unanswered, causing more panic to race through her.

Sarita crawled off Ian and signaled to Gina. From the time they'd trained as Amazons, they'd learned to communicate with hand signals and their telepathic link. Since one was lost, she used the other.

The last time Avalon was invaded, Helen had caught them unprepared. After that, Artair and Johann drilled new protocol into the Amazons' heads.

They were more than ready this time. Even the children knew what to do—they were already crawling to the trap door in the corner.

"We should protect the children," Ian whispered.

"They're heading to the safe room beneath the floor of the lodge. Beagan and Dolan will be there soon. They always protect the children."

"Those tiny men?"

"They can combine themselves into a Sasquatch."

"A what?"

She growled her impatience before remembering Ian couldn't possibly know what she was talking about. "They become a monster."

"Then send that monster after Helen."

"They can only be a Sasquatch to protect people they love, not for an attack or to protect themselves."

"Come out!" Helen shouted again. "I have a present for you, Sarita! Come and claim it or everyone here dies!"

The hair on the back of Sarita's neck prickled.

Artair was the only person armed, his sword constantly sheathed at his side. He rose to his knees, drew it and handed it to Rebecca. Then he kept his head low and headed toward the arsenal, Johann close behind. Zach had moved closer to the women. He crouched near the door with Gina and Megan as Sarita and Ian made their way over.

They needed to plan their attack, but Sarita had to know Ian was in a safe spot first.

"Go to the bunker with the kids and keep your head down," she ordered. She pointed to the trap door in the floor that Bonnie was holding open while Mina and Darian crawled inside.

"Nay," he replied. "I'll not disappear into some hidey hole. I must face her, too."

"No, *jaanu*. No."

"I'm a man—I'll nae hide with the bairns. I intend to fight at your side."

"You're a *mortal*, and if you take on Helen, you'll die."

"Then wouldn't you die, too?"

"Your life is tied to mine, not vice-versa. Just stay safe and let me do my job."

"Sarita—"

She didn't have time to argue with him, and she doubted it would do any good anyway. "Then go help Artair and Johann get our weapons and grab yourself a sword. You can watch our backs. Okay?"

An argument was in his eyes, but he nodded and hurried after the Sentinels.

Sarita kept her head low and dropped down beside her sisters and Zach.

"Any ideas?" Rebecca asked.

"I wish we knew where she was," Gina said. "Guesses?"

"My guess is the climbing tower," Sarita answered. "She'll want to be able to see everything going on in the compound."

"She'll be looking for Sarita," Rebecca said. "But you know damn well she wants to kill us all. How did she get into Avalon?"

"Her followers, I'll bet," Zach replied. "Johann and I have been watching the news networks. She made a big call for all her followers to head to their temples and pray for her to have strength, like she was sick or something. They were all worried she might be dying. It had to be a ruse to give her the power to come here."

"Oh, goddess…" Sarita's heart was pounding so hard she could barely think. "You don't think there were more human sacrifices, do you?"

Zach shrugged. "Wouldn't put it past her."

Rebecca's gaze caught Sarita's. "Even without sacrifices, the prayers will make her stronger."

"If she has every follower sending her worship," Gina added, "we'll never have the strength to kill her."

"Maybe not," Rebecca said, "but we can at least get her ass out of Avalon, have Rhiannon shift the location again and put up a stronger shield. I won't have my children in danger."

"*If* she'll help us," Zach said in a cynical tone. Not surprising after all the warnings that the goddesses were out of this fight.

Sarita tried again to connect with Gina telepathically. She groaned in frustration. "The goddesses have truly abandoned us. Could be why I suddenly can't reach any of you with my thoughts."

Gina gave her a curt nod. "Same thing I was thinking."

"What do you think Helen's *surprise* is?" Megan asked.

"I'm afraid to find out," Sarita replied. "Let me go out first. Once I see where she is, I can signal information to Gina. Then you'll know where to put Zach so he can bind Helen."

"I'm not letting you go out there alone," Gina insisted.

"All I have to do is keep her focused on me while you all get ready."

"What if she throws something wicked at you? Fireballs…or lightning?" Megan asked. "Can you hold them off?"

"I think so." Sarita wasn't sure of the extent of her new powers, yet she *was* sure she could raise some kind of defense against any weapon Helen tried to use. Already, the white magicks made her feel stronger and more confident—almost giddy with the anticipation of kicking Helen's ass. "Pretty sure I'll be okay."

"Pretty sure?" Rebecca asked. "I've faced her before, Sarita—and I was a goddess at the time. She's damned powerful."

"I can do this," Sarita retorted. "I don't know how to explain it. I just know I can hold a defense. I can block anything she tosses my way."

"Not like we have a choice," Zach added. He flexed his fingers. "Let's do this. I'm itching to tie that bitch up."

The final call was the Guardian's. Rebecca studied Sarita intently, most likely trying to re-establish their mental link. Then, with a sigh, she nodded. "Keep her occupied as long as you can. Gina will get Zach in place and protect him while he binds Helen. Megan and I will guard your back."

"With these," Johann said, setting several weapons next to them.

Artair added to the pile, handing Rebecca a sword and a dagger.

Sarita pulled out a sword. Her sari would make it difficult to move, especially if she had to run.

Ian flopped down next to her then pressed a dirk into her hand. "Try this."

She sliced through the silk until her sari was a miniskirt.

"Ian, you stay close to Artair," she ordered.

"Last chance, Sarita!" Helen's voice boomed loud enough to make the windows shake. "Come out now or else!"

When Sarita tried to rise from her crouch, Ian

grabbed her arm. "Watch yerself, loving." He cupped her neck and pulled her close for a quick, hard kiss.

She glanced at each of her sisters and got to her feet.

Confidence washed over her as she strode out of the lodge. "I'm here, Helen."

She'd been right—Helen stood atop the climbing tower. At least she thought it was Helen. The figure looming above the courtyard was draped in a black robe, reminding Sarita so much of the stereotypical portrayal of Death, she shuddered.

Did *benandantas* have premonitions? Because all she could think of was Death had come to Avalon...

"So. You *are* brave enough to face me." The confidence in Helen's voice didn't shake Sarita's confidence. "I had my doubts."

"You don't scare me, Helen."

"Today is a good day for you to die," Helen said, sending a cold chill racing the length of Sarita's spine.

"Yeah, well... I'm not planning on leaving anytime soon, so how about you show me your surprise and get the hell out of Avalon. I don't suppose you noticed we don't have a welcome mat out—especially for you."

Without being able to see Helen's face, Sarita couldn't make any guess over what she was thinking or feeling.

A bundle that resembled a rolled up Persian rug rested at Helen's feet—no doubt the promised surprise. Sarita wasn't in any hurry to see it. Judging from the size, Helen had brought a revenant along to create havoc. Once her sisters were in place, then she could tell Helen to go ahead and let her freak flag fly.

For now, she needed to keep her occupied.

"Why the robe?" Sarita asked. "Did you get tired

of trying to imitate Rhiannon and decide to go all Jedi on us?"

Thunder rumbled and storm clouds gathered. "How dare you compare me to *her*!"

Sarita had been right all along—Helen *was* jealous of Rhiannon. She stank of envy, and the way she copied all of Rhiannon's mannerisms—even wearing her style of clothing—screamed that Helen wanted to be equal to the Lady of the Lake. "Hard to compare you to anyone right now. What's with the robe?"

Lightning crackled through the darkening skies. "I came here to kill you."

"What's that got to do with the monk outfit?"

"You. I wear the robe because of *you*!" Helen threw the hood back.

Sarita swallowed a gasp. Helen's thick blond hair was now gray, hanging from her head in thin snarls and dirty tangles, making her appear more bald than not. Her face was grotesque, the skin sallow and deeply wrinkled. She looked as though someone had begun mummifying her and never completed the process.

"*You* did this to me!" Helen's shriek echoed through Avalon as thunder boomed to punctuate her words.

"How is your looking like—like—*that* my fault?"

A bolt of lightning struck Sarita's cabin, setting it afire. The action revealed Helen's greatest weakness—she had lashed out at Water's old home.

She had no idea about the recent changes in Avalon.

Beagan and Dolan were surely protecting the children now, all of the innocents tucked away safely in their room beneath the lodge. At least Helen was venting her anger on the old cabins and not the lodge where Ian and everyone else she loved waited for the right time to join the fray.

"You cursed me!" Helen screamed.

"I what?"

Another bolt of lightning, this time sizzling through the branches of one of the tallest trees in the woods surrounding the compound.

"Don't play ignorant with me! When you stole Darian MacKay, you cursed me!"

Searching her memory from her last visit to the island, Sarita could only find her fears for Ian and her sisters. Then understanding dawned, and the words that had filled her head when her anger had run hot and deep came forward.

Your rancid soul hides behind a beautiful face. I wish the world to see you as you truly are.

Being a *benandanta*, her words had carried more weight than she'd expected—or hoped for. Helen's face was a now a mirror to her soul.

Sarita smiled.

Helen slammed a bolt of lightning down against Gina's old cabin. Two buildings were being consumed by fire.

A glimpse of Zach's brown hair caught Sarita's eye. He'd pulled close enough to try to bind Helen. Her sisters had to be in place, too. How frustrating that their thoughts weren't connected. Never expecting an attack inside Avalon, they hadn't fetched their communication devices.

"Since you gifted me with this new face," Helen sneered, "I have a gift for you, as well."

She kicked hard at the tapestry, rolling it forward. When it reached the ledge of the climbing tower, the rug opened and a body spilled out, crashing to the ground with a sickening thud.

The woman didn't move. Long black and silver hair tangled around her face, which made it impossible to tell whether she was alive or dead, let alone who it was.

Sarita approached cautiously, her gaze on Helen. The body could be a revenant, but with her sword in her hand, Sarita would dispatch it with one swing. Helen, on the other hand, could do some major damage. Sarita needed to stay on guard.

The body wasn't moving, so she swept the hair away from the face. "No. It's not—" A strangled cry rose from her chest as she dropped her sword. "No!"

Her aunt Kamala had been dead long enough that Sarita could do nothing to help her. There was no life in her open eyes, no sign of her spirit hovering nearby. Her face was frozen in a painful grimace, one that made Sarita vow to repay Helen with the same pain she'd caused Kamala.

Rage blinded her as power sizzled from her chest to her fingertips. Balls of fire formed against her palms and she shoved them at Helen with a wish that they consume her.

Just before they struck, Helen held up her wrinkled hands, absorbed them and laughed.

The laughter only enraged Sarita more. Channeling the fury, she threw a shockwave that made the logs of the climbing tower crack. Helen stumbled before regaining her feet.

The arrow came from Sarita's left, and she held her breath in hopes Rebecca was as accurate as usual. But in the split second before it would have hit Helen's chest, she grabbed it from midair, clenching it in a fist.

"Nice try." Heaving it like a javelin, Helen launched the arrow at Rebecca, who stood just beside Water's burning cabin.

Rebecca stepped back, barely avoiding the arrow.

"I have a gift for you as well, Rebecca," Helen announced. She looked to the darkened sky and blinked.

From the clouds, a body fell, the sound of it hitting the ground turned Sarita's stomach. She prayed whoever it was had already been dead as long as her aunt Kamala, because healing someone after such a drop would sorely drain Sarita's powers.

Slinging her bow over her shoulder, Rebecca ran to the body. The guttural cry meant she recognized the victim. She dropped to her knees, rolled the woman to face her and screamed. "Aunt Kay! No!"

"Damn you, Helen!" Sarita shouted.

"That you did! Just look at what you did to me! Look at my face!"

"Then come after me. These women did nothing to hurt you."

"They mattered to you! They mattered to all of you!"

Two identical Zachs stepped from either side of the compound, palms raised to throw their tethers at Helen. Megan had done a stupendous job in her transformation—even Sarita couldn't tell which one was the real Zach.

Tie her good and tight, Zach. Then I'll kill her.

The rage flowed through Sarita, and she fought to hold it down. She wasn't successful, especially when her gaze went to Rebecca and she saw the anguish in her sister's eyes.

With a shudder, Rebecca stood, grabbed her bow

and plucked an arrow from her quiver. She aimed it at Hélen and shot at the same time both Zach and Megan grunted as though releasing their binding powers.

Things happened so quickly, Sarita had a hard time keeping up.

Helen grabbed the arrow mid-air and sent it hurling back at Rebecca. Before it could sink into her, the Sasquatch appeared and threw itself in the path of the arrow. It sank into the creature's chest, and an unearthly howl filled the air.

With a swish of her hand, Helen sent one of the Zachs flying into the wall of the closest cabin. Hard. By the time Megan slid to the ground, she'd shifted back into herself.

The real Zach fared no better as Helen plucked at the invisible binds the way a puppeteer pulled strings, wrapping them around her wrist and jerking until Zach stumbled forward, trying to break the links. He collided headfirst with the climbing tower and went down. He wasn't moving.

Gina hurried from her hiding place to crouch at her husband's side.

Helen raised a hand to the clouds. "You mustn't believe I forgot you, Gina." A woman's body fell close to Zach, no doubt the last of the "gifts"—Gina's aunt Carla.

With a shout, Gina sprang forward, her jump high enough to put her at Helen's level, but she never got a foothold on the tower. Helen greeted her with a raised dagger that she sank into Gina's stomach.

Sarita couldn't even scream as she watched Gina fall to lie at her husband's side.

"I'm going to kill you," Sarita whispered, letting the hate build to a crescendo.

Helen must have heard her, because she said, "Not before I give you my final offering."

"Megan's aunt Tasha is already dead, so you're out of aunts."

"Ah, but I have someone left who is as good—if not *better*—as a special punishment for *you*."

The sing-song moan of revenants filled the air, their stench following right behind. A large group of zombies began lumbering from the woods.

Sarita's heart plummeted to the ground when she saw the rotting corpse of Lalita. "Please...no."

Lumbering along, the zombie snarled, snapping her teeth several times before she fell into a stumbling walk.

Then Kamala reanimated. Watching her fall in step with Lalita made Sarita so nauseous, she feared she'd empty her stomach right then and there. Swallowing the bile rising in the back of her throat, she gripped her sword tighter as the last of the "aunts" stirred.

"Fuck you, Helen!" Sarita couldn't catch her breath, her chest heaving as she let the hatred fill her soul.

The electricity crackled through her fingers and she blasted the shocks at Helen, catching her in the chest.

Helen stumbled back but didn't fall.

Sarita channeled her wrath and hit her again.

This time Helen sank to her knees. But before Sarita could deal the death blow, Helen disappeared in a shimmer of light.

TWENTY-SIX

"DAMN IT!" HANDS CLENCHED at her side, Sarita scrambled to think of a way to chase after Helen, to follow her celestial escape and hunt her down. To kill her. "I let her get away!"

The sounds of people running and shouting and the moans of the zombies drew her back to reality.

Avalon was in the middle of an invasion—and it was being led by four people who'd meant the world to the Amazons. The first revenant Sarita had to face was the woman who had made her childhood meaningful, the woman she loved—the mother of her heart.

Lalita.

Common sense told Sarita this body stumbling toward her—mouth open in the snarl and eyes glazed with death—wasn't Lalita. This was nothing but a physical shell. Lalita had moved on to the afterlife. But the prospect of raising her weapon made Sarita's stomach twist into agonizing knots.

Swallowing hard, she whispered, "I love you. Please forgive me." Then she swung her sword and let out an agonized cry as she took Lalita's head from her shoulder.

Ian's shout echoed behind her, as did Artair's. They threw themselves into the fight, striking down revenants as Sarita took a quick inventory of what needed to be done and how quickly she had to act. She pushed her worry for Ian aside when she saw how well he wielded his sword, lopping heads from shoulders with little effort.

Gina was her major concern. Helen had stabbed her, and Zach knelt at her siding holding pressure on the wound. Before Sarita could go to her, she had to hack her way through a throng of zombies, including her aunt Kamala.

Kamala was beyond her help. Gina needed her now.

Cheeks wet with tears, Sarita faced Kamala as she had Lalita and did her distasteful job.

Ian took position at her back, and once Sarita reached Gina and Zach, he faced anything coming their way.

"Sarita," Gina rasped. "I need to get into this fight. Fix this. Now."

"Bossy pants. When I heal you, you're gonna need to rest, so fight's over for you." Sarita tried to manage a reassuring smile, but it wouldn't come. She swiped away her remaining tears and focused on the injury. Fingers wrapped around the dagger, she stared into Gina's eyes. "This is gonna hurt."

"Just do it."

Yanking the dagger out, Sarita tossed it aside and held her hands over the wound now gushing fresh blood. Her hands didn't immediately glow or warm with healing energy, so she took a couple of calming breaths, willing her power to work.

It wouldn't.

"Your eyes," Gina said, raising her bloody hand to rest on Sarita's arm.

"Don't talk. Save your strength."

"It's your eyes. Get rid of the anger."

"What are you talking about?" Sarita demanded.

Zach was the one who answered. "Your eyes are black. You're using Seior."

Gina's words echoed in her head. *"Get rid of the anger."*

So much easier said than done.

Sarita tried again, interlacing her fingers as though she would perform CPR. "C'mon. C'mon, damn it."

A hand settled on her shoulder. "Loving, let the hatred go. We'll find Helen. I promise you—we'll find her. Think about Gina, remember how much you love her."

I love my sister.

Ian leaned down to brush a kiss over Sarita's lips. "You're a good woman, Sarita. Hate isn't a part of you."

I love you, too, Ian.

Her hands suddenly flared white, and she blinked back grateful tears. Sealing the wound—one that could have easily taken Gina's life—the energy flowed from her into her sister. Exhaustion followed closely behind as the injury knit closed. There was too much happening for her to surrender to the fatigue, no matter how much healing drained her.

Sarita cast a glance around at the chaos surrounding them. Artair, Rebecca and Johann fought the remaining revenants, but their numbers weren't dwindling fast enough to bring the herd under control. Since Megan was nowhere to be seen, Sarita assumed she'd gone to watch over the children. The Sasquatch had morphed back into Beagan and Dolan—both changelings lay still on the grass.

Sure that Gina's wound was healed, Sarita closed her hands into fists to stop the light, trying to curb her

power so she'd have enough left to help the changelings. She stumbled to her feet, steadied by Ian's strong
grip.

"Go help the others," she scolded and smacked at
his hands. "I don't need your help."

When he let go, she fell on her ass, wondering when
the bones in her legs had become rubber.

"Oh, aye. I can see you're doing *verra well* on yer
own." He hauled her to her feet and swept her into his
arms. "The little men need you."

Sarita held tight to his neck as he ran to Beagan and
Dolan. When Ian put her down, she fell to her knees,
trying to figure out which one needed her more. Instead
of choosing, she held one hand over the deep wounds
in each changeling's chest.

Nothing happened.

"No. No, damn it!" Shaking her hands out, she tried
again, willing her love for Beagan and Dolan to bring
her healing power to her hands. "You can't die. You
just can't."

Ian stood at her side. She looked up, her gaze meeting his. The small shake of his head made her want to
throw up.

"No!" Rebecca screamed as she ran to Sarita's side
and fell to her knees. "Help them, Sarita!"

"I'm trying!"

"They saved my life," Rebecca said, her voice falling to a harsh whisper. She kissed each of the changeling's foreheads as tears rolled down her cheeks. "I
need them."

Nothing Sarita tried worked, which could only
mean—

I'm too late.

Ian stroked her hair. "They're gone, loving."

She wasn't giving up, not on Beagan and Dolan—the last of their kind and the most unselfish beings she'd ever known.

"Give me strength," Sarita said, hoping the Ancients—especially Rhiannon, who loved the changelings—would hear and answer her plea. "Please."

Joining her hands, she focused on Beagan, pouring every ounce of strength and power she had left into healing her friend.

But he was gone. As was Dolan.

With guttural shriek, Rebecca got to her feet and gripped her sword. Then with an agonized battle cry, she charged at the revenants that had moved closer.

Sarita took a shuddering breath and dropped to her side like a fallen tree. She couldn't summon the energy to stop her tumble.

Like it or not, she was out of this fight.

IAN KNELT NEXT to Sarita and smoothed her white hair—the color it had turned when she'd healed Gina—from her face. Her breath was deep and labored, and while he feared for her, there was little he could do. The battle raged, and Rebecca was out of control, attacking anything close to her with fury born of her pain. Artair had moved to protect his wife's back, but that had left his own exposed.

"You're safe here," he said.

Gina struggled to stand. She might not be entirely healed, but she was steady on her feet and held her weapon without trembling. Her cheeks were also wet with tears, although her expression was stoic. "I'll watch her."

He nodded his thanks.

Leaving Sarita, Ian charged a zombie that was poised to take a chunk out of Artair's shoulder. A kick to the back of the knees dropped the creature to the ground, and Ian split the dead man's skull just as Artair whirled around with wide eyes.

"I owe ye one," Artair announced as moved to protect his wife.

"Nay," Ian softly replied. "Now we are even."

The stream of revenants pouring from the woods seemed never ending, and Ian despaired at the slim chance of victory. But he dug in, figuring dying a fourth time would be sadder than those times before because he'd be giving up this life when he'd finally found something worth living for.

A loud pop sounded in the center of the courtyard, followed by an unusual comment.

"Avalon is a foul mess," Freyjr said, stepping over a couple of headless corpses. He stared at the burning cabins. "You humans should care better for the gifts you are given."

"Freyjr!" Rebecca shouted back at the god. "Do something!"

"I *am* doing something, dear Rebecca," Freyjr replied. "I have brought assistance in your fight. I have brought two of your brothers to lend you aid—Richard and Jory wished to join you."

Two more pops were followed by the shouts of two new men trying to make sense of the disorder surrounding them.

"Dick! I'm actually glad to see you!" Zach stumbled to his feet, looking pale and shaky from the hard hit he'd taken to his head. He pointed at the revenants as he grabbed his sword. "Go get 'em! I'm right behind you."

"It's *Richard*," the man replied through gritted teeth. "And you don't look like you could fight anything bigger than a squirrel. Keep an eye on Gina and Sarita." He ran toward the zombies, swinging his sword.

The second newcomer didn't speak as he moved to Ian's side, helping cull the revenants.

"Where is my niece?" Freyjr asked.

"She's in the bunker with the kids," Gina replied.

"Then I shall see to the young ones so that Megan may assist you," he announced before he disappeared again.

Despite the burning of his muscles and the sweat pouring from his body, Ian kept at his task, even though despair at ending this fight crept into his thoughts. How could so few defeat so many?

Slowly, painfully, the zombies fell.

"Fucking revenants!" Megan shouted as she ran from the lodge. "Go back to hell!"

With nothing but swipes of her arm, she sent the revenants flying into the fires that were consuming the two cabins, turning them into funeral pyres. Her movements were labored but effective, and she guarded her left side as though she had a few cracked ribs.

The acrid smell of burning flesh washed over Ian, sending agonizing memories ripping through his thoughts. With great effort, he shoved those memories aside and focused on his task.

Finally between Megan's assistance and the fighting skills of the Rebecca and the men, the last of the revenants perished.

Ian hurried back to Sarita, who was at least sitting

up now. Her hair had shifted back to black and color had returned to her cheeks, but she was more asleep than awake. She and Gina sat next to the dead changelings, and Rebecca and Megan soon knelt at their sides. Rebecca gathered Dolan into her arms and rocked him as Gina stroked Beagan's hair.

Every Amazon had tears in her eyes, and the somber expressions on the Sentinels' faces as they drew near spoke of their loss. Richard and Jory hung back for a few moments before Richard inclined his head toward the lodge and the two headed that direction.

"There wasn't anything you could do?" Megan asked Sarita.

"I tried." Sarita took a ragged sigh. "I did—I *tried*. I'm so sorry. I failed them. I failed you all."

"No one's blaming you," Gina replied. "It's Helen's fault they're dead."

"This whole fucking thing is Helen's fault!" Sparks shot from Megan's hair and fingers. "I'm going to kill her. Slowly and painfully." When she tried to get up, she winced and held tight to her left side.

Johann helped her to stand. "Broken ribs?"

"Probably just cracked, 'cause I can breathe. I don't care, though. I'm going after that bitch."

"I can heal you," Sarita offered.

Ian shook his head at Johann, hoping the Sentinel would understand how drained Sarita was.

"It's okay, Sarita," Johann said, "I'll get Megan fixed up. We'll wrap her middle good and tight and she can get some sleep."

"Are you sure?" Sarita asked.

"I'm sure. Megan, you're going to have to suffer through someone caring for you. For once."

Megan opened her mouth as if to argue, then gave her husband a brusque nod. "I'll get rested up so I can kill Helen."

Rebecca laid Dolan on the grass, got to her feet and glared down at Megan. "The hell you will! She killed the changelings! She's *mine*, and I'm going to make her suffer before she dies." With a sob, she threw herself into Artair's arms.

Artair stroked her braid. "I'm so sorry, Becca mine."

Zach plopped down beside Gina and held her hand.

"How's your head?" she asked.

"Hurts like hell," he replied. "That climbing tower is mighty hard on a skull."

"You might have a concussion. I'll have to keep an eye on you for a while."

"Says the woman who was just stabbed in the gut." He leaned in to kiss her before tossing Sarita a lopsided smile. "Thank you for healing my wife."

Sarita nodded then scrubbed the tears away from her cheeks with the back of her hand.

"Let's go see the bairns," Artair suggested, holding his wife as she cried.

After a few minutes, Rebecca pulled herself together enough to dry her eyes with his plaid. "I need to see my babies. Oh, God, Artair... How can I tell them about—about—"

"We'll find the words," he reassured.

They walked back toward the lodge, Artair's arm draped over her shoulder as she leaned against him.

"Sarita should rest," Ian said. He scanned the compound. "I shall take her home, then I'll return to help with this mess."

"We'll have to bury Beagan and Dolan." Johann's voice was as harsh as the winter wind.

"Aye," Ian replied. "I'll help see to the task once I get my wife settled."

Calling Sarita his wife seemed a bit unusual, but he'd learned to love it. He made a silent vow to do whatever he could to help her and her sisters win the day so he could spend many years with Sarita at his side.

"*All* the women will rest," Johann ordered. "Whether they want to or not. This fight isn't over. Not by a long shot."

TWENTY-SEVEN

Sparse sunlight spilled through the window when Sarita awakened, and she had no idea how long she'd been asleep. Was it dawn or dusk?

After healing Gina, she'd been amazed she could keep her eyes open long enough to watch the end of the fight. Death had been hovering, but Gina's spirit remained in her body. Had Sarita waited much longer, she could have lost her sister.

A chill raced over her skin, forcing a shudder.

Ian stopped his soft snore and pulled her tighter against him. "Are you cold, lass?"

Sarita shook her head and settled her cheek against his shoulder, grateful to have his embrace drive away her fears.

When she'd been a child, she'd suffered from nightmares—especially one that recurred far too often. In those dreams, a bolt of lightning struck her, fracturing her body as though she'd been drawn and quartered in days of old. No matter how hard she tried, she couldn't pull herself back together, and she knew she'd die if she couldn't reconnect her severed parts. It wasn't gruesome—there was no blood. But the pain was so real, so agonizing, she often awakened with her own scream echoing in her ears. Lalita came after each nightmare to soothe Sarita with gentle words and warm hugs.

And Sarita had repaid her by lopping off her head.

That wasn't Lalita.

Her heart refused to listen.

"What time is it?" Sarita asked, trying to divert her morbid thoughts.

"I'd say close to dawn."

Dawn of what day? Amazons slept when they needed to heal and recharge after a fight, sometimes for several days. "How long have I been asleep?"

"Since dawn yesterday."

Her other sorrow hit. Hard. "I couldn't help Beagan and Dolan."

Ian gave Sarita a squeeze. "It wasn't your fault, loving."

"It *was*. I saved you. I saved Gina. Why couldn't I save them?"

"Because it was their time." His deep, calm voice was soothing. "Donnae fash yourself. You tried your best."

"But—"

His hug was fierce. "You cannae save everyone. Accept it. Do good when you can and let the Fates take care of the rest. Who were the men Freyjr brought with him?"

"Not very subtle at changing the topic, are you?"

She loved the way his chest rumbled when he laughed.

"How much do you know about the Ancients?" she asked. While it was clear Helen had given Ian quite a bit of knowledge about both the modern and magical worlds, Sarita would have a hard time explaining if certain facts were lacking.

"All gods and goddesses from every culture exist. They share power so none has too much."

"Do you know who Gaia is?"

"She's the mother of the universe," he replied, "and Helen and Rebecca's mother."

This wouldn't be so hard after all. "Richard and Jory are Gaia's sons. She has *lots* of kids. Hundreds— maybe thousands. Ganga said she can give birth every day if she wants—the normal rules don't apply to her. The girls sometimes become Earth Amazons, but she's afraid of her sons."

"Why?"

"They're demigods."

"So?"

"Demigods have a nasty habit of trying to kill their parents. Gaia keeps them corralled on an island. They have everything they want or need."

"Except freedom, aye?"

"Exactly. If they leave the island, they can only live a day or so. They hate being prisoners in a gilded cage," Sarita replied. "They get pretty restless."

"Then how do the Amazons know about the sons of Gaia if they donnae live in the mortal world?" Ian asked.

"Richard was their leader. He wanted something more from life and called for help to escape. Freyjr stuck his nose into it and answered them. He set them up in an enchanted house where he could party with them."

"Freyjr." Ian grunted. "Imagine that."

"You know, he's really not a bad guy," Sarita insisted. "He's helped us more than the men want to admit. Even my sisters tolerate him since he lends a hand sometimes."

"He kissed you."

"It was his version of a payment for giving me Seior. Knowing Freyjr, he wanted to get a rise out of you." She brushed a kiss on his chest. "Let it go, Ian. I love *you*. Remember?"

"I love you, too. Do these sons of Gaia still live in Freyjr's mansion?

"Not now. When they were there they couldn't leave. They needed magical protection. But at least living in Freyjr's bachelor pad was closer to a real life."

"Then they're back on the island now?"

She nodded against his shoulder. "They're being punished since several started following the goddess Sekhmet and tried to help her destroy the world. Have you heard of her?"

"Och, aye. Egyptian. Helen brags about destroying her. Then she rants and raves about you helping Gina and Zach get away."

"Helen didn't destroy her. Zach and Gina locked her back in her tomb."

With my help.

Just thinking about how she'd frozen Helen in a block of ice made Sarita smile. "Gaia put all her sons back on the island after that. Freyjr's one of the few gods strong enough to protect them when they're off the island."

"Why don't they just leave?"

"They'll die in a few days. Unless..." Perhaps she was telling too much.

Ian prodded her. "Unless what?"

"Freya felt sorry for them and fixed it so they can stay alive if they drink magical blood every now and then."

Ian sat up on his elbow to glare down at her. "Magical blood? As in *your* magical blood? They're vampires?" He shook his head. "I'll nae allow that, *wife*."

He was jealous, and while she should soothe him, all she could do was smile.

Ian really did love her.

"They're not really *vampires*. Real vampires are disgusting. They're like rats." She shuddered for effect. "The SOGs—"

"SOGs?"

"Our nickname for the Sons of Gaia," she replied. "SOGs just need a little magical sustenance. Gina usually takes care of them. She and Richard are very close. He used to have a thing for her until she met Zach. There's a bit of friction between them."

Throwing aside the silk sheet, he crawled out of bed. "Zach shouldnae allow it."

"Did—did you bury the changelings?"

"You're nae subtle about changing topics, either." He stroked her cheek. "Nay. Rebecca wanted to wait for their burial until you could all be there. Gina and Megan have been sleeping, as well." After he brushed a quick kiss on her lips, he said, "I'm going to take a shower. Then we can go for breakfast."

Who would cook?

Beagan and Dolan had handled most of the food in Avalon. Sure, Rebecca liked to cook, and she often made meals for her family. But Amazons were too busy to be domesticated. They'd always relied on the changelings for so much. Everyone in Avalon was able to do their jobs because they could always count on Beagan and Dolan to take care of them.

The children had to be devastated.

Sarita held back her tears until she was sure Ian couldn't hear.

IAN KNOCKED ON the front door, hoping he wasn't disturbing Rebecca. The woman had to be exhausted.

She'd been running around like a woman possessed,

making arrangements for the changelings burial, cooking, caring for the children. She refused to accept help from any of the men, no matter how they all tried to lend a hand or give her comfort.

Perhaps she needed to work through her grief.

"We never knock," Sarita said. She opened the door and walked in. "Bonnie! Darian! Aunt Sarita's here!"

"They're not here right now," Rebecca called. "I'm in the kitchen. Come get some breakfast."

"You cooked?" Sarita grabbed Ian's hand and dragged him through the house.

Rebecca plucked delicious smelling biscuits from the oven, dumped them in a big bowl and set them on the table. "Someone has to feed this brood now that—" She shook her head and hurried back to the stove.

Sarita went to her and rubbed her back. "I'm sorry, Rebecca. I should have… I'm sorry."

Although Ian wanted to reassure Sarita—again—that the changelings' deaths hadn't been her fault, she'd be more likely to believe it if she heard it from the other Amazons.

Rebecca spun around and embraced Sarita. "It's not your fault."

"Where are the bairns?" Ian asked.

"They've already eaten." Rebecca smiled at Sarita, brushed away her tears and went back to cooking. "They went outside with their father."

Artair came in through the kitchen door and kissed his wife.

"The kids are okay?" she asked.

"Aye. Richard was going to help Bonnie with her bow, and Darian took his wooden sword to spar with Jory."

"Anyone home?" Gina shouted.

"In the kitchen!" Sarita called back.

Gina and Zach no sooner got settled when Megan and Johann arrived. Since Rebecca had piled enough eggs, bacon and pancakes on the kitchen table to feed an army before a battle, no one went hungry. Only when the meal ended did the idle chit-chat shift to serious topics.

"We shall bury Beagan and Dolan at sunset," Artair announced. "They shall lie next to Sparks."

"She'd like that," Megan said, swallowing hard.

"Will the goddesses come?" Gina asked.

"Doubt it," Megan replied. "My mother was pretty adamant that they're not allowed to help us."

Zach frowned. "Coming to Avalon to pay their respects to the changelings isn't helping. I can't imagine Rhiannon staying away. She loved them so much."

"You *always* take her side!" Rebecca snapped. "She doesn't love *anyone*, Zach. Not even Beagan and Dolan!" She jumped up and grabbed a nearly empty platter. It shattered when she slammed it into the sink. "Damn her. She could have saved them."

Artair went to her. "The goddesses—even Rhiannon—cannae stop all bad things, sweeting."

She didn't acknowledge him as she attacked the pile of dirty dishes.

With no warning, Freyjr popped into the kitchen, impeccably dressed and clearly full of himself. "How are you all this fine morning?" The god's gaze settled on Sarita, and a smile bowed his lips. "You are awake, little one. Are you well now? Have you recovered from battle?"

"I'm fine, Freyjr," she drawled. "Thanks for asking."

Ian grabbed Sarita's hand and squeezed it, not caring if he revealed his jealousy.

Freyjr arched an eyebrow at him. "Have I caused you worry, Darian MacKay?" He chuckled. "Ah, Sarita... I see your husband still worries you will stray. Perhaps because he realizes I will always welcome your attentions and can give you pleasure beyond what he—"

"What do you want, Freyjr?" Johann interrupted, draping his arm around Megan's shoulder.

The possessive action eased Ian's mind. He wasn't the only one who didn't trust Freyjr around his woman.

"I came with a gift." Freyjr extended his hand to Sarita. "For you, little one."

"She doesnnae need another gift from you," Ian said.

"Ah, but this gift is for *her*, not you. *She* should decide whether to accept."

Sarita cocked her head. "Why would you give me another gift?"

"I have my reasons. Shall we simply say I am fond of this world and wish to help it survive? I merely offer a gift to a woman I admire." He fixed his eyes back on Sarita. "A beautiful woman, despite the flaws."

"She isnae *flawed*," Ian said through gritted teeth.

Sarita squeezed Ian's hand but kept her eyes on Freyjr. "What's *this* one gonna cost me?"

His manicured hand settled on his chest. "Are you questioning my motives?"

She snorted a laugh. "I'd be stupid not to."

Freyjr's hand dropped away, and he grinned. "*Touché*, Sarita. This is truly a gift and bears no price. I give it in celebration of your marriage."

Artair left his wife to stand between Freyjr and the others. "What is it you wish to give her?"

If Freyjr took offense to the protective stance, it didn't show in his expression. "I wish to give her the sight."

The sight—an ability to see glimpses of the future. Not a gift Ian wanted Sarita to receive. Helen had carried on and on about wishing she had the sight. She wanted to be able to know what the Amazons were up to so she could stay a step ahead of them. Her hatred of them—especially Sarita and Rebecca—had become an obsession.

If Sarita received the sight, it might encourage the evil side of her new magicks.

Before Ian could voice an objection, Sarita asked Freyjr, "You can help me see what Helen will do next?" She got up and went to Freyjr's side.

Ian reluctantly let her go. This was her job, her life—who she was. No matter how jealous he was of Freyjr or how much he feared for her each time she faced danger, this was her destiny. Sarita was an Amazon, and he had to give her freedom. He'd have to trust that her heart was as pure as he believed and put aside his own misgivings.

"Yes," the god replied. "And no. I cannot tell you what the sight will show you. I can only give you the ability to glimpse into what *could* be."

"You mean whatever I see isn't set in stone? It can be prevented?" Sarita asked.

All he did was toss Sarita an enigmatic smile.

"You don't want to do this, lass," Artair insisted, his lips drawn thin. "Beware of gods bearing gifts."

"If he can help us kill Helen," Sarita replied, "I'd dare anything."

Rebecca went to them. Her blue eyes were filled with concern. "Sarita? Are you sure? Maybe one of us could take it instead."

"Only those with Seior may have the sight," Freyjr replied. Judging from his strained tone, he was losing patience.

"I want that bitch dead." Megan pounded her fist against the table. "If giving Sarita a peek into the future helps with that—"

"And if it doesn't harm Sarita," Gina added.

"—then I say go for it."

Freyjr gave Megan a formal bow and a crooked smile. "Thank you for that vote of trust, my loving niece."

She scoffed, leaning back in her chair and folding her arms over her chest. "I don't trust you one damn bit, Freyjr, and you know it. I just want every advantage to get Helen. She's been a problem for far too long."

Sarita's gaze searched Ian's, asking without words if he'd allow this.

He went to her and made her face him. "What do *you* want to do? The choice is yours alone, because you will have to bear the weight of it."

"What I want is to kill Helen. So I'm in."

With a concerned frown, he looked to Freyjr. "This willnae harm her?"

"Nay. The vision might be…intense. But I would never cause her harm."

"Do you give your word on that?" Artair's skeptical tone did little to ease Ian's worries.

A storm gathered on Freyjr's face. "Although I

should punish you for your insolence, I give you my word."

For some reason—perhaps the sincerity in the god's eyes as he watched Sarita—Ian believed him. He heaved a relieved sigh. "Then you should do this, loving."

With a radiant smile, she rose on tiptoes to kiss him.

The kiss wasn't long enough to satisfy Ian, but considering their audience, he fought the urge to haul her back into his arms and kiss her until she sagged against him.

With great effort, he let her go to Freyjr.

The god took her hand and led her to a sofa as everyone trailed after them. Ian stood right behind her where he could help if she needed him. The rest of the clan formed a circle around the living room as a clear sign of support.

Ian nodded to the men to thank them. They returned the gesture.

"Now, little one," Freyjr said, taking Sarita's hand in his. "You must close your eyes and clear your mind."

After one last glance at Ian, she obeyed.

He raised his other hand to press three fingers against her forehead, his thumb and pinkie touching her temples. "Open your thoughts to what will come. Let the images surround you, fill you."

She gasped and then began to pant like a hard-run hound.

"You said you wouldnae harm her!" Ian reached for Sarita.

Artair pulled his arm back. "Wait."

"But—"

"Be patient," Artair cautioned. "We'll watch her

closely, but to have the sight isnae easy. Freyjr won't
hurt her. He gave his word."

"He might be a son of a bitch," Johann added, "but
he doesn't lie."

Ian clenched his fists at his side and set his jaw.
Letting Sarita be an Amazon wasn't going to be easy.

"See what might be, what the future might hold in
store..." Freyjr pressed on.

SARITA OPENED HER EYES, but couldn't focus on anything
or anyone. Her thoughts filled with images that flashed
too quickly for her to grasp one and hold tight. "I can't
isolate anything. Everything's moving so fast."

"Focus, little one," Freyjr coaxed. "Find an object—
a face or an item—and grasp it."

"A palm tree," she whispered. "On Ian's island."

One of her favorite places in the world—until Helen
had changed it into a nightmare.

Helen's face—her new Dorian Gray face—loomed
in Sarita's mind. She was laughing as everything
around her shimmied and swayed. An earthquake. Not
surprising from a former Earth Amazon. The palm
trees began to fall, one by one, and Ian's hut was reduced to rubble.

Sarita was there, as were her sisters. Helpless to
stay on her feet as the ground rocked, she fell to her
knees. Helen strode to Rebecca and thrust her sword
through her middle. As Sarita screamed and crawled
to Rebecca, Helen tossed a fireball at Megan, who became engulfed in flames. Finally, Helen went to Gina,
who was also on her knees. After dropping her sword,
Helen pulled a dirk, tugged on Gina's hair to jerk her
head back then slit Gina's throat.

Sarita screamed, scrambling to help her sisters, but the visions suddenly changed.

Now, she was in Helen's glass temple, filled with her followers, all dressed in red. So many—too many to count. Music burst from their lips. Sumerian. They were chanting in Sumerian.

Moving slowly, reverently, they approached the front of the temple. One woman was dressed in white. She was at the front of the pack, but her steps were unsteady. Every so often, she'd sway. Someone in a red robe would steady her and then nudge her forward.

The people surrounded the altar. One tall man lifted the woman in white and laid her on the marble altar. She cried out, but many hands held her down against the stone. Her struggles were worthless.

One of Helen's priestesses—dressed in black and bedecked in diamonds—pulled a jeweled athame from under her robe. Joining in the chants, she raised the weapon high. The moment the chanting ceased, the priestess plunged the athame into the woman's heart.

Sarita felt the pain as if the knife had pierced her own body, and she'd barely caught her breath when she saw another temple in another place with the same kind of scene unfolding. And then another. And another. Again and again, the agony poured through her as the people were sacrificed to give Helen more power.

But power for *what*?

The image changed, soaring out over the blue waters of the Caribbean, pulling back as though a movie were panning to a long-distance shot. Farther still until she could see every island in the sea.

As Sarita watched in horror, Helen floated in the air, high above the Caribbean and laughed maniacally as each of the islands splintered and sank, taking with it every person who called those islands home. Their cries echoed in Sarita's ears.

Helen was now above a volcano, urging molten lava to surge forth and spill over the top. The river of smoldering magma ending more lives than Sarita could count.

Next, coastal waters rose to a wall of water, smashing into land at Helen's command. Sarita screamed in rage and despair as tsunamis claimed more lives and caused more suffering than her heart could bear.

In her mind's eye, she watched the world die—until all that remained were Helen and her followers.

TWENTY-EIGHT

"Sarita?"

A cool cloth smoothed over her cheeks, soothing the heat on her skin.

"Are you awake?"

"Ian?"

"Aye, lass. Come back to me now." His lips brushed her forehead. "Are you well?"

Sarita opened her eyes. She was on Rebecca's couch with Ian at her side.

"You're probably getting damned sick and tired of me passing out." Although she was trying to be non-chalant, the images of her premonition haunted her, making her gut twist and churn.

"You've gone pale. Don't faint on me again," Ian scolded. He folded the wet cloth and laid it over her forehead.

"I'm—I'm fine."

But she wasn't. If the vision she'd just suffered through was any indication, the world was going to end. Soon. Then Helen would be free to re-create it as she saw fit with her followers' worship feeding her power.

A chilling notion.

She looked up at her sisters. They all stood around her, staring down with concern in their eyes. Their deaths haunted her—the deaths she'd seen as though they were actual events, not shadows of what could be.

"Ian..." Rebecca stepped around to put a hand on Ian's shoulder. "Why don't you let us talk to Sarita for bit?" She nodded at the Sentinels and Zach. "How about some Amazon bonding time, gentlemen?"

"Sarita?" Ian's eyes searched her.

"It's fine," she replied. "Let me talk to my sisters."

He set his lips in a thin line before giving her a nod. Rebecca took his place as Ian followed the rest of the men out of the living room.

"What did you see?" she asked.

Taking a ragged breath, Sarita told her sisters of all that Helen had planned, including their deaths. Funny, but the thought of Armageddon didn't hurt as much as the notion of losing her sisters.

"Is it set in stone?" Gina asked. "I mean...if we can get to Helen and kick her ass, can we stop all...*that*?"

Sarita sat up so fast she got dizzy. "*You're* not gonna stop anything. *I'm* going after Helen myself."

"Not happening," Megan said.

"Not in a million years," Rebecca added.

If they wanted to be stubborn, fine. Sarita could out-last every one of them. "If any of you think I'm letting you leave Avalon after what I saw Helen do to you—"

"She hasn't done it yet." Gina put her hands on the back of the sofa and leaned in closer. "Even Freyjr said what you saw was only what *could* be. Now that we know what she's up to, we can change the premonition."

Since she'd withheld enough information to keep the rest of the Amazons from knowing exactly where Helen murdered them, Sarita held the upper hand. She intended to use it.

First, she had to—as Artair always joked before battle—gird her loins.

"Sis…" Gina watched her warily. "I don't like that look on your face. What are you planning?"

For the first time since their telepathic link was severed, Sarita was grateful for the loss. "I won't let Helen get to you. No matter what."

Rebecca studied her as intently as Gina. "Sarita, don't do something stupid."

Saving my sisters isn't stupid.

Megan took her turn scolding. "We need to make some careful plans before we do anything."

Sarita wouldn't be deterred. She had the power to stop this and she knew exactly what to do.

And that she had to do it without their help.

"Forgive me." She blinked herself into the armory.

She wasn't alone. "Dammit."

Artair whirled to face her, Rebecca's bow in his hand. "Sarita? I didnae hear you enter. Johann taught you how to walk verra quietly."

The door opened and Johann walked in. "Did I hear my name?"

"Aye. I told Sarita you taught her well. She slipped in without my noticing, but you were as loud as a stampeding bull."

While she wanted to let Artair believe she was a fantastic Amazon, she'd never been able to lie with straight face. "I teleported in."

"I thought you were talking to the girls." Johann frowned and set his hands against his hips. "You ducked out on them, didn't you?"

Artair stood next to Johann, his glare no less harsh.

"Why did you leave your sisters? I thought you were planning our attack on Helen."

"I'm not letting them anywhere near Helen." *Not after what I saw...*

Sarita grabbed a weapon from the dirks lined up in a neat row. She shoved one into her belt and grabbed a smaller dagger in a leather sheath and strapped it to her leg. If she was facing Helen, she was going loaded for bear.

Her sword—the beautiful one Ganga had given her with the sapphires—was at her new house. She wanted to bring it along, to have the strength she felt from her goddess. About to send herself there, she stopped when Johann took a hold of her arm.

"Wait," he said. "I don't know exactly what's going through that head of yours, but one thing's clear. You think you're going after Helen without help."

She dropped her gaze to stare at the hand gripping her upper arm. Whispers in her head told her she could blink herself out of his grasp. She didn't need his approval any longer, nor did she need his help—just like she didn't need her sisters' help. Not if it put them at risk.

Helen would kill them all if Sarita didn't stop them.

So why couldn't she make herself leave?

"Listen to me, Sarita," Johann said. "I've known you since the day I took Gina to get you at Sea World. I trained you. I know what you're thinking."

"No you don't! If you did, you'd understand why I have to—" She swallowed the rest of the words.

None of them could understand. None of them had seen the horrors she'd seen.

"We're stronger together," Artair said. "I know

you've been given magicks that make you powerful, especially the sight…"

"But that doesn't mean you're in this alone," Johann added. "None of us fly solo. Ever. The goddesses created four warriors—*four*, not *one*. You complement each other. You enhance each other. You need your sisters as much as they need you right now."

Emotions roiled through her, overwhelming their words of wisdom and counsel. "You don't know! If you saw what's going to happen, you'd let me go! You'd let me stop this!"

"What did you see, lass?" Artair asked. "Tell us. Then we can help."

The door to the armory flew open, and the Amazons spilled inside.

"I knew you'd be here." Gina strode over to Sarita. "You pop out on me again, and I'll smack you."

An idle threat. It always was. With the exception of blows inflicted in the name of training, none of the sisters ever raised a hand to the others.

"If you're arming up, so are we," Megan announced. "Thanks for stopping her, Joeman."

He scoffed. "I can't stop her if she really wants to go. None of us can."

"Which means," Artair said, "that she's rethinking her rash plan. Otherwise she'd be gone already."

"It's not *rash*." Sarita's words sounded weak, even to her own ears. "I'm just trying to do what's best."

Rebecca's frown was sternest. "You don't get to decide for all of us."

Sarita gave as good as she got. "Strange advice coming from you. You're a hypocrite."

"Me?"

"Yeah, *you*. I seem to remember the first time we were up against Helen, you went Earth Amazon on us when we wanted to follow."

Rebecca's cheeks reddened.

"So you *do* remember. I got swallowed by kudzu. You had an elm grab Gina. Remember *that*, Rebecca?"

The flush spread down Rebecca's neck. "That was different."

"No, it wasn't," Sarita insisted. "You were afraid for us then, and you wanted to kick Helen's ass on your own. I'm not just afraid for you, I'm *terrified*. For goddess's sake, I saw her kill you all with my own eyes!"

A warm hand grasped hers. "We're not dead." Gina's reassuring tone did little to help calm Sarita. "We're right here."

Ian joined them, walking into the armory and staring at them. "Why wasnae I invited to the party? I could've brought some ale."

Sarita snorted a laugh at his cheekiness.

"The lass was leaving on her own, aye?" he asked.

"She was," Megan announced. "We're not letting her."

Ian brushed Johann's hand away as Gina set Sarita loose, as well. Ian frowned down at her. "What did you see, loving?"

She took a couple of ragged breaths before she answered him. "I saw my sisters die at Helen's hand." Tears glistened in her eyes.

"Then Helen destroyed the world," Gina added. Her hair highlights had shifted, easing from red to a blue.

His gaze searched hers. "And you think you can stop those events?"

"I can try. I can't let them die, don't you see?"

Ian brushed the back of his knuckles over her cheek. "No, I don't see. If you go alone, it's suicide. Why wouldn't you want to take your sisters?"

"Because I can't watch another person I love die!"

Jerking away from him, Sarita stormed out of the armory, not looking back to see if anyone followed, yet knowing they would. Long strides with her short legs wouldn't get her away from them for too long.

They hadn't seen what she'd seen. One by one, her sisters had died, too, taken by a woman who should never have been given the powers of an Ancient. No, those powers had come from yet another death—the murder of Sparks, an Amazon full of heart and spirit and life.

There will be no more deaths! Not if Sarita could do anything to prevent them.

How ironic. Sparks had perished because she'd embraced Seior and it had changed her, infected her. Yet now Sarita could use Seior to save those she loved.

Her gaze settled on the hill where Sparks lay beneath the cold ground. Two small pine boxes waited there for everyone to pay their last respects.

Then Beagan and Dolan would join Sparks in eternal rest…

Anger surged inside Sarita, the power making her fingertips crackle and spark. She fisted her hands, smothering the energy and forcing aside the blackness the threatened to consume her. Yes, she would use the gift Freyjr had given her, but she wouldn't let the Seior rule her. She hurried up the hill, needing to feel close to those she'd lost along the way.

"I'm not like Helen. I'm not." She fell to her knees on Sparks's grave.

Helen had become a monster. At her hands, almost everyone in world would die. The Ancients wouldn't care. They'd sit back and watch it happen with no more emotion than one would feel watching a movie. There were other worlds for them to rule—worlds that hadn't forgotten them the way humans had.

The worst of the lot were the patron goddesses. They already had the sight—every single one of them. They could look into the future if they wanted. They just chose to remain ignorant. Because of their neglect, people—lots of people—would suffer and die.

So why had they bothered to create the Amazons? Why had they set up generation after generation to fight and die for people the four of them cared nothing about? Why had they created the evil force that would bring about Armageddon?

Looking up at the clouds, Sarita channeled her anger at the beings who most deserved her wrath. "This is all your fault! All of you! Every one of you could have stopped her any step of the way, but you didn't!

"Rhiannon, you knew what Helen held in her heart, how much she envied you. She's always wanted to be you, always wanted to be better than you! But you made her an Earth anyway.

"And, Freya, Ix Chel—even you, Ganga—you *all* knew what the future held! All you had to do was look to know what Helen would be, what she'd become and what she wants to do." Sarita slammed her fist against the grass that blanketed Sparks's grave. "You let Sparks die." She laid her palms on the rough pine of the changelings' caskets. "You let Helen kill Beagan and Dolan. And *now*? Now, you won't lift a finger to save my sisters. You'll just sit on your thrones and let that bitch *you* created destroy this world and everyone I love!"

Breathing as though she'd run a marathon, Sarita closed her eyes and collapsed to rest her forehead against her knees.

She couldn't cry. Not anymore. She'd shed far too many tears for people she'd loved. "Please help me. Please don't let this happen. I beg you all."

A hand suddenly grasped hers. Sarita blinked in surprise.

Gina knelt at her side, squeezing her hand. Then she looked up at the clouds. "We need your help, Ix Chel. We can't do this alone. Not this time."

Rebecca fell to her knees and took Sarita's other hand. She raised her voice to the sky. "Don't let Helen win, Rhiannon. You care. No matter how much you pretend you don't, you care. That's why you created us. Please don't abandon us."

Megan joined the circle, hands joined with Gina and Rebecca. "Mother! Listen to us, please! We need you now. We need all of you to help us."

"Please, Ganga," Sarita pleaded. "Don't leave us to this fate."

The clouds above them rumbled, but instead of darkening in a gathering storm, they parted. Sunlight spilled through, striking the Amazons as they stood united on their knees, appealing to the patron goddesses in a way Sarita had never imagined. Four proud women had humbled themselves for the good of the world.

But was anyone listening?

TWENTY-NINE

THE SUNLIGHT WARMING Sarita's face was in stark contrast to the chills racing the length of her spine.

The goddesses had to have heard the Amazons' pleas. Would they care enough to come to their aid? And if they did, what could they do to prevent the horrifying premonition Sarita had about her sisters' deaths?

Minutes passed slowly before Rebecca squeezed Sartia's hand. "At least we can say we tried."

Megan let out a ragged sigh. "I can't believe my mom wouldn't at least come and tell us to our faces that we're on our own for good. I always figured the goddesses would come through for us if things got too rough."

Gina kept her face to the sky. "I've always trusted you, Ix Chel. *Always.* I've given you everything I have to give. Don't abandon us now."

Us.

Not *me.*

Us.

Sarita thought back to the last time she'd faced Helen on Ian's island—the time when she'd stolen her sisters' powers and wielded the strength of four Amazons instead of just one.

She'd wounded Helen. Badly. The curse she hadn't known she leveled had taken a hefty toll. And with the powers of the four Amazons joined, Sarita had been more than Helen could handle.

She looked to her sisters, trying to find a way to explain the plan forming in her mind. "I wish there was some way we could… I don't know…combine everything that we can do."

Gina dropped her gaze to capture Sarita's. "What do you mean?"

Sarita's face flushed hot. "Back on Helen's island, I hurt her. I had the power to really hurt her. I was so much stronger than I was when she came to Avalon."

"Because you'd borrowed our powers," Rebecca said.

Megan wasn't nearly as diplomatic. "You *stole* our powers."

"I'm sorry for that," Sarita replied. "I couldn't control the Seior. The anger was in charge, and I wanted Helen dead so badly, I—I stole all of you powers." She bowed her head. "I'm sorry. We're so strong when we're together. I needed that. I just went about it the wrong way for the wrong reasons."

A loud pop echoed from the hillside.

Sarita's head whipped around to see her goddess, dressed in a silver sari, standing next to the Amazons. "Ganga! Did you come to help?"

Three more pops made Sarita's heart skip a beat.

The prayers of the Amazons had been answered.

Or had they?

Ganga was smiling, but the other three patrons threw fierce frowns at the group.

Rhiannon strode closer, the train of her pink velvet dress dragging against the grass. "So, Sarita Neeraj, you blame *me* for the crimes Helen committed?"

After years of feeding Rhiannon's vanity, Sarita was done. This problem wasn't going to go away, and telling Rhiannon what she wanted to hear wasn't going to get them anywhere.

She let honesty rule her words. "Yes. Yes, I do. You could have stopped Helen any step along the way—even when you took her from Gaia to be fostered by one of your priestesses. But you let her become what she is now—a threat to everyone. She'll destroy almost all of humanity if you allow it."

With a dismissive wave of her hand, Rhiannon said, "I care naught for humanity."

Rebecca got to her feet. "That's bullshit."

The Lady of the Lake whirled on Rebecca. "How dare you! After all I have done for you—"

"I have thanked you time and time again," Rebecca replied. "You can stop using that old excuse to try to keep me in line. This is too important for me to bow to your ego. I will have my say—and I say you care, despite your façade of indifference."

Blue eyes widening, Rhiannon breathed hard enough her nostrils flared.

"I mean it," Rebecca continued. "Come down off that high horse and be the goddess I know you can be. You've always cared about humans."

"I do not ca—"

This time, Rebecca waved the dismissive hand. "You *do* care. You think I don't know you? After all this time and after all you've done for me, I know more than you think. You care. You care about Bonnie and Darian. You cared about Beagan and Dolan. You cared about me and all the other daughters of Gaia you saved. You know what Helen is."

"Evil." Rhiannon hissed like a cat. "Just like that black witch who destroyed my Arthur."

"Can't the four of you kill her?" Megan asked.

"Nay," Freya replied. "Ancients have not the power to destroy one another. Had she not ascended by sacrificing Sparks...perhaps we could have put an end to her."

"If we could wield that kind of power," Rhiannon added, "Freya and I might have destroyed each other long ago." Her words were softened by the knowing smiles the goddesses shared.

"Well then... It's up to the Amazons. And we've got an ace hiding up our sleeves." Rebecca pulled Sarita to her feet. "We've got a white witch on our side. That makes us evenly matched."

A smile filled Freya's face. "Aye, we do. A balance, but now we need more than an equal match. We need a—what is the word you use? Ah, yes. We need a *superhero* the likes of which this world has never seen."

IAN WASN'T SURE he was welcome in this group.

The lodge was so full, surely no one—even his wife—would notice if he slipped outside. Four goddesses. Four Amazons. Two Sentinels. A genius who wielded great power. All Ian could offer to them was a good sword arm. Not much help against what they faced.

As though she'd heard his thoughts, Sarita glanced back. Then she motioned to him. Just a flick of her wrist, but he understood. Unworthy and unskilled as he was, she needed him.

Ian laced his fingers through hers and tried to focus on what was being discussed.

Rebecca was the most vocal. "Sarita should tell us everything she saw. We need to be on guard."

Rhiannon chuckled. "Oh, my dear Rebecca. Have no doubt. You shall see all that Sarita has seen—all that she will see."

"A superhero," Megan said to her mother. "When you told us to all meet you here, you said we needed a superhero. That's what we *all* are—that's what we've always been."

"Nay," Freya said. She stroked her daughter's cheek. "You are Fire, but even you, my darling, have your weaknesses."

Gina's brow knit. "If Megan's not our superhero, who is? She's the strongest Amazon."

"Nay, Sarita is." Ian blurted out without thought.

Sarita snorted a laugh. "As if." She leaned the side of her face against his arm. "That's sweet of you to say, but it's not true."

"It *is*," Ganga said with a decisive nod.

"No," Sarita insisted, "it isn't. I love that you both think so, but—"

"You have Seior," Rebecca said. "Of course you're the strongest Amazon."

With an exaggerated sigh, Sarita shook her head. "What's it matter anyway? I'm strongest. Megan's strongest. You or Gina's strongest. Who really cares? This isn't a competition. No matter who's strongest, she can't defeat Helen alone. Like Freya said, we need someone else."

Freya gave them an enigmatic grin. "Ah, I did not

say you needed *another*. I merely said you needed a superhero."

"How do you know what that means?" Megan asked.

"Please, daughter, do not mistake my keeping with ways of old for being uneducated about *this* world. I know what a superhero is, and my fellow patron goddesses and I are in agreement. 'Tis exactly what we intend to make of you—an undefeatable force."

"Me?" Megan asked.

"Aye."

"And Rebecca," Rhiannon added.

"And Gina," Ix Chel said.

Ganga smiled at Sarita. "And the smallest of all will be the vessel."

"Vessel?" Ian asked. "You mean to make Sarita and the other Amazons more powerful?"

Artair stepped into the mix. "You want to combine their strengths."

Since his brother had made a statement rather than a question, Ian tried to follow his train of thought. "The women will surrender their powers to Sarita?"

"Nay," Rhiannon replied. "They will surrender their *lives*."

"Oh, hell, no," Johann said. He grabbed Megan's hand and tugged her to his side.

"After all I have done for you, you do not trust me, Johann Hermann?" Freya asked. "After I gave you Apollo's cloak? After I gave you my Megan as a bride?"

"Of course I do, but… You're talking about Megan's life now."

"We're talking about *all* our lives." Megan looked at each woman. "I think I see the plan they're taking far too long to explain. The goddesses are going to combine our powers and our life forces in Sarita. Then the four of us—acting as one—are going to collectively kick Helen's ass. Just like when Sarita had all our powers before—she was stronger. Sound about right, Mom?"

"Very smart, my daughter," Freya replied.

"Talk about one for all and all for one," Zach said. "Either you all kill her and come back to us, or you all—you all…"

"Die." Gina filled in the last word. "We all *die*. I'd rather go down together swinging than sit on the sidelines and let Sarita try this on her own. Can you really do this, Ix Chel?"

"*Sí*. Although it is not without risk."

"If you'd seen everything I saw," Sarita said, "you wouldn't worry about the risk."

"But we *did* see," Ganga said. "That is the reason we have come to you."

"We refuse to let humanity die," Rhiannon added. "Not when the force of that destruction was our folly."

"When do ye plan to do this?" Artair asked.

"Tonight," Rhiannon replied. "'Tis time we ended this once and for all. The Amazons will meet on Gina's tower."

"We need to be able to see my moon," Ix Chel added.

Johann didn't appear appeased, but he nodded. "I'll bury Beagan and Dolan before—"

"Nay!" Rhiannon took a deep breath. "Nay. Not yet. I must…bid them farewell. We shall bury them when this distasteful task is over. Let their bodies rest where they are for now."

"May I stand at Sarita's side?" Ian asked, not sure

if any of the goddesses would bother to answer a mere mortal.

Ganga smiled at him. "I fear this is a time where the women must face their task alone. None of you men may come."

"Then I will stay here and guard the bairns. 'Twill comfort me to help them, and they're sure to know something is wrong."

"All of you men must keep yourselves inside," Freya warned. "Drink heavily if you must, but—"

"You may not interfere," Rhiannon interrupted, her tone more severe than the other goddesses.

"None of us?" Zach asked. "Can't I help with my binding power? I could go with them…"

Ix Chel shook her head. "Your power cannot help them now, Zachary. You all love your wives. That is noble."

"But we have to do this alone." Sarita gave Ian a hesitant smile. "You can all pretend we're in labor and you're not allowed in the delivery room."

Rhiannon's laugh made Ian's gut clench in fear.

"That which you plan to undertake," the Lady of the Lake warned, "will make bringing a child into the world seem a simple, painless task."

SARITA JERKED HER T-shirt over her head and tossed it onto the pile of dirty clothes no one had dealt with yet. Her eyes blurred with unshed tears at the thought that the changelings were really gone. Not because of all they'd done for her and the rest of the people in Avalon, but because they were kind and sweet and represented all that was good in the world.

The world she and her sisters would risk their lives to try and save.

Again.

"Are you sure you want to do this, loving?"

She glanced to Ian. He'd asked her that question so many times since they'd returned to her house, she'd lost track.

There were only a few precious hours before sunset, and she didn't want to waste a minute of that time worrying about what was to come. The goddesses were helping, which could only mean the Amazons would have a fighting chance at defeating Helen. That was a hell of a lot more than they'd had an hour ago.

What Sarita needed now was a pleasant distraction, and Ian obviously needed the same. She knew exactly what to do.

Facing him in nothing but her bra and panties, she crooked her finger. His responding smile made her heart do a flip-flop.

"Damn," she said, "I'm married to a handsome man."

He crossed the room. "And I'm married to a verra beautiful woman."

His hands slid up her back to pop the clasp on her bra. She dropped it to the floor. He wrapped his arms around her waist.

Looping her arms around Ian's neck, Sarita smiled. "So what are you gonna do about it?"

He shrugged as though he didn't have a clue. "Make love to her, I suppose."

"You suppose wrong." She slipped out of his embrace and took a step back.

He gaped at her. "Sarita? What's wrong?"

"Nothing. I'm just not going to let you make love to me." The hurt in his gaze made her hurry to add, "*I'm* going to make love to *you*."

She wiggled out of her panties, loving the heated look in his green eyes.

Closing the distance between them, she threw his plaid over his shoulder. Then she undid his belt and pulled it from his hips so the plaid fell to the floor.

One by one, she undid each of the buttons on his shirt, pushing it from his shoulders. His erection bobbed toward her, so she wrapped her fingers around him and stroked.

He hissed and closed his eyes.

Sarita dropped to her knees and took him in her mouth, swirling her tongue around the crown as she held tight to his hips.

Ian let out something between a groan and a gasp.

Goddess, she loved the taste of him. She loved his reaction, too. He tugged at her hair and gently thrust his hips forward.

He didn't let her play for long. Without a word, he hauled her to her feet and kissed her long and deep. They fell to the bed together, her back pressed against the blanket as Ian roughly pushed her thighs apart. "I need you now, wife."

"I'm yours, *jaanu*."

He entered her body as his tongue thrust into her mouth. She gasped against his lips, loving the fierceness, needing to feel alive.

The ride was fast and rough and exactly what she wanted. She let all her worries go and drowned in the sensations. His tongue caressing hers. The crispy hair on his chest rubbing her nipples. The length of his cock sliding almost out before thrusting deep again and again.

The familiar tightness of approaching release swelled and then burst inside her, showering her in bliss. Ian's harsh grunt in her ear made her smile and sent an aftershock to her core. His pleasure was her pleasure.

Rising on his elbows, he stared into her eyes. "Each time is heaven."

She smiled up at him, smoothing his tangled hair away from his face. "Aye. 'Tis wonderful." The more she imitated his brogue, the better she got at rolling her Rs.

"Do ye think we made a baby tonight?"

A baby?

Had the passion they shared created a new life?

While she would welcome a child—especially one created with the man she loved—she wouldn't let herself think beyond the battle that was to come.

IAN COULDN'T FIND the words to explain all he was feeling. *He* was supposed to be the warrior heading off to battle. Instead, his woman—his wife—would risk her life.

That notion didn't sit well.

He'd heard married men talk about their ferocious need to plant a seed in their wives' wombs the eve before a fight. He'd never understood why until now. Foolish though he was, considering the woman who was to bear that seed would face death, he wanted to make a child with Sarita.

Her quick dismissal of his question spoke volumes. The topic would be dropped, but that didn't mean his

heart wasn't pining to know if their lovemaking had
created a new life.

He squeezed her tighter.

Their time would come.

THIRTY

SARITA HAD NEVER liked heights, so she resisted the urge to look over the side of Gina's tower.

Ix Chel had gifted Gina with a place that was high enough to please Air and where she could always see the stars and the moon. Magicks kept clouds from forming over the tower's platform.

Four Amazons and their patron goddesses stood together, ready to do something that had never been done before.

The time had come to create a force of good that could challenge an Ancient.

No wonder the other gods and goddesses gave the patronesses so much gruff. They were preparing to endow four women with the ability to destroy one of their kind.

"Sarita," Rebecca said. "We're ready."

Sarita stepped up to stand at Gina's side.

Rhiannon was running the show. "'Tis time." She beckoned to the rest of them.

Each goddess guided her Amazon until the four women stood in a square, facing each other. The patronesses stayed behind them, hands gripping the Amazons' shoulders.

Damn, but the goddesses were tall, especially Rhiannon.

What an odd little group. Four Amazons dressed

in workout clothing, comfortable and loose. Four goddesses—two in medieval gowns and two in the dress of their cultures—all standing atop a large metal tower in the middle of the woods.

The platform was covered in pillows that had been strategically placed for when the three Amazons collapsed as they surrendered their spirits into Sarita.

Swallowing hard, she hoped she was worthy of their trust. Once their powers were inside her, she had no idea how they could work as one. They were so different—and so very stubborn—linking them couldn't be an easy task.

Rhiannon took a deep breath and began. "You must join hands."

Although Sarita found herself between Megan and Rebecca, she had no desire to switch places. Gina stood opposite her, and those brown eyes stared back with a determination that was every bit as strong as if they were holding hands.

"We call the four corners," Rhiannon said.

"We call the four corners," the other goddesses echoed.

"We call the four corners to make these women stronger." Rhiannon's tone was solemn. Determined.

Thunder rumbled in the distance as storm clouds gathered, pressing in but leaving a piece of clear sky open above the tower.

"Air for the North corner," Ix Chel said.

Lightning flashed, followed by a clap of thunder, louder than the one before.

"Fire for the East corner." Freya squeezed her daughter's shoulders.

A bolt of lightning struck one of the tallest trees,

the rolling sound of thunder followed closely by the crackling of a fire.

Ganga's voice came from behind Sarita. "Water for the South corner."

Sheets of rain began to fall from the clouds, but the platform stayed dry. Walls of rain bordered each side, yet all on the tower remained untouched.

"Earth for the West corner." Rhiannon's voice had risen to a near shout. "These women—these warriors— *are* the watchtowers, and they pledge themselves to become one force, one spirit, one will. Rebecca MacKay do you surrender your spirit to the vessel?"

"I do."

"Gina Hanson," Ix Chel asked, her voice raised against the din, "do you surrender your spirit to the vessel?"

"I do."

"Megan Herrmann, do you surrender your spirit to the vessel?" Freya's voice quivered, yet she was loud enough to be heard.

"I do."

Ganga leaned close to brush a kiss over Sarita's cheek. Then she straightened and held tight to Sarita's arms. "Sarita MacKay, do you wish to become the vessel of the watchtowers?"

The full implication of what she was agreeing to hit. Hard. Her sisters' lives would literally be in her hands—the hands that had once belonged to the weakest Amazon.

"Sarita?"

I'm not weak. I'm strong—because they love me.

"I wish to become the vessel of the watchtowers."

Lightning sizzled from the clear sky, forming a circle as it whirled around and around before slamming into the platform. The heat swept over Sarita, knocking her to her knees as the sound of the thunder roared loud enough to make her ears ring. Her vision blurred, but she was aware of her sisters collapsing as the goddesses disappeared.

Her heart slammed against her ribcage and she struggled to catch her breath. Each time she tried to pull air into her lungs, it was as if she'd sucked in acid. Her throat burned, feeling thick and clogged. She gasped, clutching at the neck of her shirt, trying to tug it loose.

No air. There's no air!

She fell forward, not able to stop the tumble with her hands. Her nose slammed into the wooden platform, making lights dot her vision. She rolled to her back, staring up at the surreal clouds, allowing a perfect square of clear sky to remain above her. Suddenly, four bright bursts of light appeared on the corners, each a different color. Green, red, white and blue.

Twinkling like stars, the corners drifted to the center, stopping short of touching. Then they shot down to slam into Sarita's chest.

She wondered if she'd died.

A few moments later, she wished she had.

Pain shot through her head only a second before her muscles cramped. All she could do was roll to her side, pull her knees to her chest and try to breathe.

Her mind was thrown in bedlam. Thought after thought swirled in a kaleidoscope, none making sense. Sounds came fast and furious, like a cacophony of birds chirping in the same tree.

No, not chirps—voices.

The voices of her sisters blending with her own.

She squeezed her eyes shut and tried to focus on one thought.

I am the vessel. I am the vessel.

The other voices drowned her out, each giving orders of what to do and trying to move different parts of her body. Megan ordering her to stand. Rebecca trying to grab a dagger. Gina wanting to know if she could still jump.

Sarita sat up and set her jaw.

Oh, for the love of… Shut up for a second!

Her sisters' voices stopped and the pain vanished.

I *am the vessel. Let me take the reins.*

And they did. The other Amazons were there in her mind and using their distinct voices, but those thoughts came as easily as her own. Just to see if that meant they could work together as well, she held out a hand, palm up, and tried to create fire. The spark began as a red light, growing into a small ball of flames. With a smile, she snuffed it by closing her fist.

Hand raised, she made the tallest tree's branches dance at her command.

Oh, yes, she was ready. *They* were ready.

Sarita got to her feet, steady and confident, with one purpose and one intent. She strode to the edge of the platform and stepped off.

FIRST THINGS FIRST.

Sarita pictured Helen's temple and blinked.

From the back of the sanctuary, Sarita waited, listening as Helen ranted at Children of the Earth who'd gathered in the temple.

The sanctuary was packed, people standing shoulder to shoulder. All ages. All sizes. Men and women who cheered each of Helen's comments. Many pumped their fists in the air, grunting or whooping when Helen told them they were the chosen ones.

Helen's beautiful face, the one that had appeared so young despite her age, beamed down from an impossibly large monitor. A glamour, no doubt, to keep the COEs from seeing her true face.

From door to the left of the altar, two followers—rather burly men—dragged a girl of no more than sixteen toward Helen. The girl's head lolled from side to side as though she'd been drugged.

"I require a sacrifice," Helen coaxed before pointing to the girl in white. "I require another sign of your faith. Only then can I bring you the riches you deserve."

Sarita couldn't watch one more minute. Neither could her sisters who clamored for her to act. Now.

"She can't bring you riches!" Sarita shouted above the din. "She'll bring you nothing but misery."

Everyone in the sanctuary whirled to face her.

A shriek spilled from Helen's lips. "It's the enemy, the one who wants to destroy me! Kill her!"

One COE, a man no older than Sarita, charged first. With a swipe of her hand, she sent him crashing into the blue velvet chairs. Two more surged forward. With a twist of her wrist, they went flying to land on the first guy.

As the rest of Helen's followers eyed her warily, Sarita spun her finger to turn the video camera and then brought it to life with a blink. Helen's image flickered and then died as Sarita's filled the screen, just as it would the screens at all of Helen's temples. Worldwide.

She gasped at what she saw, feeling her sisters' surprise, as well. Although it was her face—the familiar scar keeping her grounded—everything else had changed.

Her hair was not only white but glowing. Her eyes shimmered like enormous pearls with no visible pupils. Her casual clothes had been replaced by a white gown, light as a feather and sparkling in the sunlight.

A true benandanta.

The power was at her fingertips and the words of spells on the tip of her tongue.

She was jam-packed full of Amazon powers, too.

"I need you all to listen to me." Sarita's voice boomed through the temple, making the glass walls and ceiling rattle. "This woman isn't who she claims to be. She's not a goddess who wants to grant you favors. She's an imposter with borrowed powers. She's a murderer and a fraud."

"Kill her!" one man shouted.

"Sacrifice *her*!" a woman screamed. "Sacrifice her to our savior!"

Angry words flew from the COEs, directed at Sarita.

Instead of letting their hate touch her, she brushed it aside with little effort. All she cared about was saving lives. No humans would be sacrificed on *her* watch, and she wasn't about to let herself be led like a lamb to slaughter.

Sarita waved her hands, bringing the volume of the shouts down. Many of the COEs grabbed at their throats. With one quick swish of her arm, they were all silenced.

"She's deceiving you," Sarita said. "She's turned you into thieves and vandals. But what has it gained you anything? No!"

"They have my benevolence," Helen insisted.

"They have nothing." Sarita tried to reach these people before their souls were lost. "She's turned you into murderers, sacrificing people. And for what? For her? She can offer you nothing but misery and pain! Don't commit any more murders for a fake goddess. Let me show you her true face!"

The screen flickered until Helen's visage filled it again.

Taking a deep breath, Sarita drew on her combined powers. Every action was so natural, every word coming as though she'd always known how to wield white magicks. "I bind your glamour! Let your spell be broken so that we may all see inside your soul!" She thrust her hands out.

Helen put her hands in front of her face and screamed. Her blond hair thinned and grayed as the skin on her hands wrinkled and spotted. When she pulled her hands away, her face was back to the ancient crone who'd attacked Avalon.

The COEs began to screech. A couple of the women fainted. Sarita could only imagine the chaos in the other temples.

She tried to steer the followers in the right direction. "Look at her! This is *not* someone to die for! She's not someone to worship! Go home to your families and forget her!"

Many of the people hurried to the exits, several shedding their robes as they fled, but a few faced Sarita, coming slowly up the aisle.

Time to press her point home.

She narrowed her eyes at the glass ceiling panel hanging over the altar. It cracked, then shattered into shards. She held the pieces up with a raised hand, letting them hover over the brave souls ready to do Helen's bidding.

"You should run now," she warned. "While you have the chance."

They obeyed, fleeing the altar a moment before Sarita dropped her hand and let the glass shards rain down.

Helen shimmered and disappeared from the screen.

Sarita whirled on her heel and stalked out of the temple, letting each of her footsteps send tremors racing across the ground. Once she was outside, she stomped her foot once and sent a quake strong enough to collapse the empty temple into a pile of rubble.

THE ISLAND WAS still beautiful, and she'd always keep the memories of her times here with Ian in her heart.

Sarita stared out at the open water, watching the waves crash against the sand, recharging as she waited for the last act of this play to commence.

Her sisters were with her, and she fed all their powers. The water lapped against her toes as she curled them in the sand. She faced the setting sun, letting the heat warm her skin before the wind cooled it.

We are one.

"Now, you die."

A slow smile spread over Sarita's lips as she faced Helen.

The once powerful and beautiful Ancient had been reduced to a snarling beast. She clutched a sword in her hands, waving it as the blade sang.

"I'm unarmed," Sarita said.

"Then killing you will be easier."

The confidence of her sisters washed over her, and

her heart swelled with love as her body trembled with power.

Helen let out a rage-filled scream and charged.

Sarita sprang over her head, landing gracefully on the sand and whirled to catch the dagger Helen had thrown between her palms. She discarded it beside her. "Nice try."

The sword fell to the sand, and Helen raised her hands, palms out. Streams of fire burst at Sarita.

This one was easy. A quick gesture sent an enormous wave crashing over Helen's head, extinguishing the flames and soaking her.

Sputtering, Helen narrowed her eyes and disappeared.

Sarita saw where she'd gone in her thoughts and blocked Helen's kick.

The fight was on.

Blows and kicks were punctuated with the bursts of energy that Helen tried to throw. Each move was in Sarita's mind before it was made.

Helen finally bellowed—sounding like wounded animal—and disappeared. She popped back up close to the tree line.

The scene's familiarity hit when the ground rumbled and the first tree toppled. Had her sisters not been safely bonded inside her, Sarita might have worried about watching their deaths play out in real life. Now, there was no fear—only a certainty that her premonition had faded to nothing more than wisps of images that would never be.

A palm tree hurtled at her.

Sarita deflected it with a sweep of her arm.

Two more sailed at her.

This time, she jumped them.

Ian's hut collapsed as the ground continued to shift, and Helen fired the pieces at Sarita in an endless torrent of debris.

"Be gone!" Holding out her palms, Sarita shot streams of white energy at the rubble, burning each piece to gray ash as it came in contact with the force field.

Helen collapsed on to her hands and knees, panting for breath, as the earthquake intensified.

Sarita was ready for this to end, but her stomach rebelled when she realized the time had come to kill Helen. No matter what she'd done, the evil she'd unleashed, all that remained of the former Earth Amazon was a shell—a withered, exhausted old woman.

How could Sarita kill something so...pathetic?

A spell sprung from her lips. "I bind your magicks, Helen, from doing harm to yourself and doing harm to others."

The ground stilled.

"I bind your magicks, Helen, from doing harm to yourself and doing harm to others."

"You think that—that—*nonsense* will work against me?" Helen shouted. "I'm an Ancient—a goddess. You should grovel at my feet!"

"An Ancient with no followers to give you power." The spell had to be recited four times so that Helen was disarmed of her powers. Then they could send her to the goddesses to imprison. "I bind your magicks, Helen—"

"Die!" Helen snatched at tufts of her hair. "Why won't you *die!*"

The sky darkened, clouds gathering and winds

whipping Sarita's hair and gown. Lightning struck the beach close to her feet.

Sarita closed her eyes and absorbed the energy.

"I bind your magicks, Helen—"

Her words froze when Helen fell to her side.

Striding across the littered beach, Sarita felt pity swell in her heart. That pity grew when she saw the wretched creature lying on the dried grass. To kill Helen like this would be a crime.

"I bind your magicks, Helen—"

With an enraged snarl, Helen rose, thrusting a dagger into Sarita's chest.

THIRTY-ONE

THE ENERGY ERUPTED from Sarita's hands, a united force of four similar, destructive desires.

The shimmering beams morphed into an ethereal rope, encircling Helen, binding her arms against her sides and then lifting her until her feet dangled.

With a hoarse cry, Sarita unleashed two spirals of white fire from her eyes, hitting Helen's chest. Instead of burning her, the flames seeped inside her. Her skin seemed to shrink, cracking into long fissures. White light erupted from each crevice until Helen exploded into a blinding shower of sparks. They shot high in the air before raining down on the island like dying fireworks.

The battle was over.

Sarita looked down at the hilt of the dagger embedded between her breasts. She waited for the pain.

It never came.

She blinked herself back to Avalon, materializing in the middle of the grassy compound. Jerking the blade free, she gasped at the rush of blood staining her white gown. She tossed the dagger aside.

"Sarita!" Ian was at the door to the lodge.

He sprinted toward her as the rest of the men spilled out the door. Everyone ran her way, their faces full of concern.

"Wait." Her voice was calm, as were her thoughts.

Three spirits—and her own—told her all would be well, and she trusted her sisters' intuitions. With her life. "Just wait a minute."

"What in the hell happened?" Artair demanded.

"Helen. She's dead."

"Oh, loving," Ian said, his voice gruff. "What have you gone and done?"

When he tried to touch her, she pushed his hand away. "Wait. I—I—"

A sudden vibration rose from inside her. Heat flared in her lower belly, snaking its way up her body to her chest. Then the stab wound began to glow, the heat intensifying until it was almost unbearable. Her breathing sped as the healing energy moved through her body.

The wound closed, and the glow faded away as the heat died.

Ian reached for her with trembling hands, pulling apart the material of her gown. "Are you well?"

"I'm fine." She giggled when his fingers brushed over her healed skin. "That tickles."

"How did you do...*that*?"

"I don't know for sure, but I think I healed myself."

Lights flashed only a few yards away, and the patron goddesses appeared. Ganga strode over to Sarita and gently pushed Ian away. She lifted the edge of the blood-stained material to look at where the wound had been.

"How did it heal?" Sarita asked her goddess.

"With love," the goddess replied with a smile.

"So it was my sisters who helped the wound heal? I thought it was me. You know—my Water powers."

Ganga shook her head.

That made no sense. "Then was it Ian? He didn't touch me—"

"We shall discuss this later. Now, we must restore you and the other Amazons." She took Sarita's hand and they were suddenly on top of Gina's tower, as were the other patron goddesses.

Although her sisters' spirits were safe inside her, Sarita couldn't help but stare at their crumpled bodies.

Rhiannon stepped up to lay her cool fingers against Sarita's forehead as Ganga, Ix Chel and Freya all placed their hands on her shoulders. "The task is done. The corners must be released. We call for the watchtowers to again stand alone."

Sarita screamed at the pain shooting through her as though someone had sank a hand deep inside her chest and ripped out her heart.

Three lights floated up—green, red and white— spinning in a circle before they separated. Then they zipped across the platform to the proper Amazon, slamming into their bodies.

Mercifully, the pain disappeared, and Sarita's thoughts were now hers alone.

She tried to catch her breath as she rubbed her chest, waiting for her heart stop racing.

The groans coming from her sisters were music to her ears.

All was as it should be.

Rebecca pushed herself up on an elbow. "Did anyone get the license plate of that truck?"

Rhiannon tilted her head. "Truck? There was no truck. Are you addled?"

"It's just a saying, m'lady," Rebecca replied.

Gina rubbed her fingertips against her forehead. "I feel like my brain's too big for my skull."

Megan rolled over onto her back. "My body aches more than it did when we were training with Artair. Remember, Rebs?"

"Yeah," she replied. "I remember."

Then they grew quiet and shifted their gazes to Sarita.

"I'm fine," she replied to the curiosity flowing her way. Nice to know the connection was there, perhaps strengthened after what they'd just shared. "We should go back to the guys. They'll be worried."

"She's fine, Ian," Artair said.

"I know... I just..." Ian sighed. "How can you stand this? How can you let your women go off like that and nae worry?"

Johan chuckled. "You think we don't worry?"

"Then you've got another think coming," Zach added.

"Of course we worry," Artair said. "But they're Amazons. We have to trust them to do their job."

"How can you all be so calm? Sarita was stabbed for Jesu's sake!"

"And did ye happen to notice she healed herself?" Artair asked. "You're married to an Amazon now. Ye'll have to accept that danger is part of her life."

"But—but—" Running his hand down his face, Ian sighed. "'Twill be...difficult."

Zach slapped him on the back. "Welcome to the 'Amazon Wives Club.' Difficult doesn't come *close* to describing our lives."

Sarita popped up right in front of Ian, and after a

surprised grunt, he gave her a quick head-to-toe inspection.

She was back in her usual clothing, and her hair was black once again. That disconcerting white had left her eyes to return to the ice blue he'd grown to love.

He pressed his palm between her breasts. "Ye scared me to death."

Her smile told him all was well. "Can't have that. You're not a cat, and I can't depend on you to have six more lives left." She brushed a kiss on his lips.

The goddesses and Amazons appeared, and the women ran to their men as the goddesses strode over to Richard and Jory.

Ian hadn't decided what he thought of the Sons of Gaia. They'd been quiet since their arrival, keeping close to the children and performing some of the tasks that Beagan and Dolan used to do.

Rhiannon and Freya spoke to them in low tones, and the men nodded every so often. The expressions on the brothers' faces were serious, in contrast to the goddesses' bright smiles. Then they all marched to the lodge as the Rhiannon and Freya came over to stand close to their Amazons.

Ganga was the first to speak. "We are planning a celebration. Not only has Helen been brought to justice, but the marriage feast for Sarita and Ian was interrupted. We shall continue that this evening, with all of the patron goddesses in attendance."

"We have one more thing to do before we can celebrate," Rebecca said. She glanced over her shoulder at the pine boxes resting on the grass. "We need to say goodbye to Beagan and Dolan." Her voice caught on the names.

"We owe them a proper burial," Artair added.

Rhiannon's eyes flashed red. "To Hades with *that!* All of the women must follow me. *Now.*" She hiked up the skirts of her gown and marched up the hill, each step causing the ground to tremble.

A heartbeat later, the Amazons and goddesses obeyed.

Ian wanted to go but wasn't sure if he'd be welcome since the goddess had only asked for the women. He waited for the other men to take the lead.

"Like I'm getting left outta *this*," Zach said. He trotted after his wife.

The rest of the men, including the Sons of Gaia, followed.

The Lady of the Lake flipped the lids of the coffins away with a flick of her wrist. Her lips dropped to a frown. "My beloved changelings. Look at what that horrible creature did to my changelings." She straightened her shoulders and held her hands out. "We must make a circle and join hands. Ancients and Amazons come to me."

"Rhiannon, my friend," Freya said in a hesitant voice, "you cannot think to—"

Rhiannon narrowed her now blue eyes. "Freya of *Folkvang*, will you take my hand and assist me or nae?"

"The Ancients will be—"

With a huff, Rhiannon said, "I care not for their misgivings. These are my pets—my servants. *My* changelings. Every other one of the Ancients is a hypocrite, using skills and powers when its suits their purpose. In this place, for these creatures, I will use my powers and that of the Amazons. I need you, my friend, as well for the spell to work. Will you help?"

"Aye, Rhiannon. I will help." Freya grabbed Megan's hand as the women encircled the small caskets.

"What are they doing?" Ian whispered to his brother.

"I'm nae sure, but I hope they intend to produce a miracle."

Rhiannon started a chant. *Latin, perhaps?* The other goddesses lent their voices to the repetition of the words Ian didn't understand. About to ask Artair another question, he had barely opened his mouth when Rhiannon's shout filled the air.

"Redeo nobis!"

Bright orange flames burst from the changelings' coffins.

Ian almost reached out to grab Sarita's arm and jerk her away. But after what he'd seen her do earlier—knowing she was capable of bringing him back from the brink of death and of saving herself—he held himself back. This was her life, and it was fraught with both danger and excitement. He needed to learn restraint and acceptance. That didn't make his heart stop pounding, though.

Rhiannon pulled her hands away and crouched between the changelings. They glowed with bright lights. She lifted Beagan by the shoulders. Then she pursed her lips and blew across his face. After she lay him back down, she did the same to Dolan.

The glow faded, leaving the two changelings looking lifeless.

C'mon, little guys. Every muscle in Ian's body tensed. *Come back to us.*

The changelings both gasped a deep breath at the same time and sat up.

With a brilliant smile, Rhiannon touched each of them on the head. "'Tis good to have you back."

She rose, patted her hair and smoothed her gown. Staring at two creatures she'd just resurrected, she said, "We have a feast to plan. I need your assistance."

Arrogant as ever, Rhiannon strolled back down the hill, only pausing long enough to call over her shoulder. "Beagan! Dolan! Come along! You have had more than your share of rest and may no longer dawdle."

THIRTY-TWO

SARITA DABBED HER eyes with her napkin again. No matter how hard she tried to hold back tears, every time one of the changelings bustled past her as they served the meal, she choked up.

Thinking she'd finally pulled herself together, she glanced to Rebecca. Earth wasn't trying to hide the fact she'd been crying, which made Sarita's eyes sting with tears again—that, and she could feel Rebecca's happiness. And Megan's. And especially Gina's.

The Amazons were linked again. All was right in the world.

When either Beagan or Dolan got close to Rebecca, she'd grab him and kiss the top of his head.

Enough holding back!

Next time they drew near, Sarita was going to hug them.

Ian laid his hand over hers. "'Tis a miracle to have them back, loving."

"I'm just so—so—" A sob bubbled out.

He wrapped his arm around her shoulder and pulled her closer.

Rhiannon stood and raised her flute of champagne, making the buzz of conversation end. "We have much to discuss this fair evening. First, Ganga shall address her Amazon." She bowed to Ganga and took her seat.

Ganga stood and bowed in return. Then she faced Sarita. "I am so proud of all you have accomplished."

Sarita's face flushed hot. "Thank you, Ganga."

"There is one more task I ask of you—one that will be the most challenging of your life."

"That sounds ominous."

Ganga smiled. "I have yet to answer your question."

The turn in topic left Sarita confused. "*Which* question?"

"You asked how your wound was healed."

Since that seemed to be something Ganga hadn't wanted to discuss, Sarita had already dismissed it as a byproduct of the Amazons' combined spirits increasing Water's power to heal. "It wasn't because of my sisters being inside me?"

"It was someone else."

That made no sense. "The only people there were you goddesses and the men."

"There was someone else, my child—someone who is destined to be one of the most powerful magical creatures ever created. She shall be the daughter of two special people—the strongest of all *benandantas* and a soul who has cheated death more than once. Her spirit has also been infused with the blood and powers of three other women who shared her mother's body."

Sarita's eyes widened. "Are—are you saying—"

"Your daughter healed you. You can come to no harm so long as she rests in your womb."

Heart pounding, Sarita dropped her hands to her abdomen. When she'd been injured, the healing heat had grown from there, and now she knew why. Stupefied, she couldn't get a single word out of her mouth.

Ian's hand covered hers, and his tender smile

brought more tears to her eyes. "A daughter, loving. We're going to have a daughter."

"Conceived the night Sarita chose to gift you with her innocence," Ganga added.

Sarita nodded and sniffed, not wanting to keep crying in front of everyone. The notion that she wouldn't have conceived her daughter if she hadn't found the courage to go to Ian was sobering. Thank the goddess he'd accepted her and taken her as a lover.

As soon as she and her husband were alone, she was sure to let a river of tears flow as they shared the happy news.

Ganga wasn't done. "You must guard this child well, Sarita MacKay. She will wield magicks the like of which this world has never seen. Many will hunt her, fearing her powers or wishing to control them. I am counting on you, your husband and your sisters to protect this child."

Sarita's stomach plummeted to the floor. "She'll be in danger?"

"Aye," Rhiannon replied, standing to address her as Ganga took a seat. "But she will have protection."

"Damn right she will," Megan said, punctuating her words with a nod. "A great *benandanta* for a mother, three kick-ass Amazons for aunts, two Sentinels and a man who can bind Ancients for uncles. *No one* will get near her."

"Therein lies the problem," Rhiannon said. "Her mother and aunts will no longer be Amazons. This generation must retire."

"Retire?" Almost everyone in the group shouted the word along with Sarita.

"Aye. Retire. After using your combined powers to destroy an Ancient—"

Rebecca interrupted. "Helen wasn't a true Ancient. You said yourself that the rest of the gods and goddesses resented her and wanted her gone. Surely they're grateful we killed her."

"Aye, they are." Freya jumped into the discussion. "However, they also now fear your combined threat. Few creatures have the strength to kill an Ancient. Should you remain active Amazons, you would represent a perpetual danger."

Megan folded her arms over her breasts. "Then just tell them we won't combine again, Mother."

"Works for me," Gina added. "Not really happy about the idea of going through that kind of pain again anyway."

"It hurt you, too?" Sarita asked. She'd been so busy trying to cope with the agony of having her sisters' spirits shoved inside her, she hadn't thought about how difficult the process must have been to have those spirits jerked out of them.

"Hell, yeah," Rebecca said.

"Like a son of a bitch," Megan added.

"Well, there you have it," Gina said. "The rest of the Ancients don't have anything to worry about. Besides, we need to stay strong. There are children—especially Sarita's daughter—to protect. We have to keep our powers."

"You shall do *that*," Freya said. "No one shall take away your powers so long as these goddesses and I have any say. 'Tis just… Well…you must take a lower profile."

Ix Chel wasn't as diplomatic. "You may hunt no longer."

Artair was the only one who didn't seem disturbed by the news. "Will you call the next generation?"

"Nay," Rhiannon replied. "I fear the time of the Amazons has come to an end. For now."

"At least 'til the memories of many Ancients fade," Freya added, "and a potential threat necessitates another generation be given their powers."

"Bonnie." Rebecca whispered her daughter's name. *No wonder.* Sarita had always worried about Bonnie as well, knowing that she was a potential Earth Amazon.

Artair wasn't quite as subtle. "Will my daughter serve?"

"I do not know the future, Arthur," Rhiannon replied.

Sarita's snorted laugh was echoed by her sisters.

Rhiannon shot them a nasty glare. "The Amazons must now become quiet. Stay in Avalon. Raise your families. And come to aid those who fight only when you are truly needed."

"If we're not going to fight, who is?" Rebecca asked.

"Some as worthy as you," Freya replied. She stood at Rhiannon's side as Ganga and Ix Chel took their seats. "'Tis clear we must continue to thwart the threats to this world since other Ancients are content to let humanity teeter on the brink of annihilation. We need a force as strong as the Amazons—perhaps *stronger*."

Rhiannon turned her attention to Jory and Richard. "Sons of Gaia, rise. 'Tis time to learn your fate."

They stood, both with faces full of curiosity.

"I thought now that Beagan and Dolan were back,

we'd have to go back to our island," Richard said. "I mean, didn't you bring us here to be Avalon's caretakers?"

"Aye," Rhiannon replied. "'Twas the plan. Yet now, I see more purpose in you being here. Unless… Did you wish to return to your island?"

"Fuck, no," Jory answered.

A grin lit Rhiannon's face. "Well then, I see a greater future for you—and any of your brothers who wish to serve—although 'twill be a life full of danger."

"And adventure," Freya added with a grin.

Rhiannon came around to the head of the table. "You must pledge your fealty to me."

"To *us*." Freya wagged a finger at Rhiannon. "I shall not allow you to monopolize these intriguing men."

Rhiannon heaved a weary sigh. "So be it."

"The Sons of Gaia will serve us both," Freya insisted. Then she turned to Richard and Jory. "You will pledge your allegiance to me, as well."

"Just you two?" Gina asked. "Not the rest of the patron goddesses?"

With a shake of her head, Ix Chel said, "The time has come to go our separate ways."

Ganga nodded. "We can no longer risk the anger and wrath of our kind, not after what we had to do to defeat Helen."

"But humanity is in need of champions." Freya swept her hand to Jory and Richard. "These men have been wronged by their mother—and by the rest of the Ancients—for allowing their imprisonment because they are demigods. 'Tis time the Sons of Gaia find their place in this world."

Sarita looked to Ganga. "But you'll still be there for us if we need you?"

"Of course, my child. We will always keep watch over you and yours. Rebecca's brothers will have need of your wisdom—and perhaps your fighting skills—on occasion."

"And we'll give them both," Rebecca said.

Rhiannon gave a cool smile to Jory and Richard. "Do you wish to leave your island paradise to pledge your lives to our service?"

Richard scoffed. "I want off that place so badly, I'd do just about anything."

"Be careful what you wish for, Richard," Freya said. "For it will surely be granted and bring with you more than you anticipated."

"And you, Jory?" Rhiannon asked. "Do you also choose a life of service?"

"Oh, hell, yeah," he replied.

A flash of light and a loud pop brought Freyjr into the mix. "A celebration? In my sister's sanctuary?" His gaze settled on the Sons of Gaia. "With men who worship me?"

"Worship?" Jory shook his head. "Not even close."

Freyjr's eyes hardened. "'Ware, Jory."

Not looking at all worried, Jory inclined his head to Freya. "Your sister offers me her protection."

"Is that true?" Freyjr asked his twin.

"Aye, my brother. The Sons of Gaia are now in my service."

"And mine," Rhiannon reminded. "The Amazons are no more. Their swords shall be taken up by these men, and they will answer to me." A beat passed before she added, "Oh, and your sister, as well."

Stroking his chin with his thumb and index finger, Freyjr considered the men for a long moment. "'Twill be an amusement."

"An amusement?" Sarita asked. "What are you talking about?"

"Ah, little one. Can you not see how much enjoyment we shall get by watching these powerful demigods jump to the commands of my twin and the Lady of the Lake? I, for one, will relish the conflicts to come."

Sarita rolled her eyes. Jory and Richard had no idea what they'd just opened themselves up to. But Freyjr was right—seeing the Sons of Gaia try to take over the Amazons' jobs while dealing with the constant feud between Freya and Rhiannon could be downright hilarious.

She kept that thought to herself—at least she believed she had until Gina's gaze caught hers and Sarita saw the grin on her sister's face. Her own smile bloomed as she silently thanked her goddess for restoring their telepathic link.

Rhiannon stared at the men. "Then pledge your fealty to us as the Sentinels do."

"You're Rhiannon, right?" Jory asked.

Gathering herself to her full height, Rhiannon glowered down at him. "You do not know who I am?" Her booming voice made the windows shake.

"I—I—"

"I am Rhiannon. The Lady of the Lake. The Guardian of—"

The crowd joined in. "Excalibur. The Goddess of the Isle. The Divine Queen." Everyone broke into laughter.

Sarita couldn't help but chuckle, hoping Rhiannon took the good-natured teasing as it was clearly intended—with affection.

"Aye." Rhiannon gave them a brilliant smile. "'Tis good of you *all* to remember."

Richard and Jory both fisted their hands and thumped them against their hearts.

"Kneel before us."

As soon as the words were out of her mouth, both men dropped to their knees.

Rhiannon tilted her head back and lifted her right hand high above her head. Thunder roiled in the distance as the lights inside the lodge dimmed.

"What's going on?" Ian whispered in Sarita's ear.

"Not sure, but I suspect we might see the famous—"

A hole suddenly opened in the ceiling, a perfect circle of flames that didn't spread beyond the portal.

"Come to me, I bid you." Rhiannon's words echoed through the lodge, followed by another clap of thunder.

A glowing sword—a silver blade with a gold, jewel-encrusted hilt—descended through the opening in the ceiling. The hilt settled in Rhiannon's palm.

"Excalibur," Sarita said in a breathless murmur.

The goddess took Freya's hand in hers and set the flat of the blade first against Richard's shoulder and then Jory's. "I anoint these Sons of Gaia as the new protectors of the realm. You will be the ones to hunt the demons that stalk this world. We grant you life beyond your island so you no longer need to feed on magical blood to survive."

Freya took over. "We grant you whatever funds you shall need to pursue the enemies of humanity. We grant you homes where you may rest with no fear of attack."

"We allow you to keep the powers granted by your

mother, Gaia," Rhiannon said. "And we gift you with that which I have always given the Amazons—you may not die by bullet. Your powers may grow, as the Amazons always have—"

"But," Freya interrupted, "we leave that growth to the purity of your souls."

Rhiannon raised Excalibur high. "So we have said, so may it be done."

Lightning flashed through the opening, striking the tip of Excalibur and then forking to hit Richard and Jory square in the chests. Both men gasped, throwing their heads back.

Sarita looked to Gina, knowing how close her sister was to Richard.

Gina's lips were pulled into a tight line, but she didn't react. She wasn't afraid for her friend—nor did Sarita feel any fear from her other sisters.

But Sarita was afraid—for both Sons of Gaia and any of their brothers who chose to serve the goddesses. Being hit by whatever energy Rhiannon was pumping into them had to hurt like bloody hell, but neither man cried out. She held her breath, waiting to see if she'd have to hurry to them to heal whatever injuries would be inflicted in this miraculous transformation.

The lightning faded as the men collapsed back against the floor boards, panting for air.

Rhiannon released her grip on the sword, and it floated back out through the ceiling. The hole repaired itself after Excalibur disappeared.

Beagan and Dolan hurried over to Richard and Jory as they sat up, groaning. Only then did Sarita relax enough to accept that they were fine. The changelings helped them back to their chairs and handed them glasses of water.

"No time to tarry, my new warriors," Rhiannon said with a wave of her hand. "You two must be about business."

"What business?" Richard asked, a bit breathless.

"Marbas has escaped again. You must find him and return him to the jailer, Kampe."

"Who's Marbas?" Jory asked.

"A fire-breathing lion," Sarita replied. "Nasty one at that."

"And he has been spotted near a school, so you must hurry." With a snap of Freya's divine fingers, Jory and Richard disappeared.

"Just like that?" Gina asked. "We at least had Johann to train us before you sent us on a mission."

Rhiannon chuckled. "They shall have to learn *as* they perform their jobs."

Freyjr was the only one to laugh in response. "I believe I shall follow along to witness their first mission. Should be...amusing." He snapped his fingers and disappeared.

Rebecca stood up and raised her champagne glass. "What a night!"

"You can say that again," Megan added.

Artair stood at Rebecca's side. "We should all raise our glasses in a toast. First, to the patron goddesses. Their benevolence will allow us to remain in this beautiful place."

"And," Rebecca added, "to their kindness in letting us keep our powers so that we can protect ourselves and our children as well as help my brothers."

Glasses clinked before everyone sipped their champagne.

Sarita almost choked when she drank because her champagne had been replaced with apple juice. Her gaze quickly found the changelings. They laughed, their cheeks blushing.

She couldn't stop herself. She put her glass down, crooked her finger and waited for them to come to her. Then she crouched, gathered them both in her arms and hugged them.

"I'm so glad you're back. I love you guys."

After she turned them loose, Beagan smiled at her. "We will do all we can to protect and care for your child, mistress."

Dolan nodded. "No harm will come to her so long as we are near."

She burst into tears.

The changelings each pulled a handkerchief from the pockets in their velvet vests and held them out to her.

Sarita's tears changed to laughter.

Ian came to her and grabbed her elbow to help her back to her feet. "Are you well?"

"I'm fine, *jaanu*. Just...happy. Happier than I thought possible."

SARITA STOOD ON a hill overlooking Avalon.

Things had changed—probably for the better—but nothing would ever be the same again.

She felt her sisters before she saw them. Of course, she knew they'd come. The bond they'd always shared had only been strengthened by their joining. Their hearts were now linked in a way no one but the Amazons could understand.

Gina was the first to reach her, and Sarita hugged her sister.

Megan and Rebecca laughed as they wrapped their arms around the two women so that all four were included in the embrace. Then they faced Avalon. Together.

"How's it feel to be retired?" the Guardian asked her charges.

"I'm too young to be retired," Megan replied. "Besides, it's not like they took our powers away or anything."

"Richard and Jory will surely need us," Gina added.

"They can always call on their other brothers," Sarita pointed out. "I'm sure several of them would trade the safety of their island for the chance of living in the world—even if it's a dangerous place to be."

"But we'll always be close just in case," Rebecca said. "After all, they're my brothers. And we might be *retired*, but we'll always be able to help if needed."

"I don't know how to feel," Sarita admitted. "I mean, no more revenant attacks."

"No more demons to chase," Gina said.

"No more puzzles to solve," Megan added.

"Sounds…boring." Then Sarita remembered her condition. "We'll have to stay sharp to protect this little one." She caressed her stomach. "Wonder what Lalita will be capable of doing?"

"Lalita?" Megan asked. "Ah…after your nanny."

"Such a pretty name," Rebecca said.

Gina elbowed Sarita lightly in the ribs. "After what

Ganga and Rhiannon said, I imagine Lalita will make us look like lightweights."

Rebecca put her hand over Sarita's that rested against her abdomen. "We'll be there for her, Sarita."

Another hand—Megan's—was added. "Just like you've always been there for our kids."

Gina completed the set, putting her palm over the joined hands. "Since we were called, we've always helped each other. Now, we'll help your daughter."

Sarita's heart was full of love—for her husband, her child and her sisters. She wiped away a stray tear. "Goddess, seems like all I can do today is cry."

"It's the hormones," Rebecca said. "I cried at the drop of a hat when I was pregnant with Darian."

Megan knit her brows. "Speak for yourself. I wasn't emotional at all when I had Mina."

"Are you kidding me?" Gina chuckled. "You threw fireballs at Johann at least ten times a day."

"Doesn't count. He had it coming." Then Megan laughed. "Okay…maybe I was *a little* emotional."

Sarita let her gaze settle on her new home. Ian would be waiting there, and they would celebrate their child, this daughter who had the ability to change the world. Lalita MacKay—a child who was not only gifted with incredible power, but one who had ties to so many different cultures. She was truly blessed. "I need to go. Ian's waiting."

Her sisters' knowing laughter followed her as she popped from the hill to the fountain in her courtyard. The sight that greeted her came as a welcome surprise.

"Sile! Old Ewan! You're here!"

The servants both bowed to her.

Ian strode over to take her hand. "Yer goddess

dropped them off a few minutes ago. She said we'd need more help now that our family is growing. She also said loyalty like theirs needed to be rewarded. Ye do realize they're ghosts, right?"

"Duh. Of course I do. How else could they have been serving you after so long? And Ganga's right. They deserved a reward," Sarita said to her husband before looking to the ghosts. "It's so good to have you both here."

"'Tis wonderful to be here, m'lady," Sile replied. "Me and Old Ewan got a wee bit lonely at *dorcha àite*. 'Twill be a pleasure to tend ye and m'laird in this home."

"And a bairn," Old Ewan said, grinning. "We can help ye with the new bairn."

"I'd like that." Sarita returned his smile.

"We'll leave ye now." Old Ewan took Sile's hand, and the two of them floated away from the courtyard.

Ian led Sarita to the fountain. "Did you see yer sisters?"

"I did. They've all pledged to protect our daughter."

"Our daughter."

"I'd like to name her Lalita…after the woman who raised me."

"'Tis fitting, loving. A beautiful name."

Quick as a cat, he grabbed her around the waist and set her against the stone edge of the fountain. He dropped to kneel before her, putting his hands on her thighs. Then he leaned in to kiss her stomach.

"I love you," she said, stroking his hair, letting her fingers slide through the silky strands.

"As I love ye. And I'll be a good father."

"I know that."

"You saved me."

She nodded, thinking of how afraid she'd been when he'd taken that sword in her place. "I couldn't let you die, not when you were wounded to protect me from being cut down."

"Nay, 'tis not the sword wound I meant, although I thank ye kindly for that deed, as well."

She cocked her head. "Then what—"

"I was a drowning man, loving. I needed revenge, and I let all that anger eat at my soul like a cancer. Until you came into my life."

Cupping his cheeks in her hands, she smiled down at him. "You saved me, too, Ian."

He tried to shake his head.

She held him fast. "You *did*. I always thought I was the weakest Amazon, but you showed me I'm strong. Your love for me makes me strong—just like my love makes you strong."

"Is it not a wee bit funny?"

"What's funny?"

Ian's smile reached all the way to Sarita's soul. "It took Water to save a drowning man."

* * * * *

ABOUT THE AUTHOR

SANDY LIVES IN a quiet suburb of Indianapolis with her husband of over thirty years. She's a high school social studies teacher who especially loves psychology and United States history. Since she and her husband own a small stable of harness racehorses, they often spend time together at the two Indiana racetracks.